STEFAN ZWEIG was born in 1881 in Vienna, into a wealthy Austrian-Jewish family. He studied in Berlin and Vienna and was first known as a poet and translator, then as a biographer. Zweig travelled widely, living in Salzburg between the wars, and was an international bestseller with a string of hugely popular novellas including *Letter from an Unknown Woman*, *Amok* and *Fear*. In 1934, with the rise of Nazism, he moved to London, and later on to Bath, taking British citizenship after the outbreak of the Second World War. With the fall of France in 1940 Zweig left Britain for New York, before settling in Brazil, where in 1942 he and his wife were found dead in an apparent double suicide. Much of his work is available from Pushkin Press.

STEFAN ZWEIG

THE INVISIBLE COLLECTION

Tales of
Obsession and Desire

Translated from the German by
Anthea Bell

PUSHKIN PRESS

LONDON

Pushkin Press
71–75 Shelton Street
London WC2H 9JQ

Original texts © Williams Verlag AG Zurich
English translations © Anthea Bell

This edition first published by Pushkin Press in 2015

0 0 2

ISBN 978 1 782271 49 9

Set in 10.25 on 14 Monotype Baskerville
by Tetragon, London

Printed and bound by CPI Group (UK) Ltd, Croydon CR0 4YY

www.pushkinpress.com

CONTENTS

THE INVISIBLE
COLLECTION

An episode from the time of German inflation

T WO STATIONS AFTER DRESDEN an elderly gentleman got into our compartment, passed the time of day civilly and then, looking up, expressly nodded to me as if I were an old acquaintance. At first I couldn't remember him; however, as soon as he mentioned his name, with a slight smile, I recollected him at once as one of the most highly regarded art dealers in Berlin. In peacetime I had often viewed and bought old books and autograph manuscripts from him. We talked of nothing much for a while, but suddenly and abruptly he said: "I must tell you where I've just come from—this is the story of about the strangest thing that I've ever encountered, old art dealer that I am, in the thirty-seven years I've been practising my profession." And the story as he told it follows.

You probably know for yourself what it's like in the art trade these days, since the value of money started evaporating like gas; all of a sudden people who have just made their fortunes have discovered a taste for Gothic Madonnas, and incunabula, old engravings and pictures. You can't conjure up enough such things to satisfy them—why, you have to be careful they don't clear out your house and home. They'd happily buy the cufflinks from your sleeves and the lamp from your desk. It's getting harder and harder to find new wares all the time—forgive me for suddenly describing as *wares* items that, to the likes of you and me, usually mean something to be revered—but these philistines have accustomed even me to regard a wonderful Venetian incunabulum only as if it were a coat costing such-and-such a sum in dollars, and a drawing by Guercino as the embodiment of a few hundred franc notes. There's no resisting the insistent urging of those who are suddenly mad to buy art. So I was right out of stock again overnight, and I felt like putting up the shutters, I was so ashamed of seeing our old business that my father took over from my grandfather with nothing for sale but wretched trash, stuff that in the past no street trader in the north would have bothered even to put on his cart.

In this awkward situation, the idea of consulting our old business records occurred to me, to look up former customers from whom I might be able to get a few items if they happened to have duplicates. A list of old customers is always something of a graveyard, especially in times like the present, and it did not really tell me much: most of those who had bought from us in the past had long ago had to get rid of their possessions in auction sales, or had died, and I could not hope for much from the few who remained. But then I suddenly came upon a bundle of letters from a man who was probably our oldest customer, and who had surfaced from my memory only because after 1914 and the outbreak of the World War, he had never turned to us with any orders or queries again. The correspondence—and I really am not exaggerating!—went back over almost sixty years; he had bought from my father and my grandfather, yet I could not remember him ever coming into our premises in the thirty-seven years of my personal involvement with the family business. Everything suggested that he must have been a strange, old-fashioned oddity, one of that lost generation of Germans shown in the paintings and graphic art of such artists as Menzel and Spitzweg, who survived here and there as rare phenomena in little provincial towns until just before our own times. His letters were pure calligraphy, neatly written, the items he was ordering underlined in red ink, with a ruler, and he always wrote out the sum of money involved in words as well as figures, so that there could be no mistake. That, as well as his exclusive use of blank flyleaves from books as writing paper

10

and old, reused envelopes, indicated the petty mind and fanatical thrift of a hopeless provincial. These remarkable documents were signed not only with his name but with the elaborate title: Forestry and Economic Councillor, retd; Lieutenant, retd; Holder of the Iron Cross First Class. Being a veteran of the Franco-Prussian War, he must therefore, if still alive, be at least eighty. However, as a collector of old examples of graphic art this ridiculously thrifty oddity showed unusual acumen, wide knowledge and excellent taste. As I slowly put together his orders from us over almost sixty years, the first of them still paid for in silver groschen, I realized that in the days when you could still buy a stack of the finest German woodcuts for a taler, this little provincial must have been assembling a collection of engravings that would probably show to great advantage beside those so loudly praised by the *nouveaux riches*. For what he had bought from us alone in orders costing him a few marks and pfennigs represented astonishing value today, and in addition it could be expected that his purchases at auction sales had been acquired equally inexpensively.

Although we had had no further orders from him since 1914, I was too familiar with all that went on in the art trade to have missed noticing the auction or private sale of such a collection. In that case, our unusual customer must either be still alive, or the collection was in the hands of his heirs.

The case interested me, and on the next day, that's to say yesterday evening, I set off for one of the most provincial towns in Saxony; and as I strolled along the main street from the station it seemed to me impossible that here, in the middle of these undistinguished little houses with their tasteless contents, a man could live who owned some of the finest prints of Rembrandt's etchings, as well as engravings by Dürer and Mantegna in such a perfectly complete state. To my surprise, however, when I asked at the post office if a forestry or economic councillor of his name lived here, I discovered that the old gentleman really was still alive, and in the middle of the morning I set off on my way to him—with my heart, I confess, beating rather faster.

I had no difficulty in finding his apartment. It was on the second floor of one of those cheaply built provincial buildings that might have been hastily constructed by some builder on spec in the 1860s. A master tailor lived on the first floor, to the left on the second floor I saw the shiny nameplate of a civil servant in the post office, and on the right, at last, a porcelain panel bearing the name of the Forestry and Economic Councillor. When I tentatively rang the bell, a very old white-haired woman wearing a clean little black cap immediately answered it. I gave her my card and asked if I might speak to the Forestry Councillor. Surprised, and with a touch of suspicion, she looked first at me and then at the card; a visitor from the outside world seemed to be an unusual event in this little town at the back of beyond and this old-fashioned building. But she asked me in friendly tones to wait, took my card and went into the room beyond the front door; I heard her whispering quietly, and then, suddenly, a loud male voice. "Oh, Herr R. from Berlin, from the great antiques dealers there… bring him in, bring him in, I'll be very glad to meet him!" And the little old lady came tripping out to me again and asked me into the living room.

I took off my coat and followed her. In the middle of the modest little room an old but still-vigorous man stood erect. He had a bushy moustache and wore a frogged, semi-military casual jacket, and he was holding out both hands in heartfelt welcome. But this gesture, unmistakably one of happy and spontaneous greeting, contrasted with a curious rigidity in the way he held himself. He did not come a step closer to me, and I was obliged—feeling slightly alienated—to approach him myself in order to take his hand. As I was about to grasp it, however, the way he held both hands out horizontally, not moving them, told me that they were not searching for my own but expecting mine to find them. And the next moment I understood it all: this man was blind.

Even from my childhood I had always been uncomfortable facing someone blind; I was never able to fend off a certain shame and embarrassment in sensing that the blind person was entirely alive and knowing, at the same time, that he did not experience our meeting in the same way as I did. Now, yet again, I had to overcome my initial shock at seeing those dead eyes, staring fixedly into space under bushy white brows. However, the blind man himself did not leave me feeling awkward for long; as soon as my hand touched his he shook it powerfully, and repeated his welcome with strong and pleasingly heartfelt emotion. "A rare visitor," he said, smiling broadly at me, "really, it's a miracle, one of the great Berlin antiques dealers making his way to our little town… however, it behoves us to be careful when one of those gentlemen boards the train. Where I come from, we always say: keep your gates and your purses closed when the gypsies are in town… yes, yes, I can guess why you seek me out… business is going badly these days in our poor country; now that our unhappy land of Germany's come down in the world, there are no buyers left, so the great gentlemen of the art world think of their old customers and go in search of those little lambs. But I'm afraid you won't have much luck here, we poor old retired folk are glad if we can put a meal on the table. We can't match the crazy prices you ask these days… the likes of us are finished with all that for ever."

I told him at once that he had misunderstood me; I had not come to sell him anything, I just happened to be in this neighbourhood, and didn't want to miss my chance of calling on him, as a customer of our house over many years, and paying my respects to one of the greatest collectors in Germany. As soon as I said, "one of the greatest collectors in Germany", a remarkable change came over the old man's face. He was still standing upright and rigid in the middle of the room, but now there was an expression of sudden brightness and deep pride in his attitude. He turned towards the place where he thought his wife was, as if to say, "Did you hear that?" and his voice as he then turned to me was full of delight, with not a trace of the brusque, military tone in which he had spoken just now; instead it was soft, positively tender.

"That's really very, very good of you… and you will find you have not come here in vain. You shall see something that can't be seen every day, even in the grandeur of Berlin… a few pieces as fine as any in the Albertina in Vienna or in that damn city of Paris… yes, if a man collects for sixty years he comes upon all kinds of things that aren't to be found on every street corner. Luise, give me the key to the cupboard, please!"

But now something unexpected happened. The little old lady standing beside him, listening courteously and with smiling, quietly attentive friendliness to our conversation, suddenly raised both hands to me in an imploring gesture, at the same time shaking her head vigorously, a sign that at first I failed to understand.

Only then did she go over to her husband and lightly laid both hands on his shoulder. "Oh, Herwarth," she admonished him, "you haven't even asked the gentleman if he has time to spare to look at your collection. It's nearly lunchtime, and after lunch you must rest for an hour, you know the doctor expressly said so. Wouldn't it be better to show our visitor your things after lunch, and Annemarie will be here as well then, she understands it all much better than I do, she can help you!"

And once again, as soon as the words were out of her mouth, she repeated that urgently pleading gesture as if over her husband's head, leaving him unaware of it. Now I understood her. I could tell that she wanted me to decline an immediate viewing, and I quickly invented a lunch engagement. It would be a pleasure and an honour to be allowed to see his collection, I said, but it wouldn't be possible for me to do so before three in the afternoon. Then, however, I would happily come back here.

Cross as a child whose favourite toy has been taken away, the old man made a petulant gesture. "Oh, of course," he grumbled, "those Berlin gentlemen never have time for anything. But today you'll have to find the time, because it's not just three or five good pieces I have, there are twenty-seven portfolios, one for each master of the graphic arts, and all of them full. So come back at three, but mind you're punctual or we'll never get through the whole collection."

Once again he put out his hand into the air, in my direction. "I warn you, you may like it, or you may be jealous. And the more jealous you are the better I'll be pleased. That's collectors for you: we want it all for ourselves and nothing for anyone else!" And once again he shook my hand vigorously.

The little old lady accompanied me to the door. I had noticed a certain discomfort in her all this time, an expression of anxious embarrassment. But now, just before we reached the way out, she stammered in a low voice, "Could you... could you... could my daughter Annemarie join you before you come back to us? That would be better for... for various reasons... I expect you are lunching at the hotel?"

"Certainly, and I will be delighted to meet your daughter first. It will be a pleasure," I said.

And sure enough, an hour later when I had just finished my lunch in the little restaurant of the hotel on the market square, a lady not in her first youth, simply dressed, came in and looked enquiringly around. I went up to her, introduced myself and said I was ready to set out with her at once to see the collection. However, with a sudden blush and the same confused embarrassment that her mother had shown, she asked if she could have a few words with me first. I saw at once that this was difficult for her. Whenever she was bringing herself to say something, that restless blush rose in her face, and her hand fidgeted with her dress. At last she began, hesitantly, overcome by confusion again and again.

"My mother has sent me to see you… she told me all about it, and… and we have a request to make. You see, we would like to inform you, before you go back to see my father… of course Father will want to show you his collection, and the collection… the collection, well, it isn't entirely complete any more… there are several items missing… indeed, I'm afraid quite a number are missing…"

She had to catch her breath again, and then she suddenly looked at me and said, hastily: "I must speak to you perfectly frankly… you know what these times are like, I'm sure you'll understand. After the outbreak of war Father went blind. His vision had been disturbed quite often before, but then all the agitation robbed him of his eyesight entirely. You see, even though he was seventy-six at the time he wanted to go to France with the army, and when the army didn't advance at once, as it had in 1870, he was dreadfully upset, and his sight went downhill at terrifying speed. Otherwise he's still hale and hearty: until recently he could walk for hours and even go hunting, his favourite sport. But now he can't take long walks, and the only pleasure he has left is his collection. He looks at it every day… that's to say, he can't see it, he can't see anything now, but he gets all the portfolios out so that he can at least touch the items in them, one by one, always in the same order; he's known their order by heart for decades. Nothing else interests him these days, and I always have to read the accounts of all the auction sales in the newspaper to him. The higher the prices he hears about the happier he is, because… this is the worst of it, Father doesn't understand about prices nowadays… he doesn't know that we've lost everything, and his pension will keep us for only two days in the month… in addition, my sister's husband fell in the war, leaving her with four small children. But Father has no idea of the material difficulties we're in. At first we saved hard, even more than before, but that didn't help. Then we began selling things—we didn't touch his beloved collection, of course, we sold the little jewellery we had, but dear God, what did that amount to? After all, for sixty years Father had spent every pfennig he could spare on his prints alone. And one day there was nothing for us to sell, we didn't know what to do, and then... then Mother and I sold one of the prints. Father would never have allowed it, after all, he doesn't know how badly off we are, how hard it is to buy a little food on the black market, he doesn't even know that we lost the war, and Alsace and Lorraine are part of France now, we don't read those things to him when they appear in the paper, so that he won't get upset.

"It was a very valuable item that we sold, a Rembrandt etching. The dealer offered us many, many thousands of marks for it, and we hoped that would provide for us for years. But you know how money melts away these days... we had deposited most of it in the bank, but two months later it was all gone. So we had to sell another work, and then another, and the dealer was always so late sending the money that it was already devalued when it arrived. Then we tried auctions, but there too we were cheated, although the prices were in millions... by the time the millions reached us they were nothing but worthless paper. And so gradually the best of his collection left us, except for a few good items, just so that we could lead the most frugal of lives, and Father has no idea of it.

"That's why my mother was so alarmed when you came today— because if he opens the portfolios and shows them to you, it will all come out... you see, we put reprints or similar sheets of paper in the old mounts instead of the prints we had sold, so that he wouldn't notice when he touched them. If he can only touch them and enumerate them (he remembers their order of arrangement perfectly), he feels just the same joy as when he could see them in the past with his own eyes. There's no one else in this town whom Father would think worthy of seeing his treasures... and he loves every single print so fanatically that I think his heart would break if he guessed that they all passed out of his hands long ago. You are the first he has invited to see them in all these years, since the death of the former head of the engravings department in the Dresden gallery—he meant to show his portfolios to him. So I beg you…"

And suddenly the ageing woman raised her hands, and tears gleamed in her eyes.

"…We beg you… don't make him unhappy… don't make us all unhappy… don't destroy his last illusion, help us to make him believe that all the prints he will describe to you are still there… he wouldn't survive it if he only suspected. Maybe we have done him an injustice, but we couldn't help it. One must live, and human lives, the lives of four orphaned children as well as my sister, are surely worth more than sheets of printed paper. To this day, what we did hasn't taken any of his pleasure from him; he is happy to be able to leaf through his portfolios for three hours every afternoon, talking to every print as if it were a human being. And today… today would perhaps be the happiest day of his life; he's been waiting years for a chance to show a connoisseur his darlings. Please… I beg and pray you, please don't destroy his happiness!"

My account of her plea cannot express the deep distress with which she told me all this. My God—as a dealer I have seen many such people despicably robbed, infamously deceived by the inflation, people who were persuaded to part with their most precious family heirlooms for the price of a sandwich—but here Fate added a touch of its own, one that particularly moved me. Of course I promised her to keep the secret and do my best.

So we went back to the apartment together—on the way, still full of my bitter feelings, I heard about the trifling amounts that these poor women, who knew nothing of the subject, had been paid, but that only confirmed me in my decision to help them as well as I could. We went up the stairs, and as soon as we opened the door we heard the old man's cheerfully hearty voice from the living room. "Come in, come in!" With a blind man's keen hearing, he must have heard our footsteps as we climbed the stairs.

"Herwarth hasn't been able to sleep at all, he is so impatient to show you his treasures," said the little old lady, smiling. A single glance at her daughter had already set her mind at rest: I would not give them away. Piles of portfolios were arranged on the table, waiting for us, and as soon as the blind man felt my hand he took my arm, without further greeting, and pressed me down into an armchair.

"There, now let's begin at once—there's a great deal to see, and I know you gentlemen from Berlin never have much time. The first portfolio is devoted to that great master Dürer and, as you'll see for yourself, pretty well complete—each of my prints finer than the last. Well, you can judge for yourself, look at this one!" he said, opening the portfolio at the first sheet it contained. "There—the Great Horse!"

And now, with the tender caution one would employ in handling something fragile, his fingertips touching it very lightly to avoid wear and tear, he took out of the folio a mount framing a blank, yellowed sheet of paper, and held the worthless scrap out in front of him with enthusiasm. He looked at it for several minutes, without of course really seeing it, but in his outstretched hand he held the empty sheet up level with his eyes, his expression ecstatic, his whole face magically expressing the intent gesture of a man looking at a fine work. And as his dead pupils stared at it—was it a reflection from the paper, or a glow coming from within him?—a knowledgeable light came into his eyes, a brightness borrowed from what he thought he saw.

"There," he said proudly, "did you ever see a finer print? Every detail stands out so sharp and clear—I've looked at it beside the Dresden copy, which was flat and lifeless by comparison. And as for its provenance! There—" and he turned the sheet over and pointed to certain places on the back, which was also blank, so that

I instinctively looked at it as if the marks he imagined were really there after all—"there you see the stamp of the Nagler collection, here the stamps of Remy and Esdaile; I dare say the illustrious collectors who owned this print before me never guessed that it would end up in this little room some day."

A cold shudder ran down my back as the old man, knowing nothing of what had happened, praised an entirely blank sheet of paper to the skies; and it was a strange sight to see him pointing his finger, knowing the right places to the millimetre, to where the invisible collectors' stamps that existed only in his imagination would have been. My throat constricted with the horror of it, and I didn't know what to say; but when, in my confusion, I looked at his wife and daughter I saw the old woman's hands raised pleadingly to me again, as she trembled with emotion. At this I got a grip on myself and began to play my part.

"Extraordinary!" I finally stammered. "A wonderful print." And at once his entire face glowed with pride. "But that's nothing to all I still have to show you," he said triumphantly. "You must see my copy of the Melancholia, or the Passion—there, this one is an illuminated copy, you won't see such quality in one of those again. Look at this—and again his fingers tenderly moved over an imaginary picture—"that freshness, that warm, grainy tone. All the fine dealers in Berlin, and the doctors who run the museums there, they'd be bowled over."

And so that headlong, eloquent recital of his triumphs went on for another good two hours. I can't say how eerie it was to join him in looking at a hundred, maybe two hundred blank sheets of paper or poor reproductions, but in the memory of this man, who was tragically unaware of their absence, the prints were so incredibly real that he could describe and praise every one of them unerringly, in precise detail, just as he remembered the order of them: the invisible collection that in reality must now be dispersed to all four corners of the earth was still genuinely present to the blind man, so touchingly deceived, and his passion for what he saw was so overwhelming that even I almost began to believe in it.

Only once was the somnambulistic certainty of his enthusiasm as he viewed the collection interrupted, alarmingly, by the danger of waking to reality; in speaking of his copy of Rembrandt's *Antiope* (the print of the etching was a proof and must indeed have been inestimably valuable), he had once again been praising the sharpness of the print, and as he did so his nervously clairvoyant fingers lovingly followed the line of it, but his ultra-sensitive nerves of touch failed to feel an indentation that he expected on the blank sheet. The suggestion of a shadow descended on his brow. His voice became confused. "But surely… surely this is the *Antiope?*" he murmured, with some awkwardness, whereupon I immediately summoned up all my powers, quickly took the mounted sheet from his hands, and enthusiastically described the etching, which I myself knew well, in every detail. The tension in the blind man's expression relaxed again. And the more I praised the merits of the collection, the more did a jovial warmth bloom in that gnarled old man's face, a simple depth of feeling.

"Here's someone who understands these things for once," he rejoiced, turning triumphantly to his family. "At last, at long last a man who can tell you what my prints are worth. You've always been so cross with me for putting all the money I had to spare into my collection, that's the truth of it: over sixty years no beer, no wine, no tobacco, no travelling, no visits to the theatre, no books—I was always saving and saving for these prints. But one day, when I'm gone, you'll see—you two will be rich, richer than anyone in this town, as rich as the richest in Dresden, then for a change you'll be glad of my folly. However, as long as I live not a single one of these prints leaves the house—they'll have to carry me out first and only then my collection."

And as he spoke, his hand passed lovingly over the portfolios that had been emptied of their contents long ago, as if they were living things—I found it terrible, yet at the same time touching, for in all the years of the war I had not seen so perfect and pure an expression of bliss on any German face. Beside him stood the women, looking mysteriously like the female figures in that etching by the German master, who, coming to visit the tomb of the Saviour, stand in front of the vault, broken open and empty, with an expression of fearful awe and at the same time joyous ecstasy. As the women disciples in that picture are radiant with their heavenly presentiment of the Saviour's closeness, these two ageing, worn, impoverished ladies were irradiated by the childish bliss of the old man's joy—half laughing, half in tears, it was a sight more moving than any I had ever seen. As for the old man himself, he could not hear enough of my praise, he kept stacking the portfolios up again and turning them, thirstily drinking in every word I said, and so for me it was a refreshing change when at last the deceitful portfolios were pushed aside and, protesting, he had to let the table be cleared for the coffee things. But what was my sense of guilty relief beside the swelling, tumultuous joy and high spirits of a man who seemed to be thirty years younger now! He told a hundred anecdotes of his purchases, his fishing trips in search of them, and rejecting any help tapped again and again on one of the sheets of paper, getting out another and then another print; he was exuberantly drunk as if on wine. When I finally said I must take my leave, he was positively startled, he seemed as upset as a self-willed child, and stamped his foot defiantly: this wouldn't do, I had hardly seen half his treasures. And the women had a difficult time making him understand, in his obstinate displeasure, that he really couldn't keep me there any longer or I would miss my train.

When, after desperate resistance, he finally saw the sense of that, and we were saying goodbye, his voice softened. He took both my hands, and his fingers caressed the joints of mine with all the expressiveness conveyed by the touch of a blind man, as if they wanted to know more of me and express more affection than could be put into words. "You have given me the greatest pleasure—at long, long last I have been able to look through my beloved prints again with a connoisseur. But you'll find that you haven't come to see me, old and blind as I am, in vain. I promise you here and now, before my wife as my witness, that I will add a clause to my will entrusting the auction of my collection to your old-established house. You shall have the honour of administering these unknown treasures"—and he placed his hand lovingly on the plundered portfolios—"until the day when they go out into the world and are dispersed. Just promise me to draw up a handsome catalogue: it will be my tombstone, and I couldn't ask for a better memorial."

I looked at his wife and daughter, who were holding each other close, and sometimes a tremor passed from one to the other, as if they were a single body trembling in united emotion. I myself felt a sense of solemnity in the touching way the old man, unaware of the truth, consigned the invisible and long-gone collection to my care as something precious. Greatly moved, I promised him what I could never perform; once again his dead pupils seemed to light up, and I felt his inner longing to feel me physically; I could tell by the tender, loving pressure of his fingers as they held mine in thanks and a vow.

The women went to the door with me. They dared not speak, for his keen hearing would have picked up every word, but their eyes beamed at me, warm with tears and full of gratitude! Feeling dazed, I made my way down the stairs. I was in fact ashamed of myself; like the angel in the fairy tale I had entered a poor family's house, I had restored a blind man's sight, if only for an hour, by helping him with what amounted to a white lie, when in truth I had gone to see him only as a mean-minded dealer hoping to get a few choice items out of someone by cunning. But what I took away with me was more: I had once again felt a sense of pure and lively enthusiasm in a dull, joyless time, a kind of spiritually irradiated ecstasy bent entirely on art, something that people these days seem to have forgotten entirely. And I felt—I can't put it any other way—I felt a sense of reverence, although I was still ashamed of myself, without really knowing why.

I was already out in the street when I heard an upstairs window open, and my name was called; the old man had not wanted to miss looking with his blind eyes in the direction where he thought I would be standing. He leant so far forwards that the two women had to support him, waved his handkerchief and called, "*Bon voyage!*" with the cheerful, fresh voice of a boy. It was an unforgettable moment: the white-haired old man's happy face up at the window, high above all the morose, driven, busy people in the street, gently elevated from what in truth is our dismal world on the white cloud of a well-meant delusion. And I found myself remembering the old saying—I think it was Goethe's—"Collectors are happy men."

TWILIGHT

M ADAM DE PRIE, returning from her morning drive on the day when the King dismissed her lover the Duke of Bourbon from his position as prime-minister in charge of the affairs of state, thought, as the two footmen at the door bowed low to her, that she caught them suppressing a smile at the same time, which vexed her. She did not let it show for the moment, and walked past them and up the steps with composure. But when she reached the first landing on the stairs she abruptly turned her head back, and she saw a broad grin on the lips of the garrulous pair, although it rapidly disappeared as they bowed again in alarm.

Now she knew enough. And up in her salon, where an officer of the royal bodyguard with much gold braid about his person was waiting for her with a letter, she appeared to be in as serene and almost exuberant a mood as if this were merely a conventional call on a friend. Although she noticed the royal seal on the letter and the rather awkward manner of the officer who was aware of the embarrassing nature of his message, she showed neither curiosity nor concern. Without opening the letter or even examining it more closely she made light conversation with the aristocratic young soldier, and on recognising him as a Breton by his accent told him the story of a lady who could never stand Bretons, because one of his countrymen had once become her lover against her will. She was in high spirits and made risqué jokes, partly from a deliberate intention of showing how carefree she was, partly from habit, for in general a careless and easy levity made all her dissimulations seem natural, even transforming them into sincerity. She talked until she really forgot the royal letter, which she creased as she held it in her hands. But finally, after all, she broke the seal.

The letter contained the royal order, expressed briefly and with remarkably little civility, for her to leave court at once and retire to her estate of Courbépine in Normandy. She had fallen into disfavour, her enemies had won at last; even before the King's message arrived she had known it from the smiles of her footmen at the door. But she did not give herself away. The officer carefully observed her eyes as they ran along the lines. They did not flicker, and now that she turned to him again a smile sparkled in them. "His Majesty is very anxious about my health, and would like me to leave the heat of the city and retire to my château. Tell his Majesty that I will comply with his wishes immediately." She smiled as she spoke, as if there were some secret meaning in her words. The officer raised his hat to her and left, with a bow.

But the door had hardly closed behind him before the smile fell from her lips like a withered leaf. She angrily crumpled up the letter. How many such missives, each sealing a human fate, had been sent out into the world under the royal name when she herself had dictated their contents! And now, after she had ruled all France for two years, her enemies dared to banish her from court with a sheet of paper like this! She hadn't expected so much courage from them. To be sure, the young King had never liked her and was ill-disposed towards her, but had she made Marie Leszczynska Queen of France only to be exiled now, just because a mob had rioted outside her windows and there was some kind of famine in the country? For a moment she wondered whether to resist the King's command: the Regent of France, the Duke of Orléans, had been her lover, and anyone who now held power and a high position at court owed it all to her. She did not lack for friends. But she was too proud to appear as a beggar where she was known as a mistress; no one in France was ever to see her with anything but a smiling face. Her exile couldn't last more than a few days, until tempers had calmed down, and then her friends would make sure she was recalled. In her mind, she was already looking forward to her revenge, and soothed her anger with that idea.

Madame de Prie went about her departure with the utmost secrecy. She gave no one a chance to feel sorry for her and received no callers, to avoid having to tell them she was going away. She wanted to disappear suddenly, in mysterious and dashing style, leaving a riddle calculated to confuse the whole court permanently linked to her absence, for it was a peculiarity of her character that she always wished to deceive, to veil whatever she was really doing with a lie. The only person she herself visited was the Count of Belle-Isle, her mortal enemy and the man behind her banishment. She sought him out to show him her smile, her unconcern, her self-confidence. She told him how she welcomed the opportunity of a rest from the stress of life at court, she told blatant lies that clearly showed him the depth of her hatred and contempt. The Count only smiled coldly and said he thought that she would find it hard to bear so long a period of solitude, and he gave the word "long" a strange emphasis that alarmed her. But she controlled herself, and civilly invited him to come and hunt on her estate.

In the afternoon she did meet one of her lovers in her little house in the rue Apolline, and told him to keep her well informed about everything that went on at court. She left that evening. She did not want to drive through the city in her open chaise during the day, because the common people had been hostile to her since the riot that cost human lives, and in addition she was determined to keep her disappearance a mystery. She intended to leave by night and return by day. She left her house just as it was, as if she were going away for only a day or so, and at the moment when the carriage began to move off she said out loud—knowing that her words would find their way back to court—that she was taking a short journey for the sake of her health and would soon be back. And she had schooled herself to wear the mask of dissimulation so well that, genuinely reassured by her own lie, she soon fell into an easy sleep in the jolting carriage, and woke only when she was well outside Paris and past the first posting station, surprised to find herself in a carriage at all, bound for something new, not knowing yet whether it would be good or bad. She felt only that the wheels were turning under her and she had no control over them, that she was gliding into the unknown, but she could not feel any serious anxiety, and soon fell asleep again.

The journey to Normandy was long and tedious, but her first day in Courbépine restored her cheerfulness. Her restless, fanciful mind, always lusting after novelty, discovered an unaccustomed charm in giving itself up to the crystalline purity of a summer's day in the country. She lost herself in a thousand follies, amused herself by walking down the avenues of the park, jumping hedges and trying to catch fluttering butterflies, clad in a dress white as blossom with pale ribbons in her hair, like the little girl she had once been and whom she had thought long dead in her. She walked and walked, and for the first time in years felt the pleasure of letting her limbs relax in the rhythm of her pace, just as she delightedly rediscovered everything about the simple life that she had forgotten in her days at court. She lay in the emerald grass and looked up at the clouds. How strange it was: she hadn't looked at a cloud for years, and she wondered whether clouds were as beautifully outlined, as fluffily white, as pure and airy above the buildings of Paris. For the first time she saw the sky as something real, and its blue vault, sprinkled with white, reminded her of the wonderful Chinese vase that a German prince had recently given her as a present, except that the sky was even lovelier, bluer, more rounded, and full of mild, fragrant air that felt as soft as silk. After hurrying from one entertainment to the next in Paris, she delighted in doing nothing, and the silence around her was as delicious as a cool drink. She now realised, for the first time, that she felt nothing for all the people who had flocked around her at Versailles, she neither loved nor hated any of them, she felt no more for them than for the peasants standing there on the outskirts of the wood with their large, flashing scythes, sometimes shading their eyes with a hand to peer curiously at her. She became more and more exuberant; she played with the young trees, jumped in the air until she could catch the hanging branches, let them spring up again, and laughed out loud when a few white blossoms, as if struck by an arrow, fell into the hand she held out to catch them or the hair she was wearing loose for the first time in years. With the wonderful facility of forgetfulness available to women of no great depth throughout their lives, she did not remember that she was in exile and before that had ruled France, playing with the fate of others as casually as she played now with butterflies and glimmering trees. She cast aside five, ten, fifteen years of her life and was Mademoiselle Pleuneuf again, daughter of the Geneva banker, playing in the convent garden, a small, thin, high-spirited girl of fifteen who knew nothing of Paris and the wide world.

In the afternoon she helped the maids with the harvest: she thought it uncommonly amusing to bind up the big sheaves and fling them exuberantly up to the farm cart. And she sat among them—they had been awestruck at first and behaved shyly—on top of the fully loaded wagon, dangling her legs, laughing with the young fellows and then, when the dancing began, whirling around with the best. It all felt to her like a successful masquerade at court, and she looked forward to telling everyone in Paris how charmingly she had spent her time, dancing with wild flowers in her hair and drinking from the same pitcher as the peasants. She noticed the reality of these things as little as she had felt, at Versailles, that the games of shepherds and shepherdesses were only pretence. Her heart was lost to the pleasure of the moment, it lied in telling the truth and was honest even while it intended to deceive, for she only ever knew what she felt. And what she felt now was delight and rapture running through her veins. The idea that she was out of favour was laughable.

But next morning a dark vestige of ill humour seeped in, mingling with the crystalline merriment of her hours. Waking itself was painful; she tumbled from the black night of dreamless sleep into day as if from warm, sultry air into icy water. She didn't know what had woken her. It was not the light, for a dull, rainy day was dawning outside the tear-stained windows. And it was not the noise either, for there were no voices here, only the fixed, piercing eyes of the dead looking down at her from their pictures on the wall. She was awake and didn't know why or what for; nothing appealed to her here or tempted her.

And she thought how different waking up in Paris had been. She had danced and talked all evening, had spent half the night with her friends, and then came the wonderful sleep of exhaustion, with bright images still flickering on in her excited mind. And in the morning, with her eyes closed and as if still in a dream, she heard muted voices in the anterooms, and no sooner did her *levée* begin than they came streaming in: the royal dukes of France, petitioners, lovers, friends, all vying for her favour and bringing the suitor's gift of solicitous cheerfulness. Everyone had a story to tell, laughed, chattered, all the latest news and gossip came to her bedside, and her moment of waking carried her straight from those bright dreams into the full tide of life. The smile she had worn on her sleeping lips did not vanish but remained at the corners of her mouth, hovering there in high spirits like a bird swinging in its cage.

The day led her on from these images of her friends to those friends themselves, and they stayed with her as she dressed, as she drove out, as she ate, until far into the night again. She felt herself constantly carried on by this murmuring torrent, restless as the waves, dancing in never-ending rhythm and rocking the flowery boat of her life.

Here, however, the torrent cast her moment of awakening upon a rock, where it lay stranded on the beach of the hours, immobile and useless. Nothing tempted her to get up. Yesterday's innocent amusements had lost their charm; her curiosity, used to being indulged, was of the kind that quickly wore off. Her room was empty, as if airless, and she felt empty too in this solitude where no one asked for her: empty, useless, washed out and drained; she had to remind herself slowly why and how she had come to be here. What did she expect of the day that made her stare so hard at the clock, as it paced indefatigably through the silence with its gentle, tremulous gait?

At last she remembered. She had asked the Prince of Alincourt, the only one of her former lovers for whom she felt any real affection, to send her news from court daily by a mounted messenger. All yesterday she had forgotten what a sensation her disappearance must have been in Paris; now she longed to enjoy that triumph. And the messenger soon arrived, but not the message. Alincourt wrote her a few indifferent banalities, news of the King's health, visits from foreign princes, and let the letter peter out in friendly wishes for her well-being. Not a word about herself and her disappearance. She was angry. Hadn't the news been made public? Or had no one really believed her pretence that she was coming to this tedious place for the sake of her health?

The messenger, a simple, bull-necked groom, shrugged his shoulders. He knew nothing. She concealed her annoyance and wrote back to Alincourt—without showing her displeasure—to thank him for his news and urge him to continue writing to her, telling her everything, all the details. She hoped not to stay in the country long, she said, although she liked it here very well. She didn't even notice that she was lying to him.

But then the rest of the day was so long. The hours here, like the people themselves, seemed to go at a more sedate pace, and she knew no means of making them pass any faster. She didn't know what to do with herself: everything in her was mute, all the brilliant music of her heart dead as a musical clock when the key has been lost. She tried all kinds of things, she sent for books, but even the wittiest of them seemed to her mere printed pages. Disquiet came over her, she missed all the people among whom she had lived for years. She sent the servants hither and thither to no good purpose with imperious commands: she wanted to hear footsteps on the stairs, to see people, to create an illusion of the busy hum of messages, to deceive herself, but like all her plans at present, it didn't work. Eating disgusted her, like the room and the sky and her servants: all she wanted now was night and deep, black, dreamless sleep until morning, when a more satisfactory message would arrive.

At last evening came, but it was dismal here! Nothing but the coming of darkness, the disappearance of everything, the extinction of the light. Evening here was an end, whereas in Paris it had been the beginning of all pleasures. Here it let the night pour in, there it lit gilded candles in the royal halls, made the air sparkle in your eyes, kindled, warmed, intoxicated and inspired the heart. Here it only made you more anxious. She wandered from room to room: silence lurked in all of them, like a savage animal sated with all the years when no one had been here, and she feared it might leap on her. The floorboards groaned, the books creaked in their bindings as soon as you touched them; something in the spinet moaned in fright like a beaten child when she touched the keys and summoned up a tearful sound. Everything joined in the darkness to resist her, the intruder.

Then, shivering, she had lights lit all over the house. She tried to stay in one room, but she was constantly impelled to move on, she fled from room to room as if that would calm her. But everywhere she came up against the invisible wall of the silence that had ruled this place by right for years, and would not be dismissed. Even the lights seemed to feel it; they hissed quietly and wept hot drops of wax.

Seen from outside, however, the château shone brightly with its thirty sparkling windows, as if there were great festivities here. Groups of villagers stood outside, amazed and wondering aloud where so many people had suddenly come from. But the figure that they saw flitting like a shadow past first one window and then another was always the same: Madame de Prie, pacing desperately up and down like a wild beast in the prison of her inner solitude, looking through the window for something that never came.

On the third day she lost control of her impatience and it turned violent. The solitude oppressed her; she needed people, or at least news of people, of the court, the natural home of her whole being with all its ramifications, of her friends, something to excite or merely touch her. She couldn't wait for the messenger, and early in the morning she rode for three hours to meet him. It was raining, and there was a high wind; her hair, heavy with water, pulled her head back, and the wind blew rain in her face so hard that she saw nothing. Her freezing hands could hardly hold the reins. Finally she galloped back, had her wet clothes stripped off, and took refuge in bed again. She waited feverishly, clenching her teeth on the covers. Now she understood the Count of Belle-Isle's menacing smile as he said that she would find so long a period of solitude hard to bear. And it had been only three days!

At last the courier came. She did not pretend any longer, but avidly tore the seal off the letter with her nails, like a starving man tearing the husk off a fruit. There was a great deal about the court in it: her eye ran down the lines in search of her name. Nothing, nothing. But one name did stand out like fire: her position as lady-in-waiting had been given to Madame de Calaincourt.

For a moment she trembled and felt quite weak. So it was not a case of fleeting disfavour but permanent exile: it was her death sentence, and she loved life. She leaped suddenly out of bed, feeling no shame in front of the courier, and half-naked, shaking with the cold, she wrote letter after letter with a wild craving. She abandoned her show of pride. She wrote to the King, although she knew he hated her; she promised in the humblest, most pitifully grovelling of terms never to try meddling in affairs of state again. She wrote to Marie Leszczynska, reminding her that she was Queen of France only through the agency of Madame de Prie; she wrote to the ministers, promising them money; she turned to her friends. She urged Voltaire, whom she had saved from the Bastille, to write an elegy on her departure from court and to read it aloud. She ordered her secretary to commission lampoons on her enemies and have them distributed in pamphlet form. She wrote twenty such letters with her fevered hand, all begging for just one thing: Paris, the world, salvation from this solitude. They were no longer letters but screams. Then she opened a casket, gave the courier a handful of gold pieces, told him that even if he rode his horse to death he must be in Paris tonight. Only here had she learned what an hour really meant. Startled, he was going to thank her, but she drove him out.

Then she sought shelter in bed again. She was freezing. A harsh cough shook her thin frame. She lay staring ahead, always waiting for the clock on the mantelpiece to reach the hour and strike at last. But the hours were stubborn, they were not to be hounded with curses, with pleas, with gold, they went sleepily around. The servants came, she sent them all out, she would show no one her despair, she did not want food, or words, she wanted nothing from anyone. The rain fell incessantly outside, and she was as chilly as if she were standing out there shivering like the shrubs with their arms helplessly outstretched. One question went up and down in her mind like the swing of a pendulum: why, why, why, why? Why had God done this to her? Had she sinned so much?

She tugged at the bell-pull and told them to fetch the local priest. It soothed her to think that someone lived here to whom she could talk and confide her fears.

The priest did not delay, more particularly as he had been told that madame was ill. She could not help smiling when he came in, thinking of her abbé in Paris with his fine and delicate hands, the bright glance that rested on her almost tenderly, his courtly conversation which made you quite forget that he was taking confession. The abbé of Courbépine was portly and broad-shouldered, and his boots creaked as he trudged through the doorway. Everything about him was red: his plump hands, his face, weathered by the wind, his big ears, but there was something friendly about him as he offered her his great paw in greeting and sat down in an armchair. The horror in the room seemed to fear his weighty presence and cringed in a corner: filled by his loud voice the room appeared warmer, livelier, and it seemed to Madame de Prie that she breathed more easily now that he was here. He did not know exactly why he had been summoned, and made clumsy conversation, spoke of his parish work, and Paris which he knew only by hearsay, he demonstrated his scholarship, spoke of Descartes and the dangerous works of the sieur de Montaigne. She put in a word here and there, abstractedly; her thoughts were buzzing like a swarm of flies, she just wanted to listen, to hear a human voice, to raise it like a dam holding back the sea of loneliness that threatened to drown her. When, afraid he was disturbing her he was about to stop talking, she encouraged him with ardent kindness which was really nothing but fear. She promised to call on the reverend gentleman, invited him to visit her often; the seductive side of her nature, which had cast such a spell in Paris, emerged extravagantly from her dreamy silence. And the abbé stayed until it was dark.

But as soon as he left she felt as if the weight of the silence were descending on her twice as heavily as before, as if she alone had to hold up the high ceiling, she alone must keep back the advancing darkness. She had never known how much a single human being can mean to another, because she had never been lonely before. She had never thought more of other people than of air, and one does not feel the air, but now that solitude was choking her, only now did she realise how much she needed them, recognising how much they meant to her even when they deceived and told lies, how she herself drew everything from their presence, their easy manners, their confidence and cheerfulness. She had been immersed for decades in the tide of society, never knowing that it nourished and bore her up, but now, stranded like a fish on the beach of solitude, she flinched in despair and convulsive pain. She was freezing and feverishly hot at once. She felt her own body, was startled to find how cold it was; all its sensuous warmth seemed to have died away, her blood surged sluggishly through her veins like gelatine, she felt as if she were lying here in the silence inside the coffin of her own corpse. And suddenly a hot sob of despair tore through her. Alarmed at first, she tried to suppress it, but there was no one here, here she did not have to dissimulate, she was alone with herself for the first time. And she willingly abandoned herself to the sweet pain of feeling hot tears run down her icy cheeks, while she heard her own sobbing in the terrible silence.

She made haste to return the abbé's visit. The house was deserted, no letters came—she herself knew that no one in Paris had much time for petitioners, and she had to do something, anything, even if it was just playing backgammon, or talking, or simply finding out how someone else talked. Somehow she must defy the tedium advancing ever more menacingly and murderously on her heart. She hurried through the village; she felt nauseated by everything that partook in any way of the name of Courbépine and reminded her of her exile. The abbé's little house lay at the end of the village street, surrounded by green countryside. It was not much higher than a barn, but flowers framed the tiny windows and their tangled foliage hung down over the door, so that she had to bend down to avoid being caught in their fragrant toils.

The abbé was not alone. With him at his desk sat a young man whom, in great confusion at the honour of such a visit, he introduced as his nephew. The abbé was preparing him for his studies, although he was not to be a priest—a vocation for which so much must be given up! This was meant as a gallant jest. Madame de Prie smiled, not so much at the rather clumsy compliment as at the amusing embarrassment of the young man, who blushed red and didn't know where to look. He was a tall country fellow with a bony, red-cheeked face, yellow hair and a rather artless expression: he seemed clumsy and brutish with his awkward limbs, but at the moment his extreme respect for her kept his boorishness within bounds and made him look childishly helpless. He scarcely dared to answer her questions, stuttered and stammered, put his hands in his pockets, took them out again, and Madame de Prie, enchanted by his embarrassment, asked him question after question—it did her good to find someone who was confused and small in her presence again, who felt that he was a supplicant, subservient to her. The abbé spoke for him, praised his passion for the noble vocation of scholarship, his other good qualities, and told her it was the boy's great wish to be able to complete his studies at the university in Paris. He himself, to be sure, was poor and could not help his nephew much, the boy also lacked the patronage that alone smoothed the path to high office, and he pressingly recommended him to her favour. He knew that she was all-powerful at court; a single word would suffice to make the young student's boldest dreams come true.

Madame de Prie smiled bitterly into the darkness: so she was supposed to be all-powerful at court, and couldn't even compel anyone to answer a single letter or grant a single request. Yet it was good to feel that no one here knew of her helplessness and her fall from grace. Even the semblance of power warmed her heart now. She controlled herself: yes, she would certainly recommend the young man, who from what so estimable an advocate as the abbé said of him must surely be worthy of every favour. She asked him to come and talk to her tomorrow so that she could assess his qualities. She would recommend him at court, she said, she would give him a letter of introduction to her friend the Queen and the members of the Academy (reminding herself, as she said so, that not one of them had sent a single line in reply to her letters).

The old abbé was quivering with delight, and tears ran down his fat cheeks. He kissed her hands, wandered around the room as if drunk, while the young fellow stood there with a dazed expression, unable to utter a word. When Madame de Prie decided to leave he did not budge, but stayed rooted to the spot, until the abbé surreptitiously indicated, with a vigorous gesture, that he should escort his benefactress back to the château. He walked beside her, stammering out thanks, and tangling his words up whenever she looked at him. It made her feel quite cheerful. For the first time she felt the old relish, mingled with slight contempt, of seeing a human being powerless before her. It revived the desire to toy with others which had become a necessity of life to her during her years of power. He stopped at the gateway of the château, bowed clumsily and strode away with his stiff, rustic gait, hardly giving her time to remind him to come and see her tomorrow.

She watched him go, smiling to herself. He was clumsy and naïve, but all the same he was alive and passionate, not dead like everything else around her. He was fire, and she was freezing. Her body was starved here too, accustomed as it was to caresses and embraces; her eyes, if they were to have any lively brilliance, must reflect the sparkling desires of the young that came her way daily in Paris. She watched for a long time as he walked away: this could be a toy, admittedly made of hard wood, rough-hewn and artless, but still a toy to help her pass the time.

*

Next morning the young man called. Madame de Prie, who weary as she was with inactivity and discontent did not usually rise until late in the afternoon, decided to receive the caller in her bed. First she had herself carefully adorned by her lady's maid, with a little red colour on her lips, which were getting paler and paler. Then she told the maid to admit her visitor.

The door slowly creaked open. Hesitantly and very awkwardly, the young man made his way in. He had put on his best garments, which nonetheless were the Sunday clothes of a rustic, and smelled rather too strongly of various greasy ointments. His gaze wandered searchingly from the floor to the ceiling of the darkened room, and he seemed relieved to find no one there, until an encouraging greeting came from beneath the pink cloud of the canopy over the bed. He started, for he either did not know or had forgotten that great ladies in Paris received visitors at their *levée*. He made some kind of backwards movement, as if he had stepped into deep water, and his cheeks flushed a deep red, betraying embarrassment which she enjoyed to the full and which charmed her. In honeyed tones, she invited him to come closer. It amused her to treat him with the utmost civility.

He carefully approached, as if walking a narrow plank with great depths of foaming water to right and left of him. And she held out her small, slim hand, which he cautiously took in his sturdy fingers as if he were afraid of breaking it, raising it reverently to his lips. With a friendly gesture, she invited him to sit in a comfortable armchair beside her bed, and he dropped into it as if his knees had suddenly been broken.

He felt a little safer sitting there. Now the whole room couldn't go on circling wildly around him, the floor couldn't rock like waves. However, the unusual sight still confused him, the loose silk of the covers seemed to mould the shape of her naked body, and the pink cloud of the canopy hovered like mist. He dared not look, yet he felt that he couldn't keep his eyes fixed on the floor for ever. His hands, his useless large, red hands, moved up and down the arms of the chair as if he had to hold on tight. Then they took fright at their own restlessness, and lay in his lap, frozen like heavy clods. There was a burning, almost tearful sensation in his eyes, fear tore at all his muscles, and his throat felt powerless to utter a word.

She was delighted by his awkwardness. It pleased her to let the silence drag mercilessly on, to watch, smiling, as he struggled to utter his first word, repeatedly unable to bring out anything but a stammer. She liked to see a young man as strong as an ox trembling and looking helplessly around him. Finally she took pity on him, and began asking him about his intentions, in which she contrived to pretend an uncommon amount of interest, so that he gradually plucked up his courage again. He talked about his studies, the church fathers and philosophers, and she chatted to him without knowing much about it. And when the self-important sobriety with which he put forward his opinions and expanded on them began to bore her, she amused herself by making little movements to discompose him. Sometimes she plucked at the bedspread as if it were about to slide off; at an abrupt gesture from the speaker she suddenly raised a bare arm from the crumpled silk; she wriggled her feet under the covers; and every time she did this he stopped, became confused, stumbled over his words or brought them out tumbling over each other, his face assumed an increasingly tortured and tense expression, and now and then she saw a vein run swift as a snake across his forehead. The game entertained her. She liked his boyish confusion a thousand times better than his well-turned rhetoric. And now she sought to discomfit him verbally too.

"You mustn't keep thinking so much of your studies and your sterling qualities! There are certain skills that matter more in Paris. You must learn to put yourself forward. You're an attractive man; be clever, make good use of your youth, above all, don't neglect women. Women mean everything in Paris, so our weakness must be your strength. Learn to choose your lovers and exploit them well, and you'll become a minister. Have you ever had a lover here?"

The young man started. All of a sudden his face was dark as blood. An overpowering sense of intolerable strain urged him to run to the door, but there was a heaviness in him, as if he were dazed by the fragrance of this woman's perfume, by her breath. All his muscles felt cramped, his chest was tense, he felt himself running crazily wild.

Then there was a crack. His clutching fingers had broken the arm of the chair. He jumped up in alarm, unspeakably humiliated by this mishap, but she, charmed by his elemental passion, just smiled and said, "Oh, you mustn't take fright like that when you're asked a question that you're not used to. You'll find it often happens in Paris. But you must learn a few more courtly manners, and I'll help you. I find it difficult to do without my secretary anyway; I would like it if you'd take his place here."

His eyes shining, he stammered effusive thanks and pressed her hand so hard that it hurt. She smiled, a sad smile—here it was again, the old delusion of imagining herself loved, when the reality was that one man had a position in mind, another his vanity, a third his career. All the same, it was so delightful to keep forgetting that. And here she had no one to delude but herself. Three days later he was her lover.

But the dangerous boredom had only been scared away, not mortally wounded. It dragged itself through the empty rooms again, lying in wait behind their doors. Only unwelcome news came from Paris. The King did not reply to her at all; Marie Leszczynska sent a few frosty lines inquiring after her health and carefully avoiding any hint of friendly feeling. She thought the lampoons were tasteless and offensive, besides showing too clearly who had commissioned them, which was enough to make her position at court even worse, in so far as anyone there still remembered her. Nor was there a word in the letter she received from her friend Alincourt about any return, not even a glimmer of hope. She felt like a woman who was thought dead but wakes in her coffin underground, screaming and raving and hammering on its sides, while no one hears her up above, men and women walk lightly over the ground, and her voice chokes alone in the solitude. Madame de Prie wrote a few more letters, but with the same feeling that she was buried alive and screaming, well aware that no one would hear her, that she was hammering helplessly against the walls of her isolation. However, writing them passed the time, and here in Courbépine time was her bitterest enemy.

Her game with the young man soon bored her too. She had never shown any constancy in her affections (it was the main reason behind her fall from favour), and this young fellow's few words of love, the awkwardness that he soon forgot once she had given him good clothes, silk stockings and fine buckles for his shoes, could not keep her mind occupied. Her nature was so sated with the company of crowds that she soon wearied of a single man, and as soon as she was alone she seemed to herself repulsive and wretched. Seducing this timid peasant, schooling his clumsy caresses, making the bear dance had been a pretty game; she found possessing him was tedious, indeed positively embarrassing.

And furthermore, he no longer pleased her. She had been charmed by the adoration he had shown her, his devotion, his confusion. But he soon shed those qualities and developed a familiarity that repelled her; his once humble gaze was now full of relish and self-satisfaction. He preened in his fine clothes, and she suspected that he showed off to the village in them. A kind of hatred gradually arose in her, because he had gained all this from her unhappiness and loneliness, because he was healthy and ate with a hearty appetite, while she ate less and less out of rage and her injured feelings, and grew thin and weak. He took her for granted as his lover, oaf that he was, he lolled contentedly in the idle bed of his conquest, instead of showing his first amazement when she gave him the gift of herself, he grew apathetic and lazy, and she, bitterly envious, burning with unhappiness and ignominy, hated his repellent satisfaction, his boorish avarice and base pride. And she hated herself for sinking so low that she must reach out to such crude folk if she was not to founder in the mud of solitude.

She began to provoke and torment him. She had never really been vicious, but she felt a need to avenge herself on someone for everything, for her enemies' triumph, her exile from Paris, her unanswered letters, for Courbépine. And she had no one else to hand. She wanted to rouse him from his lethargic ease, make him feel small again, not so happy, make him cringe. She mercilessly reproached him for his red hands, his lack of sophistication, his bad manners, but he, with a man's healthy instinct, took little notice now of the woman who had once summoned him to her. He was defiant, he laughed, and indignantly shook off her sarcasm. But she did not stop: irritating someone made a nice game to relieve her boredom. She tried to make him jealous, told him on every occasion about her lovers in Paris, counted them on her fingers for him. She showed him presents she had been given, she exaggerated and told lies. But he merely felt flattered to think that, after all those dukes and princes, she had chosen him. He smacked his lips with satisfaction and was not discomposed. That enraged her even more. She told him other, worse things, she lied to him about the grooms and valets she had had. His brow darkened at last. She saw it, laughed, and went on. Suddenly he struck the table with his fist.

"That's enough! Why are you telling me all this?"

Her expression was perfectly innocent. "Because I like to."

"But I don't want to hear it."

"I do, my dear, or I wouldn't do it."

He said nothing, but bit his lip. She had so naturally commanding a tone of voice that he felt like a servant. He clenched his fists. How like an animal he is when he's angry, she thought, feeling both revulsion and fear. She sensed the danger in the atmosphere. But there was too much anger pent up in her, she couldn't stop tormenting him. She began again.

"What strange ideas you have of life, my dear. Do you think Parisians live as you do in your hovels here, where one is slowly bored to death?"

His nostrils flared; he snorted. Then he said, "People don't have to come here if they think it's so boring."

She felt the pang deep within her. So he knew about her exile too. She supposed the valet had spread the news. She felt weaker now that he knew, and smiled to veil her fear.

"My dear, there are reasons that you may not necessarily understand even if you've learned a little Latin. Perhaps you would have found it more useful to study better manners."

He said nothing, but she heard him snorting quietly with rage. That aroused her even more and she felt something like a sensual desire to hurt him.

"And there you stand proud as a cockerel on the dunghill. Why do you snort like that? You're acting like a lout!"

"We can't all be princes or dukes or grooms."

He was red in the face and had clenched his fists. She, however, poisoned by unhappiness, leaped to her feet.

"Be quiet! You forget who I am. I won't be spoken to like that by a rustic oaf!"

He made a gesture.

"Be quiet! Or else…"

"Or else?"

He impudently faced her. And it occurred to her that she had no "or else" left. She couldn't have anyone sent to the Bastille, or reduced to the ranks or dismissed, she couldn't command or forbid anyone to do or not to do something. She was nothing, only a defenceless woman like hundreds of thousands in France, vulnerable to any insult, any injustice.

"Or else," she said, fighting for breath, "I'll have you thrown out by the servants."

He shrugged his shoulders and turned. He was going to leave.

But she wouldn't let him. He was not to be the one to throw her over! Another man rejecting her—least of all must it be this one. All her anger suddenly broke out, the accumulated bitterness of days, and she went for him as if she were drunk.

"Get out! Do you think I need you, you fool of a peasant, just because I felt sorry for you? Go away! Don't soil my floors any more. Go where you like but not to Paris, and not to me. Get out! I hate you, your avarice, your simplicity, your stupid satisfaction—you disgust me. Get out!"

Then the unexpected happened. As she so suddenly flung her hatred at him, he had been holding his fists clenched in front of him like an invisible shield, but now they suddenly came down on her with the impact of falling stones. She screamed and stared at him. But he struck and struck in blind, vengeful rage, intoxicated by the awareness of his strength, he struck her, taking out on her all a peasant's envy of the distinguished and clever aristocrat, all the hatred of a man despised for a woman, he hammered it all into her weak, flinching, convulsed body. She screamed at first, then whimpered quietly and fell silent. The humiliation hurt her more than the blows. She fell silent, felt his rage, and still preserved her silence.

Then he stopped, exhausted, and horrified by what he had done. A shudder ran through her body. He thought she was about to stand up, and he fled, afraid of her glance. But it was only the weeping that she had held back suddenly tearing convulsively through her body.

And so she broke her last toy herself.

The door had closed behind him long ago, and still she did not move. She lay there like an animal hunted to death, breathing quietly but stertorously, and quite without fear, without feelings, without any sense of pain or shame. She was full of an unspeakable weariness, she felt no wish for revenge, no indignation, just weariness, an unspeakable weariness as if all her blood had flowed out of her together with her tears and only her lifeless body lay here, held down by its own weight. She did not try to stand up, she didn't know what to do with herself after such an experience.

The evening slowly entered the room, and she did not feel it. For evening comes quietly. It does not look boldly through the window like mid-day, it seeps from the walls like dark water, raises the ceiling into a void, brings everything gently floating down into its soundless torrent. When she looked up, there was darkness around her and silence, except for the sound of the little clock mincing along into infinity somewhere. The curtains fell in dark folds as if some fearful monster were hiding behind them, the doors seemed to have sunk into the wall in some way, making the room look sealed and black around her, like a nailed-up coffin. There was no way in or out any more, it was all boundless yet barred, everything seemed to weigh down, compressing the air so that she could gasp, not breathe.

At the far end of the room shone a path into the unknown: the tall mirror there gleamed faintly in the dark like the nocturnal surface of a marshy pool, and now, as she rose, something white swirled out of it. She got to her feet, went closer, it surged from the mirror like smoke, a ghostly creature: she herself, coming closer and quickly withdrawing again.

She felt dread. Something in her cried out for light, but she did not want to call anyone. She struck the tinder herself, and then one by one lit the candles in the dully glowing bronze candelabrum standing on its marble console. The flames flickered, quivering as they felt their way into the dark, like someone overheated stepping into a cool bath; they retreated, came forward again, and at last a trembling, circular cloud of light rose above the candelabrum and hovered there, casting more and more circles of light on the ceiling. High above, where delicate *amoretti* with wings of cloud usually rocked in the blue sky, grey, misty shadows now lay, with the soft lightning of the quivering candle-flames flashing fitfully through them. The objects all around seemed to have been roused from sleep; they stood there motionless, with shadows creeping high behind them as if animals had been crouching there, giving them a fearful look.

However, the mirror enticed and allured her. Something was always moving in it when she looked. Otherwise, all around her was silent and hostile, the objects were sleepy, human beings rejected her. She could ask no questions, couldn't complain to anyone, but there was something in the mirror that gave an answer, did not remain indifferent, moved and looked significantly at her. But what should she ask it? She had seldom asked if she was beautiful in Paris. The bright eyes of the men who desired her had been her mirror. She knew she was beautiful from her triumphs, her passionate nights, from the amazement of the common people when she drove to Versailles in her carriage. She had believed them even when they lied, for confidence in her own power was the secret of her strength. But now, what was she now that she had been humbled?

She looked anxiously into the flickering light in the glass, as if her fate stood in the mirror looking back at her. She started in alarm: was that really herself? Her cheeks looked hollow and dull, a bitter set to her mouth mocked her, her eyes lay deep in their sockets and looked out in fear as if searching for help. She shook herself. This was just a nightmare. And she smiled at the mirror. But the smile was returned frostily, scornfully. She felt her body: no, the mirror did not lie, she had grown thin, thin as a child, and the rings hung loose on her fingers. She felt the blood flow more coldly in her veins. She was full of dread. Was everything over, youth as well? A furious desire came over her to mock herself, celebrated as she was, the mistress of France, and as if in a dream she spoke the lines that Voltaire had written when dedicating his play to her, the lines that her flatterers liked to repeat:

> Vous qui possedez la beauté
> Sans être vaine et coquette
> Et l'extrème vivacité
> Sans être jamais indiscrète,
> Vous à qui donnèrent les Dieux
> Tant des lumières naturelles
> Un esprit juste, gracieux,
> Solide dans le sérieux
> Et charmant dans les bagatelles. *

Every word now seemed to express derision, and she stared and stared into the mirror to see if the woman there was not mocking her too.

She raised the candelabrum to get a better view of herself. And the closer she held it the more she seemed to age. Every minute she spent looking into the mirror seemed to put years on her life, she saw herself grow paler and paler, becoming more wan, sicklier, older all the time, she felt herself aging, her whole life seemed to be passing away. She trembled. She saw her fate horribly revealed

---

* Lady, yours is a beauty bright, never flirtatious, never vain; your liveliness will show no spite, and never seeks to inflict pain. Yours, all the bounty of the mind, a spirit gracious, full of love. In graver questions wise you prove, in matters light, charming and kind.

in the mirror, the entire story of her decline, and she couldn't take her eyes off it, but stared and stared at the white, distorted mask of the old woman who was herself.

Then, suddenly, the candles all flickered at once as if in alarm, the flames turned blue and tried to fly up from their wicks. A dark figure stood in the mirror, its hand reaching out to her.

She uttered a piercing scream, and in self-defence flung the bronze candelabrum at the mirror. A thousand sparks sprang from the glass. The candles fell to the floor and went out. There was darkness around her and in her as she collapsed unconscious. She had seen her fate.

The courier who had entered the room with news from Paris, and whose sudden appearance in the mirror-frame had so alarmed Madame de Prie, saw only the shimmering of the broken shards of glass, and heard the sound of a fall in the darkness. He ran to fetch the servants. They found Madame de Prie lying motionless on the floor among the sparkling glass splinters and the extinguished candles, her eyes closed. Only her bluish lips trembled slightly, showing a sign of life. They carried her to her bed, and a servant set out to ride to Amfreville and fetch the doctor.

But the sick woman soon came round, and with difficulty brought herself back to reality amidst the frightened faces. She did not know exactly how she had come here, but she controlled her fear and weariness in front of the others, kept her ever-ready smile on her bloodless lips, although her face had now frozen to a mask, and asked in a voice that endeavoured to be carefree, even cheerful, what had happened to her. In alarm, and evasively, the servants told her. She did not reply, but smiled and reached for the letter.

However, it was difficult for her to keep that smile on her face. Her friend wrote to say that he had succeeded in speaking to the

King at last. The King was still extremely angry with her, because she had wrecked the country's finances and roused the people against her, but there was some hope of having her recalled to Paris in two or three years' time. The letter shook in her hands. Was she to live away from Paris for two years without people around her, without power? She was not strong enough to bear such solitude. It was her death sentence. She knew that she couldn't breathe without happiness, without power, without youth, without love; after ruling France, she couldn't live here like a peasant woman.

And all of a sudden she understood the figure in the mirror that had reached out for her, and the extinguishing of the flames: she must put an end to it before she grew really old, wholly ugly and wholly unhappy. She refused to see the doctor, who had now arrived; only the King could have helped her. And as he would not, she must help herself. The thought no longer hurt her. She had died long ago, on the day when the officer stood in her room and took everything from her that kept her alive: the air of Paris, the only place where she could breathe; the power that was her plaything; the admiration and triumph to which she owed her strength. The woman who roamed these empty rooms, lonely, bored, and humiliated, was no longer Madame de Prie, was an aging, unhappy, ugly creature whom she must kill so that it would not dishonour the name that had once shone brightly over France.

Now that the exiled woman had decided to put an end to it herself, her sense of frozen heaviness, her urgent disquiet had left her. She had a purpose again, an occupation, something that kept her going, excited her and intrigued her with the various possibilities it offered. For she would not die here like an animal breathing its last in a corner; she wanted an aura of the mysterious and mystical to hover around her death. She would come to a heroic, legendary end like the queens of antiquity. Her life had burned bright, and so must her death; it must arouse the somnolent admiration of the multitude once again. No one in Paris was to guess that she died here in torment, choked by loneliness and disfavour, burnt up by her unsatisfied greed for power; she would deceive them all by staging her death as a drama. Deception, the delight of her life, opened up her heart again. She would end it all in a blazing fire of merriment, as if at random, she wouldn't die squirming like a discarded wax taper coiling on the ground, trodden out in pity. She would go down into the abyss dancing.

Next day a number of notes flew away from her desk: affectionate, appealing, seductive, imperious, promising and softly perfumed lines. She scattered her invitations around Paris and the provinces, she held out the prospect of their favourite occupations to everyone, offered some hunting, others gaming, others again masked balls. She had actors, singers and dancers hired by her agents in Paris, she ordered expensive costumes, announced the founding of a second court in France, with all the refinements and pleasures of Versailles. She enticed and invited strangers and acquaintances, the distinguished and the less distinguished, but she must have people here, a great many people, an audience for the comedy of happiness and satisfaction that she was going to stage before the end came.

And soon a new life began in Courbépine. Parisian society, always craving pleasure, sought out this novelty. In addition, its members all felt a secret, slightly contemptuous curiosity to see how the former mistress of France, now toppled, took her exile. One festivity followed another. Carriages came emblazoned with noble coats of arms, large country coaches arrived crammed with high-spirited passengers, army officers came on horseback—more visitors flooded in every day, and with them an army of hangers-on and servants. Many had brought pastoral costumes with them, as if for a rustic game, others came in great pomp and ceremony. The little village was like a military camp.

And the château awoke, its once unlighted windows shining proudly, for it was enlivened by talking and laughter, games and music. People walked up and down, couples whispered in corners where only grey silence had lurked. Women's dresses glowed in bright hues in the shade of the shrubberies, the cheerfully plangent tunes of risqué songs were plucked on mandolins far into the night. Servants hurried along the corridors, the windows were framed by flowers, coloured lights sparkled among the bushes. They lived out the carefree life of Versailles, the light charm of heedlessness. The absence of the real court did take a little of the bloom off it all, but increased the exuberance that encouraged the guests to dance, free from all constraints of etiquette.

At the centre of this whirlwind of activity, Madame de Prie felt her sluggish blood begin to circulate feverishly again. She was one of those women, and they are not rare, who are shaped entirely by other people's attitudes. She was beautiful when she was desired, witty in clever company, proud when she was flattered, in love when she was loved. The more that was expected of her, the more she gave. But in solitude, where no one saw her, spoke to her, heard her or wanted anything of her, she had become ugly, dull-witted, helpless, unhappy. She could be lively only in the midst of life; in isolation she dwindled to a shadow. And now that the reflected light of her earlier life shone around her, all her merriment and her carefree charm sparkled in the air again, she was witty once more, agreeable, she wove her enchantments, made conversation, caught fire from the glances that lingered on her. She forgot that she meant to deceive these people with her cheerfulness, and was in genuine high spirits, she took every smile as a piece of good fortune, every word as true, plunged feverishly into enjoying the company she had been deprived of so long, as if falling into the arms of a lover.

She made the festivities wilder and wilder, she summoned more and more guests, enticing them to Courbépine. And more and more came. For at the time, after the failure of John Law's financial system, the land was impoverished, but she herself was rich, and she was casting the millions she had extorted during her time of power to the wind. Money was thrown down on the gaming tables, went up in smoke in expensive firework displays, was squandered on exotic fancies, but she threw it away more and more wildly, like a woman desperate. The guests were amazed, surprised by her lavish expenditure and the magnificence of the festivities; no one knew in whose honour they were really given. And in all the wild merriment, she herself almost forgot.

The festivities continued unabated for the whole month of August. September came, the trees wore colourful fruits in their hair, and the evening clouds were shot with gold. The guests were fewer now; time was pressing.

But amidst the pleasures, Madame de Prie had almost forgotten her purpose. Wishing to deceive others with such magnificent frenzies, she deceived herself; her carefree mood matched this imitation of her former life so well that she took it for real, and even believed in her power, her beauty, her *joie de vivre*.

To be sure, one thing was different, and that hurt. People were all kinder to her now that she was of no importance, they were warmer and yet cooler. The women no longer envied her, did not inflict malicious little pinpricks, the men did not flock around her. They all laughed with her, treated her as a good friend, but they told no more lies about love, they did not beg, they did not flatter, they did not make an enemy of her, and that was what made her feel that she was quite powerless. A life without envy, hatred and lies was not a life worth living. She realised, with horror, that in fact she had already been forgotten; the social whirl was as wild as ever, but she was not at its centre now. The men laughed with other women, whose freshness and youth they saw for the first time; the moment had come to remind the world of herself again before she grew old and a stranger to them all.

She put off her decision from day to day. A sensation quivered within her, half fear, half hope that something might yet hold her back, might keep her from that despairing leap into the irrevocable. Among all those pairs of hands reaching for the food on her tables, holding women close in the dance, rolling gold coins over the gaming tables, might there not be one who could hold her back, would want to hold her back, one who loved her so much that she could happily dispense with the bright show of a large company, and exchange the unstable possession of royal power for him? Without knowing it, she was looking for such a thing; she courted the passion of all the men, for she was courting her own life. But they all passed her by.

Then, one day, she met a young captain in the royal guard, a handsome, amusing fellow whom she had noticed before. They met as twilight fell over the park, and she saw him walking up and down among the trees, his eyes wild, his teeth clenched, and sometimes he struck the tree trunks with his fist. She spoke to him. He gave her a distracted answer; she saw that some secret was troubling him, and asked the reason for his desperation. At last he confessed that he had lost a hundred *louis d'or* at the gaming table, money entrusted to him by his regiment. That made him a thief, and now he must carry out sentence on himself. She felt it strangely ominous that here, amidst this happy tumult, someone else had come to the same dark conclusion too. But this man was young, had rosy cheeks, could laugh again; there was still help for him. She summoned him to her room and gave him five hundred *louis d'or*. Trembling with joy, he kissed her hands. She kept him there a long time, but that was all he wanted from her, he asked no more with any glance or gesture.

She was shaken; she couldn't even buy love now. That fortified her in her decision.

She sent him away, and stepped quickly out into the hall. Laughter met her as she opened the door, happy voices and lively people filled the room like a cloud. Suddenly she felt that she hated them all, cheerful as they were, dancing and laughing on her grave. Envy took hold of her when she thought that they would all live on, and be happy.

She was burning with a malicious desire to disturb her guests, alarm and confuse them, stop their laughter. And suddenly, when their exuberance died down for a second and silence fell, she said directly, "Don't you notice that there's a death in the house?"

For a moment confusion reigned. Even to a drunk, the word "death" is like a hammer falling on his heart. Baffled, they asked each other who was dead. "I am," Madame de Prie said coldly, without any change of expression, "I shall not see this winter come."

She spoke so gravely, in so sombre a tone, that they all looked at one another in silence. But only for a second. Then a jest flew from somewhere in the room like a coloured ball, someone else threw it back, and as if enlivened by the curious notion of death the wave of exuberance surged foaming and high again, and buried the discomfort of that initial surprise.

Madame de Prie remained very calm. She felt that there was no going back now. But it amused her to stage her prophecy even more dramatically. She went up to one of the round tables where her guests were playing faro, and waited for the next card to be turned over. It was a seven of one of the black suits, clubs or spades. "The seventh of October, then." Without meaning to, she had said it out loud under her breath.

"What's the seventh of October?" one of the onlookers asked casually.

She looked at him calmly. "The day of my death."

They all laughed. The joke was passed on. Madame de Prie was delighted to find that no one believed her. If they didn't trust her in life any more, then at least they should see how she and her comedy had fooled them in death. A wonderful sense of superiority, pleasure and ease ran through her limbs. She felt as if she must rejoice aloud in high spirits and derision.

In the next room music was playing. A dance had just begun. She joined the dancers, and had never danced better.

From that moment on, her life had meaning again. She knew she was preparing to do something that would certainly make her immortal. She imagined the King's amazement, the horror of her guests when her prophecy of her death came true to the very day. And she was staging the comedy most carefully; she invited more and more guests, doubled her expenditure, worked on the multifarious magnificence of these last days as if it were a work of art, something that would make her sudden fall even more keenly felt. She aired the prediction of her death again at every opportunity, but always drew a glittering curtain of merriment over it; she wanted everyone to know that it had been announced, and no one to believe it. Only death would raise her name once again to the ranks of those who could never be forgotten, from which the King had cast her down.

Two days before she was to carry out her irrevocable purpose, she gave the last and most magnificent festivities of all. Since the Persian and other Islamic embassies had set up for the first time in Paris, all things Oriental had been the fashion in France: books were written in Eastern guise, the fairy tales and legends of the Orient were translated, Arab costume was popular, and people imitated the flowery style of Eastern language. At enormous expense, Madame de Prie had turned the whole château into an Oriental palace. Costly rugs lay on the floor, squawking parrots and white-feathered cockatoos rocked on their perches on the window bars, held there by silver chains; servants hurried soundlessly down the corridors in turbans and baggy silk trousers, taking Turkish sweetmeats and other refreshments entirely unknown at the time to the guests, who were dazzled by such daring splendour. Coloured tents were erected in the garden, boys cooled them by waving broad fans, music rang out from the dark shadows of the shrubberies, everything possible was done to make the evening an unforgettable fairy-tale experience, and the silvery half-moon hanging in the starry sky that night encouraged the imagination to conjure up the mysteriously sultry atmosphere of a night by the Bosphorus.

But the real surprise was a particularly spacious tent, containing a stage hung with red velvet curtains. Wishing to appear to her guests in the full radiance of her fame and beauty, Madame de Prie had decided to act a play herself; a final display of all the merriment and levity of her life to an audience was to be her last and finest deception. In the few days she still had left, she had commissioned a young author to write a play to her exact requirements. Time was short and his alexandrines bad, but that was not what mattered to her. The tragedy was set in the Orient, and she herself was to play the part of Zengane, a young queen whose realm is captured by enemies and who goes proudly to her death, although the magnanimous victor offers to share all his royal power with her if she will be his wife. She had insisted on these details: she wanted to give a dress rehearsal of her voluntary death in front of the unsuspecting audience before she put the plan into practice.

And in addition she wanted to experience the past once more, if only in game, she wanted to be queen again, and show that she was born to it and must die once she was deprived of power.

Her aim was to be beautiful and royal in the eyes of others on that last evening; she would adorn her past image with an invisible crown, ensuring that her name aroused that pure shiver of veneration which attends all that is sublime. Cosmetics veiled the pallor of her sunken cheeks, her thin figure was concealed by the flowing

Oriental robes she wore, the confusing brightness of the jewels gleaming on her hair, like dew on a dark flower in the morning moisture, outshone her tired eyes. And when she appeared like this in the brightness behind the curtain as it swept back, a brightness further intensified by her passion, when she appeared on stage surrounded by kneeling servants and the awe-stricken populace, a rustle passed through the ranks of her guests. Her heart was thudding: for the first time in these bitter weeks she felt the delightful wave of admiration that had borne her life up for so long surging towards her, and a wonderful feeling arose in her, a sweet sadness mingled with melancholy pleasure, a regret that kept receding, flowing back into a great sense of happiness. Before her, the surf of the wave flickered, she did not see individuals any more, only a great crowd, perhaps her guests, perhaps all France, perhaps generations yet to come, perhaps eternity. And she felt only, and blissfully, one thing: she was standing on a great height again, envied, admired, the cynosure of all those curious and nameless eyes, and at last, after such a long time, she felt aware of living again, of being really alive. Death was not too high a price to pay for this second of life.

She played her part magnificently, although she had never tried acting before. She had shed everything that prevents most people from making a show of emotion to others—fear, timidity, shame, awkwardness—she had shed all that, and was now playing only with objects. She wanted to be queen, and she was queen again for the length of an hour. Only once did her breath fail her, when she spoke the line, "*Je vais mourir, oh ne me plaignez pas!*"*, for she felt that she was expressing her deep wish for life, and was afraid they might not be deceived, might understand her, warn her, hold her back. But in fact the pause after that cry seemed in itself to be acted with such irresistible credibility that a shudder ran through the audience. And when, with a wild gesture, she turned the dagger against her heart,

---

* Now I shall die, oh do not mourn for me!

fell, and seemed to die smiling, when the play was over—although only now did it really begin—they stormed to applaud her, paying her tribute with an enthusiasm that she had not known even in the days of her greatest power.

However, she had only a smile for all the uproar, and when she was complimented on her magnificent performance of the death of Zengane, she said calmly, "I suppose that, today, I should know how to die. Death dwells in me already. It will all be over the day after tomorrow."

They laughed again, but it no longer hurt her. There was blessed, painless merriment inside her, and such a childishly exuberant joy at having deceived all these enthusiastic people that she instinctively joined in the peals of laughter. Once she had played only with men and power; now she saw that there was no better toy than death.

Next day, the last full day of her life, the guests went away; she meant to receive death alone. The coaches churned up white dust like clouds in the distance, the horsemen trotted away, the halls were emptied of light and laughter, a restless wind howled down the chimney. She felt as if the blood were slowly flowing out of her veins with the departing guests, she felt herself becoming colder and colder, weaker, more defenceless, more fearful. Death had seemed to her so easy yesterday, just a game; now that she was alone again, it suddenly showed her its horror and its power once more.

And everything that she thought she had tamed and trodden underfoot awoke again. The last evening came, and once more the snake-like shadows that, alarmed by the light, had hidden behind objects came crawling out of hiding with flickering tongues. Dread, stifled by laughter and veiled by the bright images of human company, gradually returned all-powerful to the deserted rooms. The silence had only been cowering under the surging sound of voices; now it spread abroad again like mist, filled the rooms, the halls, the stairways, the corridors, and her shuddering heart as well.

She would have liked to make an end of it at once. But she had chosen the seventh of October, and must not destroy the deception, that artificial, glimmering, lying construct of her triumph, just for the sake of a whim. She must wait. It was worse than being dead, though, to wait for the hour of death while the wind outside mocked her, and dark shadows in here reached for her heart. How could she bear this long last night before death, this endless time until dawn? Dark objects, spectre-like, pressed closer and closer, all the shades of her past life rose from their burial vaults—she fled before them from room to room, but they stared at her from the pictures, grinned behind the windows, crouched down behind cupboards. The dead reached out to her, though she was still alive and wanted human company, company just for one night. She longed for a human being as if for a coat in which to wrap her shivering form until day dawned.

Suddenly she rang the bell, which screeched shrilly like a wounded animal. A servant, drowsy with sleep, came upstairs to her. She told him to go at once to the priest's nephew, wake him and bring him here. She had important news for him.

The servant stared as if she were mad. But she did not feel it, she felt nothing at all, every emotion had died in her. She was not ashamed to summon the man who had beaten her, she did not hesitate to summon a man to her bedroom at night in front of the servant. There was only a cold void in her, she felt that her poor shivering body needed warmth if it were not to freeze. Her soul was dead already; she had only to kill her body now.

After a while the door opened. Her former lover came in. His face was chilly and contemptuous, he seemed unspeakably strange to her. And yet the horror shrank back slightly under the objects in the room, just because he opened the door and she was no longer entirely alone with them.

He took pains to seem very decided and not betray his inner astonishment, since this summons was entirely unexpected. For days, while the festivities were in full swing in the château, he had slunk around the barred gateways of the park, his eyes narrowed with rage; he had eaten his heart out with self-reproaches, for he, as her lover, should have been able to stride through the midst of this brilliance. He was consumed with anger for having so humiliated her; those extravagant festivities had suddenly made the power of the wealth that he had failed to exploit very clear to him again. And moreover, his hours with Madame de Prie had made him desire these fine, fragrant, spoilt ladies with their delicate, fragile limbs, their strangely provocative lusts, their rustling silken dresses. He had taken himself back to the priest's poverty-stricken house, where everything suddenly seemed to him crude, dirty and worn. His greed, once roused, made him look avidly at all the ladies who came from Paris, but none of them looked back at him, their coaches scornfully splashed him with the mud their wheels threw up, and the great lords didn't even see him when he humbly raised his hat to them. A hundred times he had felt impelled to go into the château and fling himself at Madame de Prie's feet, and every time fear had held him back.

But now she had summoned him, and that made him arrogant. Inwardly, he straightened his back: it was the proudest moment of his life to think that she needed him again after all.

For a moment they looked at one another, barely able to hide the hatred in their eyes. At that moment, each despised the other because each intended to misuse the other. Madame de Prie controlled herself. Her voice was very cool.

"The Duke of Berlington asked me yesterday if I could recommend him a secretary. If you would like the post, I'll send you to Paris tomorrow with a letter for him."

The young man trembled. He had already assumed a haughty bearing, intending to be condescending and gracious if she was seeking his favours. But all that was gone now. Greed overcame him. Paris gleamed before his eyes.

"If madame were to be so kind—I—I can't think of anything that would make me happier," he stammered. His eyes had the pleading expression of a beaten dog in them.

She nodded. Then she looked at him, commandingly yet milder again. He understood. Everything would be the way it had once been...

And not for a second of that passionate night did she forget that she hated him, despised him, and was deceiving him—for there was no Duke of Berlington —she knew how contemptible she herself was, driven to buy a man's caresses with a lie, yet it was life, real life that she felt in his limbs, drank from his lips, not the darkness and silence already coming to hold her fast. She felt the warmth of his youth driving death away, and knew at every moment that she was trying to deceive death itself, the death that was coming closer and closer, and of whose power she now, for the first time, had some inkling.

The morning of the seventh of October was clear. Sunlight shimmered above the fields, even the shadows were translucent and pure. Madame de Prie dressed carefully, as if for a great feast, put her affairs in order, burned letters. She locked her jewellery, which was very valuable, in an ebony casket, tore up all her promissory notes and contracts. Now that it was day again, everything in her was clear and determined once more, and she wanted clarity above all else.

Her lover came in. She spoke to him kindly and without resentment; it pained her to think that she was so pitilessly deceiving the last man who had meant anything to her, even if he had not meant much. She did not want anyone to speak of her with resentment, only with admiration and gratitude. And she felt an urge to lavish the jewellery from the casket on him, in return for that one last night. It was a fortune.

But he was half-asleep and inattentive. In his boorish greed for gain, he thought of nothing but his position, his future. The memory of their passionate caresses made him yet bolder. Abruptly, he said he must set off for Paris at once, or he might arrive too late, and he demanded rather than requested the letter of recommendation. Something froze inside her. She had hired him, and now he was asking for payment.

She wrote the letter, a letter to a man who did not exist and whom he could never find. But she still hesitated to give it to him. Once more she put off her decision. She asked if he couldn't stay one day longer; she would like that very much, she said. And as she spoke she balanced the casket in her hand. She felt that if he said yes it might yet save her. But all their decisions led the same way. He was in a hurry. He didn't want to stay. If he had not said it in such a surly manner, making her feel so clearly that he had let himself be bought only for one night, she would have given him the jewellery, which was worth hundreds of thousands of livres. But he was brusque, his glance impudent and with no love in it. So she took a single, very small jewel with only a dull glow to it—dull as his eyes—and gave it to him in return for taking the casket, of whose contents he had no idea, to the Ursuline convent in Paris. She added a letter asking the nuns to say Masses for her soul. Then she sent the impatient young man off to find the Duke of Berlington.

He thanked her, not effusively, and left, unaware of the value of the casket that he himself was carrying. And so, after acting out a comedy of her feelings in front of them all, she deceived even the last man to cross her path.

Then she closed the door and quickly took a small flask from a drawer. It was made of fine Chinese porcelain, with strange, monstrous dragons coiling and curling in blue on it. She looked at it with curiosity, toyed with it as carelessly as she had toyed with her fellow men and women, with princes, with France, with love and death. She unscrewed the stopper and poured the clear liquid into a small dish. For a moment she hesitated, really just from a childish fear that it might have a bitter flavour. Cautiously, like a kitten sniffing warm milk, she touched it with her tongue; no, it didn't taste bad. And so she drank the contents of the dish down in a single draught.

The whole thing, at that moment, seemed to her somehow amusing and extremely ludicrous: to think that you had only to take that one tiny sip, and tomorrow you wouldn't see the clouds, the fields, the woods any more, messengers would go riding, the King would be horrified and all of France amazed. So this was the great step that she had feared taking so much. She thought of the astonishment of her guests, of the legends that would be told of the way she had foretold the day of her death, and failed to understand only one thing: that she had given herself to death because she missed the company of humans, those same gullible humans who could be deceived with such a little comedy. Dying seemed to her altogether easy, you could even smile as you died—yes, you could indeed, she tried it—you could perfectly well smile, and it wasn't difficult to preserve a beautiful and tranquil face in death, a face radiant with unearthly bliss. It was true, even after death you could act happiness. She hadn't known that. She found everything, human beings, the world, death and life, suddenly so very amusing that the smile she had prepared sprang involuntarily to her carefree lips. She straightened up, as if there were a mirror opposite her somewhere, waited for death, and smiled and smiled and smiled.

But death was not to be deceived, and broke her laughter. When Madame de Prie was found her face was distorted into a terrible grimace. Those dreadful features showed everything that she had really suffered in the last few weeks: her rage, her torment, her aimless fear, her wild and desperate pain. The deceptive smile for which she had struggled so avidly had been helpless, had drained away. Her feet were twisted together in torment, her hands had clutched a curtain so convulsively that scraps of it were left between her fingers, her mouth was open as if in a shrill scream.

And all that show of apparent merriment, the mystic prophecy of the day of her death had been for nothing too. The news of her suicide arrived in Paris on the evening when an Italian conjuror was displaying his arts at court. He made rabbits disappear into a hat, he brought grown geese out of eggshells. When the message arrived people were slightly interested, were surprised, whispered, the name of Madame de Prie went around for a few minutes, but then the conjuror performed another amazing trick and she was forgotten, just as she herself would have forgotten someone else's fate at such a moment. Interest in her strange end did not last long in France, and her desperate efforts to stage a drama that would never be forgotten were in vain. The fame she longed for, the immortality she thought to seize by force with her death, passed her name by: her story was buried under the dust and ashes of trivial events. For the history of the world will not tolerate intruders; it chooses its own heroes and implacably dismisses those not summoned to that rank, however hard they may try; someone who has fallen off the carriage of fate as it goes along will never catch up with it again. And nothing was left of the strange end of Madame de Prie, her real life and the ingeniously devised deception of her death but a few dry lines in some book of memoirs or other, conveying to their reader as little of the passionate emotions of her life as a pressed flower allows one to guess at the fragrant marvel of its long-forgotten spring.

THE MIRACLES
OF LIFE

To my dear friend Hans Müller

G REY MIST LAY LOW over Antwerp, enveloping the city entirely in its dense and heavy swathes. The shapes of houses were blurred in the fine, smoky vapour, and you could not see to the end of the street, but overhead there was ringing in the air, a deep sound like the word of God coming out of the clouds, for the muted voices of the bells in the church towers, calling their congregations to prayer, had also merged in the great, wild sea of mist filling the city and the countryside around, and encompassing the restless, softly roaring waters of the sea far away in the harbour. Here and there a faint gleam struggled against the damp grey mist, trying to light up a gaudy shop sign, but only muffled noise and throaty laughter told you where to find the taverns in which freezing customers gathered, complaining of the weather. The alleys seemed empty, and any passers-by were seen only as fleeting impressions that soon dissolved into the mist. It was a dismal, depressing Sunday morning.

Only the bells called and pealed as if desperately, while the mist stifled their cries. For the devout were few and far between; foreign heresy had found a foothold in this land, and even those who had not abandoned their old faith were less assiduous and zealous in the service of the Lord. Heavy morning mists were enough to keep many away from their devotions. Wrinkled old women busily telling their beads, poor folk in their plain Sunday best stood looking lost in the long, dark aisles of the churches, where the shining gold of altars and chapels and the priests' bright chasubles shone like a mild and gentle flame. But the mist seemed to have seeped through the high walls, for here, too, the chilly and sad mood of the deserted streets prevailed. The morning sermon itself was cold and austere, without a ray of sunlight to brighten it. It was preached against the Protestants, and the driving force behind it was furious rage, hatred along with a strong sense of power, for the time for moderation was over, and good news from Spain had reached the clerics—the new king served the work of the Church with admirable fervour. In his sermon, the preacher united graphic descriptions of the Last Judgement with dark words of admonition for the immediate future. If there had been a large congregation, his words might have been passed on by the faithful murmuring in their pews to a great crowd of hearers, but as it was they dropped into the dark void with a dull echo, as if frozen in the moist, chilly air.

During the storm two men had quickly entered the main porch of the cathedral, their faces obscured at first by wind-blown hair and voluminous coats with collars turned up high. The taller man shed his damp coat to reveal the honest but not especially striking features of a portly man in the rich clothing suitable for a merchant. The other was a stranger figure, although not because of anything unusual in his clothing; his gentle, unhurried movements and his rather big-boned, rustic but kindly face, surrounded by abundant waving white hair, lent him the mild aspect of an evangelist. They both said a short prayer, and then the merchant signed to his older companion to follow him. They went slowly, with measured steps, into the side aisle, which was almost entirely in darkness because dank air made the candles gutter, and heavy clouds that refused to lift still obscured the bright face of the sun. The merchant stopped at one of the small side chapels, most of which contained devotional items promised to the Church as donations by the old families of the city, and pointing to one of the little altars he said, "Here it is."

The other man came closer and shaded his eyes with his hand to see it better in the dim light. One wing of the altarpiece was occupied by a painting in clear colours made even softer by the twilight, and it immediately caught the old painter's eye. It showed the Virgin Mary, her heart transfixed by a sword, and despite the pain and sorrow of the subject it was a gentle work with an aura of reconciliation about it. Mary had a strangely sweet face, not so much that of the Mother of God as of a dreaming girl in the bloom of youth, but with the idea of pain tingeing the smiling beauty of a playful, carefree nature. Thick black hair tumbling down softly surrounded a small, pale but radiant face with very red lips, glowing like a crimson wound. The features were wonderfully delicate, and many of the brushstrokes, for instance in the assured, slender curve of the eyebrows, gave an almost yearning expression to the beauty of the tender face. The Virgin's dark eyes were deep in thought, as if dreaming of another brighter and sweeter world from which her pain was stealing her away. The hands were folded in gentle devotion, and her breast still seemed to be quivering with slight fear at the cold touch of the sword piercing her. Blood from her wound ran along it. All this was bathed in a wonderful radiance surrounding her head with golden flame, and even her heart glowed like the mystical light of the chalice in the stained glass of the church windows when sunlight fell through them. And the twilight around it took the last touch of worldliness from this picture, so that the halo around the sweet girlish face shone with the true radiance of transfiguration.

Almost abruptly, the painter tore himself away from his lengthy admiration of the picture. "None of our countrymen painted this," he said.

The merchant nodded in agreement.

"No, it is by an Italian. A young painter at the time. But there's quite a long story behind it. I will tell it all to you from the beginning, and then, as you know, I want you to complete the altarpiece by putting the keystone in place. Look, the sermon is over. We should find a better place to tell stories than this church, well as it may suit our joint efforts. Let's go."

The painter lingered for a moment longer before turning his eyes away from the picture. It seemed even more radiant as the smoky darkness outside the windows lifted, and the mist took on a golden hue. He almost felt that if he stayed here, rapt in devout contemplation of the gentle pain on those childish lips, they would smile and reveal new loveliness. But his companion had gone ahead of him already, and he had to quicken his pace to catch up with the merchant in the porch. They left the cathedral together, as they had come.

The heavy cloak of mist thrown over the city by the early spring morning had given way to a dull, silvery light caught like a cobweb among the gabled roofs. The close-set cobblestones had a steely, damp gleam, and the first of the flickering sunlight was beginning to cast its gold on them. The two men made their way down narrow, winding alleys to the clear air of the harbour, where the merchant lived. And as they slowly walked towards it at their leisure, deep in thought and lost in memory, the merchant's story gathered pace.

"As I have told you already," he began, "I spent some time in Venice in my youth. And to cut a long story short, my conduct there was not very Christian. Instead of managing my father's business in the city, I sat in taverns with young men who spent all day carousing and making merry, drinking, gambling, often bawling out some bawdy song or uttering bitter curses, and I was just as bad as the others. I had no intention of going home. I took life easy and ignored my father's letters when he wrote to me more and more urgently and sternly, warning me that people in Venice who knew me had told him that my licentious life would be the end of me. I only laughed, sometimes with annoyance, and a quick draught of sweet, dark wine washed all my bitterness away, or if not that then the kiss of a wanton girl. I tore up my father's letters, I had abandoned myself entirely to a life of intoxicated frenzy, and I did not intend to give it up. But one evening I was suddenly free of it all. It was very strange, and sometimes I still feel as if a miracle had cleared my path. I was sitting in my usual tavern; I can still see it today, with its smoke and vapours and my drinking companions. There were girls of easy virtue there as well, one of them very beautiful, and we seldom made merrier than that night, a stormy and very strange one. Suddenly, just as a lewd story aroused roars of laughter, my servant came in with a letter for me brought by the courier from Flanders. I was displeased. I did not like receiving my father's letters, which were always admonishing me to do my duty and be a good Christian, two notions that I had long ago drowned in wine. But I was about to take it from the servant when up jumped one of my drinking companions, a handsome, clever fellow, a master of all the arts of chivalry. 'Never mind the croaking old toad. What's it to you?' he cried, throwing the letter up in the air, swiftly drawing his sword, neatly spearing the letter as it fluttered down and pinning it to the wall. The supple blue blade quivered as it stuck there. He carefully withdrew the sword, and the letter, still unopened, stayed where it was. 'There clings the black bat!' he laughed. The others applauded, the girls clustered happily around him, they drank his health. I laughed myself, drank with them, and forgetting the letter and my father, God and myself, I forced myself into wild merriment. I gave the letter not a thought, and we went on to another tavern, where our merriment turned to outright folly. I was drunk as never before, and one of those girls was as beautiful as sin."

The merchant instinctively stopped and passed his hand several times over his brow, as if to banish an unwelcome image from his mind. The painter was quick to realise that this was a painful memory, and did not look at him, but let his eyes rest with apparent interest on a galleon under full sail, swiftly approaching the harbour that the two men had reached, and where they now stood amidst all its colourful hurry and bustle. The merchant's silence did not last long, and he soon continued his tale.

"You can guess how it was. I was young and bewildered, she was beautiful and bold. We came together, and I was full of urgent desire. But a strange thing happened. As I lay in her amorous embrace, with her mouth pressed to mine, I did not feel the kiss as a wild gesture of affection willingly returned. Instead, I was miraculously reminded of the gentle evening kisses we exchanged in my parental home. All at once, strange to say, even as I lay in the whore's arms I thought of my father's crumpled, mistreated, unread letter, and it was as if I felt my drinking companion's sword-thrust in my own bleeding breast. I sat up, so suddenly and looking so pale that the girl asked in alarm what the matter was. However, I was ashamed of my foolish fears, ashamed in front of this woman, a stranger, in whose bed I lay and whose beauty I had been enjoying. I did not want to tell her the foolish thoughts of that moment. Yet my life changed there and then, and today I still feel, as I felt at the time, that only the grace of God can bring such a change. I threw the girl some money, which she took reluctantly because she was afraid I despised her, and she called me a German fool. But I listened to no more from her, and instead stormed away on that cold, rainy night, calling like a desperate man over the dark canals for a gondola. At last one came along, and the price the gondolier asked was high, but my heart was beating with such sudden, merciless, incomprehensible fear that I could think of nothing but the letter, miraculously reminded of it as I suddenly was. By the time I reached the tavern my desire to read it was like a devouring fever; I raced into the place like a madman, ignoring the cheerful, surprised cries of my companions, jumped up on a table, making the glasses on it clink, tore the letter down from the wall and ran out again, taking no notice of the derision and angry curses behind me. At the first corner I unfolded the letter with trembling hands. Rain was pouring down from the overcast sky, and the wind tore at the sheet of paper in my hands. However, I did not stop reading until, with overflowing eyes, I had deciphered the whole of the letter. Not that the words in it were many—they told me that my mother was sick and likely to die, and asked me to come home. Not a word of the usual blame or reproach. But how my heart burnt with shame when I saw that the sword blade had pierced my mother's name…"

"A miracle indeed, an obvious miracle, one to be understood not by everyone but certainly by the man affected," murmured the painter as the merchant, deeply moved, lapsed into silence. For a while they walked along side by side without a word. The merchant's fine house was already visible in the distance, and when he looked up and saw it he quickly went on with his tale.

"I will be brief. I will not tell you what pain and remorseful madness I felt that night. I will say only that next morning found me kneeling on the steps of St Mark's in ardent prayer, vowing to donate an altar to the Mother of God if she would grant me the grace to see my mother again alive and receive her forgiveness. I set off that same day, travelling for many days and hours in despair and fear to Antwerp, where I hurried in wild desperation to my parental home. At the gate stood my mother herself, looking pale and older, but restored to good health. On seeing me she opened her arms to me, rejoicing, and in her embrace I wept tears of sorrow pent up over many days and many shamefully wasted nights. My life was different after that, and I may almost say it was a life well lived. I have buried that letter, the dearest thing I had, under the foundation stone of this house, built by the fruits of my own labour, and I did my best to keep my vow. Soon after my return here I had the altar that you have seen erected, and adorned as well as I could. However, as I knew nothing of those mysteries by which you painters judge your art, and wanted to dedicate a worthy picture to the Mother of God, who had worked a miracle for me, I wrote to a good friend in Venice asking him to send me the best of the painters he knew, to paint me the work that my heart desired.

"Months passed by. One day a young man came to my door, told me what his calling was, and brought me greetings and a letter from my friend. This Italian painter, whose remarkable and strangely sad face I well remember to this day, was not at all like the boastful, noisy drinking companions of my days in Venice. You might have thought him a monk rather than a painter, for he wore a long, black robe, his hair was cut in a plain style, and his face showed the spiritual pallor of asceticism and night watches. The letter merely confirmed my favourable impression, and dispelled any doubts aroused in me by the youthfulness of this Italian master. The older painters of Italy, wrote my friend, were prouder than princes, and even the most tempting offer could not lure them away from their native land, where they were surrounded by great lords and ladies as well as the common people. He had chosen this young master because, for some reason he did not know, the young man's wish to leave Italy weighed more with him than any offer of money, but the young painter's talent was valued highly and honoured in his own country.

"The man my friend had sent was quiet and reserved. I never learnt anything about his life beyond hints that a beautiful woman had played a painful part in his story, and it was because of her that he had left his native Italy. And although I have no proof of it, and such an idea seems heretical and unchristian, I think that the picture you have seen, which he painted within a few weeks without a model, working with careful preparation from memory, bears the features of the woman he had loved. Whenever I came to see him at work I found him painting another version of that same sweet face again, or lost in dreamy contemplation of it. Once the painting was finished, I felt secretly afraid of the godlessness of painting a woman who might be a courtesan as the Mother of God, and asked him to choose a different model for the companion piece that I also wanted. He did not reply, and when I went to see him next day he had left without a word of goodbye. I had some scruples about adorning the altar with that picture, but the priest whom I consulted felt no such doubt in accepting it."

"And he was right," interrupted the painter, almost vehemently. "For how can we imagine the beauty of Our Lady if not from looking at the woman we see in the picture? Are we not made in God's image? If so, such a portrayal, if only a faint copy of the unseen original, must be the closest to perfection that we can offer to human eyes. Now, listen—you want me to paint that second picture. I am one of those poor souls who cannot paint without a living model. I do not have the gift of painting only from within myself, I work from nature in trying to show what is true in it. I would not choose a woman whom I myself loved to model for a portrait worthy of the Mother of God—it would be sinful to see the immaculate Virgin through her face—but I would look for a lovely model and paint the woman whose features seem to me to show the face of the Mother of God as I have seen it in devout dreams. And believe me, although those may be the features of a sinful human woman, if the work is done in pious devotion none of the dross of desire and sin will be left. The magic of such purity, like a miraculous sign, can often be expressed in a woman's face. I think I have often seen that miracle myself."

"Well, however that may be, I trust you. You are a mature man, you have endured and experienced much, and if you see no sin in it…"

"Far from it! I consider it laudable. Only Protestants and other sectarians denounce the adornment of God's house."

"You are right. But I would like you to begin the picture soon, because my vow, still only half-fulfilled, still burns in me like a sin. For twenty years I forgot about the second picture in the altarpiece. Then, quite recently, when I saw my wife's sorrowful face as she wept by our child's sickbed, I thought of the debt I owed and renewed my vow. And as you are aware, once again the Mother of God worked a miracle of healing, when all the doctors had given up in despair. I beg you not to leave it too long before you start work."

"I will do what I can, but to be honest with you, never in my long career as an artist has anything struck me as so difficult. If my picture is not to look a poor daub, carelessly constructed, beside the painting of that young master—and I long to know more about his work—then I shall need to have the hand of God with me."

"God never fails those who are loyal to him. Goodbye, then, and go cheerfully to work. I hope you will soon bring good news to my house."

The merchant shook hands cordially with the painter once again outside the door of his house, looking confidently into the artist's clear eyes, set in his honest German, angular face like the waters of a bright mountain lake surrounded by weathered peaks and rough rocks. The painter had another parting remark on his lips, but left it unspoken and firmly clasped the hand offered to him. The two parted in perfect accord with each other.

The painter walked slowly along beside the harbour, as he always liked to do when his art did not keep him to his studio. He loved the busy, colourful scene presented by the place, with the hurry and bustle of work at the waterside, and sometimes he sat down on a bollard to sketch the curious physical posture of a labourer, or practice the difficult knack of foreshortening a path only a foot wide. He was not at all disturbed by the loud cries of the seamen, the rattling of carts and the monotonous sound of the sea breaking on shore. He had been granted those insights that do not reflect images seen only in the mind's eye, but can recognise in every living thing, however humble or indifferent, the ray of light to illuminate a work of art. For that reason he always liked places where life was at its most colourful, offering a confusing abundance of different delights. He walked among the sailors slowly, with a questing eye, and no one dared to laugh at him, for among all the noisy, useless folk who gather in a harbour, just as the beach is covered with empty shells and pebbles, he stood out with his calm bearing and the dignity of his appearance.

This time, however, he soon gave up his search and got to his feet. The merchant's story had moved him deeply. It touched lightly upon an incident in his own life, and even his usual devotion to the magic of art failed him today. The mild radiance of that picture of the Virgin painted by the young Italian master seemed to illuminate the faces of all the women he saw today, even if they were only stout fishwives. Dreaming and thoughtful, he wandered indecisively for a while past the crowd in its Sunday best, but then he stopped trying to resist his longing to go back to the cathedral and look at the strange portrayal of that beautiful woman again.

A few weeks had passed since the conversation in which the painter agreed to his friend's request for a second picture to complete the altarpiece for the Mother of God, and still the blank canvas in his studio looked reproachfully at the old master. He almost began to fear it, and spent a good deal of time out and about in the streets of the city to keep himself from brooding on its stern admonition and his own despondency. In a life full of busy work—perhaps he had in fact worked *too* hard, failing to keep an enquiring eye on his true self—a change had come over the painter since he first set eyes on the young Italian's picture. Future and past had been wrenched abruptly apart, and looked at him like an empty mirror reflecting only darkness and shadows. And nothing is more terrible than to feel that your life's final peak of achievement already lies just ahead if only you stride on boldly, and then be assailed by a brooding fear that you have taken the wrong path, you have lost your power, you cannot take the last, least step forward. All at once the artist, who had painted hundreds of sacred pictures in the course of his life, seemed

to have lost his ability to portray a human face well enough for him
to think it worthy of a divine subject. He had looked at women who
sold their faces as artist's models to be copied by the hour, at others
who sold their bodies, at citizens' wives and gentle girls with the light
of inner purity shining in their faces, but whenever they were close to
him, and he was on the point of painting the first brushstroke on the
canvas, he was aware of their humanity. He saw the blonde, greedy
plump figure of one, he saw another's wild addiction to the game of
love; he sensed the smooth emptiness behind the brief gleam of a
girlish brow, and was disconcerted by the bold gait of whores and the
immodest way they swung their hips. Suddenly a world full of such
people seemed a bleak place. He felt that the breath of the divine
had been extinguished, quenched by the exuberant flesh of these
desirable women who knew nothing about mystical virginity, or the
tremor of awe in immaculate devotion to dreams of another world.
He was ashamed to open the portfolios containing his own work, for
it seemed to him as if he had, so to speak, made himself unworthy
to live on this earth, had committed a sin in painting pictures where
sturdy country folk modelled for the Saviour's disciples and stout
countrywomen as the women who served him. His mood became
more and more sombre and oppressive. He remembered himself as
a young man following his father's plough, long before he took to art
instead, he saw his hard peasant hands thrusting the harrow through
the black earth, and wondered if he would not have done better to
sow yellow seed corn and work to support a family, instead of touching
secrets and miraculous signs, mysteries not meant for him, with his
clumsy fingers. His whole life seemed to be turned upside down, he
had run aground on the fleeting vision of an hour when he saw an
image that came back to him in his dreams, and was both torment
and blessing in his waking moments. For he could no longer see the
Mother of God in his prayers except as she was in the picture that
presented so lovely a portrayal of her. It was so different from the

beauty of all the earthly women he met, transfigured in the light of feminine humility touched with a presentiment of the divine. In the deceptive twilight of memory, the images of all the women he had ever loved came together in that wonderful figure. And when he tried, for the first time, to ignore reality and create a Mother of God out of the figure of Mary with her child that hovered before his mind's eye, smiling gently in happy, unclouded bliss, then his fingers, wielding the brush, sank powerless as if numbed by cramp. The current was drying up, the skill of his fingers in interpreting the words spoken by the eye seemed helpless in the face of his bright dream, although he saw as clearly in his imagination as if it were painted on a solid wall. His inability to give shape to the fairest and truest of his dreams and bring it into reality was pain that burnt like fire now that reality itself, in all its abundance, did not help him to build a bridge. And he asked himself a terrible question—could he still call himself an artist if such a thing could happen to him, had he been only a hardworking craftsman all his life, fitting colours together as a labourer constructs a building out of stones?

Such self-tormenting reflections gave him not a day's rest, and drove him with compelling power out of his studio, where the empty canvas and carefully prepared tools of his trade reproached him like mocking voices. Several times he thought of confessing his dilemma to the merchant, but he was afraid that the latter, while a pious and well-disposed man, would never understand him, and would think it more of a clumsy excuse than real inability to begin such a work. After all, he had already painted many sacred pictures, to the general acclaim of laymen and master painters alike. So he made it his habit to wander the streets, restless and at his wits' end, secretly alarmed when chance or a hidden magic made him wake from his wandering dreams again and again, finding himself outside the cathedral with the altarpiece in its chapel, as if there were an invisible link between him and the picture, or a divine power ruled his soul even in dreams.

Sometimes he went in, half-hoping to find some flaw in the picture and thus break free of its spell, but in front of it he entirely forgot to assess the young artist's creation enviously, judging its art and skill. Instead, he felt the rushing of wings around him, bearing him up into spheres of calm, transfigured contemplation. It was not until he left the cathedral and began thinking of himself and his own efforts that he felt the old pain again, redoubled.

One afternoon he had been wandering through the colourful streets once more, and this time he felt that his tormenting doubt was eased. The first breath of spring wind had begun to blow from the south, bringing with it the brightness, if not the warmth, of many fine spring days to come. For the first time the dull grey gloom that his own cares had cast over the world seemed to leave the painter, and a sense of the grace of God poured into his heart, as it always did when fleeting signs of spring announced the great miracle of resurrection. A clear March sun washed all the rooftops and streets clean, brightly coloured pennants fluttered down in the harbour, the water shone blue between the ships rocking gently there, and the never-ending noise of the city was like jubilant song. A troop of Spanish cavalry trotted over the main square. No hostile glances were cast at them today; the townsfolk enjoyed the sight of the sun reflected from their armour and shining helmets. Women's white headdresses, tugged wilfully back by the wind, revealed fresh, highly coloured complexions. Wooden clogs clattered on the cobblestones as children danced in a ring, holding hands and singing.

And in the usually dark alleys of the harbour district, to which the artist now turned feeling ever lighter at heart, something shimmering flickered like a falling rain of light. The sun could not quite show its bright face between the gabled roofs here as they leant towards each other, densely crowded together, black and crumpled like the hoods of a couple of little old women standing there chattering, one each side of the street. But the light was reflected from window to window, as if sparkling hands were waving in the air, passing back and forth in a high-spirited game. In many places the light remained soft and muted, like a dreaming eye in the first evening twilight. Down below in the street lay darkness where it had lain for years, hidden only occasionally in winter by a cloak of snow. Those who lived there had the sad gloom of constant dusk in their eyes, but the children who longed for light and brightness trusted the enticement of these first rays of spring, playing in their thin clothing on the dirty, potholed streets. The narrow strip of blue sky showing between the rooftops, the golden dance of the sunlight above made them deeply, instinctively happy.

The painter walked on and on, never tiring. He felt as if he, too, were granted secret reasons to rejoice, as if every spark of sunlight was the fleeting reflection of the radiance of God's grace going to his heart. All the bitterness had left his face. It now shone with such a mild and kindly light that the children playing their games were amazed, and greeted him with awe, thinking that he must be a priest. He walked on and on, with never a thought for where he was going. The new force of springtime was in his limbs, just as flower buds tap hopefully at the bast holding old, weather-beaten trees together, willing it to let their young strength shoot out into the light. His step was as spry and light as a young man's, and he seemed to be feeling fresher and livelier even though he had been walking for hours, putting stretches of the road behind him at a faster and more flexible pace.

Suddenly the painter stopped as if turned to stone and shaded his eyes with his hand to protect them, like a man dazzled by a flashing light or some awesome, incredible event. Looking up at a window, he had felt the full beam of sunlight reflected back from it strike his eyes painfully, but through the crimson and gold mist forming in front of them a strange apparition, a wonderful illusion had appeared—there was the Madonna painted by that young Italian master, leaning back dreamily and with a touch of sorrow as she did in the picture. A shudder ran through him as the terrible fear of disappointment united with the trembling ecstasy of a man granted grace, one who had seen a vision of the Mother of God not in the darkness of a dream but in bright daylight. That was a miracle of the kind to which many had borne witness, but few had really seen it! He dared not look up yet, his trembling shoulders did not feel strong enough to bear the shattering effect of finding that he was wrong, and he was afraid that this one moment could crush his life even more cruelly than the merciless self-torment of his despairing heart. Only when his pulse was beating more steadily and slowly, and he no longer felt it like a hammer blow in his throat, did he pull himself together and look up slowly from the shelter of his hand at the window where he had seen that seductive image framed.

He had been mistaken. It was not the girl from the young master's Madonna. Yet all the same, his raised hand did not sink despondently. What he saw also appeared to him a miracle, if a sweeter, milder, more human one than a divine apparition seen in the radiant light of a blessed hour. This girl, looking thoughtfully out of the sunlit window frame, bore only a distant resemblance to the altarpiece in the chapel—her face too was framed by black hair, she too had a delicate complexion of mysterious, fantastic pallor, but her features were harder, sharper, almost angry, and around the mouth there was a tearful defiance that was not moderated even by the lost expression of her dreaming eyes, which held an old, deep grief. There was a childlike wilfulness and a legacy of hidden sorrow in their bright restlessness, which she seemed to control only with difficulty. He felt that her silent composure could dissolve into abrupt and angry movement at any time, and her mood of gentle reverie did not hide it. The painter felt a certain tension in her features, suggesting that this child would grow to be one of those women who live in their dreams and are at one with their longings, whose souls cling to what they love with every fibre of their being, and who die if they are forced away from it. But he marvelled not so much at all this strangeness in her face as at the miraculous play of nature that made the sunny glow behind her head, reflected in the window, look like a saint's halo lying around her hair until it shone like black steel. And he thought he clearly felt here the divine hand showing him how to complete his work in a manner worthy of the subject and pleasing to God.

A carter roughly jostled the painter as he stood in the middle of the street, lost in thought. "God's wrath, can't you watch out, old man, or are you so taken with the lovely Jew girl that you stand there gaping like an idiot and blocking my way?"

The painter started with surprise, but took no offence at the man's rough tone, and indeed he had scarcely noticed it in the light of the information provided by this gruff and heavily clad fellow. "Is she Jewish?" he asked in great surprise.

"So it's said, but I don't know. Anyway, she's not the child of the folk here, they found her or came by her somehow. What's it to me? I've never felt curious about it, and I won't neither. Ask the master of the house himself if you like. He'll know better than me, for sure, how she comes to be here."

The 'master' to whom he referred was an innkeeper, landlord of one of those dark, smoky taverns where the liveliness and noise never quite died down, because it was frequented by so many gamblers and seamen, soldiers and idlers that the place was seldom left entirely empty. Broad-built, with a fleshy but kindly face, he stood in the narrow doorway like an inn sign inviting custom. On impulse the painter approached him. They went into the tavern, and the painter sat down in a corner at a smeared wooden table. He still felt rather agitated, and when the landlord put the glass he had ordered in front of him, he asked him to sit at the table with him for a few moments. Quietly, so as not to attract the attention of a couple of slightly tipsy sailors bawling out songs at the next table, he asked his question. He told the man briefly but with deep feeling of the miraculous sign that had appeared to him—the landlord listened in surprise as his slow understanding, somewhat clouded by wine, tried to follow the painter—and finally asked if he would allow him to paint his daughter as the model for a picture of the Virgin Mary. He did not forget to mention that by giving permission her father too would be taking part in a devout work, and pointed out several times that he would be ready to pay the girl good money for her services.

The innkeeper did not answer at once, but kept rubbing his broad nostrils with a fat finger. At last he began.

"Well, sir, you mustn't take me for a bad Christian, by God no, but it's not as easy as you think. If I was her father and I could say to my daughter, off you go and do as I say, well, sir, the bargain would soon be struck. But with that child, it's different... Good God, what's the matter?"

He had jumped up angrily, for he did not like to be disturbed as he talked. At another table a man was hammering his empty tankard on the bench and demanding another. Roughly, the landlord snatched the tankard from his hand and refilled it, suppressing a curse. At the same time he picked up a glass and bottle, went back to join his new guest, sat down and filled glasses for them both. His own was soon gulped down, and as if well refreshed he wiped his bristling moustache and began his tale.

"I'll tell you how I came by that Jewish girl, sir. I was a soldier, fighting first in Italy, then in Germany. A bad trade, I can tell you, never worse than today, and it was bad enough even back then. I'd had enough of it, I was on my way home through Germany to take up some honest calling, because I didn't have much left to call my own. The money you get as loot in warfare runs through your fingers like water, and I was never a skinflint. So I was in some German town or other, I'd only just arrived, when I heard a great to-do that evening. What set it off I don't know, but the townsfolk had ganged up together to attack the local Jews and I went along with them, partly hoping to pick something up, partly out of curiosity to see what happened. The townsfolk went to work with a will, there was storming of houses, killing, robbing, raping, and the men of the town were roaring with greed and lust. I'd soon had enough of that kind of thing, and I left them to it. I wasn't going to sully my honourable sword with women's blood, or wrestle with whores for what loot I could find. Well then, as I'm about to go back down a side alley, I see an old Jew with his long beard a-quiver, his face distorted, holding in his arms a small child just woken from sleep. He runs to me and stammers out a torrent of words I can't make out. All I understood of his Yiddish German was that he'd give me a good sum of money in return for saving the pair of them. I felt sorry for the child, looking at me all alarmed with her big eyes. And it didn't seem a bad bargain, so I threw my cloak over the old man and took them to my lodgings. There were a few people standing in the alleys, looking like they were inclined to go for the old man, but I'd drawn my sword, and they let all three of us pass. I took them to the inn where I was staying, and when the old man went on his knees to plead with me we left the town that same evening, while the fire-raising and murder went on into the night. We could still see the firelight when we were far away, and the old man stared at it in despair, but the child, she just slept on calmly. The three of us weren't together for long. After a few days the old man fell mortally sick, and he died on the way. But first he gave me all the money he'd brought away with him, and a piece of paper written in strange letters—I was to give a broker in Antwerp, he said, and he told me the man's name. He commended his granddaughter to my care as he died. Well, I came here to Antwerp and showed that piece of paper, and a strange effect it had too—the broker gave me a handsome sum of money, more than I'd have expected. I was glad of it, for now I could be free of the wandering life, so I bought this house and the tavern with the money and soon forgot the war. I kept the child. I was sorry for her, and then I hoped that as she grew up she'd do the work about the place for me, old bachelor that I am. But it didn't turn out like that.

"You saw her just now, and that's the way she is all day. She looks out of the window at empty air, she speaks to no one, she gives timid answers as if she was ducking down expecting someone to hit her. She never speaks to men. At first I thought she'd be an asset here in the tavern, bringing in the guests, like the landlord's young daughter over the road, she'll joke with his customers and encourage them to drink glass after glass. But our girl here's not bold, and if anyone so much as touches her she screams and runs out of the door like a whirlwind. And then if I go looking for her she's sure to be sitting huddled in a corner somewhere, crying fit to break your heart, you'd think God know what harm had come to her. Strange folk, the Jews!"

"Tell me," said the painter, interrupting the storyteller, who was getting more and more thoughtful as he went on, "tell me, is she still of the Jewish religion, or has she converted to the true faith?"

The landlord scratched his head in embarrassment. "Well, sir," he said, "I was a soldier. I couldn't say too much about my own Christianity. I seldom went to church and I don't often go now, though I'm sorry, and as for converting the child, I never felt clever enough for that. I didn't really try, seemed to me it would be a waste of time with that truculent little thing. Folk set the priest on me once, and he read me a right lecture, but I was putting it off until the child reached the age of reason. Still, I reckon we'll be waiting a long time yet for that, although she's past fifteen years old now, but she's so strange and wilful. Odd folk, these Jews, who knows much about them? Her old grandfather seemed to me a good man, and she's not a bad girl, hard as it is to get close to her. And as for your idea, sir, I like it well enough, I think an honest Christian can never do too much for the salvation of his soul, and everything we do will be judged one day... but I'll tell you straight, I have no real power over the child. When she looks at you with those big black eyes you don't have the heart to do anything that might hurt her. But see for yourself. I'll call her down."

He stood up, poured himself another glass, drained it standing there with his legs apart, and then marched across the tavern to some sailors who had just come in and were puffing at their short-stemmed white clay pipes, filling the place with thick smoke. He shook hands with them in friendly fashion, filled their glasses and joked with them. Then he remembered what he was on his way to do, and the painter heard him make his way up the stairs with a heavy tread.

He felt strangely disturbed. The wonderful confidence he had drawn from that happy moment of emotion on seeing the girl began to cloud over in the murky light of this tavern. The dust of the street and the dark smoke were imposed on the shining image he remembered. And back came his sombre fear that it was a sin to take the solid, animal humanity that could not be separated from earthly women, mingling it with sublime ideas and elevating it to the throne of his pious dreams. He shuddered, wondering from what hands he was to receive the gift to which miraculous signs, both secret and revealed, had pointed his way.

The landlord came back into the tavern, and in his heavy, broad black shadow the painter saw the figure of the girl, standing in the doorway indecisively, seeming to be alarmed by the noise and the smoke, holding the doorpost with her slender hands as if seeking for help. An impatient word from the landlord telling her to hurry up alarmed her, and sent her shrinking further back into the darkness of the stairway, but the painter had already risen to approach her. He took her hands in his—old and rough as they were, they were also very gentle—and asked quietly and kindly, looking into her eyes, "Won't you sit down with me for a moment?"

The girl looked at him, astonished by the kindness and affection in the deep, bell-like sound of his voice on hearing it for the first time there in the dark, smoky tavern. She felt how gentle his hands were, and saw the tender goodness in his eyes with the sweet diffidence of a girl who has been hungering for affection for weeks and years, and is amazed to receive it. When she saw his snow-white head and kindly features, the image of her dead grandfather's face rose suddenly before her mind's eye, and forgotten notes sounded in her heart, chiming with loud jubilation through her veins and up into her throat, so that she could not say a word in reply, but blushed and nodded vigorously—almost as if she were angry, so harshly abrupt was the sudden movement. Timidly, she followed him to his table and perched on the edge of the bench beside him.

The painter looked affectionately down at her without saying a word. Before the old man's clear gaze, the tragic loneliness and proud sense of difference that had been present in this child from an early age flared up suddenly in her eyes. He would have liked to draw her close and press a reassuring kiss of benediction on her brow, but he was afraid of alarming her, and he feared the eyes of the other guests, who were pointing the strange couple out to each other and laughing. Before even hearing a word from this child he understood her very well, and warm sympathy rose in him, flowing freely, for he understood the painful defiance, harsh and brusque and defensive, of someone who wants to give an infinite wealth of love, yet who feels rejected. He gently asked, "What is your name, child?"

She looked up at him with trust, but in confusion. All this was still too strange and alien to her. Her voice shook shyly as she replied quietly, half turning away, "Esther."

The old man sensed that she trusted him but dared not show it yet. He began, in a quiet voice, "I am a painter, Esther, and I would like to paint a picture of you. Nothing bad will happen to you, you will see a great many beautiful things in my studio, and perhaps we will sometimes talk to each other like good friends. It will only be for one or two hours a day, as long as you please and no more. Will you come to my studio and let me paint you, Esther?"

The girl blushed even more rosily and did not know what to say. Dark riddles suddenly opened up before her, and she could not find her way to them. Finally she looked at the landlord, who was standing curiously by, with an uneasy, questioning glance.

"Your father will allow it and likes the idea," the painter made haste to say. "The decision is yours alone, for I cannot and do not want to force you into it. So will you let me paint you, Esther?"

He held out his large, brown, rustic hand invitingly. She hesitated for a moment, and then, bashfully and without a word, placed her own small white hand in the painter's to show her consent. His hand enclosed hers for a moment, as if it were prey he had caught. Then he let it go with a kindly look. The landlord, amazed to see the bargain so quickly concluded, called over some of the sailors from the other tables to point out this extraordinary event. But the girl, ashamed to be at the centre of attention, quickly jumped up and ran out of the door like lightning. The whole company watched her go in surprise.

"Good heavens above," said the astonished landlord, "that was a masterstroke, sir. I'd never have expected that shy little thing to agree."

And as if to confirm this statement he poured another glassful down his throat. The painter, who was beginning to feel ill at ease in the company here as it slowly lost its awe of him, threw some money on the table, discussed further details with the landlord, and warmly shook his hand. However, he made haste to leave the tavern; he did not care for its musty air and all the noise, and the drunk, bawling customers repelled him.

When he came out into the street the sun had just set, and only a dull pink twilight lingered in the sky. The evening was mild and pure. Walking slowly, the old man went home musing on events that seemed to him as strange and yet as pleasing as a dream. There was reverence in his heart, and it trembled as happily as when the first bell rang from the church tower calling the congregation to prayers, to be answered by the bells of all the other towers nearby, their voices deep and high, muffled and joyful, chiming and murmuring, like human beings calling out in joy and sorrow and pain. It seemed to him extraordinary that after following a sober and straightforward path all his life, his heart should be inflamed at this late hour by the soft radiance of divine miracles, but he dared not doubt it, and he carried the grace of that radiance for which he had longed home through the dark streets, blessedly awake and yet in a wonderful dream.

Days had passed by, and still the blank canvas stood on the painter's easel. Now, however, it was not despondency paralysing his hands, but a sure inner confidence that no longer counted the days, was in no hurry, and instead waited in serene silence while he held his powers in restraint. Esther had been timid and shy when she first visited the studio, but she soon became more forthcoming, gentler and less timid, basking in his fatherly warmth as he bestowed it on the simple, frightened girl. They spent these days merely talking to each other, like friends meeting after long years apart who have to get acquainted again before putting ardent feeling into heartfelt words and reviving their old intimacy. And soon there was a secret bond between these two people, so dissimilar and yet so like each other in a certain simplicity—one of them a man who had learnt that clarity and silence are at the heart of life, an experienced man schooled in simplicity by long days and years; the other a girl who had never yet truly felt alive, but had dreamt her days away as if surrounded by darkness, and who now felt the first ray from a world of light reach her heart, reflecting it back in a glow of radiance.

The difference between the sexes meant nothing to the two of them; such thoughts were now extinguished in him and merely cast the evening light of memory into his life, and as for the girl, her dim sense of her own femininity had not fully awoken and was expressed only as vague, restless longing that had no aim as yet. A barrier still stood between them, but might soon give way—their different races and religions, the discipline of blood that has learnt to see itself as strange and hostile, nurturing distrust that only a moment of great love will overcome. Without that unconscious idea in her mind the girl, whose heart was full of pent-up affection, would long ago have thrown herself in tears on the old man's breast, confessing her secret terrors and growing longings, the pains and joys of her lonely existence. As it was, however, she showed her feelings only in glances and silences, restless gestures and hints. Whenever she felt everything in her trying to flow towards the light and express itself in clear, fluent words of ardent emotion, a secret power took hold of her like a dark, invisible hand and stifled them. And the old man did not forget that all his life he had regarded Jews if not with hatred, at least with a sense that they were alien. He hesitated to begin his picture because he hoped that the girl had been placed in his path only to be converted to the true faith. The miracle was not to be worked for him; he was to work it for her. He wanted to see in her eyes the same deep longing for the Saviour that the Mother of God must herself have felt when she trembled in blessed expectation of his coming. He would like to fill her with faith before painting a Madonna who still felt the awe of the Annunciation, but had already united it with the sweet confidence of coming fulfilment. And around his Madonna he imagined a mild landscape, a day just before the coming of spring, with white clouds moving through the air like swans drawing the warm weather along on invisible threads, with the first tender green showing as the moment of resurrection approached, flowers opening their buds to announce the coming of blessed spring as if in high, childlike voices. But the girl's eyes still seemed to him too timid and humble. He could not yet kindle the mystic flame of the Virgin's Annunciation and her devotion to a sombre promise in those restless glances; the deep, veiled suffering of her race still showed there, and sometimes he sensed the defiance of the Chosen People at odds with their God. They did not yet know humility and gentle, unearthly love.

With care and caution he tried to find ways to bring the Christian faith closer to her heart, knowing that if he showed it to her glowing in all its brightness, like a monstrance with the sun sparkling in it to show a thousand colours, she would not sink down before it in awe but turn brusquely away, seeing it as a hostile sign. There were many pictures taken from the Scriptures in his portfolios, works painted when he was an apprentice and sometimes copied again later when he was overcome by emotion. He took them out now and looked at the pictures side by side, and soon he felt the deep impression that many of them made on his mind in the trembling of his hands, and the warmth of his breath on his cheeks as it came faster. A bright world of beauty suddenly lay before the eyes of the lonely girl, who for years had seen only the swollen figures of guests at the tavern, the wrinkled faces of old, black-clad women, the grubby children shouting and tussling with each other in the street. But here were gentlewomen of enchanting beauty wearing wonderful dresses, ladies proud and sad, dreamy and desirable, knights in armour with long and gorgeous robes laughing or talking to the ladies, kings with flowing white locks on which golden crowns shone, handsome young men who had suffered martyrdom, sinking to the ground pierced by arrows or bleeding to death under torture. And a strange land that she did not know, although it touched her heart sweetly like an unconscious memory of home, opened up before her—a land of green palms and tall cypress trees, with a bright blue sky, always the same deep hue, above deserts and mountains, cities and distant prospects. Its radiant glow seemed much lighter and happier than this northern sky of eternal grey cloud.

Gradually he began telling her little stories about the pictures, explaining the simple, poetic legends of the Bible, speaking of the signs and wonders of that holy time with such enthusiasm that he forgot his own intentions, and he described, in ecstatic terms, the confidence in his faith that had brought him grace so recently. And the old man's deeply felt faith touched the girl's heart; she felt as if a wonderful country were suddenly revealed to her, opening its gates in the dark. She was less and less certain of herself as her life woke from the depths of the dark to see crimson light. She herself was feeling so strange that nothing seemed to her incredible—not the story of the silver star followed by three kings from distant lands, with their horses and camels bearing bright burdens of precious things—nor the idea that a dead man, touched by a hand in blessing, might wake to life again. After all, she felt the same wonderful power at work in herself. Soon the pictures were forgotten. The old man told her about his own life, connecting the old legends with many signs from God. He was bringing to light much that he had thought and dreamt of in his old age, and he himself was surprised by his own eloquence, as if it were something strange taken from another's hand to be tested. He was like a preacher who begins with a text from the word of God, meaning to explain and interpret it, and who then suddenly forgets his hearers and his intentions and gives himself up to the pleasure of letting all the springs of his heart flow into a deep torrent of words, as if into a goblet containing all the sweetness and sanctity of life. And then the preacher's words rise higher and higher above the heads of the humble members of his congregation, who cannot reach up to the world he now inhabits, but murmur and stare at him as he approaches the heavens in his bold dream, forgetting the force of gravity that will weigh down his wings again...

The painter suddenly looked around him as if still surrounded by the rosy mists of his inspired words. Reality showed him its cold and ordered structure once more. But what he saw was itself as beautiful as a dream.

Esther was sitting at his feet looking up at him. Gently leaning on his arm, gazing into the still, blue, clear eyes that suddenly seemed so full of light, she had gradually sunk down beside him, and in his devout emotion he had never noticed. She was crouching at his knees, her eyes turned up to him. Old words from her own childhood were suddenly present in her confused mind, words that her father, wearing his solemn black robe and frayed white bands, had often read from an old and venerable book. Those words too had been so full of resonant ceremony and ardent piety. A world that she had lost, a world of which she now knew little came back to life in muted colours, filling her with poignant longing and bringing the gleam of tears to her eyes. When the old man bent down to those sad eyes and kissed her forehead, he felt a sob shaking her tender, childlike frame in a wild fever. And he misunderstood her. He thought the miracle had happened, and God, in a wonderful moment, had given his usually plain and simple manner of speech the glowing, fiery tongue of eloquence as he once gave it to the prophets when they went out to his people. He thought this awe was the shy, still timorous happiness of one who was on her way home to the true faith, in which all bliss was to be found, and she was trembling and swaying like a flame suddenly lit, still feeling its way up into the air before settling into a clear, steady glow. His heart rejoiced at his mistake; he thought that he was suddenly close to his aim. He spoke to her solemnly.

"I have told you about miracles, Esther. Many say that miracles only happened long ago, but I feel and I tell you now that they still happen today. However, they are quiet miracles, and are only to be found in the souls of those who are ready for them. What has happened here is a miracle—my words and your tears, rising from our blind hearts, have become a miracle of enlightenment worked by an invisible hand. Now that you have understood me you are one of us; at the moment when God gave you those tears you became a Christian..."

He stopped in surprise. When he uttered that word Esther had risen from where she knelt at his feet, putting out her hands to ward off the mere idea. There was horror in her eyes, and the angry, wild truculence that her foster father had mentioned. At that moment, when the severity of her features turned to anger, the lines around her mouth were as sharp as the cut of a knife, and she stood in a defensive attitude like a cat about to pounce. All the ardour in her broke out in that moment of wild self-defence.

Then she calmed down. But the barrier between them was high and dark again, no longer irradiated by supernatural light. Her eyes were cold, restless and ashamed, no longer angry, but no longer full of mystic awe; only reality was in them. Her hands hung limp like wings broken in soaring too high. Life was still a mystery of strange beauty to her, but she dared not love the dream from which she had been so shatteringly woken.

The old painter too felt that his hasty confidence had deceived him, but it was not the first disappointment in his long and questing life of faith and trust. So he felt no pain, only surprise, and then again almost joy to see how quickly *she* felt ashamed. He gently took her two childish hands, still feverishly burning as they were. "Esther, your sudden outburst almost alarmed me. But I do not hold it against you... is that what you are thinking?"

Ashamed, she shook her head, only to raise it again next moment. Again her words were almost defiant.

"But I don't want to be a Christian. I don't want to. I—" She choked on the words for some time before saying, in a muted voice. "I... I hate Christians. I don't know them but I hate them. What you told me about love embracing everything is more beautiful than anything I have ever heard in my life. But the people in the tavern say that they are Christians too, although they are rough and violent. And… I don't even remember it clearly, it's all so long ago… but when they talked about Christians at home, there was fear and hatred in their voices. Everyone hated the Christians. I hate them too… when I was little and went out with my father they shouted at us, and once they threw stones at us. One of the stones hit me and made me bleed and cry, but my father made me go on, he was afraid, and when I shouted for help… I don't remember any more about all that. Or yes, I do. Our alleys were dark and narrow, like the one where I live here. And only Jews lived there. But higher up, the town was beautiful. I once looked down at it from the top of a house… there was a river flowing through it, so blue and clear, and a broad bridge over the river with people crossing it in brightly coloured clothes like the ones you showed me in the pictures. And the houses were decorated with statues and with gilding and gable ends. Among them there were tall, tall towers, where bells rang, and the sun shone all the way down into the streets there. It was all so lovely. But when I told my father he ought to go and see the lovely town with me he looked very serious and said, 'No, Esther, the Christians would kill us.' That frightened me… and ever since then I have hated the Christians."

She stopped in the middle of her dreams, for all around her seemed bright again. What she had forgotten long ago, leaving it to lie dusty and veiled in her soul, was sparkling once again. She was back there walking down the dark alleys of the ghetto to the house she was visiting. And suddenly everything connected and was clear, and she realised that what she sometimes thought was a dream had been reality in her past life. Her words came tumbling out in pursuit of the images hurrying through her mind.

"And then there was that evening… I was suddenly snatched up out of my bed… I saw my grandfather, he was holding me in his arms, his face was pale and trembling… the whole house was in uproar, shaking, there was shouting and noise. Oh, now it's coming back to me. I hear what they were shouting again—it's the others, they were saying, it's the Christians. My father was shouting it, or my mother, or… I don't remember. My grandfather carried me down into the darkness, through black streets and alleys… and there was always that noise and the same shouting—the others, the Christians! How could I have forgotten? And then we went away with a man… when I woke up we were far out in the country, my grandfather and the man I live with now… I never saw that town again, but the sky was very red back where we had come from… and we travelled on…"

Again she stopped. The pictures seemed to be disappearing, getting slowly darker.

"I had three sisters. They were very beautiful, and every evening they came to my bedside to kiss me goodnight… and my father was tall, I couldn't reach up to him, so he often carried me in his arms. And my mother… I never saw her again. I don't know what happened to them, because my grandfather looked away and wouldn't tell me when I asked him. And when he died there was no one I dared to ask."

She stopped once more, and a painful, violent sob burst from her throat. Very quietly, she added, "But now I know it all. How could it all be so dark to me? I feel as if my father were standing beside me saying the words he used to say at that time, it is all so clear in my ears. I won't ask anyone again…"

Her words turned to sobs, to silent, miserable weeping that died away in deep, sad silence. Only a few minutes ago life had shown her an enticing image; now it lay dark and sombre before her again. And the old man had long ago forgotten his intention of converting her as he watched her pain. He stood there in silence, feeling as sad himself as if he must sit down and weep with her, for there were some things that he could not put into words, and with his great love of humanity he felt guilty for unknowingly arousing such pain in her. Shuddering, he felt the fullness of blessing and the weight of a burden to be borne, both coming at the same hour; it was as if heavy waves were rising and falling, and he did not know whether they would raise his life or drag it down into the menacing deeps. But wearily, he felt neither fear nor hope, only pity for this young life with so many different paths opening up before it. He tried to find words; but they were all as heavy as lead and had the ring of false coin. What was all they could express, in the face of such a painful memory?

Sadly, he stroked the hair on her trembling head. She looked up, confused and distracted; then mechanically tidied her hair and rose, her eyes wandering this way and that as if getting used to reality again. Her features became wearier, less tense, and there was only darkness now in her eyes. Abruptly, she pulled herself together, and quickly said, to hide the sobs still rising inside her, "I must go now. It's late. And my father is expecting me."

With a brusque gesture of farewell she shook her head, picked up her skirts and turned to leave. But the old man, who had been watching her with his steady, understanding gaze, called after her. She turned back reluctantly, for there were still tears in her eyes. And again the old man took both her hands in his forceful manner and looked at her. "Esther, I know that you want to go now and not come back again. You do not and will not believe me, because a secret fear deceives you."

He felt her hands relax in his gently, softer now. He went on more confidently, "Come back another day, Esther! We will forget all of this, the happy and the sad part of it alike. Tomorrow we will begin on my picture, and I feel as if it will succeed. And don't be sad any more, let the past rest, don't brood on it. Tomorrow we will begin a new work with new hope—won't we, Esther?"

In tears, she nodded. And she went home again, still timid and uncertain, but with a new and deeper awareness of many things.

The old man stayed there, lost in thought. His belief in miracles had not deserted him, but they had seemed more solemn before; were they only a case of a divine hand playing with life? He abandoned the idea of seeing faith in a mystical promise light up a face when perhaps its owner's soul was too desperate to believe. He would no longer presume to bring God and his own ideas to anyone, he would only be a simple servant of the Lord painting a picture as well as he could, and laying it humbly on God's altar as another man might bring a gift. He felt that it was a mistake to look for signs and portents instead of waiting until they were revealed to him in their own good time.

Humbled, his heart sank to new depths. Why had he wanted to work a miracle on this child when no one had asked him to? Wasn't it enough that when his life was taking bleak and meaningless root, like the trunk of an old tree with only its branches aspiring to reach the sky, another life, a young life full of fear, had come to cling trustfully to him? One of life's miracles, he felt, had happened to him; he had been granted the grace to give and teach the love that still burnt in him in his old age, to sow it like a seed that may yet come to wonderful flower. Hadn't life given him enough with that? And hadn't God shown him the way to serve him? He had wanted a female figure in his picture, and the model for it had come to meet him, wasn't it God's will for him to paint her likeness, and not try converting her to a faith that she might never be able to understand? Lower and lower sank his heart.

Evening and darkness came into his room. The old man stood up, feeling a restlessness unusual to him in his late days, for they were usually as mild as cool rays of autumn sunlight. He slowly kindled a light. Then he went to the cupboard and looked for an old book. His heart was weary of restlessness. He took the Bible, kissed it ardently, and then opened it and read until late into the night.

*

He began work on the picture. Esther sat leaning thoughtfully back in a soft, comfortable armchair, sometimes listening to the old man as he told her all kinds of stories from his own life and the lives of others, trying to while away the monotonous hours of sitting still for her. Sometimes she just sat calmly dreaming in the large room where the tapestries, pictures and drawings adorning the walls attracted her gaze. The painter's progress was slow. He felt that the studies he was doing of Esther were only first attempts, and had not yet caught the final conviction that he wanted. There was still something lacking in the idea behind his sketches; he could not put it into words, but he felt it deep within him so clearly that feverish haste often drove him on from sketch to sketch, and then, comparing them with each other, he was still not content, faithful as his likenesses of Esther were. He did not mention it to the girl, but he felt as if the harsh set of her lips, a look that never entirely left them even when she was gently dreaming, would detract from the serene expectation that was to transfigure his Madonna. There was too much childish defiance in her for her mood to turn to sweet contemplation of motherhood. He did not think any words would really dispel that darkness in her; it could change only from within. But the soft, feminine emotion he wanted would not come to her face, even when the first spring days cast red-gold sunlight into the room through every window and the whole world stirred as it revived, when all colours seemed to be even softer and deeper, like the warm air wafting through the streets. Finally the painter grew weary. He was an experienced old man, he knew the limits of his art, and he knew he could not overcome them by force. Obeying the insistent voice of sudden intuition, he soon gave up his original plan for the painting. And after weighing up the possibilities, he decided not to paint Esther as the Madonna absorbed in thoughts of the Annunciation, since her face showed no signs of devoutly awakening femininity, but as the most straightforward but deeply felt symbol of his faith, the Madonna with her child. And he wanted to begin it at once, because hesitation was making inroads on his soul, again now that the radiance of the miracle he had dreamt of was fading, and had almost disappeared entirely into darkness. Without telling Esther, he removed the canvas, which bore a few fleeting traces of over-hasty sketches, and replaced it with a fresh one as he tried to give free rein to his new idea.

When Esther sat down in her usual way next day and waited, leaning gently back, for him to begin his work—not an unwelcome prospect to her, since it brought inspiring words and happy moments into the bleakness of her lonely day—she was surprised to hear the painter's voice in the next room, in friendly conversation with a woman whose rough, rustic voice she did not recognise. Curious, she pricked up her ears, but she could not hear what they were saying distinctly. Soon the woman's voice died away, a door latched, and the old man came in and went over to her carrying something pale in his arms. She did not realise at once what it was. He carefully placed a small, naked, sturdy child a few months old on her lap. At first the baby wriggled, then he lay still. Esther stared wide-eyed at the old man—she had not expected him to play such a strange trick on her. But he only smiled and said nothing. When he saw that her anxious, questioning eyes were still fixed on him, he calmly explained, in a tone that asked her approval, his intention of painting her with the child on her lap. All the warm kindliness of his eyes went into that request. The deep fatherly love that he had come to feel for this strange girl, and his confidence in her restless heart, shone through his words and even his eloquent silence.

Esther's face had flushed rosy red. A great sense of shame tormented her. She hardly dared to look timidly sideways at the healthy little creature whom she reluctantly held on her trembling knees. She had been brought up among people who had a stern abhorrence of the naked human body, and it made her look at this healthy, happy and now peacefully sleeping baby with revulsion and secret fear; she instinctively hid her own nakedness even from herself, and shrank from touching the little boy's soft, pink flesh as if it were a sin. She was afraid, and didn't know why. All her instincts told her to say no, but she did not want to respond so brusquely to the old man's kindly words, for she increasingly loved and revered him. She felt that she could not deny him anything. And his silence and the question in his waiting glance weighed so heavily on her that she could have cried out with a loud, wordless animal scream. She felt unreasonable dislike of the peacefully slumbering child; he had intruded into her one quiet, untroubled hour and destroyed her dreamy melancholy. But she felt weak and defenceless in the face of the calm old man's kindly wisdom. He was like a pale and lonely star above the dark depths of her life. Once again, as she did in answer to all his requests, she bowed her head in humble confusion.

He said no more, but set about beginning the picture. First he only sketched the outline, for Esther was still far too uneasy and bewildered to embody the meaning of his work. Her dreamy expression had entirely disappeared. There was something tense and desperate in her eyes as she avoided looking at the sleeping, naked infant on her lap, and fixed them instead in endless scrutiny on the walls full of pictures and ornaments to which she really felt indifferent. Her stiff hand showed that she was afraid she might have to bring herself to touch the little body. In addition, the weight on her knees was heavy, but she dared not move. However, the tension in her face showed more and more strongly what a painful effort she was making. In the end the painter himself began to have some inkling of her discomfort, although he ascribed it not to her inherited abhorrence of nakedness but to maidenly modesty, and he ended the sitting. The baby himself went on sleeping like a replete little animal, and did not notice when the painter carefully took him off the girl's lap and put him down on the bed in the next room, where he stayed until his mother, a sturdy Dutch seaman's wife brought to Antwerp for a while by chance, came to fetch him. But although Esther was free of the physical burden she felt greatly oppressed by the idea that she would now have to suffer the same alarm every day.

For the next few days she both came to the studio and left it again uneasily. Secretly, she hoped that the painter would give up this plan as well, and her decision to ask him to do so with a few calm words became compelling and overwhelming. Yet she could never quite bring herself do it; personal pride or a secret sense of shame kept the words back even as they came to her lips like birds ready to take flight. However, as she came back day after day, even though she was so restless, her shame gradually became an unconscious lie, for she had already come to terms with it, as you might come to terms with an unwelcome fact about yourself. She simply did not understand what had happened. Meanwhile the picture was making little progress, although the painter described it cautiously to her. In reality the frame of his canvas contained only the empty and unimportant lines of the figures, and a few fleeting attempts at choosing shades of colour. The old man was waiting for Esther to reconcile herself to his idea, and as his hope that she would verged on certainty he did not try to hurry matters along. For the time being, he made her sittings shorter, and talked a great deal of unimportant matters, deliberately ignoring the presence of the baby and Esther's uneasiness. He seemed more confident and cheerful than ever.

And this time his confidence was well-founded. One morning it was bright and warm, the rectangle of the window framed a light, translucent landscape—towers that were far away, yet the golden gleam on them made them look close; rooftops from which smoke rose in a leisurely fashion, curling up into the deep damask blue of the sky and losing itself there; white clouds very close, as if they were about to descend like downy fluttering birds into the darkly flowing sea of roofs. And the sun cast great handfuls of gold on everything, rays and dancing sparks, circles of light like little clinking coins, narrow strips of it like gleaming daggers, fluttering shapes without any real form that leapt nimbly over the floorboards as if they were bright little animals. This dappled, sparkling play of light had woken the baby from sleep as it tapped at his closed eyelids, until his eyes opened and he blinked and stared. He began moving restlessly on Esther's lap as she reluctantly held him. However, he was not trying to get away from her, only grabbing awkwardly with his clumsy little hands at the sparkling light dancing and playing around them, although he could not seize them, and his failure only made him try harder. His fat little fingers tried to move faster and faster. The sunny light showed the warm flow of blood shining rosily through them, and this simple game made the child's clumsy little body such a charming sight that it cast a spell even on Esther. Smiling with her superior knowledge at the baby's vain attempts to catch and hold the light, she watched his endless game without tiring, quite forgetting her reluctance to hold the innocent, helpless infant. For the first time she felt that there was true human life in the smooth little body—all she had felt before was his naked flesh and the dull satisfaction of his senses—and with childish curiosity of her own she followed all his movements. The old man watched in silence. If he spoke he feared he might revive her truculence and the shame she had forgotten, but his kindly lips wore the satisfied smile of a man who knows the world and its creatures. He saw nothing startling in this change, he had expected and counted on it, confident of the deep laws of nature that never fail. Once again he felt very close to one of those miracles of life that are always renewing themselves, a miracle that can suddenly use children to call forth the devoted kindness of women, and they then give it back to the children, so the miracle passes from being to being and never loses its own childhood but lives a double life, in itself and in those it encounters. And was this not the divine miracle of Mary herself, a child who would never become a woman, but would live on in her child? Was that miracle not reflected in reality, and did not every moment of burgeoning life have about it an ineffable radiance and the sound of what can never be understood?

The old man felt again, deeply, that proximity to the miraculous the idea of which, whether divine or earthly, had obsessed him for weeks. But he knew that he stood outside a dark, closed gate, from which he must humbly turn away again, merely leaving a reverent kiss on the forbidden threshold. He picked up a brush to work, and so chase away ideas that were already lost in clouded gloom. However, when he looked to see how close his copy came to reality, he was spellbound for a moment. He felt as if all his searching so far had been in a world hung about with veils, although he did not know it, and only now that they were removed did its power and extravagance burn before him. The picture he had wanted was coming to life. With shining eyes and clutching hands, the healthy, happy child turned to the light that poured its soft radiance over his naked body. And above that playful face was a second, tenderly bent over the child, and itself full of the radiance cast by that bright little body. Esther held her slender, childish hands on both sides of the baby to protect and avert all misfortune from him. And above her head was a fleeting light caught in her hair and seeming to shine out of it from within. Gentle movement united with moving light, unconsciousness joined dreaming memory, they all came together in a brief and beautiful image, airy and made of translucent colours, an image that could be shattered by a moment's abrupt movement.

The old man looked at the couple as if at a vision. The swift play of light seemed to have brought them together, and as if in distant dreams he thought of the Italian master's almost forgotten picture and its divine serenity. Once again he felt as if he heard the call of God. But this time he did not lose himself in dreams, he put all his strength into the moment. With vigorous strokes, he set down the play of the girl's childish hands, the gentle inclination of her bent head, her attitude no longer harsh. It was as if, although the moment was transitory, he wanted to preserve it for ever. He felt creative power in him like hot young blood. His whole life was in flux and flow, light and colour flowed into that moment, forming and holding his painting hand. And as he came closer to the secret of divine power and the unlimited abundance of life than ever before, he did not think about its signs and miracles, he lived them out by creating them himself.

The game did not last long. The child at last got tired of constantly snatching at the light, and Esther was surprised to see the old man suddenly working with feverish haste, his cheeks flushed. His face showed the same visionary light as in the days when he had talked to her about God and his many miracles, and she felt fervent awe in the presence of a mind that could lose itself so entirely in worlds of creation. And in that overwhelming feeling she lost the slight sense of shame she had felt, thinking that the painter had taken her by surprise at the moment when she was entirely fulfilled by the sight of the child. She saw only the abundance of life, and its sublime variety allowed her to feel again the awe that she had first known when the painter showed her pictures of distant, unknown people, cities as lovely as a dream, lush landscapes. The deprivations of her own life, the monotony of her intellectual experience took on colour from the sound of what was strange and the magnificence of what was distant. And a creative longing of her own burnt deep in her soul, like a hidden light burning in darkness.

That day was a turning point in the history of Esther and the picture. The shadows had fallen away from her. Now she walked fast, stepping lightly, to those hours in the studio that seemed to pass so quickly; they strung together a whole series of little incidents each of which was significant to her, for she did not know the true value of life and thought herself rich with the little copper coins of unimportant events. Imperceptibly, the figure of the old man retreated into the background of her mind by comparison with the baby's helpless little pink body. Her hatred had turned to a wild and almost greedy affection, such as girls often feel for small children and little animals. Her whole being was poured into watching and caressing him; unconsciously and in a passionate game, she was living out a woman's most sublime dream, the dream of motherhood. The purpose of her visits to the studio eluded her. She came, sat down in the big armchair with the healthy little baby, who soon recognised her and would laugh back at her, and began her ardent flirtation with him, quite forgetting that she was here for the sake of the picture, and that she had once felt this naked child was nothing but a nuisance. That time seemed as far away as one of the countless deceptive dreams that she used to spin in her long hours in the dark, dismal alley; their fabric dissolved at the first cautious breath of a wind of reality. Only in those hours at the studio did she now seem to live, not in the time she spent at home or the night into which she plunged to sleep. When her fingers held the baby's plump little hands, she felt that this was not an empty dream. And the smile for her in his big blue eyes was not a lie. It was life, and she drank it in with an avidity for abundance that was a rich, unconscious part of her heritage, and also a need to give of herself, a feminine longing before she was a woman yet. This game already had in it the seed of deeper longing and deeper joy. But it was still only a flirtatious dance of affection and admiration, playful charm and foolish dream. She cradled the baby like a child cuddling her doll, but she dreamt as women and mothers dream—sweetly, lovingly, as if in some boundless distant space.

The old man felt the change with all the fullness of his wise heart. He sensed that he was further from her now, but not stranger, and that he was not at the centre of her wishes but left to one side, like a pleasant memory. And he was glad of this change, much as he also loved Esther, for he saw young, strong, kind instincts in her which, he hoped, would do more than his own efforts to break through the defiance and reserve of the nature she had inherited. He knew that her love for him, an old man at the end of his days, was wasteful, although it could bring blessing and promise to her young life.

He owed wonderful hours to the love for the child that had awakened in Esther. Images of great beauty formed before him, all expressing a single idea and yet all different. Soon it was an affectionate game—his sketches showed Esther playing with the child, still a child herself in her unbounded delight, they showed flexible movements without harshness or passion, mild colours blending gently, the tender merging of tender forms. And then again there were moments of silence when the child had fallen asleep on her soft lap, and Esther's little hands watched over him like two hovering angels, when the tender joy of possession lit in her eyes, and a silent longing to wake the sleeping face with loving play. Then again there were seconds when the two pairs of eyes, hers and the baby's, were drawn to each other unconsciously, unintentionally, each seeking the other in loving devotion. Again, there were moments of charming confusion when the child's clumsy hands felt for the girl's breast, expecting to find his mother's milk there. Esther's cheeks would flush bashfully at that, but she felt no fear now, no reluctance, only a shy surge of emotion that turned to a happy smile.

These days were the creative hours that went into the picture. The painter made it out of a thousand touches of tenderness, a thousand loving, blissful, fearful, happy, ardent maternal glances. A great work full of serenity was coming into being. It was plain and simple—just a child playing and a girl's head gently bending down. But the colours were milder and clearer than he had ever painted colours before, and the forms stood out as sharply and distinctly as dark trees against the glow of an evening sky. It was as if there must be some inner light hidden in the picture, shedding that secret brightness, as if air blew in it more softly, caressingly and clearly than in any other earthly work. There was nothing supernatural about it, and yet it showed the mystical mind of the man who had created it. For the first time the old man felt that in his long and busy creative life he had always been painting, brushstroke after brushstroke, some being of which he really knew nothing. It was like the old folk tale of the magical imps who do their work in hiding, yet so industriously that people marvel in the morning to see all they did overnight. That was how the painter felt when, after moments of creative inspiration, he stepped back from the picture and looked critically at it. Once again the idea of a miracle knocked on the door of his heart, and this time he hardly hesitated to let it in. For this work seemed to him not only the flower of his entire achievement, but something more distant and sublime of which his humble work was not worthy, although it was also the crown of his artistic career. Then his cheerful creativity would die away and turn to a strange mood when he felt fear of his own work, no longer daring to see himself in it.

So he distanced himself from Esther, who now seemed to him only the means of expressing the earthly miracle that he had worked. He showed her all his old kindness, but once again his mind was full of the pious dreams that he had thought far away. The simple power of life suddenly seemed to him so wonderful. Who could give him answers? The Bible was old and sacred, but his heart was earthly and still bound to this life. Where could he ask whether the wings of God descended to this world? Were there signs of God still abroad today, or only the ordinary miracles of life?

The old man did not venture to wish for the answer, although he had seen strange things during his life. But he was no longer as sure of himself as in the old days when he believed in life and in God, and did not stop to wonder which of them was really true. Every evening he carefully covered up the picture, because once recently, on coming home to see silver moonlight resting on it like a blessing, he felt as if the Mother of God herself had shown him her face, and he could almost have thrown himself down in prayer before the work of his own hands.

Something else, however, happened at this time in Esther's life, nothing in itself strange or unlikely, but it affected the depths of her being like a rising storm and left her trembling in pain that she did not understand. She was experiencing the mystery of maturity, turning from a child into a woman. She was bewildered, since no one had taught her anything about it in advance; she had gone her own strange way alone between deep darkness and mystical light. Now longing awoke in her and did not know where to turn. The defiance that used to make her avoid playing with other children or speaking an unnecessary word burnt like a dark curse at this time. She did not feel the secret sweetness of the change in her, the promise of a seed not yet ready to come to life, only a dull, mysterious pain that she had to bear alone. In her ignorance, she saw the legends and miracles of which the old painter had spoken like lights leading her astray, while her dreams followed them through the most unlikely of possibilities. The story of the mild woman whose picture she had seen, the girl who became a mother after a wonderful Annunciation, suddenly struck her with almost joyful fear. She dared not believe it, because she had heard many other things that she did not understand. However, she thought that some miracle must be taking place inside her because she felt so different in every way, the world and everyone in it also suddenly seemed so different, deeper, stranger, full of secret urges. It all appeared to come together into an inner life trying to get out, then retreating again. There was some common factor at work; she did not know where it lay, but it seemed to hold everything that had once been separate together. She herself felt a force that was trying to take her out into life, to other human beings, but it did not know where to turn, and left behind only that urgent, pressing, tormenting pain of unspent longing and unused power.

In these hours when she was overwhelmed by desperation and needed some kind of support to cling to, Esther tried something that she had thought impossible before. She spoke to her foster father. Until now she had instinctively avoided him, because she felt the distance between them. But now she was driven over that threshold. She told him all about it, and talked about the picture, she looked deep into herself to find something gleaned from those hours that could be useful to her. And the landlord, visibly pleased to hear of the change in her, patted her cheeks with rough kindness and listened. Sometimes he put in a word, but it was as casual and impersonal as the way he spat out tobacco. Then he told her, in his own clumsy fashion, what had just happened to her. Esther listened, but it was no use. He didn't know what else to say to her and didn't even try. Nothing seemed to touch him except outwardly, there was no real sympathy between them, and his words suggested an indifference that repelled her. She knew now what she had only guessed before—people like him could never understand her. They might live side by side, but they did not know each other; it was like living in a desert. And in fact she thought her foster father was the best of all those who went in and out of this dismal tavern, because he had a certain rough plainness about him that could turn to kindness.

However, this disappointment could not daunt the power of her longings, and they all streamed back towards the two living beings she knew who spanned the morning and evening of human life. She desperately counted the lonely night hours still separating her from morning, and then she counted the morning hours separating her from her visit to the painter. Her ardent longings showed in her face. And once out in the street she abandoned herself entirely to her passion like a swimmer plunging into a foaming torrent, and raced through the hurrying crowd, stopping only when, with flushed face and untidy hair, she reached the door of the house she longed to see. In this time of the change in her, she was overcome by an instinctive urge to make free, passionate gestures, and it gave her a wild and desirable beauty.

That greedy, almost desperate need for affection made her prefer the baby to the old man, in whose friendly kindness there was a serenity that rejected stormy passion. He knew nothing about the feminine change in Esther, but he guessed it from her demeanour, and her sudden ecstatic transports made him uneasy. Sensing the nature of the elemental urge driving her on, he did not try to rein it in. Nor did he lose his fatherly love for this lonely child, although his mind had gone back to contemplation of the abstract interplay of the secret forces of life. He was glad to see her, and tried to keep her with him. The picture was in fact finished, but he did not tell Esther so, not wishing to part her from the baby on whom she lavished such affection. Now and then he added a few brushstrokes, but they were minor details—the design of a fold, a slight shading in the background, a fleeting nuance added to the play of light. He dared not touch the real idea behind the picture any more, for the magic of reality had slowly retreated, and he thought the dual aspect of the painting conveyed the spiritual nature of the wonderful creativity that now, as the memory of his execution of it faded, seemed to him less and less like the work of earthly powers. Any further attempt at improvement, he thought, would be not only folly but a sin. And he made up his mind that after this work, in which his hand had clearly been guided, he would do no more paintings, for they could only be lesser works, but spend his days in prayer and in searching for a way to reach those heights whose golden evening glow had rested on him in these late hours of his life.

With the fine instinct that the orphaned and rejected harbour in their hearts, like a secret network of sensitive fibres encompassing everything said and unsaid, Esther sensed the slight distance that the old man who was so dear to her had placed between them, and his mild tenderness, which was still the same, almost distressed her. She felt that at this moment she needed his whole attention and the free abundance of his love so that she could tell him all that was in her heart, all that now troubled it, and ask for answers to the riddles around her. She waited for the right moment to let out the words to express her mental turmoil, but the waiting was endless and tired her out. So all her affection was bent on the child. Her love concentrated on that helpless little body; she would catch the baby up and smother him with warm kisses so impetuously, forgetting his vulnerability, that she hurt him and he began to cry. Then she was less fiercely loving, more protective and reassuring, but even her anxieties were a kind of ecstasy, just as her feelings were not truly maternal, but more of a surge of longing erotic instincts dimly sensed. A force was trying to emerge in her, and her ignorance led her to turn it on the child. She was living out a dream, in a painful dazed state; she clung convulsively to the baby because he had a warm, beating heart, like hers, because she could lavish all the tenderness in her on his silent lips, because with him, unconsciously longing for a human touch, she could clasp another living creature without fearing the shame that came over her if she said a single word to a stranger. She spent hours and hours like that, never tiring, and never realising how she was giving herself away.

For her, all the life for which she longed so wildly was now contained in the child. These were dark times, growing even darker, but she never noticed. The citizens of Antwerp gathered in the evenings and talked of the old liberties and good King Charles, who had loved his land of Flanders so much, with regret and secret anger. There was unrest in the city. The Protestants were secretly uniting. Rabble who feared the daylight assembled, as ominous news arrived from Spain. Minor skirmishes and clashes with the soldiers became more frequent, and in this uneasy, hostile atmosphere the first flames of war and rebellion flared up. Prudent people began to look abroad, others consoled and reassured themselves as well as they could, but the whole country was in a state of fearful expectation, and it was reflected in all faces. At the tavern, the men sat together in corners talking in muted voices, while the landlord spoke of the horrors of war, and joked in his rough way, but no one felt like laughing. The carefree cheerfulness of easy-going folk was extinguished by fear and restless waiting.

Esther felt nothing of this world, neither its muted alarms nor its secret fevers. The child was contented as always, and laughed back at her in his own way—and so she noticed no change in her surroundings. Confused as she was, her life followed a single course. The darkness around her made her fantastic dreams seem real, and it was a reality so distant and strange that she was incapable of any sober, thoughtful understanding of the world. Her femininity, once awakened, cried out for a child, but she did not know the dark mystery involved. She only dreamt a thousand dreams of having a child herself, thinking of the simple marvels of biblical legends and the magical possibility conjured up by her lonely imagination. If anyone had explained this everyday miracle to her in simple words, she might perhaps have looked at the men passing her by with the bashful but considering gaze that was to be seen in the eyes of girls at that time. As it was, however, she never thought of men, only of the children playing in the street, and dreamt of the miracle that might, perhaps, give her a rosy, playful baby some day, a baby all her own who would be her whole happiness. So wild was her wish for one that she might even have given herself to the first comer, throwing aside all shame and fear, just for the sake of the happiness she longed for, but she knew nothing about the creative union of man and woman, and her instincts led her blindly astray. So she returned, again and again, to the other woman's baby. By now she loved him so deeply that he seemed like her own.

One day she came to visit the painter, who had noticed with secret uneasiness her extreme, almost unhealthily passionate love of the child. She arrived with a radiant face and eagerness sparkling in her eyes. The baby was not there as usual. That made her anxious, but she would not admit it, so she went up to the old man and asked him about the progress of his picture. As she put this question the blood rose to her face, for all at once she felt the silent reproach of the many hours when she had paid neither him nor his work any attention. Her neglect of this kindly man weighed on her conscience. But he did not seem to notice.

"It is finished, Esther," he said with a quiet smile. "It was finished long ago. I shall be delivering it tomorrow."

She turned pale, and felt a terrible presentiment that she dared not consider more closely. Very quietly and slowly she asked, "Then I can't come and see you any more?"

He put out both hands to her in the old, warm, compelling gesture that always captivated her. "As often as you like, my child. And the more often that is the happier I shall be. As you see, I am lonely here in this old room of mine, and when you are here it is bright and cheerful all day. Come to see me often, Esther, very often."

All her old love for the old man came welling up, as if to break down all barriers and pour itself out in words. How good and kind he was! Was he not real, and the baby only her own dream? At that moment she felt confident again, but other ideas still hung over that budding confidence like a storm cloud. And the thought of the child tormented her. She wanted to suppress her pain, she kept swallowing the words, but they came out at last in a wild, desperate cry. "What about the baby?"

The old man said nothing, but there was a harsh, almost unsparing expression on his face. Her neglect of him at this moment, when he had hoped to make her soul entirely his own, was like an angry arm warding him off. His voice was cold and indifferent as he said, "The baby has gone away."

He felt her glance hanging on his lips in wild desperation. But a dark force in him made him cruel. He added nothing to what he had said. At that moment he even hated the girl who could so ungratefully forget all the love he had given her, and for a second this kind and gentle man felt a desire to hurt her. But it was only a brief moment of weakness and denial, like a single ripple running away into the endless sea of his gentle kindness. Full of pity for what he saw in her eyes, he turned away.

She could not bear this silence. With a wild gesture, she flung herself on his breast and clung to him, sobbing and moaning. Torment had never burnt more fiercely in her than in the desperate words she cried out between her tears. "I want the baby back, my baby. I can't live without him, they've stolen my one small happiness from me. Why do you want to take the baby away from me? I know I've been unkind to you... Oh, please forgive me and let me have the baby back! Where is he? Tell me! Tell me! I want the baby back..."

The words died away into silent sobbing. Deeply shaken, the old man bent down to her as she clung to him, her convulsive weeping slowly dying down, and she sank lower and lower like a dying flower. Her long, dark hair had come loose, and he gently stroked it. "Be sensible, Esther, and don't cry. The baby has gone away, but—"

"It's not true, oh no, it can't be true!" she cried.

"It *is* true, Esther. His mother has left the country. Times are bad for foreigners and heretics here—and for the faithful and God-fearing as well. They have gone to France, or perhaps England. But why so despairing? Be sensible, Esther, wait a few days and you'll see, you will feel better again."

"I can't, I won't," she cried through more tears. "Why have they taken the baby away from me? He was all I had... I must have him back, I must, I must. He loved me, he was the only creature in the world who was mine, all mine... how am I to live now? Tell me where he is, oh, tell me..."

Her mingled sobs and lamentations became confused, desperate murmuring growing softer and more meaningless, and finally turning to hopeless weeping. Ideas shot like lightning through her tormented mind, she was unable to think clearly and calm down. All she thought and felt circled crazily, restlessly and with pitiless force around the one painful thought obsessing her. The endless silent sea of her questing love surged with loud, despairing pain, and her words flowed on, hot and confused, like blood running from a wound that would not close. The old man had tried to calm her distress with gentle words, but now, in despair, he could say nothing. The elemental force and dark fire of her passion seemed to him stronger than any way he knew of pacifying her. He waited and waited. Sometimes her torrent of feeling seemed to hesitate briefly and grow a little calmer, but again and again a sob set off words that were half a scream, half weeping. Her young soul, rich with love to give, was bleeding to death in her pain.

At last he was able to speak to Esther, but she wouldn't listen. Her eyes were fixed on a single image, and a single thought filled her heart. She stammered it all out, as if she were seeing hallucinations. "He had such a sweet laugh... he was mine, all mine for all those lovely days, I was his mother... and now I can't have him any more. If only I could see him again, just once... if I could only see him just once." And again her voice died away in helpless sobs. She had slowly slipped down from her resting place against the old man's breast, and was clinging to his knees with weary, shaking hands, crouching there surrounded by the flowing locks of her dark hair. As she stooped down, moving convulsively, her face hidden by her hair, she seemed to be crushed by pain and anger. Monotonously, her desperate mind tiring now, she babbled those words again and again. "Just to see him again… only once… if I could see him again just once!"

The old man bent over her.

"Esther?"

She did not move. Her lips went on babbling the same words, without meaning or intonation. He tried to raise her. When he took her arm it was powerless and limp like a broken branch, and fell straight back again. Only her lips kept stammering, "Just to see him again… see him again, oh, see him again just once…"

At that a strange idea came into his baffled mind as he tried to comfort her. He leant down close to her ear. "Esther? You *shall* see him again, not just once but as often as you like."

She started up as if woken from a dream. The words seemed to flow through all her limbs, for suddenly her body moved and straightened up. Her mind seemed to be slowly clearing. Her thoughts were not quite lucid yet, for instinctively she did not believe in so much happiness revealing itself after such pain. Uncertainly she looked up at the old man as if her senses were reeling. She did not entirely understand him, and waited for him to say more, because everything was so indistinct to her. However, he said nothing, but looked at her with a kindly promise in his eyes and nodded. Gently, he put his arm around her, as if afraid of hurting her. So it was not a dream or a lie spoken on impulse. Her heart beat fast in expectation. Willing as a child, she leant against him as he moved away, not knowing where he was going. But he led her only a few steps across the room to his easel. With a swift movement, he removed the cloth covering the picture.

At first Esther was motionless. Her heart stood still. But then, her glance avid, she ran up to the picture as if to snatch the dear, rosy, smiling baby out of his frame and bring him back to life, cradle him in her arms, caress him, feel the tenderness of his clumsy limbs and bring a smile to his comical little mouth. She did not stop to think that this was only a picture, a piece of painted canvas, only a dream of real life; in fact she did not think at all, she only felt, and her eyelids fluttered in blissful ecstasy. She stood close to the painting, never moving. Her fingers trembled and tingled, longing to feel the child's sweet softness again, her lips burnt to cover the little body with loving kisses again. A fever, but a blessed one, ran through her own body. Then warm tears came to her eyes, no longer angry and despairing, but happy as well as melancholy, the overflowing expression of many strange feelings that suddenly filled her heart and must come out. The convulsions that had shaken her died down, and an uncertain but mild mood of reconciliation enveloped her and gently, sweetly lulled her into a wonderful waking dream far from all reality.

The old man again felt a questioning awe in the midst of his delight. How miraculous was this work that could mysteriously inspire even the man who had created it himself, how unearthly was the sublimity that radiated from it! Was this not like the signs and images of the saints whom he honoured, and who could suddenly make the poor and oppressed forget their troubles and go home liberated and inspired by a miracle? And did not a sacred fire now burn in the eyes of the girl looking at her own portrait without curiosity or shame, in pure devotion to God? He felt that these strange paths must have some destination, there must be a will at work that was not blind like his own, but clear-sighted and master of all its wishes. These ideas rejoiced in his heart like a peal of bells, and he felt he had been touched by the grace of Heaven.

Carefully, he took Esther's hand and led her away from the picture. He did not speak, for he too felt warm tears coming to his eyes and did not want to show them. A warm radiance seemed to rest on her head as it did in the picture of the Madonna. It was as if something great beyond all words was in the room with them, rushing by on invisible wings. He looked into Esther's eyes. They were no longer tearfully defiant, but shadowed only by a gentle reflective bloom. Everything around them seemed to him brighter, milder, transfigured. God's sanctity, miraculously close, was revealing itself to him in all things.

They stood together like that for a long time. Then they began to talk as they used to do, but calmly and sensibly, like two human beings who now understood each other entirely and had no more to search for. Esther was quiet. The sight of the picture had moved her strangely, and made her happy because it restored the happiness of her dearest memory to her, because she had her baby back, but her feelings were far more solemn, deeper and more maternal than they had ever been in reality. For now the child was not just the outward appearance of her dream but part of her own soul. No one could take him away from her. He was all hers when she looked at the picture, and she could see it at any time. The old man, shaken by mystical portents, had willingly answered her desperate request. And now she could feel the same blessed abundance of life every day, her longings need no longer be timid and fearful, and the little childlike figure who to others was the Saviour of the world also, unwittingly, embodied a God of love and life to the lonely Jewish girl.

She visited the studio several more days running. But the painter was aware of his commission, which he had almost forgotten. The merchant came to look at the picture and he too, although he knew nothing about the secret miracles of its creation, was overwhelmed by the gentle figure of the Mother of God and the simple expression of an eternal symbol in its execution. He warmly shook hands with his friend, who, however, turned away his lavish praise with a modest, pious gesture, as if he were not standing in front of his own work. The two of them decided not to keep the altar deprived of this adornment any longer.

Next day the picture occupied the other wing of the altarpiece, and the first was no longer alone. And the pair of Madonnas, strangers but with a slight similarity, were a curious sight. They seemed like two sisters, one of them still confidently abandoning herself to the sweetness of life, while the other had already tasted the dark fruit of pain and knew a terror of times yet to come. But the same radiance hung over both their heads, as if stars of love shone above them, and they would take their path through life with its joy and pain under those stars.

Esther herself followed the picture to church, as if she found her own child there. Gradually the memory that the child was a stranger to her was dying away, and true maternal feelings were aroused in her, making her dream into reality. For hours on end she would lie prostrated before the painting, like a Christian before the image of the Saviour. But hers was another faith, and the deep voices of the bells called the congregation to devotions that she did not know. Priests whose words she could not understand sang, loud choral chanting swept like dark waves through the church, rising into the mystic twilight above the pews like a fragrant cloud. And men and women whose faith she hated surrounded her, their murmured prayers drowning out the quiet, loving words she spoke to her baby. However, she was unaware of any of that. Her heart was too bewildered to look around and take any notice of other people; she merely gave herself up to her one wish, to see her child every day, and thought of nothing else in the world. The stormy weather of her budding youth had died down, all her longings had gone away or had flowed into the one idea that drew her back to the picture again and again, as if it were a magical magnet that no other power could withstand. She had never been so happy as she was in those long hours in the church, sensing its solemnity and its secret pleasures without understanding them. She was hurt only when some stranger now and then knelt in front of the picture, looking adoringly up at the child who was hers, all hers. Then she was defiantly jealous, with anger in her heart that made her want to hit out and shed tears. At such moments her mind was increasingly troubled, and she could not distinguish between the real world and the world of her dreams. Only when she lay in front of the picture again did stillness return to her heart.

Spring passed on, the mild, warm weather in which the picture had been finished still held, and it seemed that after all her stormy suffering, summer too would give her the same great and solemn gift of quiet maternal love. The nights were warm and bright, but her fever had died away, and gentle, loving dreams came over Esther's mind. She seemed to be at peace, rocking to a rhythm of calm passion as the regular hours went by, and all that had been lost in the darkness now pointed her ahead along a bright path into the future.

At last the summer approached its climax, the Feast of St Mary, the greatest day in Flanders. Long processions decked out with pennants blowing in the breeze and billowing banners went through the golden harvest fields that were usually full of busy workers. The monstrance held above the seed corn in the priest's hands as he blessed it shone like the sun, and voices raised in prayer made a gentle sound, so that the sheaves in the fields shook and humbly bowed down. But high in the air clear bells rang in the distance, to be answered joyfully from church towers far away. It was a mighty sound, as if the earth itself were singing together with the woods and the roaring sea.

The glory of the day flowed back from the fertile land into the city and washed over its menacing walls. The noise of craftsmen at work died down, the day labourers' hoarse voices fell silent, only musicians playing fife and bagpipes went from street to street, and the clear silvery voices of dancing children joined the music-making. Silken robes trimmed with yellowing lace, kept waiting in wardrobes all the last year, saw the light of day again, men and women in their best clothes, talking cheerfully, set out for church. And in the cathedral, with its doors open to invite in the pious with clouds of blue incense and fragrant coolness, a springtime of scattered flowers bloomed, pictures and altars were adorned with lavish garlands made by careful hands. Thousands of candles cast magical light into the sweet-scented darkness where the organ roared, and singing, mysterious radiance and mystical twilight reached the heights and depths of the great building.

And then, suddenly a pious and God-fearing mood seemed to flow out into the streets. A procession of the devout formed; up by the main altar the priests raised the famous portrait of St Mary, which seemed to be surrounded by whispered rumours of many miracles, it was borne aloft on the shoulders of the pious, and a solemn procession began. The picture being carried along brought silence to the noisy street, for the crowd fell quiet as people bowed down, and a broad furrow of prayer followed the portrait until it was returned to the cool depths of the cathedral that received it like a fragrant grave.

That year, however, the pious festival was under a dark cloud. For weeks the country had been bearing a heavy burden. Gloomy and as yet unconfirmed news said that the old privileges were to be declared null and void. The freedom fighters known as the Beggars who opposed Spanish rule were making common cause with the Protestants. Dreadful rumours came from the countryside of Protestant divines preaching to crowds of thousands in open places outside the towns and cities, and giving Communion to the armed citizens. Spanish soldiers had been attacked, and churches were said to have been stormed to the sound of the singing of the Geneva Psalms. There was still no definite word of any of this, but the secret flickering of a coming conflagration was felt, and the armed resistance planned by the more thoughtful at secret meetings in their homes degenerated into wild violence and defiance among the many who had nothing to lose.

The festival day had brought the first wave of rioting to Antwerp in the shape of a rabble united in nothing but an instinct to join sudden uprisings. Sinister figures whom no one knew suddenly appeared in the taverns, cursing and uttering wild threats against Spaniards and clerics. Strange people of defiant and angry appearance who avoided the light of day emerged from nooks and crannies and disreputable alleys. There was more and more trouble. Now and then there were minor skirmishes. They did not spill over into a general movement, but were extinguished like sparks hissing out in isolation. The Prince of Orange still maintained strict discipline, and controlled the greedy, quarrelsome and ill-intentioned mob who were joining the Protestants only for the sake of profit.

The magnificence of the great procession merely provoked repressed instincts. For the first time coarse jokes mingled with the singing of the faithful, wild threats were uttered and scornful laughter. Some sang the text of the Beggars' song to a pious melody, a young fellow imitated the croaking voice of the preacher, to the delight of his companions, others greeted the portrait of the Virgin by sweeping off their hats with ostentatious gallantry as if to their lady love. The soldiers and the few faithful Catholics who had ventured to take part in the procession were powerless, and had to grit their teeth and watch this mockery as it became ever wilder. And now that the common people had tasted defiant power, they were becoming less and less amenable. Almost all of them were already armed. The dark impulse that had so far broken out only in curses and threats called for action. This menacing unrest lay over the city like a storm cloud on the feast day of St Mary and the days that followed.

Women and the more sober of the men had kept to their houses since the angry scenes had endangered the procession. The streets now belonged to the mob and the Protestants. Esther, too, had stayed at home for the last few days. But she knew nothing of all these dark events. She vaguely noticed that there were more and more people crowding into the tavern, that the shrill sound of whores' voices mingled with the agitated talk of quarrelling, cursing men, she saw distraught women, she saw figures secretly whispering together, but she felt such indifference to all these things that she did not even ask her foster father about them. She thought of nothing but the baby, the baby who, in her dreams, had long ago become her own. All memory paled beside this one image. The world was no longer so strange to her, but it had no value because it had nothing to give her; her loving devotion and youthful need of God were lost in her thoughts of the child. Only the single hour a day when she stole out to see the picture—it was both her God and her child—breathed real life into her. Otherwise she was like a woman lost in dreams, passing everything else by like a sleepwalker. Day after day, and even once on a long summer night heavy with warm fragrance, when she had fled the tavern and made sure she was shut up in the cathedral, she prostrated herself before the picture on her knees. Her ignorant soul had made a God of it.

And these days were difficult for her, because they kept her from her child. While festive crowds thronged the tall aisles on the Feast of St Mary, and surging organ music filled the nave, she had to turn back and leave the cathedral with the rest of the people crowding it, feeling humbled like a beggar woman because worshippers kept standing in front of the two pictures of St Mary in the chapel that day, and she feared she might be recognised. Sad and almost despairing, she went back, never noticing the sunlight of the day because she had been denied a sight of her child. Envy and anger came over her when she saw the crowds making pilgrimage to the altarpiece, piously coming through the tall porch of the cathedral into that fragrant blue darkness.

She was even sadder next day, when she was not allowed to go out into the streets, now so full of menacing figures. Her room, to which the noise of the tavern rose like a thick, ugly smoke, became intolerable to her. To her confused heart, a day when she could not see the baby in the picture was like a dark and gloomy sleepless night, a night of torment. She was not strong enough yet to bear deprivation. Late in the evening, when her foster father was sitting in the tavern with his guests, she very quietly went down the stairs. She tried the door, and breathed a sigh of relief; it was not locked. Softly, already feeling the mild fresh air that she had missed for a long time, she slipped through the door and hurried to the cathedral.

The streets through which she swiftly walked were dark and full of muffled noise. Single groups had come together from all sides, and news of the departure of the Prince of Orange had let violence loose. Threatening remarks, heard only occasionally and uttered at random in daytime, now sounded like shouts of command. Here and there drunks were bawling, and enthusiasts were singing rebel songs so loud that the windows echoed. Weapons were no longer hidden; hatchets and hooks, swords and stakes glinted in the flickering torchlight. Like a greedy torrent, hesitating only briefly before its foaming waves sweep away all barriers, these dark troops whom no one dared to resist gathered together.

Esther had taken no notice of this unruly crowd, although she once had to push aside a rough arm reaching for her as she slipped by when its owner tried to grab her headscarf. She never wondered why such madness had suddenly come into the rabble; she did not understand their shouting and cries. She simply overcame her fear and disgust, and quickened her pace until at last, breathless, she reached the tall cathedral deep in the shadow of the houses, white moonlit cloud hovering in the air above it.

Reassured, shivering only slightly, she came into the cathedral through a side door. It was dark in the tall, unlit aisles, with only a mysterious silvery light trembling around the dull glass of the windows. The pews were empty. No shadow moved through the wide, breathless expanses of the building, and the statues of the saints stood black and still before the altars. And like the gentle flickering of a glow-worm there came, from what seemed endless depths, the

swaying light of the eternal flame above the chapels. All was quiet
and sacred here, and the silent majesty of the place so impressed
Esther that she muted her tapping footsteps. Carefully, she groped
her way towards the chapel in the side aisle and then, trembling,
knelt down in front of the picture in boundless quiet rejoicing. In
the flowing darkness, it seemed to look down from dense, fragrant
clouds, endlessly far away yet very close. And now she did not think
any more. As always, the confused longings of her maturing girlish
heart relaxed in fantastic dreams. Ardour seemed to stream from every
fibre of her being and gather around her brow like an intoxicating
cloud. These long hours of unconscious devotion, united with the
longing for love, were like a sweet, gently numbing drug; they were
a dark wellspring, the blessed fruit of the Hesperides containing and
nourishing all divine life. For all bliss was present in her sweet, vague
dreams, through which tremors of longing passed. Her agitated
heart beat alone in the great silence of the empty church. A soft,
bright radiance like misty silver came from the picture, as if shed
by a light within, carrying her up from the cold stone of the steps
to the mild warm region of light that she knew in dreams. It was
a long time since she had thought of the baby as a stranger to her.
She dreamt of the God in him and the God in every woman, the
essence of her own body, warm with her blood. Vague yearning for
the divine, questing ecstasy and the rise of maternal feelings in her
spun the deceptive network of her life's dream between them. For
her, there was brightness in the wide, oppressive darkness of the
church, gentle music played in the awed silence that knew nothing of
human language and the passing of the hours. Above her prostrated
body, time went its inexorable way.

Something suddenly thudded against the door, shaking it. Then
came a second and a third thud, so that she leapt up in alarm, staring into the dreadful darkness. Further thunderous crashing sounds
shook the whole tall, proud building, and the isolated lamps rolled

like fiery eyes in the dark. Someone was filing through the bolt of the door, now knocked half off its hinges, with a shrill sound like helpless screams in the empty space. The walls flung back the terrifying sounds in violent confusion. Men possessed by greedy rage were hammering at the door, and a roar of excited voices boomed through the hollow shell of the church as if the sea had broken its bounds to come roaring in, and its waves were now beating against the groaning walls of the house of God.

Esther listened, distraught, as if woken suddenly from sleep. But at last the door fell in with a crash. A dark torrent of humanity poured in, filling the mighty building with wild bawling and raging. More came, and more. Thousands of others seemed to be standing outside egging them on. Torches suddenly flared drunkenly up like clutching, greedy hands, and their mad, blood-red light fell on wild faces distorted by blind excitement, their swollen eyes popping as if with sinful desires. Only now did Esther vaguely sense the intentions of the dark rabble that she had already met on her way. The first axe-blows were already falling on the wood of the pulpit, pictures crashed to the floor, statues tipped over, curses and derisive cries swirled up out of this dark flood, above which the torches danced unsteadily as if alarmed by such crazy behaviour. In confusion, the torrent poured onto the high altar, looting and destroying, defiling and desecrating. Wafers of the Host fluttered to the floor like white flower petals, a lamp with the eternal flame in it, flung by a violent hand, rushed like a meteor through the dark. And more and more figures crowded in, with more and more torches burning. A picture caught fire, and the flame licked high like a coiling snake. Someone had laid hands on the organ, smashing its pipes, and their mad notes screamed shrilly for help in the dark. More figures appeared as if out of a wild, deranged dream. A fellow with a bloodstained face smeared his boots with holy oil, to the raucous jubilation of the others, ragged villains strutted about in richly embroidered episcopal vestments, a squealing whore had perched the golden circlet from a statue in her tousled, dirty hair. Thieves drank toasts in wine from the sacred vessels, and up by the high altar two men were fighting with bright knives for possession of a monstrance set with jewels. Prostitutes performed lascivious, drunken dances in front of the shrines, drunks spewed in the fonts of holy water. Angry men armed with flashing axes smashed anything within reach, whatever it was. The sounds rose to a chaotic thunder of noise and screaming voices; like a dense and repellent cloud of plague vapours, the crowd's raging reached to the black heights of the cathedral that looked darkly down on the leaping flames of torches, and seemed immovable, out of reach of this desperate derision.

Esther had hidden in the shadow of the altar in the side chapel, half fainting. It was as if all this must be a dream, and would suddenly disappear like a deceptive illusion. But already the first torches were storming into the side aisles. Figures shaking with fanatical passion as if intoxicated leapt over gratings or smashed them down, overturned the statues and pulled pictures off the shrines. Daggers flashed like fiery snakes in the flickering torchlight, angrily tearing into cupboards and pictures, which fell to the ground with their frames smashed. Closer and closer came the crowd with its smoking, unsteady lights. Esther, breathless, stayed where she was, retreating further into the dark. Her heart missed a beat with alarm and dreadful anticipation. She still did not know quite what was happening, and felt only fear, wild, uncontrollable fear. A few footsteps were coming closer, and then a sturdy, furious fellow broke down the grating with a blow.

She thought she had been seen. But next moment she saw the intruders' purpose, when a statue of the Madonna on the next altar crashed to the floor in pieces. A terrible new fear came to her—they would want to destroy her picture too, her child—and the fear became certainty when picture after picture was pulled down in the flickering torchlight to the sound of jubilant derision, to be torn and trampled underfoot. A terrible idea flashed through her head—they were going to murder the picture, and in her mind it had long ago become her own living child. In a second everything in her flared up as if bathed in dazzling light. One thought, multiplied a thousand times over, inflamed her heart in that single second. She must save the baby, *her* baby. Then dream and reality came together in her mind with desperate fervour. The destructive zealots were already making for the altar. An axe was raised in the air—and at that moment she lost all conscious power of thought and leapt in front of the picture, arms outstretched to protect it…

It was like a magic spell. The axe crashed to the floor from the now powerless hand holding it. The torch fell from the man's other hand and went out as it fell. The sight struck these noisy, frenzied people like lightning. They all fell silent, except for one in whose throat the gasping cry of "The Madonna! The Madonna!" died away.

The mob stood there white as chalk, trembling. A few dropped to their knees in prayer. They were all deeply shaken. The strange illusion was compelling. For them, there was no doubt that a miracle had happened, one of the kind often authenticated, told and retold—the Madonna, whose features were obviously those of the young mother in the picture, was protecting her own likeness. Pangs of conscience were aroused in them when they saw the girl's face, which seemed to them nothing short of the picture come to life. They had never been more devout that in that fleeting moment.

But others were already storming up. Torches illuminated the group standing there rigid and the girl pressing close to the altar, hardly moving herself. Noise flooded into the silence. At the back a woman's shrill voice cried, "Go on, go on, it's only the Jew girl from the tavern." And suddenly the spell was broken. In shame and rage, the humiliated rioters stormed on. A rough fist pushed Esther aside. She swayed. But she kept on her feet, she was fighting for the picture as if it really were her own warm life. Swinging a heavy silver candlestick, she hit out furiously at the iconoclasts with her old defiance; one of them fell, cursing, but another took his place. A dagger glinted like a short red lightning flash, and Esther stumbled and fell. Already the pieces of the splintered altar were raining down on her, but she felt no more pain. The picture of the Madonna and Child, and the picture of the Madonna of the Wounded Heart both fell under a single furious blow from an axe.

And the raving crowd stormed on; from church to church went the looters, filling the streets with terrible noise. A dreadful night fell over Antwerp. Terror and trembling made its way into houses with the news, and hearts beat in fear behind barred gates. But the flame of rebellion was waving like a banner over the whole country.

The old painter, too, shuddered with fear when he heard the news that the iconoclasts were abroad. His knees trembled, and he held a crucifix in his imploring hands to pray for the safety of his picture, the picture given him by the revelation of God's grace. For a whole wild, dark night dreadful ideas tormented him. And at first light of dawn he could not stay at home any longer.

Outside the cathedral, his last hope faded and fell like one of the overturned statues. The doors had been broken down, and rags and splinters showed where the iconoclasts had been like a bloody trail left behind them. He groped his laborious way through the dark to his picture. His hands went out to the shrine, but they met empty air, and sank wearily to his sides again. The faith in his breast that had sung its pious song in praise of God's grace for so many years suddenly flew away like a frightened swallow.

At last he pulled himself together and struck a light, which flared briefly from his tinder, illuminating a scene that made him stagger back. On the ground, among ruins, lay the Italian master's sweetly sad Madonna, the Madonna of the Wounded Heart, transfixed by a dagger thrust. But it was not the picture, it was the figure of the

Madonna herself. Cold sweat stood out on his brow as the flame went out again. He thought this must be a bad dream. When he struck his tinder again, however, he recognised Esther lying there dead of her wound. And by a strange miracle she, who in life had been the embodiment of his own picture of the Virgin, revealed in death the features of the Italian master's Madonna and her bleeding, mortal injury.

Yes, it was a miracle, an obvious miracle. But the old man would not believe in any more miracles. At that hour, when he saw the girl who had brought mild light into the late days of his life lying there dead beside his smashed picture, a string broke in his soul that had so often played the music of faith. He denied the God he had revered for seventy years in a single minute. Could this be the work of God's wise, kind hand, giving so much blessed creativity and bringing splendour into being, only to snatch them back into darkness for no good purpose? This could not be a benign will, only a heartless game. It was a miracle of life and not of God, a coincidence like thousands of others that happen at random every day, coming together and then moving apart again. No more! Could good, pure souls mean so little to God that he threw them away in his casual game? For the first time he stood in a church and doubted God, because he had thought him good and kind, and now he could not understand the ways of his creator.

For a long time he looked down at the dead girl who had shed such gentle evening light over his old age. And when he saw the smile of bliss on her broken lips, he felt less savage and did God more justice. Humility came back into his kindly heart. Could he really ask who had performed this strange miracle, making the lonely Jewish girl honour the Madonna in her death? Could he judge whether it was the work of God or the work of life? Could he clothe love in words that he did not know, could he reject God because he did not understand his nature?

The old man shuddered. He felt poor and needy in that lonely hour. He felt that he had wandered alone between God and earthly life all these long years, trying to understand them as twofold when they were one and yet defied understanding. Had it not been like the work of some miraculous star watching over the tentative path of this young girl's soul—had not God and Love been at one in her and in all things?

Above the windows the first light of dawn was showing. But it did not bring light to him, for he did not want to see new days dawning in the life he had lived for so many years, touched by its miracles yet never really transfigured by them. And now, without fear, he felt close to the last miracle, the miracle that ceases to be dream and illusion, and is only the dark eternal truth.

A STORY TOLD
IN TWILIGHT

HAS RAIN BEEN SWEEPING over the city again in the wind? Is that what suddenly makes it so dim in our room? No. The air is silvery clear and still, as it seldom is on these summer days, but it is getting late, and we didn't notice. Only the dormer windows opposite still smile with a faint glow, and the sky above the roof ridge is veiled by golden mist. In an hour's time it will be night. That will be a wonderful hour, for there is no lovelier sight than the slow fading of sunset colour into shadow, to be followed by darkness rising from the ground below, until finally its black tide engulfs the walls, carrying us away into its obscurity. If we sit opposite one another, looking at each other without a word, it will seem, at that hour, as if our familiar faces in the shadows were older and stranger and farther away, as if we had never known them like that, and each of us was now seeing the other across a wide space and over many years. But you say you don't want silence now, because in silence one hears, apprehensively, the clock breaking time into a hundred tiny splinters, and our breathing will sound as loud as the breathing of a sick man. You want me to tell you a story. Willingly. But not about me, for our life in these big cities is short of experience, or so it seems to us, because we do not yet know what is really our own in them. However, I will tell you a story fit for this hour that really loves only silence, and I would wish it to have something about it of the warm, soft, flowing twilight now hovering mistily outside our windows.

I don't remember just how I came to know this story. All I do know is that I was sitting here for a long time early this afternoon, reading a book, then putting it down again, drowsing in my dreams, perhaps sleeping lightly. And suddenly I saw figures stealing past the walls, and I could hear what they were saying and look into their lives. But when I wanted to watch them moving away, I found myself awake again and on my own. The book lay at my feet. When I picked it up to look for those characters in it, I couldn't find the story any more; it was as if it had fallen out of the pages into my hands, or as if it had never been there at all. Perhaps I had dreamt it, or seen it in one of those bright clouds that came to our city today from distant lands, to carry away the rain that has been depressing us for so long. Did I hear it in the artless old song that an organ-grinder was playing with a melancholy creaking sound under my window, or had someone told it to me years ago? I don't know. Such stories often come into my mind, and I let them take their playful course, running through my fingers, which I allow to drop them as you might caress ears of wheat and long-stemmed flowers in passing without picking them. All I do is dream them, beginning with a sudden brightly coloured image and moving towards a gentler end, but I do not hold and keep them. However, you want me to tell you a story today, so I will tell it to you now, when twilight fills us with a longing to see some bright, lively thing before our eyes, starved as they are in this grey light.

How shall I begin? I feel I must pluck a moment out of the darkness, an image and a character, because that is how those strange dreams of mine begin. Yes, now I remember. I see a slender youth walking down a broad flight of steps leading out of a castle. It is night, and a night of dim moonlight, but I see the whole outline of his supple body, and his features stand out clearly. He is remarkably good-looking. His black hair falls smoothly over his high—almost too high—forehead, combed in a childish style, and his hands, reaching out before him in the dark to feel the warmth of the air after a sunlit day, are delicate and finely formed. His footsteps are hesitant. Dreamily, he climbs down to the large garden, where the rounded treetops rustle; the white path of a single broad avenue leads through it.

I don't know when all this is set, whether yesterday or fifty years ago, and I don't know where; but I think it must be in England or Scotland, the only places where I am sure there are such tall, massive stone castles. From a distance they look menacing, like fortresses, and reveal their bright gardens full of flowers only to an eye familiar with them. Yes, now I know for certain: it is to the north, in Scotland. Only there are the summer nights so light that the sky has a milky, opalescent glow, and the fields are never entirely dark, so that everything seems full of a soft radiance, and only the shadows drop, like huge black birds, down to pale expanses of countryside. Yes, it's in Scotland, I remember that now for certain; and if I racked my brain I would also find the names of this baronial castle and the boy, because now the darkness around my dream is beginning to peel away, and I feel it all as distinctly as if it were not memory but experience. The boy has come to spend the summer with his married sister, and in the hospitable way of distinguished British families he finds that he is not alone; in the evening there is a whole party of gentlemen who have come for the field sports of shooting and fishing, and their wives, with a few young girls, tall, handsome people, who in their cheerfulness and youth play laughing, but not noisily, to the sound of the echo from the ancient walls. By day they ride horses, there are dogs about, two or three boats glitter on the river, and liveliness without frantic activity helps the day to pass quickly and pleasantly.

But it is evening now, the company around the dinner table has broken up. The gentlemen are sitting in the great hall, smoking and playing cards; until midnight, white light, quivering at the edges, spills out of the bright windows into the park, sometimes accompanied by a full-throated, jocular roar of laughter. Most of the ladies have already gone to their rooms, although a few of them may still be talking to each other in the entrance hall of the castle. So the boy is on his own in the evening. He is not allowed to join the gentlemen yet, or only briefly, and he feels shy in the presence of ladies because when he opens a door they suddenly lower their voices, and he senses that they are discussing matters he isn't meant to hear. And he doesn't like their company anyway, because they ask him questions as if he were still a child, and only half-listen to his answers; they make use of him to do them all sorts of small favours, and then thank him in the tone they would use with a good little boy. He thought he would go to bed, but his room was too hot, full of still, sultry air. They had forgotten to close the windows during the day, so the sun had made itself at home in here, almost setting light to the table, leaving the bedstead hot to the touch, clinging heavily to the walls, and its warm breath still comes out of the corners and from behind curtains. And moreover it was still so early—and outside, the summer night shone like a white candle, peaceful, with no wind, as motionless as if it longed for nothing. So the boy goes down the tall castle steps again and towards the garden, which is rimmed by the dark sky like a saint's halo. Here the rich fragrance given off by many invisible flowers comes enticingly to meet him. He feels strange. In all the confused sensations of his fifteen years of life, he couldn't have said exactly why, but his lips are quivering as if he has to say something in the night air, or must raise his hands and close his eyes for a long time. He seems to have some mysterious familiarity with this summer night, now at rest, something that calls for words or a gesture of greeting.

Then, all of a sudden, as he goes deeper into the darkness, an extraordinary thing happens. The gravel behind him crunches slightly, and as he turns, startled, all he sees is a tall white form, bright and fluttering, coming towards him, and in astonishment he feels strong and yet caught, without any violence, in a woman's embrace. A soft, warm body presses close to his, a trembling hand quickly caresses

144

his hair and bends his head back; reeling, he feels a stranger's open mouth like a fruit against his own, quivering lips fastening on his. The face is so close to him that he cannot see its features. And he dares not look, because shudders are running through his body like pain, so that he has to close his eyes and give himself up to those burning lips without any will of his own; he is their prey. Hesitantly, uncertainly, as if asking a question, his arms now go round the stranger's body, and, suddenly intoxicated, he holds it close to his own. Avidly, his hands move over its soft outline, fall still and then tremble as they move on again more and more feverishly, carried away. And now the whole weight of her body, pressing ever more urgently against him, bending forward, a delightful burden, rests on his own yielding breast. He feels as if he were sinking and flowing away under her fast-breathing urgency, and is already weak at the knees. He thinks of nothing, he does not wonder how this woman came to him, or what her name is, he merely drinks in the desire of those strange, moist lips with his eyes closed, until he is intoxicated by them, drifting away with no will or mind of his own on a vast tide of passion. He feels as if stars had suddenly fallen to earth, there is such a shimmering before his eyes, everything flickers in the air like sparks, burning whatever he touches. He does not know how long all this lasts, whether he has been held in this soft chain for hours or seconds; in this wild, sensual struggle he feels that everything is blazing up and drifting away, he is staggering in a wonderful kind of vertigo.

Then suddenly, with an abrupt movement, the chain of heat holding them breaks. Brusquely, almost angrily, the woman loosens the embrace that held him so close; she stands erect, and already a shaft of white light is running past the trees, clear and fast, and has gone before he can raise his hands to seize it and stop her.

Who was she? And how long had it lasted? Dazed, with a sense of oppressive uneasiness, he stands up, propping himself against a tree. Slowly, cool thought returns to the space between his fevered temples: his life suddenly seems to him to have moved forward a thousand hours. Could his confused dreams of women and passion suddenly have come true? Or was it only a dream? He feels himself, touches his hair. Yes, it is damp at his hammering temples, damp and cool from the dew on the grass into which they had fallen. Now it all flashes before his mind's eye again, he feels those burning lips once more, breathes in the strange, exciting, sensual perfume clinging to her dress, tries to remember every word she spoke—but none of them come back to him.

And now, with a sudden shock of alarm, he remembers that in fact she said nothing at all, not even his name; that he heard only her sighs spilling over and her convulsively restrained sobs of desire threatening to break out, that he knows the fragrance of her tousled hair, the hot pressure of her breasts, the smooth enamel of her skin, he knows that her figure, her breath, all her quivering feelings were his—and yet he has no idea of the identity of this woman who has overwhelmed him with her love in the dark. He knows that he must now try to find a name to give to his happy astonishment.

And then the extraordinary experience that he has just shared with a woman seems to him a poor thing, very petty compared to the sparkling mystery staring at him out of the dark with alluring eyes. Who was she? He swiftly reviews all the possible candidates, assembling in his mind's eye the images of all the women staying here at the castle; he recalls every strange hour, excavates from his memory every conversation he has had with them, every smile of the only five or six women who could be part of this puzzle. Young Countess E., perhaps, who so often quarrelled violently with her ageing husband, or his uncle's young wife, who had such curiously gentle yet iridescent eyes, or—and he was startled by this idea—one of the three sisters, his cousins, who are so like each other in their proud, haughty, abrupt manner. No—these were all cool, circum-spect people. In recent years he had often felt sick, or an outcast, when secret stirrings in him began disturbing and flickering in his dreams. He had envied all who were, or seemed to be, so calm, so well-balanced and lacking in desires, had been afraid of his awakening passion as if it were an infirmity. And now?… But who, which of them all could be so deceptive?

Slowly, that insistent question drives the frenzy out of his blood. It is late now, the lights in the hall where guests were playing cards are out, he is the only guest in the castle still awake, he—and perhaps also that unknown woman. Slowly, weariness comes over him. Why go on thinking about it? A glance, a spark glimpsed between someone's eyelids, the secret pressure of his hand must surely tell him everything tomorrow. Dreamily, he climbs the steps, as dreamily as he climbed down them, but he feels so very different now. His blood is still slightly agitated, but the warm room seems to him clearer and cooler than it was.

When he wakes next morning, the horses down outside the castle are already stamping and scraping their hooves on the ground; he hears voices, laughter, and his name is called now and then. He quickly leaps out of bed—he has missed breakfast—dresses at high speed and runs downstairs, where the rest of the party cheerfully wish him a good morning. "What a late riser you are!" laughs Countess E., and there is laughter in her clear eyes as well. His avid look falls on her face; no, it couldn't be the Countess, her laughter is too carefree. "I hope you had sweet dreams," the young woman teases him, but her delicate build seems to him too slight for his companion last night. With a question in his eyes, he looks from face to face, but sees no smiling reflection answering it on any of them.

They ride out into the country. He assesses each voice, his eyes dwell on every line and undulation of the women's bodies as they move on horseback, he observes the way they bend, the way they raise their arms. At the luncheon table he leans close to them in conversation, to catch the scent of their lips or the sultry warmth of their hair, but nothing, nothing gives him any sign, not a fleeting trail for his heated thoughts to pursue. The day draws out endlessly towards evening. If he tries to read a book, the lines run over the edge of the pages and suddenly lead out into the garden, and it is night again, that strange night, and he feels the unknown woman's arms embracing him once more. Then he drops the book from his trembling hands and decides to go down to the little pool. But suddenly, surprised by himself, he finds that he is standing on that very spot again. He feels feverish at dinner that evening, his hands are distracted, moving restlessly back and forth as if pursued, his eyes retreat shyly under their lids. Not until the others—at last, at last!—push back their chairs is he happy, and soon he is running out of his room and into the park, up and down the white path that seems to shimmer like milky mist beneath his feet, going up and down it, up and down hundreds, thousands of times. Are the lights on in the great hall yet? Yes, they come on at last, and at last there is light in a few of the first-floor windows. The ladies have gone upstairs. Now, if she is going to come, it can be only a matter of minutes; but every minute stretches to breaking point, fuming with impatience. Up and down the path, up and down, he is moving convulsively back and forth as if worked by invisible wires.

And then, suddenly, the white figure comes hurrying down the steps, fast, much too fast for him to recognize her. She seems to be made of glinting moonlight, or a lost, drifting wisp of mist among the trees, chased this way by the wind and now, now in his arms. They close firmly as a claw around that wild body, heated and throbbing from her fast running. It is the same as yesterday, a single moment with this warm wave beating against his breast, and he thinks he will faint with the sweet throbbing of her heart and flow away in a stream of dark desire. But then the frenzy abruptly dies down, and he holds back his fiery feelings. He must not lose himself in that wonderful pleasure, give himself up to those lips fixed on his, before he knows what name to give this body pressed so close that it is as if her heart were beating loudly in his own chest! He bends his head back from her kiss to see her face, but shadows are falling, mingling with her hair; the twilight makes it look dark. The tangled trees grow too close together, and the light of the moon, veiled in cloud, is not strong enough for him to make out her features. He sees only her eyes shining, glowing stones sprinkled deep down somewhere, set in faintly gleaming marble.

Now he wants to hear a word, just one splinter of her voice breaking away. "Who are you?" he demands. "Tell me who you are!" But that soft, moist mouth offers only kisses, no words. He tries to force a word out of her, a cry of pain, he squeezes her arm, digs his nails into its flesh; but he is aware only of his own gasping, heated breath, and of the sultry heat of her obstinately silent lips that only moan a little now and then—whether in pain or pleasure he does not know. And it sends him nearly mad to realize that he has no power over this defiant will, that this woman coming out of the dark takes him without giving herself away to him, that he has unbounded power over her body and its desires, yet cannot command her name. Anger rises in him and he fends off her embrace; but she, feeling his arms slacken and aware of his uneasiness, caresses his hair soothingly, enticingly with her excited hand. And then, as her fingers move, he feels something make a slight ringing sound against his forehead, something metal, a medallion or coin that hangs loose from her bracelet. An idea suddenly occurs to him. As if in the transports of passion, he presses her hand to him, and in so doing embeds the coin deep in his half-bared arm until he feels its surface digging into his skin. He is sure of having a sign to follow now, and with it burning against him he willingly gives himself up to the passion he has held back. Now he presses deep into her body, sucks the desire from her lips, falling into the mysteriously pleasurable ardour of a wordless embrace.

And then, when she suddenly jumps up and takes flight, just as she did yesterday, he does not try to hold her back, for he is already feverish with curiosity to see the sign. He runs to his room, turns up the dim lamplight until it is bright, and bends avidly over the mark left by the coin in his arm.

It is no longer entirely clear, the full outline is indistinct; but one corner is still engraved red and sharp on his flesh, unmistakably precise. There are angular corners; the coin must have eight sides, medium-sized like a penny but with more of a raised surface, because the impression here is still deep, corresponding to the height of the surface. The mark burns like fire as he examines it so greedily; it suddenly hurts him, like a wound, and only now that he dips his hand in cold water does the painful burning go away. So the medallion is octagonal; he feels certain of that now. Triumph sparkles in his eyes. Tomorrow he will know everything.

Next morning he is one of the first down at the breakfast table. The only ladies present are an elderly old maid, his sister and Countess E. They are all in a cheerful mood, and their lively conversation passes him by. He has all the more opportunity for his observations. His glance swiftly falls on the Countess's slim wrist; she is not wearing a bracelet. He can speak to her without agitation now, but his eyes keep going nervously to the door. Then his cousins, the three sisters, come in together. Uneasiness stirs in him again. He catches a glimpse of the jewellery they wear pushed up under their sleeves, but they sit down too quickly for a good view: Kitty with her chestnut-brown hair opposite him; blonde Margot; and Elisabeth, whose hair is so fair that it shines like silver in the dark and flows golden in the sun. All three, as usual, are cool, quiet and reserved, stiff with the dignity he dislikes so much about them; after all, they are not much older than he is, and were his playmates for years. His uncle's young wife has not come down yet. The boy's heart is more and more restless now that he feels the moment of revelation is so close, and suddenly he decides that he almost likes the mysterious torment of secrecy. However, his eyes are full of curiosity; they move around the edge of the table, where the women's hands lie at rest on the white cloth or wander slowly like ships in a bright bay. He sees only their hands, and they suddenly seem to him like creatures with a life and soul of their own, characters on a stage. Why is the blood throbbing at his temples like that? All three cousins, he sees in alarm, are wearing bracelets, and the idea that it could be one of these three proud and outwardly immaculate young women, whom he has never known, even in childhood, as anything but unapproachable and reserved, confuses him. Which of them could it be? Kitty, whom he knows least because she is the eldest, Margot with her abrupt manner, or little Elisabeth? He dares not wish it to be any of them. Secretly, he wants it to be none of them, or he wants not to know. But now his desire carries him away.

"Could I ask you to pour me another cup of tea, please, Kitty?" His voice sounds as if he has sand in his throat. He passes her his cup; now she must raise her arm and reach over the table to him. Now—he sees a medallion dangling from her bracelet and for a moment his hand stops dead, but no, it is a green stone in a round setting that clinks softly against the porcelain. His glance gratefully rests on Kitty's brown hair.

It takes him a moment to get his breath back.

"May I trouble you for a lump of sugar, Margot?" A slender hand comes to life on the table, stretches, picks up a silver bowl and passes it over. And there—his hand shakes slightly—he sees, where the wrist disappears into her sleeve, an old silver coin dangling from a flexible bracelet. The coin has eight sides, is the size of a penny and is obviously a family heirloom of some kind. But octagonal, with the sharp corners that dug into his flesh yesterday. His hand is no steadier, and he misses his aim with the sugar tongs at first; only then does he drop a lump of sugar into his tea, which he forgets to drink.

Margot! The name is burning on his lips in a cry of the utmost surprise, but he clenches his teeth and bites it back. He hears her speaking now—and her voice sounds to him as strange as if someone were speaking from a stand at a show—cool, composed, slightly humorous, and her breath is so calm that he almost takes fright at the thought of the terrible lie she is living. Is this really the same woman whose unsteady breath he soothed yesterday, from whose moist lips he drank kisses, who falls on him by night like a beast of prey? Again and again he stares at those lips. Yes, the pride, the reserve, could be taking refuge there and nowhere else, but what is there to show the fire within her?

He looks harder at her face, as if seeing it for the first time. And for the first time he really feels, rejoicing, trembling with happiness and almost near tears, how beautiful she is in her pride, how enticing in her secrecy. His gaze traces, with delight, the curving line of her eyebrows suddenly rising to a sharp angle, looks deep into the cool, gemstone hue of her grey-green eyes, kisses the pale, slightly translucent skin of her cheeks, imagines her lips, now sharply tensed, curving more softly for a kiss, wanders around her pale hair, and, quickly moving down again, takes in her whole figure with delight. He has never known her until this moment. Now he rises from the table and finds that his knees are trembling. He is drunk with looking at her as if on strong wine.

Then his sister calls down below. The horses are ready for the morning ride, prancing nervously, impatiently champing at the bit. One guest after another mounts, and then they ride in a bright cavalcade down the broad avenue through the garden. First at a slow trot, with a sedate harmony that is out of tune with the racing rhythm of the boy's blood. But then, beyond the gate, they give the horses their heads, storming down the road and into the meadows to left and right, where a slight morning mist still lingers. There must have been a heavy fall of dew overnight, for under the veil of mist, trembling dewdrops glitter like sparks, and the air is deliciously cool, as if chilled by a waterfall somewhere near. The close-packed group soon strings out, the chain breaks into colourful separate links and a few riders have already disappeared into the woods among the hills.

Margot is one of the riders in the lead. She loves the wild exhilaration, the passionate tug of the wind at her hair, the indescribable sense of pressing forward at a fast gallop. The boy is storming on behind her; he sees her proud body sitting very erect, tracing a beautiful line in her swift movement. He sometimes sees her slightly flushed face, the light in her eyes, and now that she is living out her own strength with such passion he knows her again. Desperately, he feels his love and longing flare vehemently up. He is overcome by an impetuous wish to take hold of her all of a sudden, sweep her off her horse and into his arms, to drink from those ravenous lips again, to feel the shattering throb of her agitated heart against his breast. He strikes his horse's flank, and it leaps forward with a whinny. Now he is beside her, his knee almost touching hers, their stirrups clink slightly together. He must say it now, he must.

"Margot," he stammers.

She turns her head, her arched brows shoot up. "Yes, what is it, Bob?" Her tone of voice is perfectly cool. And her eyes are cool as well, showing no emotion.

A shiver runs all the way down him to his knees. What had he been going to say? He can't remember. He stammers something about turning back.

"Are you tired?" she says, with what sounds to him like a touch of sarcasm.

"No, but the others are so far behind," he manages to say. Another moment, he feels, and he will be impelled to do something senseless—reach his arms out to her, or begin shedding tears, or strike out at her with the riding crop that is shaking in his hand as if it were electrically charged. Abruptly he pulls his horse back, making it rear for a moment. She races on ahead, erect, proud, unapproachable.

The others soon catch up with him. There is a lively conversation in progress to both sides of him, but the words and laughter pass him by, making no sense, like the hard clatter of the horses' hooves. He is tormenting himself for his failure to summon up the courage to tell her about his love and force her to confess hers, and his desire to tame her grows wilder and wilder, veiling his eyes like a red mist above the land before him. Why didn't he answer scorn with scorn? Unconsciously he urges his horse on, and now the heat of his speed eases his mind. Then the others call out that it is time to turn back. The sun has crept above the hills and is high in the midday sky. A soft, smoky fragrance wafts from the fields, colours are bright now and burn the eyes like molten gold. Sultry, heavy heat billows out over the land, the sweating horses are trotting more drowsily, with warm steam rising from them, breathing hard. Slowly the procession forms again, cheerfulness is more muted than before, conversation more desultory.

Margot too is in sight again. Her horse is foaming at the mouth, white specks of foam cling trembling to her riding habit, and the round bun into which she has pinned up her hair threatens to come undone, held in place only loosely by its clasps. The boy stares as if enchanted at the tangle of blonde hair, and the idea that it might suddenly all come down, flowing in wild tresses, maddens him with excitement. Already the arched garden gate at the end of the avenue is in sight, and beyond it the broad avenue up to the castle. Carefully, he guides his horse past the others, is the first to arrive, jumps down, hands the reins to a groom and waits for the cavalcade. Margot comes last. She trots up very slowly, her body relaxed, leaning back, exhausted as if by pleasure. She must look like that, he senses, when she has blunted the edge of her frenzy, she must have looked like that yesterday and the evening before. The memory makes him impetuous again. He goes over to her and, breathlessly, helps her down from the horse.

As he is holding the stirrup, his hand feverishly clasps her slender ankle. "Margot," he groans, murmuring her name softly. She does not so much as look at him in answer, taking the hand he is holding out casually as she gets down.

"Margot, you're so wonderful," he stammers again.

She gives him a sharp look, her eyebrows rising steeply again. "I think you must be drunk, Bob! What on earth are you talking about?"

But angry with her for pretending, blind with passion, he presses the hand that he is still holding firmly to himself as if to plunge it into his breast. At that, Margot, flushing angrily, gives him such a vigorous push that he sways, and she walks rapidly past him. All this has happened so fast and so abruptly that no one has noticed, and now it seems to him, too, like nothing but an alarming dream.

He is so pale and distracted all the rest of the day that the blonde Countess strokes his hair in passing and asks if he is all right. He is so angry that when his dog jumps up at him, barking, he chases it away with a kick; he is so clumsy in playing games that the girls laugh at him. The idea that now she will not come this evening poisons his blood, makes him bad-tempered and surly. They all sit out in the garden together at teatime, Margot opposite him, but she does not look at him. Magnetically attracted, his eyes keep tentatively glancing at hers, which are cool as grey stone, returning no echo. It embitters him to think that she is playing with him like this. Now, as she turns brusquely away from him, he clenches his fist and feels he could easily knock her down.

"What's the matter, Bob? You look so pale," says a voice suddenly. It is little Elisabeth, Margot's sister. There is a soft, warm light in her eyes, but he does not notice it. He feels rather as if he were caught in some disreputable act, and says angrily, "Leave me alone, will you? You and your damned concern for me!" Then he regrets it, because the colour drains out of Elisabeth's own face, she turns away and says, with a hint of tears in her voice, "How oddly you're behaving today." Everyone is looking at him with disapproval, almost menacingly, and he himself feels that he is in the wrong. But then, before he can apologize, a hard voice, bright and sharp as the blade of a knife, Margot's voice, speaks across the table. "If you ask me, Bob is behaving very badly for his age. We're wrong to treat him as a gentleman or even an adult." This from Margot, Margot who gave him her lips only last night! He feels everything going round in circles, there is a mist before his eyes. Rage seizes him. "You of all people should know!" he says in an unpleasant tone of voice, and gets up from the table. His movement was so abrupt that his chair falls over behind him, but he does not turn back.

And yet, senseless as it seems even to him, that evening he is down in the garden again, praying to God that she may come. Perhaps all that had been nothing but pretence and waywardness—no, he wouldn't ask her any more questions or be angry with her, if only she would come, if only he could feel once again the bitter desire of those soft, moist lips against his mouth, sealing all its questions. The hours seem to have gone to sleep; night, an apathetic, limp animal, lies in front of the castle; time drags out to an insane length. The faintly buzzing grass around him seems to be animated by mocking voices; the twigs and branches gently moving, playing with their shadows and the faint glow of evening light, are like mocking hands. All sounds are confused and strange, they irritate him more painfully than silence. Once a dog begins barking out in the countryside, and once a shooting star crosses the sky and falls somewhere behind the castle. The night seems brighter and brighter, the shadows of the trees above the garden path darker and darker, and those soft sounds are more and more confused. Drifting clouds envelop the sky in sombre, melancholy darkness. This loneliness falls on his burning heart.

The boy walks up and down, more and more vigorously, faster and faster. Sometimes he angrily strikes a tree, or rubs a piece of its bark in his fingers, rubbing so furiously that they bleed. No, she is not going to come, he knew it all along, but he doesn't want to believe it because then she will never come again, never. It is the bitterest moment of his life. And he is still so youthfully passionate that he flings himself down hard in the damp moss, digging his hands into the earth, tears on his cheeks, sobbing softly and bitterly as he never wept as a child, and as he will never be able to weep again.

Then a faint cracking sound in the undergrowth suddenly rouses him from his despair. And as he leaps up, blindly holding out his searching hands, he finds that he is holding—and how wonderful is its sudden, warm impact on his breast—he is holding the body of which he dreamt so wildly in his arms again. A sob breaks from his throat, his whole being is dissolved in a vast convulsion, and he holds her tall, curving body so masterfully to his that a moan comes from those strange, silent lips. As he feels her groan, held in his power, he knows for the first time that he has mastered her and is not, as he was yesterday and the day before, the prey of her moods; a desire overcomes him to torment her for the torment he has felt for what seems like a hundred hours, to chastise her for her defiance, for those scornful words this evening in front of the others, for the mendacious game she is playing. Hatred is so inextricably intertwined with his burning desire that their embrace is more of a battle than a loving encounter. He catches hold of her slim wrists so that her whole breathless body writhes, trembling, and then holds her so stormily against him again that she cannot move, only groan quietly again and again, whether in pleasure or pain he does not know. But he cannot get a word out of her. Now, when he forces his lips on hers, sucking at them to stifle that faint moaning, he feels something warm and wet on them, blood, blood running where her teeth have bitten so hard into his lips. And so he torments her until he suddenly feels his strength flagging, and the hot wave of desire rises in him, and now they are both gasping, breast to breast. Flames have fallen overnight, stars seem to flicker in front of his eyes, everything is crazy, his thoughts circle more wildly, and all of it has only one name: Margot. Muted, but from the depths of his heart, he finally, in a burning torrent, gets out her name in mingled rejoicing and despair, expressing longing, hatred, anger and love at the same time. It comes out in a single cry filled with his three days of torment: Margot, Margot. And to his ears, all the music in the world lies in those two syllables.

A shock passes through his body. All at once the fervour of their embrace dies down, a brief, wild thrust, a sob, weeping comes from her throat, and again there is fire in her movements, but only to tear herself away as if from a touch she hates. Surprised, he tries to hold her, but she struggles with him; as she bends her face close he feels tears of anger running down her cheeks, and her slender body writhes like a snake. Suddenly, with an embittered movement of violence, she throws him off and runs. Her white dress shows among the trees, and is then drowned in darkness.

So there he stands, alone again, shocked and confused as he was the first time, when warmth and passion suddenly fell into his arms. The stars gleam with moisture before his eyes, and his blood thrusts sharp sparks into his brow from within. What has happened? He makes his way through the row of trees, growing less densely here, and farther into the garden, where he knows the little fountain will be playing. He lets its water soothe his hand, white, silvery water that murmurs softly to him and shines beautifully in the reflection of the moon as it slowly emerges from the clouds again. And then, now that he sees more clearly, wild grief comes over him as if the mild wind had blown it down out of the trees. His warm tears rise, and now he feels, more strongly and clearly than in those moments of their convulsive embrace, how much he loves Margot. Everything that went before has fallen away from him, the shuddering frenzy of possession, his anger at her withholding of her secret; love in all its fullness, sweetly melancholy, surrounds him, a love almost without longing; but it is overpowering.

Why did he torment her like that? Hasn't she shown him incredible generosity on these three nights, hasn't his life suddenly emerged from a gloomy twilight into a sparkling, dangerously bright light since she taught him tenderness and the wild ardour of love? And then she left him, in tears of anger! A soft, irresistible wish for reconciliation wells up in him, for a mild, calm word, a wish to hold her quiet in his arms, asking nothing, and tell her how grateful he is to her. Yes, he will go to her in all humility and tell her how purely he loves her, saying he will never mention her name again or force an answer out of her that she does not want to give.

The silvery water flows softly, and he thinks of her tears. Perhaps she is all alone in her room now, he thinks, with only this whispering night to listen to her, a night that listens to all and consoles no one. This night when he is both far from her and near her, without seeing a glimmer of her hair, hearing a word in her voice half lost on the wind, and yet he is caught inextricably, his soul in hers—this night becomes unbearable agony to him. And his longing to be near her, even lying outside her door like a dog or standing as a beggar below her window, is irresistible.

As he hesitantly steals out of the darkness of the trees, he sees that there is still light in her window on the first floor. It is a faint light; its yellow shimmering scarcely even illuminates the leaves of the spreading sycamore tree that is trying to knock on the window with its branches as if they were hands, stretching them out, then withdrawing them again in the gentle breeze, a dark, gigantic eavesdropper outside the small, shining pane. The idea that Margot is awake behind the shining glass, perhaps still shedding tears or

159

thinking about him, upsets the boy so much that he has to lean against the tree to keep himself from swaying.

He stares up as if spellbound. The white curtains waft restlessly out, playing in the light wind, seeming now deep gold in the radiance of the warm lamplight, now silvery when they blow forward into the shaft of moonlight that seeps, flickering, through the leaves. And the window, opening inward, mirrors the play of light and shade as a loosely strung tissue of light reflections. But to the fevered boy now staring up out of the shadows, hot-eyed, dark runes telling a tale seem to be written there on a blank surface. The flowing shadows, the silvery gleam that passes over that black surface like faint smoke—these fleeting perceptions fill his imagination with trembling images. He sees Margot, tall and beautiful, her hair—oh, that wild, blonde hair—flowing loose, his own restlessness in her blood, pacing up and down her room, sees her feverish in her sultry passion, sobbing with rage. As if through glass, he now sees, through the high walls, the smallest of her movements when she raises her hands or sinks into an armchair, and her silent, desperate staring at the starlit sky. He even thinks, when the pane lights up for a moment, that he sees her face anxiously bend to look down into the slumbering garden, looking for him. And then his wild emotion gets the better of him; keeping his voice low, and yet urgent, he calls up her name: Margot! Margot!

Wasn't that something scurrying over the blank surface like a veil, white and fast? He thinks he saw it clearly. He strains his ears, but nothing is moving. The soft breath of the drowsy trees and the silken whispering in the grass swell, carried on the gentle wind, now farther away, now louder again, a warm wave gently dying down. The night is peaceful, the window is silent, a silver frame round a darkened picture. Didn't she hear him? Or doesn't she want to hear him any more? That trembling glow around the window confuses him. His heart beats hard, expressing the longing in his breast, beats against the bark of the tree, and the bark itself seems to tremble at such passion. All he knows is that he must see her now, must speak to her now, even if he were to call her name so loud that people came to see what was going on, and others woke from sleep. He feels that something must happen at this point, the most senseless of ideas seems to him desirable, just as everything is easily achieved in a dream. Now that his glance moves up to the window again, he suddenly sees the tree leaning against it reach out a branch like a signpost, and his hand clings harder to its trunk. Suddenly it is all clear to him: he must climb up there—the trunk is broad, but feels soft and silken—and once up the tree he will call to her just outside her window. Close to her up there, he will talk to her, and he won't come down again until she has forgiven him. He does not stop to think for a second, he sees only the window, enticing him, gleaming faintly, and feels that the tree is on his side, sturdy and broad enough to take his weight. With a couple of quick movements he swings himself up, and already his hands are holding a branch. He energetically hauls his body after them, and now he is high in the tree, almost at the top of the leaf canopy swaying beneath him as it might do in alarm. The rustling sound of the leaves ripples on to the last of them, and the branch bends closer to the window as if to warn the unsuspecting girl. Now the boy, as he climbs, can see the white ceiling of her room, and in the middle of it, sparkling gold, the circle of light cast by the lamp. And he knows, trembling slightly with excitement, that in a moment he will see Margot herself, weeping or still sobbing or in the naked desire of her body. His arms slacken, but he catches himself again. Slowly, he makes his way along the branch turned to her window; his knees are bleeding a little, there is a cut on his hand, but he climbs on, and is now almost within the light from the window. A broad tangle of leaves still conceals the view, the final scene he longs so much to see, and the ray of light is already falling on him as he bends forward, trembling—and his body rocks, he loses his balance and falls tumbling to the ground.

He hits the grass with a soft, hollow impact, like a heavy fruit falling. Up in the castle, a figure leans out of the window, looking around uneasily, but nothing moves in the darkness, which is still as a millpond that has swallowed up a drowning man. Soon the light at the window goes out and the garden is left to itself again, in the uncertain twilight gleam above the silent shadows.

After a few minutes the fallen figure wakes to consciousness. His eyes stare up for a second to where a pale sky with a few wandering stars in it looks coldly down on him. But then he feels a sudden piercing, agonizing pain in his right foot, a pain that almost makes him scream at the first movement he attempts. Suddenly he knows what has happened to him. He also knows that he can't stay lying here under Margot's window, he can't call for help to anyone, must not raise his voice or make much noise as he moves. Blood is running from his forehead; he must have hit a stone or a piece of wood on the turf, but he wipes it away with his hand to keep it from running into his eyes. Then, curled on his left side, he tries slowly working his way forward by ramming his hands into the earth. Every time something touches or merely jars his broken leg, pain flares up, and he is afraid of losing consciousness again. But he drags himself slowly on. It takes him almost half an hour to reach the steps, and his arms already feel weak. Cold sweat mingles on his brow with the sticky blood still oozing out. The last and worst of it is still to come: he must get to the top of the steps, and he works his way very slowly up them, in agony. When he is right at the top, reaching for the balustrade, his breath rattles in his throat. He drags himself a little farther, to the door into the room where the gentlemen play cards, and where he can hear voices and see a light. He hauls himself up by the handle, and suddenly, as if flung in, he falls into the brightly lit room as the door gives way.

He must present a gruesome sight, stumbling in like that, blood all over his face, smeared with garden soil, and then falling to the floor like a clod of earth, because the gentlemen spring up wildly. Chairs fall over backwards with a clatter, they all hurry to help him. He is carefully laid on the sofa. He just manages to babble something about tumbling down the steps on his way to go for a walk in the park, and then it is as if black ribbons fall on his eyes, waver back and forth, and surround him entirely. He falls into a faint, and knows no more.

A horse is saddled, and someone rides to the nearest town to fetch a doctor. The castle, startled into wakefulness, is full of ghostly activity: lights tremble like glow-worms in the corridors, voices whisper, asking what has happened from their bedroom doors, the servants timidly appear, drowsy with sleep, and finally the unconscious boy is carried up to his room.

The doctor ascertains that he has indeed broken his leg, and reassures everyone by telling them that there is no danger. However, the victim of the accident will have to lie motionless with his leg bound up for a long time. When the boy is told, he smiles faintly. It does not trouble him much. If you want to dream of someone you love, it is good to lie alone like this for lengthy periods—no noise, no other people, in a bright, high-ceilinged room with treetops rustling outside. It is sweet to think everything over in peace, dream gentle dreams of your love, undisturbed by any arrangements and duties, alone and at your ease with the tender dream images that approach the bed when you close your eyes for a moment. Love may have no more quietly beautiful moments than these pale, twilight dreams.

He still feels severe pain for the first few days, but it is mingled with a curious kind of pleasure. The idea that he has suffered this pain for the sake of his beloved Margot gives the boy a highly romantic, almost ecstatic sense of self-confidence. He wishes he had a wound, he thinks, a blood-red injury to his face that he could have taken around openly, all the time, like a knight wearing his lady's favours; alternatively, it would have been good never to wake up

again at all but stay lying down there, broken to pieces outside her
window. His dream is already under way; he imagines her awakened in the morning by the sound of voices under her window, all
talking together, sees her bending curiously down and discovering
him—him!—shattered there below the window, dead for her sake.
He pictures her collapsing with a scream; he hears that shrill cry in
his ears, and then sees her grief and despair as she lives on, sad and
serious all her life, dressed in black, her lips quivering faintly when
she is asked the reason for her sorrow.

He dreams like this for days, at first only in the dark, then with
open eyes, getting accustomed to the pleasant memory of her dear
image. Not an hour is so bright or full of activity as to keep her picture
from coming to him, a slight shadow stealing over the walls, or her
voice from reaching his ears through the rippling rustle of the leaves
and the crunch of sand outside in the strong sunlight. He converses
with Margot for hours like this, or dreams of accompanying her on
their travels, on wonderful journeys. Sometimes, however, he wakes
from these reveries distraught. Would she really mourn for him if
he were dead? Would she even remember him?

To be sure, she sometimes comes in person to visit the invalid.
Often, when he is talking to her in his mind and seems to see her
lovely image before him, the door opens and she comes in, tall and
beautiful, but so different from the being in his dreams. For she is
not gentle, nor does she bend down with emotion to kiss his brow,
like the Margot of his dreams; she just sits down beside his chaise
longue, asks how he is and whether he is in any pain, and then tells
him a few interesting stories. He is always so sweetly startled and
confused by her presence that he dares not look at her; often he closes
his eyes to hear her voice the better, drinking in the sound of her
words more deeply, that unique music that will then hover around
him for hours. He answers her hesitantly, because he loves the silence
when he hears only her breathing, and is most profoundly alone

with her in this room, in space itself. And then, when she stands up and turns to the door, he stretches and straightens up with difficulty, despite the pain, so that he can memorize the outline of her figure in movement, see her in her living form before she lapses into the uncertain reality of his dreams.

Margot visits him almost every day. But doesn't Kitty visit him too, and Elisabeth, little Elisabeth who always looks so startled, and asks whether he feels better yet in such kind tones of concern? Doesn't his sister come to see him daily, and the other women, and aren't they all equally kind to him? Don't they stay with him, telling him amusing stories? In fact they even stay too long, because their presence drives away his mood of reverie, rouses it from its meditative peace and forces him to make casual conversation and utter silly phrases. He would rather none of them came except for Margot, and even she only for an hour, only for a few minutes, and then he would be on his own again to dream of her undisturbed, uninterrupted, quietly happy as if buoyed up on soft clouds, entirely absorbed in the consoling images of his love.

So sometimes, when he hears a hand opening the door, he closes his eyes and pretends to be asleep. Then the visitors steal out again on tiptoe, he hears the handle quietly closing, and knows that now he can plunge back into the warm tide of his dreams gently bearing him away to enticingly faraway places.

And one day a strange thing happens: Margot has already been to visit him, only for a moment, but she brought all the scents of the garden in her hair, the sultry perfume of jasmine in flower, and the bright sparkling of the August sun was in her eyes. Now, he knew, he could not expect her again today. It would be a long, bright afternoon, shining with sweet reverie, because no one would disturb him; they had all gone riding. And when the door moves again, hesitantly, he squeezes his eyes shut, imitating sleep. However, the woman coming in—as he can clearly hear in the breathless stillness of the room—does not retreat, but closes the door without a sound so as not to wake him. Now she steals towards him, stepping carefully, her feet barely touching the floor. He hears the soft rustle of a dress, and knows that she is sitting down beside him. And through the crimson mist behind his closed eyelids, he feels that her gaze is on his face.

His heart begins to thud. Is it Margot? It must be. He senses it, but it is sweeter, wilder, more exciting, a secret, intriguing pleasure not to open his eyes yet but merely guess at her presence beside him. What will she do now? The seconds seem to him endless. She is only looking at him, listening to him sleeping, and that idea sends an electric tingling through his pores, the uncomfortable yet intoxicating sense of being vulnerable to her observation, blind and defenceless, to know that if he opened his eyes now they would suddenly, like a cloak, envelop Margot's startled face in tender mood. But he does not move, although his breath comes unsteadily from a chest too constricted for it, and he waits and waits.

Nothing happens. He feels as if she were bending down closer to him, as if he sensed, closer to his face now, her faint perfume, a soft, moist lilac scent that he knows from her lips. And now she has placed her hand on the chaise longue and is gently stroking his arm above the rug spread over him—the blood surges from that hand in a hot wave through his whole body—stroking his arm calmly and carefully. He feels that her touch is magnetic, and his blood flows in response to it. This gentle affection, intoxicating and intriguing him at the same time, is a wonderful feeling.

Slowly, almost rhythmically, her hand is still moving along his arm. He peers up surreptitiously between his eyelids. At first he sees only a crimson mist of restless light, then he can make out the dark, speckled rug, and now, as if it came from far away, the hand caressing him; he sees it very, very dimly, only a narrow glimpse of something white, coming down like a bright cloud and moving away again. The gap between his eyelids is wider and wider now. He sees her fingers clearly, pale and white as porcelain, sees them curving gently to stroke forward and then back again, dallying with him, but full of life. They move on like feelers and then withdraw; and at that moment the hand seems to take on a life of its own, like a cat snuggling close to a dress, a small white cat with its claws retracted, purring affectionately, and he would not be surprised if the cat's eyes suddenly began to shoot sparks. And sure enough, isn't something blinking brightly in that white caress? No, it's only the glint of metal, a golden shimmer. But now, as the hand moves forward again, he sees clearly that it is the medallion dangling from her bracelet, that mysterious, giveaway medallion, octagonal and the size of a penny. It is Margot's hand caressing his arm, and a longing rises in him to snatch up that soft, white hand—it wears no rings—carry it to his lips and kiss it. But then he feels her breath, senses that Margot's face is very close to his, and he cannot keep his eyelids pressed together any longer. Happily, radiantly, he turns his gaze on the face now so close, and sees it retreat in alarm.

And then, as the shadows cast by the face bent down to him disperse and light shows her features, stirred by emotion, he recognizes—it is like an electric shock going through his limbs—he recognizes Elisabeth, Margot's sister, that strange girl young Elisabeth. Was this a dream? No, he is staring into a face now quickly blushing red, she is turning her eyes away in alarm, and yes, it is Elisabeth. All at once he guesses at the terrible mistake he has made; his eyes gaze avidly at her hand, and the medallion really is there on her bracelet.

Mists begin swirling before his eyes. He feels exactly as he did when he fainted after his fall, but he grits his teeth; he doesn't want to lose his ability to think straight. Suddenly it all passes rapidly before his mind's eye, concentrated into a single second: Margot's surprise and haughty attitude, Elisabeth's smile, that strange look of hers touching him like a discreet hand—no, there was no possible mistake about it.

He feels one last moment of hope, and stares at the medallion; perhaps Margot gave it to her, today or yesterday or earlier.

But Elisabeth is speaking to him. His fevered thinking must have distorted his features, for she asks him anxiously, "Are you in pain, Bob?"

How alike their voices are, he thinks. And he replies only, without thinking, "Yes, yes… I mean no… I'm perfectly all right!"

There is silence again. The thought keeps coming back to him in a surge of heat: perhaps Margot has given it to her, and that's all. He knows it can't be true, but he has to ask her.

"What's that medallion?"

"Oh, a coin from some American republic or other, I don't know which. Uncle Robert gave it to us once."

"Us?"

He holds his breath. She must say it now.

"Margot and me. Kitty didn't want one, I don't know why."

He feels something wet flowing into his eyes. Carefully, he turns his head aside so that Elisabeth will not see the tear that must be very close to his eyelids now; it cannot be forced back, it slowly, slowly rolls down his cheek. He wants to say something, but he is afraid that his voice might break under the rising pressure of a sob. They are both silent, watching one another anxiously. Then Elisabeth stands up. "I'll go now, Bob. Get well soon." He shuts his eyes, and the door creaks quietly as it closes.

His thoughts fly up like a startled flock of pigeons. Only now does he understand the enormity of his mistake. Shame and anger at his folly overcome him, and at the same time a fierce pain. He knows now that Margot is lost to him for ever, but he feels that he still loves her, if not yet, perhaps, with a desperate longing for the unattainable. And Elisabeth—as if in anger, he rejects her image, because all her devotion and the now muted fire of her passion cannot mean as much to him as a smile from Margot or the touch of her hand in passing. If Elisabeth had revealed herself to him from the first he would have loved her, for in those early hours he was still childlike in his passion; but now, in his thousand dreams of Margot, he has burnt her name too deeply into his heart for it to be extinguished now.

He feels everything darkening before his eyes as his constantly whirling thoughts are gradually washed away by tears. He tries in vain to conjure up Margot's face in his mind as he has done in all the long, lonely hours and days of his illness; a shadow of Elisabeth always comes in front of it, Elisabeth with her deep, yearning eyes, and then he is in confusion and has to think again, in torment, of how it all happened. He is overcome by shame to think how he stood outside Margot's window calling her name, and again he feels sorry for quiet, fair-haired Elisabeth, for whom he never had a word or a look to spare in all these days, when his gratitude ought to have been bent on her like fire.

Next morning Margot comes to visit him for a moment. He trembles at her closeness, and dares not look her in the eye. What is she saying to him? He hardly hears it; the wild buzzing in his temples is louder than her voice. Only when she leaves him does he gaze again, with longing, at her figure. He feels that he has never loved her more.

Elisabeth visits him in the afternoon. There is a gentle familiarity in her hands, which sometimes brush against his, and her voice is very quiet, slightly sad. She speaks, with a certain anxiety, of indifferent things, as if she were afraid of giving herself away if she talked about the two of them. He does not know quite what he feels for her. Sometimes he feels pity for her, sometimes gratitude for her love, but he cannot tell her so. He hardly dares to look at her for fear of lying to her.

She comes every day now, and stays longer too. It is as if, since the hour when the nature of their shared secret dawned on them, their uncertainty has disappeared as well. Yet they never dare to talk about those hours in the dark of the garden.

One day Elisabeth is sitting beside his chaise longue again. The sun is shining brightly outside, a reflection of the green treetops in the wind trembles on the walls. At such moments her hair is as fiery as burning clouds, her skin pale and translucent, her whole being shines and seems airy. From his cushions, which lie in shadow, he sees her face smiling close to him, and yet it looks far away because it is radiant with light that no longer reaches him. He forgets everything that has happened at this sight. And when she bends down to him, so that her eyes seem to be more profound, moving darkly inward, when she leans forward he puts his arm round her, brings her head close to his and kisses her delicate, moist mouth. She trembles like a leaf but does not resist, only caresses his hair with her hand. And then she says, merely breathing the words, with loving sorrow in her voice, "But Margot is the only one you love." He feels that tone of devotion go straight to his heart, that gentle, unresisting despair, and the name that shakes him with emotion strikes at his very soul. But he dares not lie at that minute. He says nothing in reply.

She kisses him once more, very lightly, an almost sisterly kiss on the lips, and then she goes out without a word. That is the only time they talk about it. A few more days, and then the convalescent is taken down to the garden, where the first faded leaves are already chasing across the path and early evening breathes an autumnal melancholy. Another few days, and he is walking alone with some difficulty, for the last time that year, under the colourful autumn canopy of leaves. The trees speak louder and more angrily now than on those three mild summer nights. The boy, in melancholy mood himself, goes to the place where they were once together. He feels as if an invisible, dark wall were standing here behind which, blurred in twilight already, his childhood lies; and now there is another land before him, strange and dangerous.

He said goodbye to the whole party that evening, looked hard once more at Margot's face, as if he had to drink enough of it in to last for the rest of his life, placed his hand restlessly in Elisabeth's, which clasped it with warm ardour, almost looked past Kitty, their friends and his sister—his heart was so full of the realization that he loved one of the sisters and the other loved him. He was very pale, with a bitter expression on his face that made him seem more than a boy; for the first time, he looked like a man.

And yet, when the horses were brought up and he saw Margot turn indifferently away to go back up the steps, and when Elisabeth's eyes suddenly shone with moisture, and she held the balustrade, the full extent of his new experience overwhelmed him so entirely that he gave himself up to tears of his own like a child.

The castle retreated farther into the distance, and through the dust raised by the carriage the dark garden looked smaller and smaller. Then came the countryside, and finally all that he had experienced was hidden from his eyes—but his memory was all the more vivid. Two hours of driving took him to the nearest railway station, and next morning he was in London.

A few more years and he was no longer a boy. But that first experience had left too strong an impression ever to fade. Margot and Elisabeth had both married, but he did not want to see them again, for the memory of those hours sometimes came back to him so forcefully that his entire later life seemed to him merely a dream and an illusion by comparison with its reality. He became one of those men who cannot find a way of relating to women, because in one second of his life the sensation of both loving and being loved had united in him entirely; and now no longing urged him to look for what had fallen into his trembling, anxiously yielding boyish hands so early. He travelled in many countries, one of those correct, silent Englishmen whom many consider unemotional because they are so reserved, and their eyes look coolly away from the faces and smiles of women. For who thinks that they may bear in them, inextricably mingled with their blood, images on which their gaze is always fixed, with an eternal flame burning around them as it does before icons of the Madonna? And now I remember how I heard this story. A card had been left inside the book that I was reading this afternoon, a postcard sent to me by a friend in Canada. He is a young Englishman whom I met once on a journey. We often talked in the long evenings, and in what he said the memory of two women sometimes suddenly and mysteriously flared up, as if they were distant statues, and always in connection with a moment of his youth. It is a long time, a very long time since I spoke to him, and I had probably forgotten those conversations. But today, on receiving that postcard, the memory was revived, mingling dreamily in my mind with experiences of my own; and I felt as if I had read his story in the book that slipped out of my hands, or as if I had found it in a dream.

But how dark it is now in this room, and how far away you are from me in the deep twilight! I can see only a faint pale light where I think your face is, and I do not know if you are smiling or sad. Are you smiling because I make up strange stories for people whom I knew fleetingly, dream of whole destinies for them, and then calmly let them slip back into their lives and their own world? Or are you sad for that boy who rejected love and found himself all at once cast out of the garden of his sweet dream for ever? There, I didn't mean my story to be dark and melancholy—I only wanted to tell you about a boy suddenly surprised by love, his own and someone else's. But stories told in the evening all tread the gentle path of melancholy. Twilight falls with its veils, the sorrow that rests in the evening is a starless vault above them, darkness seeps into their blood, and all the bright, colourful words in them have as full and heavy a sound as if they came from our inmost hearts.

WONDRAK

I N THE AUTUMN OF 1899, the incredible, improbable news that
that ugly creature Ruzena Sedlak, known to everyone far and
wide as 'the Death's Head', had had a baby aroused much mirth in
the small Southern Bohemian town of Dobitzan. Her alarmingly
and indeed distressingly ugly appearance had often enough caused
amusement that none the less was more pitying than spiteful, but even
the most inventive joker would never have ventured to speculate that
such a battered, unattractive pot would ever find its lid. Now, however,
a young huntsman had vouched for what was surely a miracle, if a
miracle in the worst of taste. He had actually seen the baby in the
remote part of the forest where Ruzena Sedlak lived, had seen it
suckling happily from her breast, and the maidservants who heard
this amazing news made haste to carry it back with their buckets to
all the shops, inns and houses of Dobitzan. All that grey October
evening, no one talked of anything but the unexpected infant and
its presumed father. Forthright souls drinking at the regulars' table
dug one another meaningfully in the ribs, spluttering with laughter
as they accused each other of that unappetizing claim to fame, and
the pharmacist, who had a certain amount of medical knowledge,
described the probable course of the amorous scene in such real-
istic detail that everyone had to put back another schnapps or so
in order to recover. For the first time in her twenty-eight years, the
unfortunate Ruzena had provided her fellow citizens with piquant
and abundant material for jokes.

Of course Nature herself, long ago, had been the first to play a
cruel and ineradicable joke on the poor monstrosity, the daughter
of a syphilitic brewer's man, by squashing her nose while she was

still in the womb, and the derisive nickname that clung so terribly came into the world with her. For as soon as the midwife, who had seen plenty of strange and ugly creatures born in forty years, set eyes on the newborn baby she hastily made the sign of the cross and cried, losing all control of herself, "A death's head!" For where the arch of the nose normally rises clear and distinct in a human face, protecting the eyes and shading the lips, dividing light and shadow on the human countenance, there yawned in this child only a deep-set, empty Nothing: just two breathing holes, black as bullet wounds and shockingly empty in the pink surface of flesh. The sight, which no one could stand for long, reminded people forcibly of a skull, where a similarly monstrous and disturbing void lies between the bony forehead and the white teeth. Then, recovering from her first shock, the midwife examined the baby and found that otherwise the little girl was well proportioned, healthy and shapely. The unfortunate child needed nothing to be the same as other babies but an inch of bone and gristle and a small amount of flesh. But Nature has made us so accustomed to the regularity of her laws that the slightest deviation from their familiar harmony seems repellent and alarming. Every mistake made by the creator arouses our bitter dislike of the failed creation—an injustice for which there is no remedy. Fatally, we feel revulsion not for the negligent designer but for the innocent thing it has designed. Every maimed and malformed being is doomed to suffer horribly not only from its own torment, but from the ill-concealed discomfort of those who are normally formed. And so a squinting eye, a twisted lip, a split palate, all of them just single mistakes of Nature, become the lasting torment of a human being, the inescapable misery of a soul—indeed, such diabolical misery that the sufferer finds it hard to believe in any sense of justice on the circling star we call the Earth.

Even as a child Ruzena Sedlak learned, to her shame, that she was known with good reason as the Death's Head, at the same

176

time as she learned to talk, and every second she was reminded yet again that because of that missing inch of bone she was mercilessly banished from the cheerful company of other human beings. Pregnant women quickly turned away if they met her in the street; farmer's wives from the local countryside, bringing their eggs to sell at market, crossed themselves on seeing her, for these simple souls could not help thinking that the Devil himself had squashed the child's nose. And even those who were more kindly disposed and talked to her kept their eyes obviously lowered as they talked; she could not remember ever having seen the pupil of an eye clearly and at close quarters, except in the eyes of animals, who sense only kindness and not ugliness in human beings. It was lucky that her mind was dull and lethargic, so that she suffered only vaguely from this injustice of God's when she was with other people. She did not have the strength to hate them, or any wish to love them; she took little notice of the whole town, which remained strange to her, so she was very pleased when kind Father Nossal put in a good word for her and found her a post as housekeeper at a hunting lodge out in the forest. It was eight hours' walk from town, and very remote from any human company. In the middle of his extensive woods, which reached from Dobitzan to the Schwarzenberg Forests, Count R had had a log cabin built in the foreign style for his guests, and apart from those few weeks in autumn when they came visiting, it was always empty. Ruzena Sedlak was installed as caretaker, with a ground-floor room to live in. Her only duties were to look after the hunting lodge, and feed the deer and the small game in hard winters. Otherwise her time was her own to use as she pleased, which she did by rearing goats, rabbits, chickens, and other small livestock, cultivating a vegetable garden, and trading a little in eggs, chickens, and kids. She lived entirely in the woods for eight years, and the animals, which she loved dearly, made her forget human beings. In their own turn human beings forgot her. Only the miraculous fact that some specimen of masculinity, either blind or dead drunk (no one could explain the aberration in any other way), had made the Death's Head pregnant, brought this forgotten creature of God back to the amused attention of the people of Dobitzan after many years.

One man in town, to be sure, did not laugh at the news but growled angrily, and that was the Mayor. For if Nature is unkind to one of her offspring now and then, and God forgets one of his creatures, an official would be no kind of official if he allowed himself to forget any human being, and there must be no omissions from a well-kept register. A child five months old and not yet registered, with no name in the records, grumbled the Mayor (who was a baker by profession) in great indignation. The priest was upset too: a child of five months and not yet baptised! These were heathen ways. After long discussion between the two of them, as representing the earthly and divine powers, the town clerk Wondrak was sent off to the forest to remind Ruzena Sedlak of her duty as a citizen. At first she told him roughly that the child was hers, no business of anyone else, and no concern of God or the Devil either. But when Wondrak, a sturdy figure and sticking to his point, replied that she was wrong there, the Devil would indeed take an interest in an unbaptised child, he'd carry its mother off to Hell if she failed to have the baby christened, the poor simple creature felt terrified of good Father Nossal, and she obediently brought the child to town next Sunday, wrapped in blue cotton. The baptism was celebrated early in the morning, to keep curious mockers away, the sponsors being a half-blind beggar woman and the good clerk Wondrak, who gave his own first name of Karel to the crying boy. The civil formalities proved a little more awkward, for when the Mayor asked as in duty bound for the father's name, a small, unseemly smile escaped both him and the kindly Wondrak. Ruzena did not reply, but bit her lip. So the unknown man's son was registered in her name, and thereafter was known as Karel Sedlak.

It was a fact that Ruzena, the Death's Head, could not have said who Karel's father was. One misty October evening the previous year, she had come back from town very late with her pannier on her back. Three fellows met her deep in the forest, out to steal timber, perhaps, or poachers or gypsies, at any rate not local men. The thick leaves cast far too much shade for her to tell their faces apart, and they could not make out who they had in front of them either (a sight which might have spared her their unwanted attentions). They saw only from her full, bell-shaped skirts that they were looking at a woman, and they attacked her. Ruzena quickly turned to run away, but one of them leaped at her from behind, moving faster than she did, and knocked her to the ground so hard that her back crashed down on her smashed pannier. Now she wanted to scream, but the three men quickly pulled her skirt up over her head, tore her shift in two, knotted the rags of it together and used them to tie her hands as she hit out wildly, punching and scratching. That was when it happened. There were three of them, she couldn't tell one from the other with her skirts up over her face, and none of them said a word. She heard only laughter, deep, rumbling and spiteful, and then satisfied grunts. She smelled tobacco, felt bearded faces, hard hands inflicting pain, weight falling on her, and more pain. When the last man had finished with her she tried to get up and free herself, but one of them hit her on the head with a cudgel so hard that she fell down. They weren't standing for any nonsense.

They must have been a long way off by the time Ruzena Sedlak ventured to get up again, bleeding, angry, abused and beaten. Her knees were trembling with exhaustion and rage. Not that she felt ashamed: her own hated body meant far too little to her, and she had known too much humiliation to feel that this vicious attack was anything out of the ordinary, but her shift was torn, her green skirt and her apron, and in addition the rogues had broken her pannier, which had cost her good money. She thought of going back to town to complain of the vagabonds, but the people there would only mock her; no one would help her. So she angrily dragged herself home, and once among her animals, good, gentle creatures who nuzzled her hands affectionately with their soft noses, she forgot all about the vile attack on her.

Only months later did she realize, in alarm, that she was going to be a mother. She immediately decided to get rid of the unwanted child. She didn't want to bring another monstrosity like herself into the world! No other innocent child should suffer as she had suffered herself. Better to kill it at once, get rid of it, bury it. For the next few weeks she avoided going to town so that no one would notice her condition, and as her pregnancy went on she dug a deep pit beside the compost heap ahead of time. She would bury the child there as soon as it was born, she thought; who would ever know? No one came into these woods.

One May night her pains began, so suddenly and savagely that she lay writhing on the floor, groaning as hot claws tore at her inside, and had no time to find a light. She bit her lips until they bled. Alone, helpless and in agony, she bore her child on the bare floor like an animal. She had just enough strength left afterwards to drag herself to her bed, where she collapsed, exhausted, in a wet and bleeding heap, and slept until it was day. Waking up when it grew light, she remembered what had happened, and the thought of what she must do now immediately came back into her mind. She hoped she wouldn't have to kill the brat, she hoped it was dead already. She listened. And then, very faintly, she heard a thin sound, a squeaking sound on the floor. She dragged herself over to it; the child was still alive. She felt it with a shaking hand: first the forehead, then the tiny ears, the chin, the nose, and she trembled worse than ever. It was a wild yet at the same time pleasant feeling, for an extraordinary thing had happened—the baby was well-formed. She, the monstrosity, had brought a real, pure, healthy child into the world. The curse had run its course. In amazement, she stared at the pink little thing. The child looked fair, she even thought beautiful, he was a little boy, not a death's head but made like other human beings, and a tiny smile was just forming on his tadpole of a mouth. She no longer had the strength to do what she had meant to do; she picked up the faintly breathing little creature and put it to her breast.

Many things altered for the better now. Life no longer went pointlessly by; it came running to her with tiny gasps and little cries, now it touched her with two small, clumsy baby hands. She had never had anything but her own malformed body; now she had something of her own. She had made a creature that would outlast and survive her, a child who needed and made use of her. For those first five months Ruzena Sedlak was perfectly happy. The baby grew for her alone, no one else knew about him, which was all to the good. And he had no father; that was good too. No one on earth knew about him, and once again that was excellent. He belonged entirely to her, and her alone.

That was why she snapped so angrily at poor Wondrak when he came from the offices in town with the message to say she had to take the baby to be baptised and registered. Her dull, rural sense of greed instinctively if vaguely felt that if people knew about her baby, he would be taken away from her. Now he was hers, all hers, but if those people in the offices, if the State and the Mayor wrote his name in one of their stupid books, a part of the baby as a human being would belong to them. They would have got a grip on his ankle, so to speak, they could summon him and order him about. And indeed, this was the one and only time that she took her Karel as a baby to town to see other people. To her own surprise, he grew to be a sturdy, brown, pretty boy with a pert, curious nose and quick straight legs, a lad with an ear for music who could whistle like a thrush, imitate the cry of the jay and the cuckoo, who climbed trees like a cat and ran races with the white dog Horcek. Knowing no one else, he was not afraid of her deformed face, and she laughed and was carefree and happy when she talked to him and his round, chestnut-brown eyes were turned on her. He was soon helping her to milk the goats, gather berries and split wood with his firm little hands. It was at this time that she, who had seldom been to church, began to pray again. She was never entirely free of the fear that he might be taken away from her as suddenly as he had arrived.

But once, when she went to town to sell a kid, Wondrak suddenly barred her way, which he was well able to do, for in these seven years his good Bohemian belly had grown even bigger and broader. It was a good thing he'd happened to meet her, he growled, that would save him another trek into the woods. He had a bone to pick with her. Didn't Ruzena Sedlak know that at the age of seven a boy ought to be at school? And when she said angrily it was none of his business how old her boy was, or where he ought to be, then Wondrak tightened his braces and his broad moon-face assumed a menacing expression of official dignity. Now the town clerk spoke forcefully; he didn't give a damn for her impertinence. Hadn't she ever heard of the law on elementary schooling for all? Why did she think the expensive new schoolhouse had been put up two years ago? She must go the Mayor at once, he'd soon make her understand that a Christian child in the Imperial state couldn't be allowed to grow up like the beasts of the field. And if she didn't like it, he supposed there was still a place in the lockup for her, and the child would be taken away and put in the orphanage.

At this last threat Ruzena turned pale. Of course the thought of school had long ago occurred to her, but she had always hoped they would forget. This was all because of that wretched book in the Mayor's office. Anyone whose name was written in it didn't own himself any more. And they were already beginning to take him away from her. For Karel, sturdy as his legs were, couldn't spend eight hours a day walking to school, and what was she to live on in the town? Finally, yet again, Father Nossal came to the rescue. He would have the boy to live with him during the week, he said, and he could go home to her every Saturday and Sunday and in the school holidays. His housekeeper would look after Karel very well. Ruzena stared angrily at the kindly, plump woman, who assured her in friendly tones that Father Nossal was right. She would have liked to strike the housekeeper—a woman who would now have more of her Karel than she did herself. But she was afraid in front of Father Nossal, so there was nothing she could do but agree. However, her skin was pale as stone, and in her hatred those terrible holes looked so black in her ruined face that the housekeeper hastily crossed herself in the kitchen, as if she had seen the Devil.

After that Ruzena often went to town. She had to walk all night, for eight hours, just to get a glimpse from the corner of her Karel and feel proud of him: neatly dressed, sponge dangling from his slate, walking to school with the other boys. He was strong, lively, and better-looking than most of them, not a fright like her, shunned by everyone. She would walk eight hours there and eight hours back for that sight of him, she brought eggs and butter with her out of the forest, and she worked harder and did more business than ever simply so that she could pay to have new clothes made for him. And now, too, she understood for the first time that Sundays were a God-given gift to man. Karel studied hard and did well, and the priest even spoke of sending him to high school in the big city at his own expense. But she balked frantically at this: no, no, he must stay here, and she found him a job with a woodcutter in the forest where she lived. It was hard work but closer to her, only four hours from her part of the woods, in a place where they were cutting rides through the forest. She was sometimes able to take him his mid-day meal and sit with him for an hour. And even when she didn't see him but just heard the firm, ringing axe strokes in the distance, they echoed cheerfully in her heart. It was her own blood she heard, her own strength.

Only Karel mattered to her. She even neglected the animals. There was no one else in the world. So she hardly noticed that a war began in the year 1914, and when she did notice it seemed to her, oddly enough, rather a good thing. The boys were paid better wages now, because the men were away, and when she took her eggs and chickens to town she didn't feel she must wait humbly for the women to arrive, as she used to, but went further and further down the road to meet them, and soon sold her shining eggs for shining coins, haggling with her customers. She already had a whole hidden drawer full of money and banknotes; another three years like this, and she would be able to move into town with her Karel. That was all she knew about the war, and all she thought of it.

But one day in this period that could hardly be measured in months, when she took her son's meal to the workmen's hut, he said, bending his head and swallowing the words along with his soup, that he couldn't come out to see her this Sunday. She was dumbfounded. Why not? It was the first time since she had given birth to him that he wouldn't be spending Sunday with her. Well, it was like this, he said, chewing, he had to go off to Budweis with the others for acceptance. Acceptance? She didn't know what he was talking about. Acceptance for military service, he explained, eighteen-year-olds were soon going to be called up, it had been in the newspapers for a long time, and yesterday they'd had official notification.

Ruzena turned pale. All at once the blood drained from her face. She had never thought of that—she had never thought that he too would turn eighteen, her own child, and then they could take him away from her. Now she saw it all: that was why they had written him down in their wretched book in the Mayor's office all that time ago, so that they could drag him off to their accursed war. She sat perfectly still, and when Karel looked at her in surprise, he was frightened of his mother for the first time, because the figure sitting there was no longer a human being. He himself felt the force of the terrible nickname of 'the Death's Head', as he never had before—he had once punched a friend in the face for thoughtlessly uttering it. Out of a face drained of blood and white as bone, her black eyes stared straight into space, and her mouth had fallen open to show an empty cavern under those two dark holes in her flesh. He shuddered. Then she stood up and took his hand.

"Come over here," she said. And her voice was brittle as hard bone too. She led him to the nearby barn where the woodcutters kept their tools. No one was there; she closed the door. "Go over there," she told him sternly, and once again her voice in the dark might have come from the world beyond. Then she unbuttoned her dress. It was some time before her trembling fingers found and took out the silver crucifix that she wore on a thong around her neck. She placed it on the window-sill.

"There," she told him. "Now swear."

"What do you want me to swear?"

"Swear on that cross, by God and all his saints and the crucified Christ, that you will do as I say!"

He would have asked questions, but her bony fingers forced his hand down on the crucifix. Outside the sound of plates clattering could be heard, the laughter and talking of the workmen, and over there the grasshoppers were chirping in the grass, but here in the barn all was silent. Only her death's head shone menacingly out of the shadows. Her dark passion made him shudder. But he swore.

She breathed a sigh of relief, and tucked the crucifix back into place. "You've sworn on the crucified Christ to obey me. You will not go to that damned war. Let them find others in Vienna. Not you!"

"But suppose they come looking for me?"

She laughed again, shrill, malicious laughter. "Those donkeys, they won't get you. If they do come in search of you, you must go out to me in the woods. Now, go back and tell everyone you're going to Budweis on Sunday, hand in your notice and say you'll be off to the war."

Karel obeyed. He had inherited her stubborn cast of mind that could cope with anything. And on Saturday night he stole out to the house in the forest—she had already taken his clothes there little by little—and she showed him a room in the attic. He must stay here during the day, she said. He could come out at night, she said (they wouldn't come then), but he must not go too close to town, and he must always take Horcek the dog with him. The dog would start barking if anyone moved within a mile of them. And he mustn't be afraid of the townsfolk, said Ruzena, no one had ever come out to her house yet except for Wondrak and the huntsman. But now the huntsman was buried somewhere in the rocks of Italy, and she could deal with that fat fool Wondrak, ha, ha.

However, she laughed only to give the lad courage. In reality, fear weighed on her breast by night like a great block of stone. Only the Count and the guests at his hunting parties, it was true, had ever made their way out to this remote and isolated house. But small, dull-minded, ignorant creature that she was, she feared the unknown in the shape of the power with which they had begun this war. What did they really have all those books for in Dobitzan, in Budweis and Vienna? What was in them? Somehow or other, thanks to those accursed books, they must know all about everyone, every single person. They had summoned the tailor Wrba's brother back from America, and someone had come from Holland too, the bastards had reached everyone. Might they perhaps lay hands on Karel after all? Might they not work out that he hadn't gone to Budweis, but was hiding here in the forest? Oh, it was so hard to be alone against everyone, without anyone to talk to! Ought she to tell the priest? Perhaps he might advise her; over the years she had become used to that. And while her son's strong breathing regularly broke the silence, its sound coming through the thin floor above her, she tormented herself: a mother on her own against the monstrosity of the world, how could she deceive all those people in town with their mean-minded books and notes and certificates? She tossed and turned, unable to sleep, and now and then bit her lip so that her child up above, knowing nothing of her fears, would not hear her groans, and then she lay there with her eyes open, a prey to all the cruel torments of dark night and horror until well into the early hours of morning. At last she thought she had an idea, and she immediately leaped out of bed, gathered up her things, and made her way fast to town.

She had eggs with her, a great many eggs, and a few young chickens, and she hurried with those from house to house. One woman wanted to buy all she had, but she would let her have only two chickens, because she wanted to talk to a large number of people—that was her cunning trick. She wanted to talk to everyone in town so that the news would spread rapidly. So everywhere she went, from house to house, she complained bitterly. It was a shame, she said, taking her child off to Budweis, her Karel. They were dragging all the young fellows off to war these days, oh, surely God couldn't suffer them to take a poor woman's breadwinner away from her. Couldn't the Emperor see that it was all over if they needed such children, wouldn't he do better to stop the war? People listened to her, sad and sympathetic, frowning gloomily. Many cautiously turned and put a finger to their lips to warn her to be careful. For long ago the whole Czech people had broken away in their hearts from the Habsburgs, those strange gentlemen in Vienna, they had been surreptitiously keeping banners and candles ready to receive the Russians and set up their own kingdom. In secret and mysterious ways, passing the news from mouth to mouth, they all knew that their leaders Kramarc and Klopitsch were in jail, that Masaryk, who was on their side, was in exile, and the soldiers had brought back from the front vague news of German legions forming in Russia and Siberia. So there had been a secret understanding at work in people's minds all over the country for a long time before any individuals ventured to take action, and by mutual consent they approved of any kind of resistance and indignation. The townsfolk therefore gave Ruzena a sympathetic hearing, and looked regretful, and with secret delight she felt that the whole town believed her lying tale. When she passed, she heard them talking behind her back: they've taken even that poor woman's son away, folk said. And good Father Nossal himself spoke to her and said, with a strange twinkle in his eye, she mustn't worry too much, because he'd heard that this business wouldn't last much longer. The poor silly creature's heart beat high when she heard people talking like that: how stupid they were! Now she had fooled the whole town, all by herself, and they would pass the news that Karel had been called up on to Budweis, and then it would go from Budweis to Vienna. So he would be forgotten, and afterwards, when the war was over, she would take the consequences on herself. And to hammer the lie home, to make other people feel sure of it, she came to town week after week and went on spinning her tale: he had written, she said, saying he had to go to Italy, and telling her how bad the food was in wartime. She sent him butter every week, she said, but God knew if it wasn't stolen on the way. Oh, if he were only back from the war, if only she had him home again!

This went on for several weeks, but one day when she had come to town yet again, and was embarking on the litany of her woes, Wondrak accosted her in a rather strange way and said, "Come along to my house and let's drink a glass of something." She dared not say no. But she felt cold all the way to her knees when she was alone with Wondrak in his parlour, and realized that he wanted to talk about one particular subject. He began by walking up and down, apparently undecided, and then he carefully closed the windows and sat down facing her.

"Well, and how's your Karel?"

She stammered that he knew Karel had joined the army, his regiment had marched off to Italy yesterday. Oh, if only the war were over, she said, she prayed for her child daily.

Wondrak did not reply, but just whistled quietly to himself. Then he rose and checked that the door was well closed. She concluded from this that he meant her no ill, although he so persistently avoided looking at her.

Well, that's all to the good, he muttered, but he, Wondrak, had just been wondering whether Karel hadn't secretly made off? No business of his, of course, and after all, you could understand a fellow who didn't want to throw his bones into another man's soup—let the Germans manage this stupid war of theirs on their own. But (and here he turned to the door again) three days ago an armed troop had arrived, a contingent of military police from Prague with Carinthian soldiers, and they were searching the houses now for lads who hadn't obeyed the call-up to join the army. There was Jennisch the locksmith, who after all had sprained his forefinger, they'd taken him out of his house and led him over the marketplace in handcuffs. It was a shame, such a good, honest man. And in the neighbouring village they were said to have shot a man who ran away, a shocking thing, it really was! They hadn't finished yet either, said Wondrak. They had brought a whole list from Budweis or Prague or somewhere, a list of the names of all the men who hadn't joined. Well, his lips were sealed on account of his official position, but maybe a number of men shouldn't be on that list at all.

As he spoke, Wondrak did not look at her, but stared with curious interest at the smoke rings rising from his pipe to the ceiling. Then he stood up and growled, unruffled, "But if your Karel really did join up, they'll have had their trouble for nothing, and it will all turn out well."

Ruzena sat there, frozen. It was all over. So her trick had done no good, they had found out, those bastards in Vienna with their books, they'd discovered that her child hadn't joined up. However, she asked no more questions, and merely got to her feet. Wondrak didn't look at her, but elaborately knocked out his pipe; they had understood one another.

"Thank you," she said quietly, and left.

She went to the end of the street with her knees stiff and cold, and then she suddenly began to run. If only she wasn't still on the way when they came—her child wouldn't defend himself, silly boy. She ran faster and faster, she threw her basket away, she tore open the dress clinging damply to her skin, she ran on and on and on, further into the forest, she ran as she had never run before in her life.

Night lay black above the house when she heard, from afar, the dog barking. That good dog Horcek, she thought, he gives us plenty of warning. All was still. Thank God, she had come in time. I'll have a Mass said, she thought, gasping for breath and only now aware of her exhaustion, two Masses, three Masses, and I'll offer candles, she added, lots of candles, all the rest of my life. Then she quietly went in, held her breath and listened. And suddenly the blood flowed strongly back into her trembling body as she heard the regular breath of the sleeping man. He was safe and sound, the child who had grown from her body. She climbed the stairs to the attic, a lighted candle in her shaking hand. Karel was fast asleep, sleeping deeply. His thick, heavy brown hair hung damp over his forehead, his broad, handsome, masculine mouth stood open to show his strong, firm white teeth. Tenderly, uncertainly, the candlelight flickered over the clear planes and shadows of that carefree boyish face. She saw again how handsome he was, and how young. His muscles stood out like white roots on his arms, which were bare, crossed above the blanket, and his shoulders might have been made of smooth marble; they were broad, strong and firm. There was power to last for decades in the flesh that she had formed from her own, there was an unimaginable wealth of life in his body, which had only just grown to manhood. And was she to give it up to Vienna for the sake of a silly piece of paper? Instinctively, she uttered a sharp laugh. Karel started up in alarm and shook himself, blinking foolishly at the light. Then, seeing her, he laughed too, his good, hearty, childlike Bohemian laugh. "What's up?" he asked, yawning and cracking his finger joints. "Is it day?"

But she shook him fully awake. He must get out of bed at once, she told him, he must get out of the house, she'd make him a place to stay for the next few days far in the forest and on no account must he move from it, even if a week passed before she came back for him. Then she tied up a great bundle of hay, put it on her back, and led him along a secret path for about quarter-of-an-hour into the thickest, most inaccessible part of the forest, to a place where a small huntsman's hide had once been erected.

He had to stay here, she told him, he mustn't show himself by day, but he could walk around at night. And she'd bring him food, she assured him of that. As usual, Karel obeyed her. He didn't understand, but he obeyed her. She would bring him food and tobacco in the middle of the day, she said. And then she went away, feeling relieved. Thank God, she had saved him. The house was cleared of his traces, so now let them come.

And come they did, quite a large troop of them. They knew their trade, they had studied it. Wondrak had done well to warn her. At five in the morning, when she had gone to bed and had been there for two hours (they must have been marching all night), the dog began to bark. She lay awake with her heart thudding. They were here. The enemy had come. But she did not stir, even when a harsh voice downstairs shouted, "Open up there!" Slowly, very slowly she dragged herself to the door, muttering in a deliberately loud voice, as if she had just been woken from deep sleep. Slow-witted she might be thought, but deception came naturally to her.

She yawned, a loud yawn. Then she opened the door. A military police officer stood outside in the wan, misty light of early morning with dew on his cap, a stranger. He had four soldiers and a dog with him, and he immediately stuck his foot in the door.

Did her son Karel Sedlak live here, he asked.

"Oh mercy me, he left long ago. He went to Budweis to join the army, all our town knows that," she was quick to answer. A little too quick—noticeably quick. As she spoke, she did not forget that she should look these men in the eye. She had worked that out for herself.

"We'll see," grunted the officer through his red moustache, which was moist from the mist. Then he barked out an order in German. Two men stationed themselves outside the door, two more went round behind the house, unslinging the guns from their shoulders. The dog leaped around sniffing at her own Horcek, who distrustfully avoided him. As soon as the soldiers had taken up their positions, the officer told them something else in German and then, turning to her, addressed her in Czech.

"Let's see the house now."

She followed him, feeling both fear and angry glee. There's nothing in the house, look as long as you like, she thought. You won't find anything.

He stepped briskly into her living-room, pushed open the shutters so that grey light fell on everything inside, and looked around. He opened the chest, looked under the bed, raised the bolster—nothing. "The other rooms," he ordered.

As if to trying to fool him and make him tired of all this, she replied, "I don't have any. The others all belong to His Excellency the Count. And His Excellency just has me here to keep house for him. I had to swear my oath on it."

He ignored this. "Open up."

She showed him the Count's dining-room, the kitchen, the servants' quarters, the bedrooms where the gentry slept. He searched the whole place. He had had practice; he tapped at the walls. Nothing. An expression of annoyance came over his face, and joy leaped up in her, sharp and full of malice.

Then he pointed to the stairs. "The attics," he ordered. Once more she felt that surge of glee. Yes, Karel had indeed been sleeping in the attics. Thank heaven that good man Wondrak had warned her, or they would have caught him there.

The officer climbed the stairs and she followed. There was his empty bed. And only now did it strike her that some of his clothes still lay there; she ought to have cleared them away, she should have stowed them in a chest. The straw was untidy too; she'd forgotten about that.

He noticed it himself. Who, he asked, slept here?

She made herself out simple-minded. "Oh, it's only the servant ever sleeps here—that's the Count's huntsman when there's a hunting party. Sometimes he has a couple of others with him."

"There's no hunting parties these days. Who last slept here?"

No one, she assured him. But the straw, he pointed out, was all churned up. Oh, she replied, the dog often lay down there to sleep in winter.

"Indeed?" said the man sharply. "The dog." And he reached for the table. There lay a pipe, half knocked-out. There were ashes on the floor. "So the dog smokes a pipe too, eh?"

Ruzena did not answer. She was lost for words. He did not wait for her to reply, but opened the chest and took out clothes. Whose, he asked, were these?

"My Karel's. He left them there when he went away to join the army."

The officer stood there, thwarted. She seemed to have an answer for everything. He knocked on the walls here too, searched the floor,

193

but there was nothing there, only the straw. At last he had finished his inspection, and her heart leaped up with relief. He stood up, adjusted his braces, and when he turned to the stairs she thought, now he'll go. Saved! And her blood began flowing again.

However, the officer stopped in the doorway, raised two fingers to his mouth, and gave a shrill whistle.

Ruzena started in alarm. The whistle went right through her ear and penetrated deep inside her. What did it mean? She was overcome by fear of the unknown. And now along came the dog, wagging his tail, carrying himself proudly because his master had called him. His paws danced on the ground, padding on it with fast, light sounds.

He was a kind of German shepherd dog, with intelligent eyes and a bushy tail. He pressed close to the officer's leg and looked up at him, thumping his tail on the floor.

"Here, Hektor," said the officer. He took clothes out of the chest, a pair of shoes, a shirt, and threw them all down. "Here, seek!"

Hektor came up, his pointed muzzle reaching a little way forward to burrow into the clothes, and sniffing a shoe as well. His nose quivered as he sniffed, and he uttered a short, sharp yelp as he took a deep breath, his sides quivering, wagging his tail hard. He was excited, his movements rapid, his flanks were heaving. He had picked up the scent, and now he had a job to do. The officer called something to him, raised his arm to point at the bed, and the dog padded over to it, sniffing. Then he put his head down and ran back and forth.

The devil must be in that dog, she thought. His eyes sparkled. He had picked up a scent on the floor and was now sniffing its trail, which led him to the top of the stairs. The officer followed him. "Seek, seek!" he encouraged the dog. Now Hektor was in the attic doorway, still following the trail, and it led him downstairs. The military police officer was following him.

Once he was down again, he shouted an order to his men. The four soldiers all assembled and followed the dog. Hektor moved swiftly from bush to bush, then back into the house. Finally he followed the scent slowly out of the door again, and at last towards the forest. Ruzena's heart missed a beat. She ran down the stairs herself and instinctively went to the door; she wanted to follow the dog, run ahead of him, scream, warn Karel, stop them... she herself didn't know just what she could do. But the officer in command of the party of military police snapped at her, standing at the door to bar her way, "You stay there! Sit down!" And he pointed to the bench around the stove. She dared not reply, she simply huddled there.

She heard the soldiers' steps, she heard the snapping sound of straps being fastened. And then she was alone with the officer, who sat down at the table as if she were not there at all. He calmly knocked out his own tobacco pipe, refilled it and began to smoke, drawing on it very slowly. He could wait patiently, he was sure of himself. It was very quiet now. Ruzena heard only the way he puffed smoke from his lungs into the air. His calm composure made her tremble. She sat and stared at him, her cold hands hanging down, feeling that her blood had congealed inside her, was frozen there. Yet everything in her was stretched to breaking point. She felt numb. She forced herself to hold her breath to listen for any sounds from the forest, then she heard her own breathing coming louder than the throbbing in her ears, and in her numb brain she wondered whether he might yet escape. Suddenly she raised her hands and felt through her blouse for the place where the crucifix hung. She clutched it and began praying, reciting the Lord's Prayer and all the intercessions she knew. Involuntarily, she uttered one word out loud. The officer half turned, looking at her sharply and, as she thought, with derision. Got you, Death's Head, just you wait, he was thinking. For at that moment she did indeed resemble a skull, with her forehead white as bone below her falling hair, her mouth open to show her white teeth, and then there were the black holes that were her eyes and her nose. He turned away again, instinctively spat on the floor, and then trod out the slimy spittle from his pipe with his foot, slowly, without haste or any agitation.

She felt as if she must scream. She couldn't bear this; time and eternity weighed down on her. She trembled, she wanted to fall down before him, beg him on her knees, plead with him, kiss his feet. He was a human being, after all, but unapproachable in his uniform, in the impregnability of his power, sent out by the enemy. But doing any such thing would surely give her away. After all, they might not find Karel. She strained her ears again, listening as if she were nothing but her sense of hearing. She listened for an eternity. This was more cruel than anything she had borne in all her forty years.

It seemed to her a longer time than the whole nine months when she was carrying her child, but in fact she waited for only half-an-hour. Then there was a clinking outside, and a footstep. More footsteps were heard, and finally a small sharp sound. The officer stood up and glanced at the door. He uttered a brief laugh, and patted the dog, who came leaping up to him. "Good dog, Hektor, good dog." Then, without looking back, he went out. Ruzena was stunned by horror.

She stood perfectly still like that for a moment. Then, with a sudden movement, she banished the leaden feeling from her legs and rushed out. Oh, how terrible, they had him! Karel, her Karel stood between them, his hands cuffed behind his back, stooping, bent, his eyes lowered in shame. They had caught him just as he was going to the stream to wash and had brought him back as he was, barefoot, in his trousers and loose shirt. His mother cried out in shrill tones, and she was already making for the officer. She fell on her knees in front of him and clutched his feet. Let her son go, she cried, he was her child, her only child! Let him go for the Saviour's sake, he was only a child still, her Karel, not yet seventeen. He was sixteen, only sixteen, she pleaded, they had made a mistake. And he was sick too, very sick, she could swear it, everyone knew, he had spent all this time lying sick in bed.

The military police officer, feeling uncomfortable (and his men were looking darkly at him too), tried to free his feet. But she only clung even more firmly, weeping and raving. The Saviour would reward him, she cried, if he spared her innocent child. Why in heaven's name take her child, who was so weak? Have pity, she begged the officer, there were others around here, tall, powerful, strong young fellows, so many of them in the country round about, why take Karel, why him? Let him leave her child to her, she begged the officer, for the Saviour's sake—God would reward him for his good deed, she herself would pray for him every day. Every day. And for his mother. She would kiss his feet—and indeed, in her frenzy she actually did fling herself down to kiss the officer's dirty, muddy shoes.

Shame made him rough. Tearing himself free, he pushed the desperate woman away. What a fuss she was making! Thousands and thousands of men had marched away for the Emperor, and none of them had uttered a squeak of protest. The doctors would soon find out if the lad was sick. She should be glad he wasn't put up against the wall at once as a deserter. A fellow who makes off like that ought by rights to be shot, and if it was up to him, the officer, he said, he knew what he'd do with him, he would...

He got no further. In the middle of this speech she leaped at him. Suddenly, from down on the floor at his feet, she sprang at him and made him stagger, both hands going for his throat like claws. He was a strong man, but he rocked back on his heels. Hitting out, he struck her, punching her flesh, her forehead. Then he seized her in his two hard hands and twisted a joint until she writhed in pain. But although she was defenceless now, she bit, snapping like an animal, bit his arm and hung there with her teeth in it. He yelled. And now his men came up, tore her away, got her down on the ground and kicked her.

The officer was shaking with pain and anger—to be shamed like this in front of his soldiers! "Handcuff her," he ordered. "We'll show you, you bitch." His arm hurt like hell. Her teeth had gone through his coat and the fabric of his shirt; red blood was running out. He felt it trickling down, but he wasn't going to show that. As they put the handcuffs on her, he bound up the place under his shirt with his handkerchief, and then, composed again, ordered the men: "Forward march. Two of you go ahead with the lad, two of you follow with her."

Her hands were fastened behind her back now, and the officer had drawn his revolver. "If either of them moves, shoot them down."

The soldiers took Karel between them. He twisted and turned, but when they told him, "March!" he marched. He walked on with fixed eyes, mechanically, without resisting; the shock had broken his strength. His mother followed without defending herself either; violence would do no good now. She would have gone anywhere with Karel, she'd have gone to the ends of the earth, just so long as she was with him, could stay with him. So long as she could see him: his fine broad back, his curly brown shock of hair above his firm neck, oh, and his hands, tortured now, bound behind his back, the hands she had known when they were tiny, with small pink nails, with sweet little folds on them. She would have walked on without any soldiers, without any orders, just so as to be with him and not leave him. All she wanted was to know that she was still near him. She felt no weariness in spite of walking for so long—eight hours. She did not feel her sore feet, although they had both gone barefoot all this time, she did not feel the pressure of her hands cuffed behind her back, all she felt was that he was close, she had him, she was with him.

They marched through the forest and along the dusty country road. Bells were pealing out over the town, striking twelve noon, all was at rest when the unusual procession made its way along the main street of Dobitzan, Karel first, with the weary soldiers trotting along to right and left of him to guard him, then Ruzena Sedlak, her eyes glazed, still dishevelled and battered from the blows, with her own hands cuffed behind her back, and bringing up the rear the military police officer, a grave, stern figure, obviously making a great effort to bear himself well. He had put his revolver back into its holster.

The buzz of noise in the marketplace died down. People came out of their doors to look darkly at the scene. Drivers on their carts cracked the whip at their horses angrily and spat, as if by chance. Men frowned and murmured, looked away and then back again, it was a shame, they muttered, first the children, the lads of seventeen, now they were dragging women off too. All the ill will and resentment of a people who had long felt that this Austrian war was nothing to do with them, yet dared not show any violent opposition, stood mute but menacing in hundreds of eyes, the eyes of the people of Dobitzan.

No one said a word; they were all silent. The steps of the marching soldiers could be heard in the street.

Somehow or other, Ruzena's animal nature must have sensed the magnetic force of that embitterment, for suddenly, in the middle of the road, the handcuffed woman flung herself down flat among the soldiers, her skirts flying, and began shouting at the top of her voice, "Help me, brothers! For God's sake help me! Don't let them do this."

The soldiers had to seize her, and then she cried out again, to Karel, "Throw yourself down! They'll have to drag us to the slaughter! Let God see this!" And Karel obediently lay down in the middle of the wet road too.

The furious military police officer intervened. "Get them up!" he shouted at his startled men. They tried to haul Ruzena and her son to their feet. But she twisted and turned, flung herself about with her bound hands like a fish landed on the bank, uttering shrill cries. She snapped and bit; it was a terrible sight. "God must see this," she howled, "God must see this." Finally the soldiers had to drag both of them away like beasts going to be butchered. But she went on shouting, her voice cracking horribly, "God must see this, God must see this!"

She was forced away as they waited for reinforcements, and was taken off to a cell under arrest, half-naked now, with her greying hair coming down. It was high time; the townsfolk were gathering together. Their looks were even darker than before. One farmer spat. Several women began talking angrily out loud. There was whistling, you could see men nudging the women and warning them; children stared, wide-eyed and alarmed, at all this tumultuous confusion.

Mother and son were taken off to the cells together, but the hatred in the air for the open display of violence was palpable.

Meanwhile, pacing furiously up and down in his office, his collar, trimmed with gold lace, torn open in his rage, the District Commissioner was bawling out the military police officer. He was a fool, he told the man, he was a godforsaken idiot to bring a deserter in along the road in broad daylight, and a woman in handcuffs with him. This kind of thing would get around the whole region, and then he personally would have trouble with Vienna. Didn't the officer think there had been quite enough of all this chasing people around here in Bohemia? This evening would have been a better time to bring the young man in. And why the devil had he brought the woman along too?

The officer showed his torn coat, pointing out that the mad bitch had attacked and bitten him. He'd had to have her arrested, he said, if only for the sake of the men's morale.

But the Commissioner was not mollified, and went on: "So did you have to drag her through the town in broad daylight? You can't treat women like that. People won't stand for it. What a mess! It gets folk really annoyed when you start in on women. Much better leave them out of it."

Finally the police officer asked, in muted tones, what he ought to do now.

"Oh, get the lad sent off tonight, send him to Budweis with the others. What business is all this of ours? Let those…" (he was about to say "bloody bureaucrats", but thought better of it in time), "let those responsible take care of it, we've done our duty. Keep the Sedlak woman under arrest until he's gone. She'll calm down in the morning. You can release her as soon as he's left. After all, women do calm down when they've had a good cry. And after that they go to church—or to some other man's bed."

The officer protested; he was most unwilling to agree. Had he marched all night for this? To himself, he vowed that this was the last time he'd go to so much trouble.

The District Commissioner had been right, it seemed. The Sedlak woman did indeed calm down in the cells. She did not move, but lay still on her bed. However, she felt no weariness. She was merely straining her ears to listen. She knew that her child was somewhere in another part of this building. Karel was still here, but she couldn't see him, couldn't hear him. She felt his presence, all the same. She knew he was close. Despite her dull nature, she felt a link with him through all these doors. Something could still make it turn out well for them. Perhaps the priest could help; he must have heard them both being dragged off under arrest. Perhaps the war was already over. Somewhere she listened for a sign, for a word. Karel was still there. As long as he was still there, there was hope. That was why everything was so quiet, so breathlessly still. The prison warder went up to see the District Commissioner, who duly noted the fact that the Sedlak woman had calmed down. Just as he'd said she would. Tomorrow they'd send Karel off, and then there would be peace and quiet again.

[*Here ends Zweig's unfinished manuscript*]

DOWNFALL
OF THE HEART

D ESTINY DOES NOT ALWAYS need the powerful prelude of a sudden violent blow to shake a heart beyond recovery. The unbridled creativity of fate can generate disaster from some small, fleeting incident. In clumsy human language, we call that first slight touch the cause of the catastrophe, and feel surprise in comparing its insignificance with the force, often enormous, that it exerts, but just as the first symptoms of an illness may not show at all, the downfall of a human heart can begin before anything happens to make it visible. Fate has been at work within the victim's mind and his blood long before his soul suffers any outward effects. To know yourself is to defend yourself, but it is usually in vain.

The old man—Salomonsohn was his name, and at home in Germany he could boast of the honorary title of Privy Commercial Councillor—was lying awake in the Gardone hotel where he had taken his family for the Easter holiday. A violent physical pain constricted his chest so that he could hardly breathe. The old man was alarmed; he had troublesome gallstones and often suffered bilious attacks, but instead of following the advice of his doctors and visiting Karlsbad to take the waters there he had decided, for his family's sake, to go further south and stay at this resort on Lake Garda instead. Fearing a dangerous attack of his disorder, he anxiously palpated his broad body, and soon realised with relief, even though he was still in pain, that it was only an ordinary stomach upset, obviously as a result of the unfamiliar Italian food, or the mild food poisoning that was apt to afflict tourists. Feeling less alarmed, he let his shaking hand drop back, but the pressure on his chest continued and kept him from breathing easily. Groaning, the old man made the effort of getting out of bed to move about a little. Sure enough, when he was standing the pressure eased, and even more so when he was walking. But there was not much space to walk about in the dark room, and he was afraid of waking his wife in the other twin bed and causing her unnecessary concern. So he put on his dressing gown and a pair of felt slippers, and groped his way out into the corridor to walk up and down there for a little while and lessen the pain.

As he opened the door into the dark corridor, the sound of the clock in the church tower echoed through the open windows—four chimes, first weighty and then dying softly away over the lake. Four in the morning.

The long corridor lay in complete darkness. But from his clear memory of it in daytime, the old man knew that it was wide and straight, so he walked along it, breathing heavily, from end to end without needing a light, and then again and again, pleased to notice that the tightness in his chest was fading. Almost entirely freed from pain now by this beneficial exercise, he was preparing to return to his room when a sound startled him. He stopped. The sound was a whispering in the darkness somewhere near him, slight yet unmistakable. Woodwork creaked, there were soft voices and movements, a door was opened just a crack and a narrow beam of light cut through the formless darkness. What was it? Instinctively the old man shrank back into a corner, not out of curiosity but obeying a natural sense of awkwardness at being caught by other people engaged in the odd activity of pacing up and down like a sleepwalker. In that one second when the light shone into the corridor, however, he had involuntarily seen, or thought he had seen, a white-clad female figure slipping out of the room and disappearing down the passage. And sure enough, there was a slight click as one of the last doors in the corridor latched shut. Then all was dark and silent again.

The old man suddenly began to sway as if he had suffered a blow to the heart. The only rooms at the far end of the corridor, where the door handle had given away a secret by clicking... the only rooms there were his own, the three-roomed suite that he had booked for his family. He had left his wife asleep and breathing peacefully only a few minutes before, so that female figure—no, he couldn't be mistaken—that figure returning from a venture into a stranger's room could have been no one but his daughter Erna, aged only just nineteen.

The old man was shivering all over with horror. His daughter Erna, his child, that happy, high-spirited child—no, this was impossible, he must be mistaken! But what could she have been doing in a stranger's room if not... Like an injured animal he thrust his own idea away, but the haunting picture of that stealthy figure still haunted his mind, he could not tear it out of his head or banish it. He had to be sure. Panting, he groped his way along the wall of the corridor to her door, which was next to his own bedroom. But he was appalled to see, at this one door in the corridor, a thin line of light showing under the door, and the keyhole was a small dot of treacherous brightness. She still had a light on in her room at four in the morning! And there was more evidence—with a slight crackle from the electric switch the white line of light vanished without trace into darkness. No, it was useless trying to pretend to himself. It was Erna, his daughter, slipping out of a stranger's bed and into her own by night.

The old man was trembling with horror and cold, while at the same time sweat broke out all over his body, flooding the pores of his skin. His first thought was to break in at the shameless girl's door and chastise her with his fists. But his feet were tottering beneath the weight of his broad body. He could hardly summon up the strength

207

to drag himself into his own room and back to bed, where he fell
on the pillows like a stricken animal, his senses dulled.

The old man lay motionless in bed. His eyes, wide open, stared at
the darkness. He heard his wife breathing easily beside him, without
a care in the world. His first thought was to shake her awake, tell her
about his dreadful discovery, rage and rant to his heart's content.
But how could he express it, how could he put this terrible thing
into words? No, such words would never pass his lips. What was he
to do, though? What *could* he do?

He tried to think, but his mind was in blind confusion, thoughts
flying this way and that like bats in daylight. It was so monstrous—
Erna, his tender, well-brought-up child with her melting eyes… How
long ago was it, how long ago that he would still find her poring over
her schoolbooks, her little pink finger carefully tracing the difficult
characters on the page, how long since she used to go straight from
school to the confectioner's in her little pale-blue dress, and then he
felt her childish kiss with sugar still on her lips? Only yesterday, surely?
But no, it was all years ago. Yet how childishly she had begged him
yesterday—*really* yesterday—to buy her the blue and gold pullover
that looked so pretty in the shop window. "Oh please, dear Papa,
please!"—with her hands clasped, with that self-confident, happy
smile that he could never resist. And now, now she was stealing away
to a strange man's bed by night, not far from his own door, to roll
about in it with him, naked and lustful.

My God, my God! thought the old man, instinctively groaning.
The shame of it, the shame! My child, my tender, beloved child—an
assignation with some man… Who is he? Who can he be? We arrived
here in Gardone only three days ago, and she knew none of those
spruced-up dandies before—thin-faced Conte Ubaldi, that Italian
officer, the baron from Mecklenburg who's a gentleman jockey…

they didn't meet on the dance floor until our second day. Has one of them already?... No, he can't have been the first, no... it must have begun earlier, at home, and I knew nothing about it, fool that I am. Poor fool! But what do I know about my wife and daughter anyway? I toil for them every day, I spend fourteen hours a day at my office just to earn money for them, more and more money so that they can have fine dresses and be rich... and when I come home tired in the evening, worn out, they've gone gadding off to the theatre, to balls, out with company, what do I know about them and what they get up to all day long? And now my child with her pure young body has assignations with men by night like a common streetwalker... oh, the shame of it!

The old man groaned again and again. Every new idea deepened his wound and tore it open, as if his brain lay visibly bleeding, with red maggots writhing in it.

But why do I put up with this, he wondered, why do I lie here tormenting myself while she, with her unchaste body, sleeps peacefully? Why didn't I go straight into her room so that she'd know *I* knew her shame? Why didn't I beat her black and blue? Because I'm weak... and a coward... I've always been weak with both of them, I've given way to them in everything, I was proud that I could make their lives easy, even if my own was ruined, I scraped the money together with my fingernails, *pfennig* by *pfennig*, I'd have torn the flesh from my hands to see them content! But as soon as I'd made them rich they were ashamed of me, I wasn't elegant enough for them any more, too uneducated... where would I have got an education? I was taken out of school aged twelve, I had to earn money, earn and earn, carry cases of samples about from village to village, run agencies in town after town before I could open my own business... and no sooner were they ladies and living in their own house than they didn't like my honourable old name any more. I had to buy the title of Councillor, so that my wife wouldn't be just Frau Salomonsohn, so that she could be Frau Commercial Councillor and put on airs. Put on airs! They laughed at me when I objected to all that putting on airs of distinction, when I objected to what they call high society, when I told them how my mother, God rest her soul, kept house quietly, modestly, just for my father and the rest of us... they called me old-fashioned. "Oh, you're so old-fashioned, Papa!" She was always mocking me... yes, old-fashioned, indeed I am... and now she lies in a strange bed with strange men, my child, my only child! Oh, the shame, the shame of it!

The old man was moaning and sighing in such torment that his wife, in the bed beside his, woke up. "What's the matter?" she drowsily asked. The old man did not move, and held his breath. And so he lay there motionless in the coffin of his torment until morning, with his thoughts eating away at him like worms.

The old man was first at the breakfast table. He sat down with a sigh, unable to face a morsel of food.

Alone again, he thought, always alone! When I go to the office in the morning they're still comfortably asleep, lazily taking their ease after all their dancing and theatre-going... when I come home in the evening they've already gone out to enjoy themselves in company, they don't need me with them. It's the money, the accursed money that's ruined them, made them strangers to me. Fool that I am, I earned it, scraped it together, I stole from myself, made myself poor and them bad with the money... for fifty pointless years I've been toiling, never giving myself a day off, and now I'm all alone...

He felt impatient. Why doesn't she come down, he wondered, I want to talk to her, I have to tell her... we must leave this place at once... why doesn't she come down? I suppose she's too tired, sleeping soundly with a clear conscience while I'm tearing my heart to pieces, old fool that I am... and her mother titivating herself for hours on end, has to take a bath, dress herself, have a manicure, get her hair arranged, she won't be down before eleven, and is it any wonder? How can a child turn out so badly? It's the money, the accursed money…

Light footsteps were approaching behind him. "Good morning, Papa, did you sleep well?" A soft cheek bent down to his side, a light kiss brushed his hammering forehead. Instinctively he drew back; repelled by the sweetly sultry Coty perfume she wore. And then…

"What's the matter, Papa… are you in a cross temper again? Oh, coffee, please, waiter, and ham and eggs… Did you sleep badly, or have you heard bad news?"

The old man restrained himself. He bowed his head—he did not have the courage to look up—and preserved his silence. He saw only her manicured hands on the table, her beloved hands, casually playing with each other like spoilt, slender little greyhounds on the white turf of the tablecloth. He trembled. Timidly, his eyes travelled up the delicate, girlish arms which she had often—but how long ago?—flung around him before she went to sleep. He saw the gentle curve of her breasts moving in time with her breathing under the new pullover. Naked, he thought grimly, stark naked, tossing and turning in bed with a strange man. A man who touched all that, felt it, lavished caresses on it, tasted and enjoyed her… my own flesh and blood, my child… that villainous stranger, oh…

Unconsciously, he had groaned again. "What's the matter with you, Papa?" She moved closer, coaxing him.

What's the matter with me? echoed a voice inside him. A whore for a daughter, and I can't summon up the courage to tell her so.

But he only muttered indistinctly, "Nothing, nothing!" and hastily picked up the newspaper, protecting himself from her questioning gaze behind a barricade of outspread sheets of newsprint. He felt increasingly unable to meet her eyes. His hands were shaking. I ought to tell her now, said his tormented mind, now while we're alone. But his voice failed him; he could not even find the strength to look up.

And suddenly, abruptly, he pushed back his chair and escaped, treading heavily, in the direction of the garden, for he felt a large tear rolling down his cheek against his will, and he didn't want her to see it.

The old man wandered around the garden on his short legs, staring at the lake for a long time. Almost blinded by the unshed tears he was holding back, he still could not help noticing the beauty of the landscape—the hills rose in undulating shades of soft green behind silver light, black-hatched with the thin spires of cypress trees, and beyond the hills were the sterner outlines of the mountains, severe, yet looking down on the beauty of the lake without arrogance, like grave men watching the light-hearted games of beloved children. How mild it all lay there outspread, with open, flowering, hospitable gestures. How it enticed a man to be kindly and happy, that timeless, blessed smile of God at the south he had created! Happy! The old man rocked his heavy head back and forth, confused.

One could be happy here, he thought. I would have liked to be happy myself, just once, feel how beautiful the world of the carefree is for myself, just once, after fifty years of writing and calculating and bargaining and haggling, I would have liked to enjoy a few bright days before they bury me… for sixty-five years, my God, death's hand is in my body now, money is no help and nor are the doctors. I wanted to breathe easily just a little first, have something for myself for once. But my late father always said: contentment is not for the likes of us, we carry our pedlar's packs on our backs to the grave… Yesterday I thought I myself might feel at ease for a change… yesterday I could have been called a happy man, glad of my beautiful, lovely child, glad to give her pleasure… and God has punished me already and taken that away from me. It's all over now for ever... I can't speak to my own child any more, I am ashamed to look her in the eye. I'll always be thinking of this at home, at the office, at night in my bed—where is she now, where has she been, what has she done? I'll never be able to come happily home again, to see her sitting there and then running to meet me, with my heart opening up at the sight of her, so young and lovely... When she kisses me I'll wonder who had her yesterday, who kissed those lips... I'll always live in fear when she's not with me, I'll always be ashamed when I meet her eyes—a man can't live like this, can't live like this...

The old man stumbled back and forth like a drunk, muttering. He kept staring out at the lake, and his tears ran down into his beard. He had to take off his pince-nez and stand there on the narrow path with his moist, short-sighted eyes revealed, looking so foolish that a gardener's boy who was passing stopped in surprise, laughed aloud and called out a few mocking words in Italian at the bewildered old man. That roused him from his turmoil of pain, and he put his pince-nez on and stole aside into the garden to sit on a bench somewhere and hide from the boy.

But as he approached a remote part of the garden, a laugh to his left startled him again... a laugh that he knew and that went to his heart. That laughter had been music to him for nineteen years, the light laughter of her high spirits... for that laughter he had travelled third-class by night to Poland and Hungary so that he could pour out money before them, rich soil from which that carefree merriment grew. He had lived only for that laughter, while inside his body his gall bladder fell sick... just so that that laughter could always ring out from her beloved mouth. And now the same laughter cut him to the heart like a red-hot saw.

Yet it drew him to it despite his reluctance. She was standing on the tennis court, twirling the racket in her bare hand, gracefully throwing it up and catching it again in play. At the same time as the racket flew up, her light-hearted laughter rose to the azure sky. The three gentlemen admiringly watched her, Conte Ubaldi in a loose tennis shirt, the officer in the trim uniform that showed off his muscles, the gentleman jockey in an immaculate pair of breeches, three sharply profiled, statuesque male figures around a plaything fluttering like a butterfly. The old man himself stared, captivated. Good God, how lovely she was in her pale, ankle-length dress, the sun dusting her blonde hair with liquid gold! And how happily her young limbs felt their own lightness as she leapt and ran, intoxicated and intoxicating as her joints responded to the free-and-easy rhythm of her movements. Now she flung the white tennis ball merrily up to the sky, then a second and a third after it, it was wonderful to see how the slender wand of her girlish body bent and stretched, leaping up now to catch the last ball. He had never seen her like that before, incandescent with high spirits, an elusive, wavering flame, the silvery trill of her laughter above the blazing of her body, like a virginal goddess escaped in panic from the southern garden with its clinging ivy and the gentle surface of the lake. At home she never stretched that slender, sinewy body in such a wild dance or played competitive games. No, he had never seen her like this within the sombre walls of the crowded city, had never heard her voice rise like lark-song set free from the earthly confines of her throat in merriment that was almost song, not indoors and not in the street. She had never been so beautiful. The old man stared and stared. He had forgotten everything, he just watched and watched that white, elusive flame. And he would have stood like that, endlessly absorbing her image with a passionate gaze, if she had not finally caught the last of the balls she was juggling with a breathless, fluttering leap, turning nimbly, and pressed them to her breast breathing fast, face flushed, but with a proud and laughing gaze. "*Brava, brava!*" cried the three gentlemen, who had been intently watching her clever juggling of the balls, applauding as if she had finished an operatic aria. Their guttural voices roused the old man from his enchantment, and he stared grimly at them.

So there they are, the villains, he thought, his heart thudding. There they are—but which of them is it? Which of those three has had her? Oh yes, how finely rigged out they are, shaved and perfumed, idle dandies... while men like me still sit in offices in their old age, in shabby trousers, wearing down the heels of their shoes visiting customers... and for all I know the fathers of these fine fellows may still be toiling away today, wearing their hands out so that their sons can travel the world, wasting time at their leisure, their faces browned and carefree, their impudent eyes bright. Easy for them to be cheerful, they only have to throw a silly, vain child a few sweet words and she'll fall into bed... But which of the three is it, which is it? One of them, I know, is seeing her naked through her dress and smacking his lips. I've had her, he's thinking, he's known her hot and naked, we'll do it again this evening, he thinks, winking at her—oh, the bastard, the dog, yes, if only I could whip him like a dog!

And now they had noticed him standing there. His daughter swung up her racket in a salutation, and smiled at him, the gentlemen wished him good day. He did not thank them, only stared at his daughter's smiling lips with brimming, bloodshot eyes. To think that you can laugh like that, he thought, you shameless creature... and one of those men may be laughing to himself, telling himself—there goes the stupid old Jew who lies snoring in bed all night... if only he knew, the old fool! Oh yes, I do know, you fine fellows laugh, you tread me underfoot like dirt... but my daughter, so pretty and willing, she'll tumble into bed with you... and as for her mother, she's a little stout now, but she goes about all dolled up with her face painted, and if you were to make eyes at her, who knows, she might yet venture to dance a step or so with you... You're right, you dogs, you're right when they run after you, those shameless women, women on heat… what's it to you that another man's heart is breaking so long as you can have your fun, fun with those shameless females… someone should take a revolver and shoot you down, you deserve to be horsewhipped… but yes, you're right, so long as no one does anything, so long as I swallow my rage like a dog returning to his vomit… you're right, if a father is so cowardly, so shockingly cowardly… if he doesn't go to the shameless girl, take hold of her, drag her away from you… if he just stands there saying nothing, bitter gall in his mouth, a coward, a coward, a coward…

The old man clutched the balustrade as helpless rage shook him. And suddenly he spat on the ground in front of his feet and staggered out of the garden.

The old man made his way unsteadily into the little town. Suddenly he stopped in front of a display window full of all kinds of things for tourists' needs—shirts and nets, blouses and angling equipment, ties, books, tins of biscuits, not in chance confusion but built up into artificial pyramids and colourfully arranged on shelves. However, his gaze went to just one object, lying disregarded amidst this elegant jumble—a gnarled walking stick, stout and solid with an iron tip, heavy in the hand; it would probably come down with a good thump. Strike him down, thought the old man, strike the dog down! The idea transported him into a confused, almost lustful turmoil of feeling which sent him into the shop, and he bought the stout stick quite cheaply. And no sooner was the weighty, heavy, menacing thing in his hand than he felt stronger. A weapon always makes the physically weak more sure of themselves. It was as if the handle of the stick tensed and tautened his muscles. "Strike him down… strike the dog down!" he muttered to himself, and unconsciously his heavy, stumbling gait turned to a firmer, more upright, faster rhythm. He walked, even ran up and down the path by the shores of the lake, breathing hard and sweating, but more from the passion spreading through him than because of his accelerated pace. For his hand was clutching the heavy handle of the stick more and more tightly.

Armed with this weapon, he entered the blue, cool shadows of the hotel lobby, his angry eyes searching for the invisible enemy. And sure enough, there in the corner they were sitting together on comfortable wicker chairs, drinking whisky and soda through straws, talking cheerfully in idle good fellowship—his wife, his daughter and the inevitable trio of gentlemen. Which of them is it, he wondered, which of them is it? And his fist clenched around the handle of the heavy stick. Whose skull do I smash in, whose, whose? But Erna, misunderstanding his restless, searching glances, was already jumping up and running to him. "So here you are, Papa! We've been looking for you everywhere. Guess what, Baron von Medwitz is going to take us for a drive in his Fiat, we're going to drive all along the lake to Desenzano!" And she affectionately led him to their table, as if he ought to thank the gentlemen for the invitation.

They had risen politely and were offering him their hands. The old man trembled. But the girl's warm presence, placating him, lay soft and intoxicating against his arm. His will was paralysed as he shook the three hands one by one, sat down in silence, took out a cigar and bit grimly into the soft end of it. Above him, the casual conversation went on, in French, with much high-spirited laughter from several voices.

The old man sat there, silent and hunched, biting the end of his cigar until his teeth were brown with tobacco juice. They're right, he thought, they're right, I deserve to be spat at... now I've shaken their hands! Shaken hands with all three, and I know that one of them's the villain. Here I am sitting quietly at the same table with him, and I don't strike him down, no, I don't strike him down, I shake hands with him civilly... they're right, quite right if they laugh at me... and see the way they talk, ignoring me as if I

217

weren't here at all! I might already be underground… and they both know, Erna and my wife, that I don't understand a word of French. They both know that, both of them, but no one asked me whether I minded, if only for form's sake, just because I sit here so foolishly, feeling so ridiculous. I might be thin air to them, nothing but thin air, a nuisance, a hanger-on, something in the way of their fun… someone to be ashamed of, they tolerate me only because I make so much money. Money, money, always that wretched, filthy lucre, the money I've spent indulging them, money with God's curse on it. They don't say a word to me, my wife, my own child, they talk away to these idlers, their eyes are all for those smooth, smartly rigged-out dandies… see how they smile at those fine gentlemen, it tickles their fancy, as if they felt their hands on bare female flesh. And I put up with it all. I sit here listening to their laughter, I don't understand what they say, and yet I sit here instead of striking out with my fists, thrashing them with my stick, driving them apart before they begin coupling before my very eyes. I let it all pass… I sit here silent, stupid, a coward, coward, coward…

"Will you allow me?" asked the Italian officer, in laborious German, reaching for his lighter.

Startled out of his heated thoughts, the old man sat up very erect and stared grimly at the unsuspecting young officer. Anger was seething inside him. For a moment his hand clutched the handle of the stick convulsively. But then he let the corners of his mouth turn down again, stretching it into a senseless grin. "Oh, I'll allow you!" he sardonically repeated. "To be sure I'll allow you, ha ha, I'll allow you anything you want—ha ha!—anything I have is entirely at your disposal… you can do just as you like."

The bewildered officer stared at him. With his poor command of German, he had not quite understood, but that wry, grinning smile made him uneasy. The gentleman jockey from Germany sat up straight, startled, the two women went white as a sheet—for a split second the air among them all was breathless and motionless, as electric as the tiny pause between a flash of lightning and the thunder that follows.

But then the fierce distortion of his face relaxed, the stick slid out of his clutch. Like a beaten dog, the old man retreated into his own thoughts and coughed awkwardly, alarmed by his own boldness. Trying to smooth over the embarrassing tension, Erna returned to her light conversational tone, the German baron replied, obviously anxious to maintain the cheerful mood, and within a few minutes the interrupted tide of words was in full flow once more.

The old man sat among the others as they chattered, entirely withdrawn; and you might have thought he was asleep. His heavy stick, now that the clutch of his hands was relaxed, dangled useless between his legs. His head, propped on one hand, sank lower and lower. But no one paid him any more attention, the wave of chatter rolled over his silence, sometimes laughter sprayed up, sparkling, at a joking remark, but he was lying motionless below it all in endless darkness, drowned in shame and pain.

The three gentlemen rose to their feet, Erna followed readily, her mother more slowly; in obedience to someone's light-hearted suggestion they were going into the music room next door, and did not think it necessary to ask the old man drowsing away there to come with them. Only when he suddenly became aware of the emptiness around him did he wake, like a sleeping man roused by the cold when his blanket has slipped off the bed in the night, and cold air blows over his naked body. Instinctively his eyes went to the chairs they had left, but jazzy music was already coming from the room next door, syncopated and garish. He heard laughter and cries of encouragement. They were dancing next door. Yes, dancing, always dancing, they could do that all right! Always stirring up the blood, always rubbing avidly against each other, chafing until the dish was cooked and ready. Dancing in the evening, at night, in bright daylight, idlers, gentlemen of leisure with time on their hands, that was how they charmed the women.

Bitterly, he picked up his stout stick again and dragged himself after them. At the door he stopped. The German baron, the gentleman jockey, was sitting at the piano, half turned away from the keyboard so that he could watch the dancers at the same time as he rattled out an American hit song on the keys, a tune he obviously knew more or less by heart. Erna was dancing with the officer; the long-legged Conte Ubaldi was rhythmically pushing her strong, sturdy mother forward and back, not without some difficulty. But the old man had eyes for no one but Erna and her partner. How that slender greyhound of a man laid his hands, soft and flattering, on her delicate shoulders, as if she belonged to him entirely! How her body, swaying, following his lead, pressed close to his, as if promising herself, how they danced, intertwined, before his very eyes, with passion that they had difficulty in restraining! Yes, he was the man—for in those two bodies moving as one there burnt a sense of familiarity, something in common already in their blood. He was the one—it could only be he, he read it from her eyes, half-closed and yet brimming over, in that fleeting, hovering movement reflecting the memory of lustful moments already enjoyed—he was the man, he was the thief who came by night to seize and ardently penetrate what his child, his own child, now concealed in her thin, semi-transparent, flowing dress! Instinctively he stepped closer to tear her away from the man. But she didn't even notice him. With every movement of the rhythm, giving herself up to the guiding touch of the dancer, the seducer leading her, with her head thrown back and her moist mouth open, she swayed softly to the beat of the music, with no sense of space or time or of the man, the trembling, panting old man who was staring at her in a frenzied ecstasy of rage, his eyes bloodshot. She felt only herself, her own young limbs as she unresistingly followed the syncopation of the breathlessly swirling dance music. She felt only herself, and the fact that a male creature so close to her desired her, his strong arm surrounded her, and she must preserve her balance and not fall against him with greedy lips, hotly inhaling his breath as she abandoned herself to him. And all this was magically known to the old man in his own blood, his own shattered being—always, whenever the dance swept her away from him, he felt as if she were sinking for ever.

Suddenly, as if the string of an instrument had broken, the music stopped in the middle of a bar. The German baron jumped up. "*Assez joué pour vous*," he laughed. "*Maintenant je veux danser moi-même.*"—"You've had your fun. Now I want to dance myself!" They all cheerfully agreed, the group stopped dancing in couples and moved into an informal, fluttering dance all together.

The old man came back to his senses—how he wanted to do something now, say something! Not just stand about so foolishly, so pitifully superfluous! His wife was dancing by, gasping slightly from exertion but warm with contentment. Anger brought him to a sudden decision. He stepped into her path. "Come with me," he said brusquely. "I have to talk to you."

She looked at him in surprise. Little beads of sweat moistened his pale brow, his eyes were staring wildly around. What did he want? Why disturb her just now? An excuse was already forming on her lips, but there was something so convulsive, so dangerous in his demeanour that, suddenly remembering the grim outburst over the lighter just now, she reluctantly followed him.

"*Excusez, messieurs, un instant!*" she said, turning back apologetically to the gentlemen. So she'll apologise to *them*, thought the agitated old man grimly, she didn't apologise to me when she got up from the table. I'm no more than a dog to her, a doormat to be trodden on. But they're right, oh yes, they're right if I put up with it.

She was waiting, her eyebrows sternly raised; he stood before her, his lip quivering, like a schoolboy facing his teacher.

"Well?" she finally asked.

"I don't want… I don't want…" he stammered awkwardly. "I don't want you—you and Erna—I don't want you mixing with those people."

"With what people?" Deliberately pretending not to understand, she looked up indignantly, as if he had insulted her personally.

"With those men in there." Angrily, he jerked his chin in the direction of the music room. "I don't like it… I don't want you to…"

"And why not, may I ask?"

Always that inquisitorial tone, he thought bitterly, as if I were a servant. Still more agitated, he stammered, "I have my reasons… I don't like it. I don't want Erna talking to those men. I don't have to tell you everything."

"Then I'm sorry," she said, flaring up, "but I consider all three gentlemen extremely well-brought up, far more distinguished company than we keep at home."

"Distinguished company! Those idlers, those… those…" Rage was throttling him more intolerably than ever. And suddenly he stamped his foot. "I don't want it, I forbid it! Do you understand that?"

"No," she said coldly. "I don't understand any of what you say. I don't know why I should spoil the girl's pleasure…"

"Her pleasure… her pleasure!" He was staggering as if under a heavy blow, his face red, his forehead streaming with sweat. His hand groped in the air for his heavy stick, either to support himself or to hit out with it. But he had left it behind. That brought him back to his senses. He forced himself to keep calm as a wave of heat suddenly passed over his heart. He went closer to his wife, as if to take her hand. His voice was low now, almost pleading. "You… you don't understand. It's not for myself… I'm begging you only because… it's the first thing I've asked you for years, let's go away from here. Just away, to Florence, to Rome, anywhere you want, I don't mind.

You can decide it all, just as you like. I only want to get away from here, please, away… away, today, this very day. I… I can't bear it any longer, I can't."

"Today?" Surprised, dismissively, she frowned. "Go away today? What a ridiculous idea! Just because you don't happen to like those gentlemen. Well, you don't have to mingle with them."

He was still standing there, hands raised pleadingly. "I can't bear it, I told you… I can't, I can't. Don't ask me any more, please… but believe me, I can't bear it, I can't. Do this for me, just for once, do something for me…"

In the music room someone had begun hammering at the piano again. She looked up, touched by his cry despite herself, but how very ridiculous he looked, that short fat man, his face red as if he had suffered a stroke, his eyes wild and swollen, his hands emerging from sleeves too short for him and trembling in the air. It was embarrassing to see him standing there in such a pitiful state. Her milder feelings froze.

"That's impossible," she informed him. "We've agreed to go out for that drive today, and as for leaving tomorrow when we've booked for three weeks… why, we'd make ourselves look ridiculous. I can't see the faintest reason for leaving early. I am staying here, and so is Erna, we are not—"

"And I can go, you're saying? I'm only in the way here, spoiling your… pleasure."

With that sombre cry he cut her short in mid-sentence. His hunched, massive body had reared up, he had clenched his hands into fists, a vein was trembling alarmingly on his forehead in anger. He wanted to get something else out, a word or a blow. But he turned abruptly, stumbled to the stairs, moving faster and faster on his heavy legs, and hurried up them like a man pursued.

*

Gasping, the old man went hastily up the stairs; he wanted only to be in his room now, alone, try to control himself, take care not to do anything silly! He had already reached the first floor when—there it came, the pain, as if a burning claw were tearing open his guts from the inside. He suddenly stumbled back against the wall, white as a sheet. Oh, that raging, burning pain kneading away at him; he had to grit his teeth to keep himself from crying out loud. Groaning, his tormented body writhed.

He knew at once what was wrong—it was his gall bladder, one of those fearful attacks that had often plagued him recently, but had never before tortured him so cruelly. Next moment, in the middle of his pain, he remembered that the doctor had prescribed 'no agitation'. Through the pain he grimly mocked himself. Easily said, he thought, no agitation—my dear good Professor, can you tell me how to avoid agitation when… oh, oh…

The old man was whimpering as the invisible, red-hot claw worked away inside his poor body. With difficulty, he dragged himself to the door of the sitting room of the suite, pushed it open, and fell on the ottoman, stuffing the cushions into his mouth. As he lay there the pain immediately lessened slightly; the hot nails of that claw were no longer reaching so infernally deep into his sore guts. I ought to make myself a compress, he remembered, I must take those drops, then it will soon be better.

But there was no one there to help him, no one. And he himself had no strength to drag himself into the next room, or even reach the bell.

There's no one here, he thought bitterly, I shall die like a dog sooner or later, because I know what it is that hurts, it's not my gall bladder, it's Death growing in me. I know it, I'm a defeated man, no professors, no drinking the waters at spas can help me… you don't recover from this sort of thing, not at sixty-five. I know what's piercing me and tearing me from the inside, it's Death, and the few years I have left will not be life, just dying, dying. But when did I ever really live? Live my own life, for myself? What kind of life have I had, scraping money together all the time, always for other people, and now, what help is it to me now? I've had a wife, I married her as a girl, I knew her body and she bore me a child. Year after year we lay together in the same bed... and now, where is she now? I don't recognise her face any more... she speaks so strangely to me, and never thinks of my life, of all I feel and think and suffer... she's been a stranger to me for years now... Where has my life gone, where did it go?... And I had a child, watched her grow up, I thought I'd begin to live again through her, a brighter, happier life than was granted to me, in her I wouldn't entirely die... and now she steals away by night to throw herself at men. There's only me, I shall die alone, all alone... I'm already dead to those two. My God, my God, I was never so much alone...

The claw sometimes closed grimly inside him and then let go again. But another pain was hammering deeper and deeper into his temples; his thoughts, harsh, sharp, were like mercilessly hot gravel in his forehead, he mustn't think just now, mustn't think! The old man had torn open his jacket and waistcoat—his bloated body quivered, plump and shapeless, under his billowing shirt. Cautiously he pressed his hand to the painful place. All that hurts there is me, he felt, it's only me, only this piece of hot skin... and only what's clawing around in it there still belongs to me, it is *my* illness, *my* death... I am all it is... I am not a Privy Commercial Councillor any more, with a wife and child and money and a house and a business... this is all I really am, what I feel with my fingers, my body and the heat inside it hurting me. Everything else is folly, makes no sense now... because what hurts in there hurts only me, what concerns me concerns me alone. They don't understand me any more, and I don't understand them... you are all alone with yourself in the end. I never felt it so much before... But now I know, now I lie here feeling Death under my skin, too late now in my sixty-fifth year, just before dying, now while they dance and go for walks or drift aimlessly about, those shameless women… now I know it, I lived only for them, not that they thank me for it, and never for myself, not for an hour. But what do I care for them now… what do I care for them… why think of them when they never think of me? Better die than accept their pity… what do I care for them now?…

Gradually receding, the pain ebbed away; the cruel hand did not grasp into the suffering man with such red-hot claws. But it left behind a dull, sombre feeling, barely perceptible as pain now, yet something alien pressing and pushing, tunnelling away inside him. The old man lay with his eyes closed, attending carefully to this soft pushing and pulling; he felt as if a strange, unknown power were hollowing something out in him, first with sharp tools, then with blunter ones. It was like something coming adrift, fibre by fibre, within his body. The tearing was not so fierce now, and did not hurt any more. But there was something quietly smouldering and rotting inside him, something beginning to die. All he had lived through, all he had loved, was lost in that slowly consuming flame, burning black before it fell apart, crumbling and charred, into the lukewarm mire of indifference. Something was happening, he knew it vaguely, something was happening while he lay like this, reflecting passionately on his life. Something was coming to an end. What was it? He listened and listened to what was going on inside him.

And slowly his heart began to fail him.

The old man lay in the twilight of the room with his eyes closed. He was still half awake, half already dreaming. And then, between sleeping and waking, it seemed to him in the confusion of his feelings as if, from somewhere or other, something moist and hot was seeping softly into him from a wound that did not hurt and that he was unaware of having suffered. It was like being drained of his own blood. It did not hurt, that invisible flow, it did not run very strongly. The drops fell only slowly, like warm tears trickling down, and each of them struck him in the middle of the heart. But his heart, his dark heart, made no sound and quietly soaked up that strange torrent. Soaked it up like a sponge, became heavier and heavier with it, his heart was already swelling with it, brimming over, it was spilling into the narrow frame of his chest. Gradually filling up, overflowing with its own weight, whatever it was began gently pulling to expand itself, pulling at taut muscles, pressing harder and harder and forcing his painful heart, gigantic by now, down after its own weight. And now (oh, how this hurt!) now the weight came loose from the fibres of flesh—very slowly, not like a stone or a falling fruit, no, like a sponge soaked with moisture it sank deeper and ever deeper into a warm void, down into something without being that was outside himself, into vast and endless night. All at once it was terribly still in the place where that warm, brimming heart had been a moment ago. What yawned empty there now was uncanny and cold. No sensation of thudding any more, no dripping now, all was very still and perfectly dead inside him. And his shuddering breast surrounded that silent and incomprehensible void like a hollow black coffin.

So strong was this dreamlike feeling, so deep his confusion, that when the old man began to wake he instinctively put his hand to the left side of his chest to see whether his heart was still here. But thank God, he felt a pulse, a hollow, rhythmical pulse beating below his groping fingers, and yet it might have been beating mutely in a vacuum, as if his heart was really gone. For strange to say, it suddenly seemed as if his body had left him of its own accord. No pain wrenched at it any more, no memory twitched painfully, all was silent in there, fixed and turned to stone. What's this, he wondered, when just now I felt such pain, such hot pressure, when every fibre was twitching? What has happened to me? He listened, as if to the sounds in a cavern, to find out whether what had been there before was still moving. But those rushing sounds, the dripping, the thudding, they were far away. He listened and listened, no echo came, none at all. Nothing hurt him any more, nothing was swelling up to torment him; it must be as empty and black in there as a hollow, burnt-out tree. And all at once he felt as if he had already died, or something in him had died, his blood was so sluggish and silent. His own body lay under him cold as a corpse, and he was afraid to feel it with his warm hand.

There in his room the old man, listening to what was happening to him, did not hear the sound of church clocks down by the lake striking the hours, each hour bringing deeper twilight. The night was already gathering around him, darkness fell on the things in the room as it flowed away into the night, at last even the pale sky visible in the rectangle of the window was immersed in total darkness. The old man never noticed, but only stared at the blackness in himself, listening to the void there as if to his own death.

Then, at last, there was exuberant laughter in the room next door. A switch was pressed, and light came through the crack of the doorway, for the door was only ajar. The old man roused himself with a start—his wife, his daughter! They would find him here on the day bed and ask questions. He hastily buttoned up his jacket and waistcoat; why should they know about the attack he had suffered, what business of theirs was it?

But the two women had not come in search of him. They were obviously in a hurry; the imperious gong was striking for the third time. They seemed to be dressing for dinner; listening, he could hear every movement through the half-open doorway. Now they were opening the shutters, now they were putting their rings down on the washstand with a light chink, now shoes were tapping on the floor, and from time to time they talked to each other. Every word, every syllable came to the old man's ears with cruel clarity. First they talked about the gentlemen, mocking them a little, about a chance incident on the drive, light, inconsequent remarks as they washed and moved around, dressing and titivating themselves. Then, suddenly, the conversation turned to him.

"Where's Papa?" Erna asked, sounding surprised that he had occurred to her so late.

"How should I know?" That was her mother's voice, instantly irritated by the mere mention of him. "Probably waiting for us down in the lobby, reading the stock prices in the Frankfurt newspaper for the hundredth time—they're all he's interested in. Do you think he's even looked at the lake? He doesn't like it here, he told me so at mid-day. He wanted us to leave today."

"Leave today? But why?" Erna's voice again.

"I really don't know. Who can tell what he has in mind? He doesn't like the other guests here, the company of those gentlemen doesn't suit him—probably he feels how little his company suits them. Really, the way he goes around here is disgraceful, with his clothes all crumpled, his collar open… you should suggest that he might look a little more *soigné*, at least in the evenings, he'll listen to you. And this morning… I thought I'd sink into the ground to hear him flare up at the lieutenant when he wanted to borrow Papa's lighter."

"Yes, Mama, what was that all about? I wanted to ask you, what was the matter with Papa? I've never seen him like that before… I was really shocked."

"Oh, he was just in a bad temper. I expect prices on the stock exchange have fallen. Or perhaps it was because we were speaking French. He can't bear other people to have a nice time. You didn't notice, but while we were dancing he was standing at the door of the music room like a murderer lurking behind a tree. Leave today! Leave on the spot! Just because that's what he suddenly feels like doing. Well, if he doesn't like it here, there's no need for him to grudge us our pleasure… but I'm not going to bother with his whims any more, whatever he says and does."

The conversation ended. Obviously they had finished dressing for dinner. Yes, the door was opened, they were leaving the room, he heard the click of the switch, and the light went out.

The old man sat perfectly still on the ottoman. He had heard every word. But strange to say, it no longer hurt, it did not hurt at all. The clockwork in his breast that had been hammering and tearing at him fiercely not so long ago had come to a standstill; it must be broken. He had felt no reaction to the sharp touch of their remarks. No anger, no hatred… nothing, nothing. Calmly, he buttoned up his clothes, cautiously made his way downstairs, and sat down at the dinner table with them as if they were strangers.

He did not speak to them that evening, and for their part they did not notice his silence, which was as concentrated as a clenched fist. After dinner he went back to his room, again without a word, lay down on the bed and put out the light. Only much later did his wife come up from the evening's cheerful entertainment, and thinking he was asleep she undressed in the dark. Soon he heard her heavy, easy breathing.

The old man, alone with himself, stared open-eyed at the endless void of the night. Beside him something lay in the dark, breathing deeply; he made an effort to remember that the body drawing in the same air in the same room was the woman whom he had known when she was young and ardent, who had borne him a child, a body bound to him through the deepest mystery of the blood; he kept forcing himself to think that the warm, soft body there—he had only to put out a hand to touch it—had once been a life that was part of his own. But strangely, the memory aroused no feelings in him any more. And he heard her regular breathing only like the murmuring of little waves coming through the open window as they broke softly on the pebbles near the shore. It was all far away and unreal, something strange was lying beside him only by chance—it was over, over for ever.

Once he found himself trembling very slightly, and stole to his daughter's door. So she was out of her room again tonight. He did feel a small, sharp pang in the heart he had thought dead. For a second, something twitched there like a nerve before it died away entirely. That was over now as well. Let her do as she likes, he thought, what is it to me?

And the old man lay back on his pillow again. Once more the darkness closed in on his aching head, and that cool, blue sensation seeped into his blood—a beneficial feeling. Soon light slumber cast its shadow over his exhausted senses.

When his wife woke up in the morning she saw her husband already in his coat and hat. "What are you doing?" she asked, still drowsy from sleep.

The old man did not turn around. He was calmly packing his night things in a small suitcase. "You know what I'm doing. I'm going home. I'm taking only the necessities; you can have the rest sent after me."

His wife took fright. What was all this? She had never heard his voice like that before, bringing each word out cold and hard. She swung both legs out of bed. "You're not going away, surely? Wait… we'll come with you, I've already told Erna that…"

He only waved this vigorously away. "No, no, don't let it disturb you." And without looking back he made his way to the door. He had to put the suitcase down on the floor for a moment in order to press down the door handle. And in that one fitful second a memory came back—a memory of thousands of times when he had put down his case of samples like that as he left the doors of strangers with a servile bow, ingratiating himself with an eye to further business. But he had no business here and now, so he omitted any greeting. Without a look or a word he picked up his suitcase again and closed the door firmly between himself and his old life.

Neither mother nor daughter understood what had happened. But the strikingly abrupt and determined nature of his departure made them both uneasy. They wrote to him back at home in south Germany at once, elaborately explaining that they assumed there had been some misunderstanding, writing almost affectionately, asking with concern how his journey had been, and whether he had arrived safely. Suddenly compliant, they expressed themselves ready and willing to break off their holiday at any time. There was no reply. They wrote again, more urgently, they sent telegrams, but there was still no reply. Only the sum of money that they had said they needed in one of the letters arrived—a postal remittance bearing the stamp of his firm, without a word or greeting of his own.

Such an inexplicable and oppressive state of affairs made them bring their own return home forward. Although they had sent a telegram in advance, there was no one to meet them at the station, and they found everything unprepared at home. In an absent-minded moment, so the servants told them, the master had left the telegram lying on the table and had gone out, without leaving any instructions. In the evening, when they were already sitting down to eat, they heard the sound of the front door at last. They jumped up and ran to meet him. He looked at them in surprise—obviously he had forgotten the telegram—patiently accepted his daughter's embrace, but without any particular expression of feeling, let them lead him to the dining room and tell him about their journey. However, he asked no questions, smoked his cigar in silence, sometimes answered

232

briefly, sometimes did not notice what they said at all; it was as if he were asleep with his eyes open. Then he got up ponderously and went to his room.

And it was the same for the next few days. His anxious wife tried to get him to talk to her, but in vain; the more she pressed him, the more evasively he reacted. Some place inside him was barred to her, inaccessible, an entrance had been walled up. He still ate with them, sat with them for a while when callers came, but in silence, absorbed in his own thoughts. However, he took no part in their lives any more, and when guests happened to look into his eyes in the middle of a conversation, they had the unpleasant feeling that a dead man's dull and shallow gaze was looking past them.

Even those who hardly knew him soon noticed the increasing oddity of the old man's behaviour. Acquaintances began to nudge each other on the sly if they met him in the street—there went the old man, one of the richest men in the city, slinking along by the wall like a beggar, his hat dented and set at a crooked angle on his head, his coat dusted with cigar ash, reeling in a peculiar way at every step and usually muttering aloud under his breath. If people greeted him, he looked up in surprise; if they addressed him he stared at them vacantly, and forgot to shake hands. At first a number of acquaintances thought he must have gone deaf, and repeated what they had said in louder tones. He was not deaf, but it always took him time to wake himself, as it were, from his internal sleep, and then he would lapse back into a strange state of abstraction in the middle of the conversation. All of a sudden the light would go out of his eyes, he would break off the discussion hastily and stumble on, without noticing the surprise of the person who had spoken to him. He always seemed to have emerged from a dark dream, from a cloudy state of self-absorption; other people, it was obvious, no longer existed for him. He never asked how anyone was; even in his own home he did not notice his wife's gloomy desperation or his daughter's baffled questions. He read no newspapers, listened to no conversations; not a word, not a question penetrated his dull and overcast indifference for a moment. Even what was closest to him became strange. He sometimes went to his office to sign letters. But if his secretary came back an hour later to fetch them, duly signed, he found the old man just as he had left him, lost in reverie over the unread letters and with the same vacant look in his eyes. In the end he himself realised that he was only in the way at the office, and stayed away entirely.

But the strangest and most surprising thing about the old man, to the whole city, was the fact that although he had never been among the most devoutly observant members of its Jewish community he suddenly became pious. Indifferent to all else, often unpunctual at meals and meetings, he never failed to be at the synagogue at the appointed hour. He stood there in his black silk cap, his prayer shawl around his shoulders, always at the same place, where his father once used to stand, rocking his weary head back and forth as he chanted psalms. Here, in the dim light of the room where the words echoed around him, dark and strange, he was most alone with himself. A kind of peace descended on his confused mind here, responding to the darkness in his own breast. However, when prayers were read for the dead, and he saw the families, children and friends of the departed dutifully bowing down and calling on the mercy of God for those who had left this world, his eyes were sometimes clouded. He was the last of his line, and he knew it. No one would say a prayer for him. And so he devoutly murmured the words with the congregation, thinking of himself as one might think of the dead.

Once, late in the evening, he was coming back from wandering the city in a daze, and was halfway home when rain began to fall. As usual, the old man had forgotten his umbrella. There were cabs for hire quite cheaply, entrances to buildings and glazed porches offered shelter from the torrential rain that was soon pouring down, but the strange old man swayed and stumbled on through the wet weather. A puddle collected in the dent in his hat and seeped through, rivulets streamed down from his own dripping sleeves; he took no notice but trudged on, the only person out and about in the deserted street. And so, drenched and dripping, looking more like a tramp than the master of a handsome villa, he reached the entrance of his house just at the moment when a car with its headlights on stopped right beside him, flinging up more muddy water on the inattentive pedestrian. The door swung open, and his wife hastily got out of the brightly lit the interior, followed by some distinguished visitor or other holding an umbrella over her, and then a second man. He drew level with them just outside the door. His wife recognised him and was horrified to see him in such a state, dripping wet, his clothes crumpled, looking like a bundle of something pulled out of the water, and instinctively she turned her eyes away. The old man understood at once—she was ashamed of him in front of her guests. And without emotion or bitterness, he walked a little further as if he were a stranger, to spare her the embarrassment of an introduction, and turned humbly in at the servants' entrance.

From that day on the old man always used the servants' stairs in his own house. He was sure not to meet anyone here, he was in no one's way and no one was in his. He stayed away from meals—an old maidservant brought something to his room. If his wife or daughter tried to get in to speak to him, he would send them away again with a vague murmur that was none the less clearly a refusal to see them. In the end they left him alone, and gradually stopped asking how he was, nor did he enquire after anyone or anything. He sometimes heard music and laughter coming through the walls from the other rooms in the house, which were already strange to him, he heard vehicles pass by until late at night, but he was so indifferent to everything that he did not even look out of the window. What was it to do with him? Only the dog sometimes came up and lay down by his forgotten master's bed.

Nothing hurt in his dead heart now, but the black mole was tunnelling on inside his body, tearing a bloodstained path into quivering flesh. His attacks grew more frequent from week to week, and at last, in agony, he gave way to his doctor's urging to have himself thoroughly examined. The professor looked grave. Carefully preparing the way, he said he thought that at this point an operation was essential. But the old man did not take fright, he only smiled wearily. Thank God, now it was coming to an end. An end to dying, and now came the good part, death. He would not let the doctor say a word to his family, the day was decided, and he made ready. For the last time, he went to his firm (where no one expected to see him any more, and they all looked at him as if he were a stranger), sat down once more in the old black leather chair where he had sat for thirty years, a whole lifetime, for thousands and thousands of hours, told them to bring him a cheque book and made out a cheque. He took it to the rabbi of the synagogue, who was almost frightened by the size of the sum. It was for charitable works and for his grave, he said, and to avoid all thanks he hastily stumbled out, losing his hat, but he did not even bend to pick it up. And so, bareheaded, eyes dull in his wrinkled face, now yellow with sickness, he went on his way, followed by surprised glances, to his parents' grave in the cemetery. There a few idlers gazed at the old man, and were surprised to hear him talk out loud and at length to the mouldering tombstones as if they were human beings. Was he announcing his imminent arrival to them, or asking for their blessing? No one could hear the words, but his lips moved, murmuring, and his shaking head was bowed deeper and deeper in prayer. At the way out of the cemetery beggars, who knew him well by sight, crowded around him. He hastily took all the coins and notes out of his pockets, and had distributed them when a wrinkled old woman limped up, later than the rest, begging for something for herself. In confusion, he searched his pockets, but there was nothing left. However, he still had something strange and heavy on his finger—his gold wedding ring. Some kind of memory came to him—he quickly took it off and gave it to the startled old woman.

And so, impoverished, empty and alone, he went under the surgeon's knife.

When the old man came round from the anaesthetic, the doctors, seeing the dangerous state he was in, called his wife and daughter, now informed of the operation, into the room. With difficulty, his eyes looked out from lids surrounded by blue shadows. "Where am I?" He stared at the strange white room that he had never seen before.

Then, to show him her affection, his daughter leant over his poor sunken face. And suddenly a glimmer of recognition came into the blindly searching eyes. A light, a small one, was kindled in their pupils—that was her, his child, his beloved child, that was his beautiful and tender child Erna! Very, very slowly the bitterly compressed lips relaxed. A smile, a very small smile that had not come to his closed mouth for a long time, cautiously began to show. And shaken by that joy, expressed as it was with such difficulty, she bent closer to kiss her father's bloodless cheeks.

But there it was—the sweet perfume that aroused a memory, or was it his half-numbed brain remembering forgotten moments?—and suddenly a terrible change came over the features that had looked happy only just now. His colourless lips were grimly tightened again, rejecting her. His hand worked its way out from under the blanket, and he tried to raise it as if to push something repellent away, his whole sore body quivering in agitation. "Get away!… Get away!"

he babbled. The words on his pale lips were almost inarticulate, yet clear enough. And so terribly did a look of aversion form on the face of the old man, who could not get away, that the doctor anxiously urged the women to stand aside. "He's delirious," he whispered. "You had better leave him alone now."

As soon as the two women had gone, the distorted features relaxed wearily again into final drowsiness. Breath was still escaping, although more and more stertorously, as he struggled for the heavy air of life. But soon his breast tired of the struggle to drink in that bitter nourishment of humanity. And when the doctor felt for the old man's heart, it had already ceased to hurt him.

LEPORELLA

HER REAL NAME WAS Crescentia Anna Aloisia Finkenhuber, she was thirty-nine years old, she had been born out of wedlock and came from a small mountain village in the Ziller valley. Under the heading of 'Distinguishing Marks' in the booklet recording her employment as a servant, a single line scored across the space available signified that she had none, but if the authorities had been obliged to give a description of her character, the most fleeting glance would have required a remark there, reading: resembles a hard-driven, strong-boned, scrawny mountain horse. For there was something unmistakably horsy about the expression of her heavy, drooping lower lip, the oval of her sun-tanned face, which was both long and harshly outlined, her dull, lashless gaze, and in particular the thick, felted strands of hair that fell greasily over her brow. Even the way she moved suggested the obstinacy and stubborn, mule-like manner of a horse used to the Alpine passes, carrying the same wooden panniers dourly uphill and downhill along stony bridleways in summer and winter alike. Once released from the halter of her work, Crescenz would doze with her bony hands loosely clasped and her elbows splayed, much as animals stand in the stable, and her senses seemed to be withdrawn. Everything about her was hard, wooden, heavy. She thought laboriously and was slow to understand anything: new ideas penetrated her innermost mind only with difficulty, as if dripping through a close-meshed sieve. But once she had finally taken in some new notion, she clung to it tenaciously and jealously. She read neither newspapers nor the prayer-book, she found writing difficult, and the clumsy characters in her kitchen records were curiously like her own heavy but angular figure, which was visibly devoid of all tangible marks of femininity. Like her bones, her brow, her hips and hands, her voice was hard too, and in spite of its thick, throaty Tyrolean accent, always sounded rusty—which was hardly surprising, since Crescenz never said an unnecessary word to anyone. And no one had ever seen her laugh. Here too she was just like an animal, for the gift of laughter, that release of feeling so happily breaking out, has not been granted to God's brute creation, which is perhaps a more cruel deprivation than the lack of language.

Brought up at the expense of the parish because of her illegitimate birth, put out to domestic service at the age of twelve, and then later a scullery maid in a carters' tavern, she had finally left that establishment, where she was known for her tenacious, ox-like capacity for work, and had risen to be cook at an inn that was popular with tourists. Crescenz rose there at five in the morning every day, worked, swept, cleaned, lit fires, brushed, cleared up, cooked, kneaded dough, strained food, washed dishes and did the laundry until late at night. She never took any holiday, she never went out in the street except to go to church; the fire in the kitchen range was her sun, the thousands and thousands of wooden logs it burned over the years her forest.

Men left her alone, whether because a quarter-century of dour, dull toil had taken every sign of femininity from her, or because she had firmly and taciturnly rejected all advances. Her one pleasure was in money, which she doggedly collected with the hamster-like instincts of the rustic labouring class, so that in her old age she would not have to eat the bitter bread of charity in the parish poorhouse yet again.

It was only for the money, in fact, that this dull-witted creature first left her native Tyrol at the age of thirty-seven. A woman who was a professional agent for domestic staff had come there on holiday, saw her working like a madwoman from morning to night in the

242

kitchen and public rooms of the inn, and lured her to Vienna with the promise of a position at double the wages. During the railway journey Crescenz hardly said a word to anyone, and in spite of the friendly offers of other passengers to put the heavy wicker basket containing all her worldly goods up in the net of the luggage rack, she held it on her knees, which were already aching, for deception and theft were the only notions that her clumsy peasant brain connected with the idea of the big city. In her new place in Vienna, she had to be accompanied to market for the first few days, because she feared all the vehicles as a cow fears a motor car. But as soon as she knew her way down the four streets leading to the marketplace she no longer needed anyone, but trotted off with her basket, never looking up, from the door of the building where her employers lived to the market stalls and home again to sweep the apartment, light fires and clear out her new kitchen range just as she had cleared the old one, noticing no change. She kept rustic hours, went to bed at nine and slept with her mouth open, like an animal, until the alarm clock went off in the morning. No one knew if she liked her job; perhaps she didn't know herself, for she approached no one, answered questions merely with a dull "Very well", or if she didn't agree, with a discontented shrug of her shoulders. She ignored her neighbours and the other maids in the building; the mocking looks of her more light-hearted companions in domestic service slipped off the leathery surface of her indifference like water. Just once, when a girl imitated her Tyrolean dialect and wouldn't stop teasing her for her taciturnity, she suddenly snatched a burning piece of wood out of the range and went for the horrified, screaming young woman with it. From that day on, everyone avoided her, and no one dared to mock someone capable of such fury again.

But every Sunday morning Crescenz went to church in her wide, pleated skirt and flat peasant hat. Only once, on her first day off in Vienna, did she try taking a walk. As she didn't want to ride on the tram, and had seen nothing but more and more stone walls in her cautious exploration of the many bewildering streets, she went only as far as the Danube Canal, where she stared at the flowing water as at something familiar, turned and went back the way she had come, always keeping close to the buildings and anxiously avoiding the carriageway. This first and only expedition must obviously have disappointed her, for after that she never left the house again, but preferred to sit at the window on Sundays either busy with her needlework or empty-handed. So the great metropolis brought no change into the routine treadmill of her days, except that at the end of every month she held four blue banknotes instead of the old two in her gnarled, tough, battered hands. She always checked these banknotes suspiciously for a long time. She unfolded the new notes ceremoniously, and finally smoothed them out flat, almost tenderly, before putting them with the others in the carved, yellow wooden box that she had brought from her home village. This clumsy, heavy little casket was her whole secret, the meaning of her life. By night she put its key under her pillow. No one ever found out where she kept it in the day.

Such was the nature of this strange human being (as we may call her, although humanity was apparent in her behaviour only in a very faint and muted way), but perhaps it took someone with exactly those blinkered senses to tolerate domestic service in the household of young Baron von F—which was an extremely strange one in itself. Most servants couldn't put up with the quarrelsome atmosphere for any longer than the legally binding time between their engagement and the day when they gave notice. The irate shouting, wound up to hysterical pitch, came from the lady of the house. The only daughter of an extremely rich manufacturer in Essen, and no longer in her first youth, she had been at a spa where she met the considerably younger Baron (whose nobility was suspect, while his financial situation was even more dubious), and had quickly married that handsome young ne'er-do-well, ready and able as he was to display aristocratic charm. But as soon as the honeymoon was over, the newly-wedded wife had to admit that her parents, who set great store by solid worth and ability, had been right to oppose the hasty marriage. For it quickly transpired that besides having many debts to which he had not admitted, her husband, whose attentions to her had soon worn off, showed a good deal more interest in continuing the habits of his bachelor days than in his marital duties. Although not exactly unkind by nature, since at heart he was as sunny as light-minded people usually are, but extremely lax and unscrupulous in his general outlook, that handsome would-be cavalier despised all calculations of interest and capital, considering them stingy, narrow-minded evidence of plebeian bigotry. He wanted an easy life; she wanted a well-ordered, respectable domestic existence of the bourgeois Rhineland kind, which got on his nerves. And when, in spite of her wealth, he had to haggle to lay hands on any large sum of money, and his wife, who had a turn for mathematics, even denied him his dearest wish, a racing stables of his own, he saw no more reason to involve himself any further in conjugal relations with the massive, thick-necked North German woman whose loud and domineering voice fell unpleasantly on his ears. So he put her on ice, as they say, and without any harsh gestures, but none the less unmistakably, he kept his disappointed wife at a distance. If she reproached him he would listen politely, with apparent compassion, but as soon as her sermon was over he would wave her passionate admonitions away like the smoke of his cigarette, and had no qualms about continuing to do exactly as he pleased. This smooth, almost formal amiability embittered the disappointed woman more than any opposition. And as she was completely powerless to do anything about his well-bred, never abusive and positively overpowering civility, her pent-up anger broke out violently in a different direction: she ranted and raged at the domestic staff, wildly venting on the innocent her indignation, which was fundamentally justified but in those quarters inappropriately expressed. Of course there were consequences: within two years she had been obliged to engage a new lady's maid no less than sixteen times, once after an actual physical scuffle—a considerable sum of money had to be paid in compensation to hush it up.

Only Crescenz stood unmoved, like a patient cab-horse in the rain, in the midst of this stormy tumult. She took no one's side, ignored all changes, didn't seem to notice the arrival of strangers with whom she shared the maids' bedroom and whose names, hair-colour, body-odour and behaviour were constantly different. For she herself talked to no one, didn't mind the slammed doors, the inter-rupted mealtimes, the helpless and hysterical outbursts. Indifferent to it all, she went busily from her kitchen to market, from market back to her kitchen, and what went on outside that enclosed circle did not concern her. Hard and emotionless as a flail, she dealt with day after day, and so two years in the big city passed her by without incident, never enlarging her inner world, except that the stack of blue banknotes in her little box rose an inch higher, and when she counted the notes one by one with a moistened finger at the end of the year, the magic figure of one thousand wasn't far off.

But Chance works with diamond drills, and that dangerously cunning entity Fate can often intervene from an unexpected quarter, shattering even the rockiest nature entirely. In Crescenz's case, the outward occasion was almost as ordinary as was she herself; after ten years, it pleased the state to hold a new census, and highly com-plicated forms were sent to all residential buildings to be filled in by their occupants, in detail. Distrusting the illegible handwriting and purely phonetic spelling of his domestic staff, the Baron decided to fill in the forms himself, and to this end he summoned Crescenz to his study. When he asked for her name, age and date of birth, it turned out that as a passionate huntsman and a friend of the owner of the local game preserves, he had often shot chamois in that very corner of the Alps from which Crescenz came. A guide from her native village had actually been his companion for two weeks. And when, extraordinarily, it turned out that this same guide was Crescenz's uncle, the chance discovery led on the Baron, who was in a cheerful mood, to further conversation, in the course of which another surprising fact came to light: on his visit to the area, he had eaten an excellent dish of roast venison at the very same inn where she was cook. None of this was of any importance, but the power of coincidence made it seem strange, and to Crescenz, for the first time meeting someone who knew her home here in Vienna, it appeared miraculous. She stood before him with a flushed, interested face, bobbed clumsily, felt flattered when he went on to crack some jokes, imitating the Tyrolean dialect and asking if she could yodel, and talked similar schoolboy nonsense. Finally, amused at himself, he slapped her hard behind with the palm of his hand in the friendly peasant way and dismissed her with a laugh. "Off you go then, my good Cenzi, and here's two crowns because you're from the Ziller valley."

In itself this was not a significant emotional event, to be sure. But that five minutes of conversation had an effect on the fish-like, underground currents of Crescenz's dull nature like that of a stone being dropped into a swamp: ripples form, lethargically and gradually at first, but moving sluggishly on until they slowly reach the edge of consciousness. For the first time in years, the obdurate and taciturn Crescenz had held a personal conversation with another human being, and it seemed to her a supernatural dispensation of Providence that this first person to have spoken to her in the midst of the stony maze of the city knew her own mountains, and had even once eaten roast venison that she herself had prepared. And then there was that casual slap on the behind, which in peasant language represents a kind of laconic courtship of a woman.

Although Crescenz did not make so bold as to suppose that such an elegant and distinguished gentleman had actually been expressing any intentions of that sort towards herself, the physical familiarity somehow shook her slumbering senses awake.

So that chance impetus set off movement in the underground realm within her, shifting stratum after stratum, until at last, first clumsily and then ever more clearly, a new feeling developed in her, like that sudden moment when one day a dog unexpectedly recognises one of the many two-legged figures around him as his master. From that hour on the dog follows him, greets the man whom Fate has set in authority over him by wagging his tail or barking, becomes voluntarily subservient and follows his trail obediently step by step. In just the same way, something new had entered the small circle of Crescenz's life, hitherto bounded by the five familiar ideas of money, the market, the kitchen range, church and her bed. That new element needed space, and brusquely pushed everything else forcefully aside. And with that peasant greed that will never let something it has seized out of its hands again, she drew it deep into herself and the confused, instinctive world of her dull senses. Of course it was some time before any change became visible, and those first signs were very insignificant: for instance, the particularly fanatical care she devoted to cleaning the Baron's clothes and shoes, while she still left the Baroness's to the lady's maid. Or she was often to be seen in the corridor of the apartment, eagerly making haste to take his hat and stick as soon as she heard the sound of the key in the front door. She redoubled her attention to the cooking, and even laboriously made her way to the big market hall so that she could get a joint of venison to roast specially for him. She was taking more care with her outward appearance too.

It was one or two weeks before these first shoots of new emotion emerged from her inner world, and many weeks more before a second idea was added to the first and grew, uncertainly in the beginning, but then acquiring distinct form and colour. This new feeling was complementary to the first: initially indistinct, but gradually appearing clear and plain, it was a sense of emergent hatred for the Baron's wife, the woman who could live with him, sleep with him, talk to him, yet did not feel the same devoted veneration for him as she herself did. Whether because she had perhaps—these days instinctively noticing more—witnessed one of those shameful scenes in which the master she idolized was humiliated in the most objectionable way by his irate wife, or whether it was that the inhibited North German woman's arrogant reserve was doubly obvious in contrast to his jovial familiarity—for one reason or another, at any rate, she suddenly brought a certain mulishness to bear on the unsuspecting wife, a prickly hostility expressed in a thousand little barbed remarks and spiteful actions. For instance, the Baroness always had to ring at least twice before Crescenz responded to the summons, deliberately slowly and with obvious reluctance, and her hunched shoulders always expressed resistance in principle. She accepted orders and errands wordlessly and with a glum expression, so that the Baroness never knew if she had actually understood her, but if she asked again to be on the safe side she got only a gloomy nod or a derisive "Sure I hears yer!" by way of answer. Or just before a visit to the theatre, while the Baroness was nervously scurrying around, an important key would prove to be lost, only to be unexpectedly discovered in a corner half-an-hour later. She regularly chose to forget about messages and phone calls to the Baroness: when charged with the omission she would offer, without the slightest sign of regret, only a brusque, "I fergot 'un". She never looked the Baroness in the face, perhaps for fear that she would not be able to hide her hatred.

Meanwhile the domestic differences between husband and wife led to increasingly unedifying scenes; perhaps Crescenz's unconsciously provocative surliness also had something to do with the hot temper of the Baroness, who was becoming more overwrought every week.

With her nerves unstable as a result of preserving her virginity too long, and embittered by her husband's indifference, the exasperated woman was losing control of herself. In vain did she try to soothe her agitation with bromide and veronal; the tension of her overstretched nerves showed all the more violently in arguments, she had fits of weeping and hysteria, and never received the slightest sympathy or even the appearance of kindly support from anyone at all. Finally, the doctor who had been called in recommended a two-month stay in a sanatorium, a proposal that was approved by her usually indifferent husband with such sudden concern for her health that his wife, suspicious again, at first balked at the idea. But in the end it was decided that she would take the trip, with her lady's maid to accompany her, while Crescenz was to stay behind in the spacious apartment to serve her master.

The news that her master was to be entrusted to her care alone affected Crescenz's dull senses like a sudden tonic. As if all her strength and zest for life had been shaken wildly up in a magic flask, a hidden sediment of passion now rose from the depths of her being and lent its colour to her whole conduct. The sluggish heaviness suddenly left her rigid, frozen limbs; it was as if since she had heard that electrifying news her joints were suddenly supple, and she adopted a quick, nimble gait. She ran back and forth between the rooms, up and down the stairs, when it was time to make preparations for the journey she packed all the cases, unasked, and carried them to the car herself. And then, when the Baron came back from the railway station late in the evening, and handed her his stick and coat as she eagerly came to his aid, saying with a sigh of relief, "She's on her way!" something strange happened. All at once a powerful stretching movement became visible around Crescenz's narrowed lips, although in the normal way, like all animals, she never laughed. Now her mouth twisted, became a wide horizontal line, and suddenly a grin appeared in the middle of her idiotically brightening face. It displayed such frank, animal lack of inhibition that the Baron, embarrassed and surprised by the sight, was ashamed of his inappropriate familiarity with the servant, and disappeared into his study without a word.

But that fleeting second of discomfort quickly passed over, and during the next few days the two of them, master and maid, were united in their sense of shared relief, enjoying the precious silence and independence that did them both good. The departure of the Baron's wife had lifted a lowering cloud, so to speak, from the atmosphere; the liberated husband, happily freed from the constant necessity to account for himself, came late home that very first evening, and the silent attentions of Crescenz were an agreeable contrast to his wife's only too voluble reception of him. Crescenz flung herself into her daily work again with passionate enthusiasm, rose particularly early, scoured everything until it shone, polished doorknobs and handles like a woman possessed, conjured up particularly delicious menus, and to his surprise the Baron noticed, when she first served him lunch, that the valuable china and cutlery kept in the silver cupboard except on special occasions had been taken out just for him. Not an observant man in general, he couldn't help noticing the attentive, almost affectionate care that this strange creature was taking, and kindly as he was at heart, he expressed his satisfaction freely. He praised her cooking, gave her a few friendly words, and when next morning, which happened to be his name-day, he found that she had made an elaborate cake with his initials and coat of arms on it in sugar icing, he smiled at her in high spirits. "You really are spoiling me, Cenzi! And what am I to do when—heaven forbid!—my wife comes home again?"

All the same, he kept a certain control over himself for a few days before casting off the last of his scruples. But then, feeling sure from various signs that she would keep silent, he began living the bachelor life again, making himself comfortable in his own apartment. On his fourth day as a grass widower he summoned Crescenz and told her, without further explanation, that he would like her to prepare a cold supper for two that evening and then go to bed; he would see to everything else himself. Crescenz received the order in silence. Not a glance, not the faintest look showed whether the real purport of what he said had penetrated her low forehead. But her master soon saw, with surprised amusement, how well she understood his real intentions, for when he came home from the theatre late that evening with a little music student who was studying opera, not only did he find the table beautifully laid and decorated with flowers, but the bed next to his own in the bedroom was invitingly if brazenly turned down, and his wife's silk dressing gown and slippers were laid out ready. The liberated husband instinctively smiled at the far-sighted thoughtfulness of that strange creature Crescenz. And with that he threw off the last of his inhibitions about letting the helpful soul into his confidence. He rang next morning for her to help the amorous intruder get dressed, and that finally sealed the silent agreement between them.

It was in those days, too, that Crescenz acquired her new name. The merry little music student, who was studying the part of Donna Elvira and in jest liked to elevate her lover to the role of Don Giovanni, had once said to him, laughing, "Now, do call for your Leporella!" The name amused him, just because it was so grotesque a parody when applied to the gaunt Tyrolean woman, and from now on he never called her anything but Leporella. Crescenz, who looked up in surprise the first time but was then enchanted by the pleasing vocal music of her new name, which she did not understand in the least, regarded it as a sign of distinction; whenever her high-spirited master called for her by that name her thin lips would part, exposing her brown, horse-like teeth, and like a dog wagging its tail, she submissively hurried to receive her lord and master's orders.

The name was intended as a joke, but the budding operatic diva had unintentionally hit the mark, throwing her a verbal dress that magically suited her. For like Don Giovanni's appreciative accomplice as depicted by Da Ponte, this bony old maid who had never known love took a curious pride and pleasure in her master's adventures. Was it just her satisfaction at seeing the bed of the wife she hated so much tumbled and desecrated every morning by now one, now another young body, or did a secret sense of conspiratorial pleasure make her own senses tingle? In any case, the stern, narrow-minded spinster showed a positively passionate readiness to be of service to her master in all his adventures. It was a long time since her own hard-worked body, now sexless after decades of labour, had felt any such urges, but she warmed herself comfortably, like a procuress, on the satisfaction of seeing a second young woman in the bedroom after a few days, and then a third; her share in the conspiracy and the exciting perfume of the erotic atmosphere worked like a stimulant on her dulled senses. Crescenz really did become Leporella, and was nimble, alert and ready to jump to attention; strange qualities appeared in her nature, as if forced into being by the flowing heat of her burning interest, all kinds of little tricks, touches of mischief, sharp remarks, a curiosity that made her eavesdrop and lurk in waiting. She was almost frolicking. She listened at doors, looked through keyholes, searched rooms and beds, flew upstairs and downstairs in excitement as soon as, like a huntswoman, she scented new prey; and gradually this alertness, this curious, interested sympathy reshaped the wooden shell of her old dull lethargy into some kind of living human being. To the general astonishment of the neighbours, Crescenz suddenly became sociable, she chatted to the maids in the building, cracked broad jokes with the postman, began chatting and gossiping with the women at the market stalls, and once in the evening, when the lights in the courtyard were out, the maidservants sleeping in the building in a room opposite hers heard a strange humming sound at the usually silent window: awkwardly, in a muted, rusty voice, Crescenz was singing one of those Alpine songs that herdswomen sing on the pastures at evening. The monotonous melody staggered out of her unpractised lips with difficulty, in a cracked tone, but it did come out, a strange and gripping sound. Crescenz was trying to sing again for the first time since her childhood, and there was something touching in those stumbling notes that rose with difficulty to the light out of the darkness of buried years.

The unconscious author of this change in the woman who was so devoted to him, the Baron, noticed it less than anyone, for who ever turns to look at his own shadow? He knows it is following faithfully and silently along behind his own footsteps, sometimes hurrying ahead like a wish of which he is not yet conscious, but he seldom tries to observe its shape imitating his, or to recognise himself in its distortion. The Baron noticed nothing about Crescenz except that she was always there at his service, perfectly silent, reliable and devoted to him to the point of self-abnegation. And he felt that her very silence, the distance she naturally preserved in all discreet situations, was specially beneficial; sometimes he casually gave her a few words of appreciation, as one might pat a dog, now and then he even joked with her, pinched her earlobe in kindly fashion, gave her a banknote or a theatre ticket—small things for him, taken from his waistcoat pocket without a moment's thought, but to her they were holy relics to be treasured in her little wooden box. Gradually he had become accustomed to thinking out loud in front of her, and even entrusting complex errands to her—and the greater the signs he gave of his confidence in her, the more gratefully and assiduously did she exert herself. An odd sniffing, searching, tracking instinct gradually appeared in her as she tried to spy out his wishes and even anticipate them; her whole life, all she did and all she wished for, seemed to pass from her own body into his; she saw everything with his eyes, listened hard to guess what he was feeling, and with almost depraved enthusiasm shared his enjoyment of all his pleasures and conquests. She beamed when a new young woman crossed the threshold, and looked downcast, as if her expectations were disappointed, if he came home at night without such amorous company—her once sluggish mind was now working as quickly and restlessly as only her hands used to, and a new, vigilant light shone in her eyes. A human being had awoken in the tired, worn-out work-horse—a human being who was reserved and sombre but cunning and dangerous, thinking and then acting on her thoughts, restless and intriguing.

Once when the Baron came home unexpectedly early, he stopped in the corridor in surprise: wasn't that giggling and laughter behind the usually silent kitchen door? And then Leporella appeared in the doorway, rubbing her hands on her apron, bold and awkward at the same time. "'Scuse us, sir," she said, eyes on the floor, "it's the pastry-cook's daughter's here, a pretty girl she be, she'd like to meet sir ever so!" The Baron looked up in surprise, not sure whether he should be angry at such outrageous familiarity or amused at her readiness to procure for him. Finally his male curiosity won the day. "Well, let her have a look at me!"

The girl, a fresh, blond sixteen-year-old, whom Leporella had gradually enticed with flattering talk, appeared, blushing, and with an embarrassed giggle as the maid firmly pushed her through the doorway, and twirled clumsily in front of the elegant gentleman, whom she had indeed often watched with half-childlike admiration from the pâtisserie opposite. The Baron thought her pretty, and invited her to take a cup of tea in his study. Uncertain whether she ought to accept, the girl turned to look for Crescenz, but she had already disappeared into the kitchen with conspicuous haste, so there was nothing the girl could do, having been lured into this adventure, but accept the dangerous invitation, flushed and excited with curiosity.

But nature cannot leap too far: though the pressure of a distorted, confused passion might have aroused a certain mental agility in her dull and angular nature, Crescenz's newly acquired and limited powers of thought were not enough to overcome the next obstacle. In that, they were still related to an animal's short-term instincts. Immured in her obsession to serve the master she loved with doglike devotion in every way, Crescenz entirely forgot his absent wife. Her awakening was all the more terrible: it was like thunder coming out of a clear sky when one morning the Baron came in with a letter in his hand, looking annoyed, and brusquely told her to set everything in the apartment to rights, because his wife was coming home from the sanatorium next day. Crescenz stood there pale-faced, her mouth open with the shock: the news had struck her like a knife. She just stared and stared, as if she didn't understand. And so immeasurably and alarmingly did this thunderclap distort her face that the Baron thought he should calm her a little with a light-hearted comment. "It looks to me as if you're not best pleased either, Cenzi, but there's nothing anyone can do about it."

Soon, however, something began to move in her rigid face again. It worked its way up from deep down in her, as if coming out of her guts, a mighty convulsion that gradually brought dark red colour to the cheeks that had been white just now. Very slowly, forced out with harsh thrusts like heartbeats, words emerged: her throat was trembling under the pressure of the effort. And at last they were there and came dully through her gritted teeth. "Could be—could be summat as 'un could do…"

It had come out harsh as the firing of a deadly shot. And so evil, so darkly determined did that distorted face look after she had vented her feelings with such violence that the Baron instinctively started, flinching back in surprise. But Crescenz had already turned away again, and was beginning to scour a copper bowl with such convulsive zeal that she looked as if she meant to break her fingers on it.

With the home-coming of the Baron's wife, stormy winds filled the apartment again, slamming doors, blowing angrily through the rooms, sweeping away the comfortable, warm atmosphere like a cold draught. Whether the deceived wife had found out, from informers among the neighbours or anonymous letters, about the despicable way in which her husband had abused the freedom of the household, or whether the nervous and obvious ill temper that he did not scruple to show on her return had upset her, no one could tell—but in any case, two months in the sanatorium seemed to have done her strained nerves no good, for weeping fits now alternated with occasional threats and hysterical scenes. Relations between the couple became more insufferable every day. For a few weeks the Baron manfully defied the storm of her reproaches with the civility he had always preserved before, and replied evasively and indirectly when she threatened him with divorce or letters to her parents. But this cool, loveless indifference of his in itself drove the friendless woman, surrounded as she was by secret hostility, further and further into her nervous agitation.

Crescenz had armoured herself entirely in her old silence. But that silence had turned aggressive and dangerous. On her mistress's arrival she defiantly stayed in the kitchen, and when she was finally summoned she avoided wishing the Baroness well on her return. Shoulders obdurately braced, she stood there like a block of wood and replied with such surliness to all questions that her impatient mistress soon turned away from her. With one glance, however, Crescenz darted all her pent-up hatred at the unsuspecting woman's back. Her greedy emotions felt wrongfully robbed by the Baroness's return; from the delights of the service she had so passionately relished, she was thrust back into the kitchen and the range, deprived of her intimate name of Leporella. For the Baron carefully avoided showing any liking for Crescenz in front of his wife. Sometimes, however, when he was exhausted by the unendurable scenes, and feeling in need of comfort and wanted to vent his feelings, he would slip into the kitchen and sit down on one of the hard wooden chairs, just so that he could groan, "I can't stand this any longer!"

These moments, when the master she idolized sought refuge with her from his excessive tension, were the happiest of Leporella's life. She never ventured to reply or say a word of consolation; silent and lost in thought, she just sat there, and only looked up sometimes with a sympathetic, receptive and tormented glance at her god, thus humiliated. Her silent sympathy did him good. But once he had left the kitchen, an angry fold would return to her brow, and her heavy hands expressed her anger by battering defenceless pieces of meat or savagely scouring dishes and cutlery.

At last the ominous atmosphere in the apartment since the wife's return discharged itself stormily; during one of the couple's intemperate scenes the Baron finally lost patience, abruptly abandoned the meekly indifferent schoolboy attitude he had adopted, and slammed the door behind him. "I've had enough of this," he shouted so angrily that all the windows in the apartment shook. And still in a furious temper, red in the face, he went out to the kitchen, where Crescenz was quivering like a bent bow. "Pack my case at once and find my sporting gun. I'm going hunting for a week. Even the Devil couldn't endure this hell any more. There has to be an end to it."

Crescenz looked at him happily: like this, he was master in his own house again! And a hoarse laugh emerged from her throat. "Sir be right, there have to be an end to 'un." And twitching with eager zeal, racing from room to room, she hastily snatched everything he would need from cupboards and tables, every nerve of the heavily built creature straining with tension and avidity. She carried the case and the gun out to the car herself. But when he was seeking words to thank her for her eager help, his eyes looked away from her in alarm. For that spiteful smile, the one that always alarmed him, had returned to her narrowed lips. When he saw her seeming to lie in ambush like that, he was instinctively reminded of the low crouching movement of an animal gathering itself to spring. But then she retreated into herself again, and just whispered hoarsely, with almost insulting familiarity, "I hopes sir has a good journey, I'll do 'un all."

Three days later the Baron was called back from his hunting trip by an urgent telegram. His cousin was waiting for him at the railway station. At his very first glance the anxious man knew that something terrible must have happened, for his cousin looked nervous and was fidgeting. After a few words solicitously designed to prepare him, he discovered what it was: his wife had been found dead in her bed that morning, with the whole room full of gas. Unfortunately a careless mistake was out of the question, said his cousin, because now, in May, the gas stove had not been lit for a long time, and his wife's suicidal frame of mind was also obvious from the fact that the unhappy woman had taken some veronal the evening before. In addition there was the statement made by the cook Crescenz, who had been alone at home that evening, and had heard her unfortunate mistress going into the room just outside the bedroom in the night, presumably on purpose to switch on the gas supply, which had been carefully turned off. On hearing this, the police doctor who had also been called in agreed that an accident was out of the question, and recorded death by suicide.

The Baron began to tremble. When his cousin mentioned the statement that Crescenz had made he suddenly felt the blood in his hands turn cold. An unpleasant, a dreadful idea rose in his mind like nausea. But he forcibly suppressed this seething, agonising sensation, and meekly let his cousin take him home. The body had already been removed; family members were waiting in the drawing room with gloomy and hostile expressions. Their condolences were cold as a knife. With a certain accusatory emphasis, they said they thought they should mention that, unfortunately, it had been impossible to hush up the 'scandal', because the maid had rushed out on the stairs that morning screaming, "The mistress has killed herself!" And they had decided on a quiet funeral—yet again that sharp, chilly blade was turned against him—because, deplorably, all kinds of rumours had aroused the curiosity of society to an unwelcome degree. The downcast Baron listened in confusion, and once instinctively raised his eyes to the closed bedroom door, but then cravenly looked away again. He wanted to think something out to the end, an unwelcome idea that kept surfacing in his mind, but all this empty, malicious talk bewildered him. The black-clad relations stood around talking for another half-hour, and then one by one they took their leave. He was left alone in the empty, dimly lit room, trembling as if he had suffered a heavy blow, with an aching head and weariness in his joints.

Then there came a knock at the door. "Come in," he said, rousing himself with a start. And along came a hesitant step, a dragging, stealthy step that he knew well. Suddenly, horror overcame him; he felt as if his cervical vertebrae were firmly screwed in place, while at the same time the skin from his temples to his knees was rippling with icy shudders. He wanted to turn, but his muscles failed him. So he stood there in the middle of the room, trembling and making no sound, his hands dropping by his sides and rigid as stone, and he felt very clearly how cowardly this guilt-ridden attitude must look. But it was useless for him to exert all his strength: his muscles just would not obey him. The voice behind him said, "I just wants ter ask, sir, will sir eat at home or out?" The Baron shivered ever more violently, and now the icy cold made its way right into his breast. He tried three times before he finally managed to get out the words, "No, I don't want anything to eat." Then the footsteps dragged themselves away, and still he didn't have the courage to turn. And suddenly the rigidity left him: he was shaking all over with spasms, or nausea. He suddenly flung himself at the door and turned the key in it, so that those dreadful footsteps following him like a ghost couldn't get at him. Then he dropped into a chair to force down an idea that he didn't want to entertain, although it kept creeping back into his mind, as cold and slimy as a snail. And this obsessive idea, though he hated the thought of coming close to it, filled all his emotions: it was inescapable, slimy, horrible, and it stayed with him all that sleepless night and during the hours that followed, even when, black-clad and silent, he stood at the head of the coffin during the funeral.

On the day after the funeral the Baron left the city in a hurry. All the faces he saw were too unendurable now: in the midst of their sympathy they had—or was he only imagining it?—a curiously observant, a painfully inquisitorial look. And even inanimate objects spoke to him accusingly, with hostility: every piece of furniture in the apartment, but more particularly in the bedroom where the sweetish smell of gas still seemed to cling to everything, turned him away if he so much as automatically opened the doors. But the really unbearable nightmare of his sleeping and waking hours was the cold, unconcerned indifference of his former accomplice, who went about the empty apartment as if nothing at all had happened. Since that moment at the station when his cousin mentioned her name, he had trembled at the thought of any meeting with her. As soon as he heard her footsteps a nervous, hasty restlessness took hold of him; he couldn't look at that dragging, indifferent gait any more, couldn't bear her cold, silent composure. Revulsion overcame him when he even thought of her—her croaking voice, her greasy hair, her dull, animal, merciless absence of feeling, and part of his anger was anger against himself because he lacked the power to break the bond between them by force, like a piece of string, although it was almost throttling him. So he saw only one way out—flight. He packed his case in secret without a word to her, leaving only a hasty note behind to say that he had gone to visit friends in Carinthia.

The Baron stayed away all summer. Returning once during that time, when he was called back to Vienna on urgent business concerning his late wife's estate, he preferred to come quietly, stay in a hotel, and send no word to that bird of ill omen waiting for him at home. Crescenz never learned of his presence because she spoke to no one. With nothing to do, dark-faced, she sat in the kitchen all day, went to church twice instead of once a week as before, received instructions and money to settle bills from the Baron's lawyer, but she heard nothing from the Baron himself. He did not write and he sent her no messages. She sat there silently, waiting: her face became harder and thinner, her movements were wooden again, and so she spent many weeks, waiting and waiting in a mysterious state of rigidity.

In autumn, however, urgent business no longer allowed the Baron to extend his stay in the country, and he had to return to his apartment. At the doorway of the building he stopped, hesitating. Two months in the company of close friends had almost made him forget a good deal of it—but now that he was about to confront his nightmare again in physical form, the person who perhaps was his accomplice, he felt exactly the same nauseating spasm as before. It made him retch. With every step he took as he went more and more slowly up the stairs, that invisible hand crept up his throat and tightened its grip. In the end he had to make a mighty effort to summon up all his will-power and force his stiff fingers to turn the key in the lock.

Surprised, Crescenz came out of the kitchen as soon as she heard the click of the key turning. When she saw him, she stood there looking pale for a moment, and then, as if ducking out of sight, bent to pick up the travelling bag he had put down. But she said not a word of greeting, and he said nothing either. In silence she carried the bag to his room; he followed in silence too. He waited in silence, looking out of the window, until she had left the room. Then he hastily turned the key in the door.

That was their first meeting after several months.

Crescenz waited. And so did the Baron, to see if that dreadful spasm of horror at the sight of her would pass off. It did not. Even before he saw her, the mere sound of her footsteps in the corridor outside his room sent the sense of discomfort fluttering up in him. He did not touch his breakfast, he was quick to leave the house every morning without a word to her, and he stayed out until late at night merely to avoid her presence. He delivered the two or three instructions that he had to give her with his face averted. It choked him to breathe the air of the same room as this spectral creature.

Meanwhile, Crescenz sat silently on her wooden stool all day. She was not cooking anything for herself. She couldn't stomach food, she avoided all human company, she just sat with timidity in her eyes, waiting for the first whistle from her master, like a beaten dog which knows that it has done something bad. Her dull mind did not understand exactly what had happened, only that her lord and master was avoiding her and didn't want her any more. That was all that reached her, and it made a powerful impression.

On the third day after the Baron's return the doorbell rang. A composed, grey-haired man with a clean-shaven face was standing there with a suitcase in his hand. Crescenz was about to send him away, but the intruder insisted that he was the new manservant here, his master had asked him to arrive at ten, and she was to announce him. Crescenz went white as a sheet; she stood there for a moment with her stiff fingers spread wide in mid-air. Then her hand fell like a bird that has been shot. "Thassa way," she abruptly told the surprised man, turned to the kitchen and slammed the door behind her.

The manservant stayed. From that day on her master no longer had to say a word to her; all messages were relayed by the calm, elderly servant. She did not know what was going on in the apartment; it all flowed over her like a cold wave flowing over a stone.

This oppressive state of affairs lasted for two weeks, draining Crescenz like an illness. Her face was thin and haggard, the hair was suddenly going grey at her temples. Her movements froze entirely. She spent almost all the time sitting on her wooden stool, like a block of wood herself, staring blankly at the empty window, and if she did work she worked furiously, like someone in a violent outbreak of rage.

After those two weeks the manservant went to his master's room, and from his tactful air of biding his time the Baron realised that there was something he particularly wanted to say. The man had already complained of the sullen manner of that 'Tyrolean clod', as he contemptuously called her, and had suggested dismissing her. But feeling in some way painfully embarrassed, the Baron had initially pretended to ignore his proposal. Although at the time the servant had bowed and left the room, this time he stuck doggedly to his opinion, and with a strange, almost awkward expression he finally stammered that he hoped sir would not think he was being ridiculous, but he couldn't… no, he couldn't put it any other way… he was *afraid* of her. That surly, withdrawn creature was unbearable, he didn't think the Baron knew what a dangerous person he had in his home.

The Baron instinctively started at this warning. What did the man mean, he asked, what was he trying to say? The manservant did soften his statement by saying that he couldn't point to anything certain, he just had a feeling that the woman was like a rabid animal… she could easily do someone harm. Yesterday he turned to give her an order, and he had unexpectedly seen a look in her eyes—well, there wasn't much you could say about a look, but it had been as if she was about to spring at his throat. And since then he had been afraid of her—even afraid to touch the food she cooked. "You wouldn't have any idea, sir," he concluded, "what a dangerous person that is. She don't speak, she don't say much, but I think she's capable of murder." Startled, the Baron cast the man a quick glance. Had he heard anything definite? Had someone passed any suspicion on to him? He felt his fingers begin to shake, and hastily put his cigar down so that the trembling of his hands would not show. But the elderly man's face was entirely unsuspecting—no, he couldn't know anything. The Baron hesitated. Then he suddenly pulled himself together, knowing what he himself wanted to do, and made up his mind. "Well, wait a little while, but if she's so unfriendly to you again then I'll just give her notice."

The manservant bowed, and the Baron sat back in relief. Every thought of that mysteriously dangerous creature darkened the day for him. It would be best to do it while he was away, he thought, at Christmas, perhaps—the mere idea of the liberation he hoped for did him good. Yes, that will be best, he told himself once more, at Christmas when I'm away.

But the very next day, as soon as he had gone to his study after dinner, there was a knock at the door. Unthinkingly looking up from his newspaper, he murmured, "Come in." And then he heard that dreaded, hard tread that was always in his dreams. He started up: like a death's head, pale and white as chalk, he saw the angular face quivering above the thin black figure. A little pity mingled with his horror when he saw how the anxious footsteps of the creature, crushed as she looked, humbly stopped short at the edge of the carpet. And to hide his bemused state, he tried to sound carefree. "Well, what is it then, Crescenz?" he asked. But it didn't come out warm and jovial, as he had intended; against his own will the question sounded hostile and unpleasant.

Crescenz did not move. She stared at the carpet. At last, as you might push a hard object away with your foot, she managed to get the words out. "That servant, sir, he come ter see 'un. He say sir be going to fire 'un."

The Baron, painfully embarrassed, rose to his feet. He had not expected it to come so soon. He began to say, stammering, that he was sure it hadn't been meant like that, she ought to try to get on with his other servant, adding whatever other unthinking remarks came to his lips.

But Crescenz stayed put, her gaze boring into the carpet, her shoulders hunched. Bitter and dogged, she kept her head bowed like an ox, letting all his kindly remarks pass her by, waiting for just one word that did not come. And when at last he fell silent, exhausted and rather repelled by the contemptible role he was obliged to adopt, trying to ingratiate himself with a servant, she remained obstinate and mute. Then at last she got out something else. "I only wants ter know if sir himself tells Anton ter fire 'un."

She somehow got it out—harshly, reluctantly, violently. And already on edge as he was, he felt it like a blow. Was that a threat? Was she challenging him? All at once all his cowardice was gone, and all his pity. The hatred and disgust that had been dammed up in him for weeks came together with his ardent wish to make an end of it at last. And suddenly changing his tone entirely, and adopting the cool objectivity that he had learned at work in the ministry, he confirmed, as if it were of no importance, that yes, that was indeed so, he had in fact given the manservant a free hand to organise the household just as he liked. He personally wished her well, and would try to persuade Anton to change his mind about dismissing her. But if she still insisted on maintaining hostilities with the manservant, well, he would just have to dispense with her services.

And summoning up all his will-power, determined not to be deterred by any sly hint or insinuating remark, he turned his glance as he spoke these last words on the woman he assumed to be threatening him and looked straight at her.

But the eyes that Crescenz now raised timidly from the floor were those of a wounded animal, seeing the pack just about to break out of the bushes ahead of her. "Th… thank 'ee, sir," she got out, very faintly. "I be goin'… I won't trouble sir no more…"

And slowly, without turning, she dragged herself out of the door with her bowed shoulders and stiff, wooden footsteps.

That evening, when the Baron came back from the opera and reached for the letters that had arrived on his desk, he saw something strange and rectangular there. As the light flared up, he made out a wooden casket with rustic carving. It was not locked: inside, neatly arranged, lay all the little things that he had ever given Crescenz: a few cards from his hunting expeditions, two theatre tickets, a silver ring, the entire heaped rectangle of her banknotes, and there was also a snapshot taken twenty years ago in the Tyrol in which her eyes, obviously taken unawares by the flashlight, stared out with the same stricken, beaten look as they had a few hours ago when she left his study.

At something of a loss, the Baron pushed the casket aside and went out to ask the manservant what these things of Crescenz's were doing on his desk. The servant immediately offered to bring his enemy in to account for herself. But Crescenz was not to be found in the kitchen or anywhere else in the apartment. And only the next day, when the police reported the suicidal fall of a woman about forty years old from the bridge over the Danube Canal, did the two men know the answer to the question of where Leporella had gone.

DID HE DO IT?

P ERSONALLY I'M AS GOOD AS CERTAIN that he was the murderer. But I don't have the final, incontrovertible proof. "Betsy," my husband always tells me, "you're a clever woman, a quick observer, and you have a sharp eye, but you let your temperament lead you astray, and then you make up your mind too hastily." Well, my husband has known me for thirty-two years, and perhaps, indeed probably, he's right to warn me against forming a judgement in too much of a hurry. So as there is no conclusive evidence, I have to make myself suppress my suspicions, especially in front of other people. But whenever I meet him, whenever he comes over to me in that forthright, friendly way of his, my heart misses a beat. And a little voice inside me says: he and no one else was the murderer.

So I am going to try reconstructing the entire course of events again, just for my own satisfaction.

About six years ago my husband had come to the end of his term of service as a distinguished government official in the colonies, and we decided to retire to some quiet place in the English countryside, to spend the rest of our days, already approaching their evening, with such pleasures of life as flowers and books. Our choice was a small village in the country near Bath. A narrow, slowly flowing waterway, the Kennet and Avon Canal, winds its way from that ancient and venerable city, passing under many bridges, towards the valley of Limpley Stoke, which is always green. The canal was built with much skill and at great expense over a century ago, to carry coal from Cardiff to London, and has many wooden locks and lock-keepers' stations along its length. Horses moving at a ponderous

271

trot on the narrow towpaths to right and left of the canal used to pull the broad, black barges along the wide waterway at a leisurely pace. It was planned and built on a generous scale, and was a good means of transport for an age when time still did not mean much. But then came the railway to bring the black freight to the capital city far more cheaply and easily. Canal traffic ground to a halt, the canal fell into decay and dilapidation, but the very fact that it is entirely deserted and serves no useful purpose makes it a romantic, enchanted place today. Waterweed grows so densely from the bottom of the sluggish, black water that the surface has a shimmer of dark green, like malachite; pale water lilies sway on the smooth surface of the canal, which reflects the flower-grown banks, the bridges and the clouds with photographic accuracy. There is barely a ripple moving on the drowsy waterway. Now and then, half sunk in the water and already overgrown with plants, a broken old boat by the bank recalls the canal's busy past, of which even the visitors who come to take the waters in Bath hardly know anything, and when we two elderly folk walked on the level towpath where the horses used to pull barges laboriously along by ropes in the old days, we would meet no one for hours on end except, perhaps, pairs of lovers meeting in secret to protect, by coming to this remote place, their youthful happiness from neighbours' gossip, before it was officially declared by their engagement or marriage.

We were delighted by the quiet, romantic waterway set among rolling hills. We bought a plot of land in the middle of nowhere, just where the slope from Bathampton falls gently to the waterside as a beautiful, lush meadow. At the top of the rise we built a little country cottage, with a pleasant garden path leading past fruit trees, vegetable beds and flower beds and on down to the canal, so that when we sat out of doors on our little garden terrace beside the water we could see the meadow, the house and the garden reflected in the canal. The house was more peaceful and comfortable than anywhere I had ever dreamt of living, and my only complaint was that it was rather lonely, since we had no neighbours.

"Oh, they'll soon come when they see what a pretty place we've found to live in," said my husband, cheering me.

And sure enough; our little peach trees and plum trees had hardly established themselves in the garden before, one day, signs of another building going up next to our house suddenly appeared. First came busy estate agents, then surveyors, and after them builders and carpenters. Within a dozen or so weeks a little cottage with a red-tiled roof was nestling beside ours. Finally a removal van full of furniture arrived. We heard constant banging and hammering in the formerly quiet air, but we had not yet set eyes on our new neighbours.

One morning there was a knock at our door. A pretty, slender woman with clever, friendly eyes, not much more than twenty-eight or twenty-nine, introduced herself as our neighbour and asked if we could lend her a saw; the workmen had forgotten to bring one. We fell into conversation. She told us that her husband worked in a bank in Bristol, but for a long time they had both wanted to live somewhere more remote, outside the city, and as they were walking along the canal one Sunday they had fallen in love with the look of our house. Of course it would mean a journey of an hour each way for her husband from home to work and back, but he would be sure to find pleasant travelling companions and would easily get used to it. We returned her call next day. She was still on her own in the house, and told us cheerfully that her husband wouldn't be joining her until all the work was finished. She really couldn't do with having him underfoot until then, she said, and after all, there was no hurry. I don't know why, but I didn't quite like the casual way she spoke of her husband's absence, almost as if she were pleased not to have him there. When we were sitting over our meal alone at home, I commented that she didn't appear to be very fond of him.

My husband told me I shouldn't keep jumping to hasty conclusions; he had thought her a very agreeable young woman, intelligent and pleasant, and he hoped her husband would be the same.

And it wasn't long before we met him. As we were taking our usual evening walk one Saturday, when we had just left our house, we heard footsteps behind us, brisk and heavy, and when we turned we saw a large, cheerful-looking man catching up with us, offering us a large, red, freckled hand. He was our new neighbour, he said, he'd heard how kind we had been to his wife. Of course he ought not to be greeting us like this in his shirtsleeves, without paying a formal visit first. But his wife had told him so many nice things about us that he really couldn't wait a minute longer to thank us. So here he was, John Charleston Limpley by name, and wasn't it a famous thing—they'd already called the valley Limpley in his honour long before he himself could ever guess that he'd be looking for a house here some day? Yes, here he was, he said, and here he hoped to stay as long as the good Lord let him live. He liked this place better than anywhere else in the world, and he would promise us here and now, hand on his heart, to be a good neighbour.

He talked so fast and cheerfully, with such a flow of words, that you hardly had a chance to get a word in. So I at least had plenty of time to scrutinise him thoroughly. Limpley was a powerful figure of a man, at least six foot tall, with broad, square shoulders that would have graced a navvy, but he seemed to have a good-natured, childlike disposition, as giants so often do. His narrowed, slightly watery eyes twinkled confidently at you from between their reddish lids. As he talked and laughed, he kept showing his perfect white teeth. He didn't know quite what to do with his big, heavy hands, and had some difficulty in keeping them still. You felt that he would have liked to clap you on the shoulder in comradely fashion with those hands, and as if to work off some of his strength he at least cracked the joints of his fingers now and then.

Could he, he asked, join us on our walk, in his shirtsleeves just as he was? When we said yes, he walked along with us talking nineteen to the dozen. He was of Scottish descent on his mother's side, he told us, but he had grown up in Canada. Now and then he pointed to a fine tree or an attractive slope; how beautiful, he said, how incomparably beautiful that was! He talked, he laughed, he expressed enthusiasm for everything almost without stopping. An invigorating current of strength and cheerfulness emanated from this large, healthy, vital man, infectiously carrying us away with it. When we finally parted, my husband and I both felt pleased with the warmth of his personality. "It's a long time since I met such a hearty, full-blooded fellow," said my husband who, as I have already indicated, is usually rather cautious and withdrawn in assessing character.

But it wasn't long before our first pleasure in finding such an agreeable new neighbour began to diminish considerably. There could not be the least objection to Limpley as a human being. He was good-natured to a fault, he was interested in others, and so anxious to be obliging that you were always having to decline his helpful offers. In addition he was a thoroughly decent man, modest, open and by no means stupid. But after a while it became difficult to put up with his effusive, noisy way of being permanently happy. His watery eyes were always beaming with contentment about anything and everything. All that he owned, all that he encountered was delightful, wonderful; his wife was the best woman in the world, his roses the finest roses, his pipe the best pipe ever seen, and he smoked the best tobacco in it. He could spend a full quarter-of-an-hour trying to convince my husband that a pipe ought to be filled just so, in exactly the way he filled his own, and that while his tobacco was a penny cheaper than more expensive brands it was even better. Always bubbling over as he was with excessive enthusiasm about the most unimportant, natural and indifferent of things, he evidently had an urge to expound the reasons for falling into such banal raptures at length. The noisy engine running inside him was never switched off. Limpley couldn't work in his garden without singing at the top of his voice, couldn't talk without laughing uproariously and gesticulating, couldn't read the paper without jumping up when he came upon a news item that aroused his interest and running round to tell us about it. His huge, freckled hands were always assertive, like his big heart. It wasn't just that he patted every horse and every dog he met; my husband had to put up with many a comradely and uninhibited Canadian slap on the knee when they sat comfortably talking together. Because his own warm, full heart, which constantly overflowed with emotion, took an interest in everything, he assumed that it was only natural for everyone else to take a similar interest, and you had to resort to all kinds of little tricks to ward off his insistent kindness. He respected no one's hours of rest or even sleep, because bursting as he was with health and strength he simply could not imagine anyone else ever feeling tired or downcast. You found yourself secretly wishing he would take a daily dose of bromide to lower his magnificent but near-intolerable vitality to a more normal level. Several times, when Limpley had spent an hour sitting with us—or rather not sitting, but leaping up and down and striding around—I caught my husband instinctively opening the window, as if the presence of that dynamic and somehow barbaric man had overheated the room. While you were with him, looking into his bright, kindly eyes—and they were indeed always brimming over with kindness—you couldn't dislike him. It was only later that you felt you were worn out and wished him at the Devil. Before we knew Limpley, we old folk had never guessed that such admirable qualities as kindness, goodness of heart, frankness and warmth of feeling could drive us to distraction in their obtrusive superfluity.

I now also understood what I had found incomprehensible at first, that it by no means showed lack of affection on his wife's part when she accepted his absence with such cheerful equanimity. For she was the real victim of his extravagant good humour. Of course he loved her passionately, just as he passionately loved everything that was his. It was touching to see him treat her so tenderly and with such care; she had only to cough once and he was off in search of a coat for her, or poking the fire to fan the flames, and if she went on an expedition to Bath he overwhelmed her with good advice as if she had to survive a dangerous journey. I never heard an unkind word pass between the two of them; on the contrary, he loved to sing her praises to the point where it became quite embarrassing. Even in front of us, he couldn't refrain from caressing her and stroking her hair, and above all enumerating her many beauties and virtues. "Have you noticed what pretty little fingernails my Ellen has?" he would suddenly ask, and in spite of her bashful protest he made her show us her hands. Then I was expected to admire the way she arranged her hair, and of course we had to taste every batch of jam she made, since in his opinion it was infinitely better than anything the most famous jam manufacturers of England could produce. Ellen, a quiet, modest woman, always sat with her eyes cast down on these embarrassing occasions, looking uncomfortable. She seemed to have given up defending herself against her husband's boisterous behaviour. She let him talk and tell stories and laugh, putting in only an occasional weary, "Oh, really?" or, "Fancy that."

"She doesn't have an easy life," commented my husband one day when we were going home. "But one can't really hold it against him. He's a good soul at heart, and she may well be happy with him."

"I'm not so sure about the happiness," I said rather sharply. "If you ask me, all that ostentatious happiness is too much to take—fancy making such a show of his feelings! I'd go mad living with so much excessive emotion. Don't you see that he's making his wife very *un*happy with all that effervescence and positively murderous vitality?"

"Oh, you're always exaggerating," said my husband, and I suppose he was right, really. Limpley's wife was by no means unhappy, or rather she wasn't even that any more. By now she was probably incapable of any pronounced feeling of her own; she was simply numbed and exhausted by Limpley's vast exuberance. When he went to his office in the morning, and his last cheery 'Goodbye' died away at the garden gate, I noticed that the first thing she did was to sit down or lie down for a little while without doing anything, just to enjoy the quiet atmosphere all around her. And there would be something slightly weary in her movements all day. It wasn't easy to get into conversation with her, for she had almost forgotten how to speak for herself in their eight years of marriage. Once she told me how they had met. She had been living with her parents in the country, he had strolled by on an outing, and in his wild way he had swept her off her feet; they were engaged and then married before she really knew what he was like or even what his profession was. A quiet, pleasant woman, she never said a word, not a syllable to suggest that she wasn't happy, and yet as a woman myself I sensed where the real crux of that marriage lay. In the first year they had taken it for granted that they would have a baby, and it was the same in the second and third years of their marriage. Then after six or seven years they had given up hope, and now her days were too empty, while her evenings were too full of his boisterous high spirits. It would be a good idea, I thought to myself, if she were to adopt a child, or take to some kind of sporting activity, or find a job. All that sitting around was bound to lead to melancholy, and melancholy in turn to a kind of hatred for his provoking cheerfulness, which was certainly likely to exhaust any normal person. She ought to have someone, anyone with her, or the tension would be too strong.

As chance would have it, I had owed an old friend of my youth who lived in Bath a visit for weeks. We had a comfortable chat, and then she suddenly remembered that she wanted to show me something charming, and took me out into the yard. At first all I could see in the dim light of a shed was a group of small creatures of some kind tumbling about in the straw, crawling over each other and mock-fighting. They were four bulldog puppies of six or seven weeks old, stumbling about on their big paws, now and then trying to utter a little squeal of a bark. They were indeed charming as they staggered out of the basket where their mother lay, looking massive and suspicious. I picked one of them up by his profuse white coat. The puppy was brown and white, and with his pretty snub nose he did credit to his distinguished pedigree, as his mistress explained to me. I couldn't refrain from playing with him, teasing him and getting him excited so that he snapped clumsily at my fingers. My friend asked if I would like to take him home with me; she loved the puppies very much, she said, and she was ready to give them away if she could be sure they were going to good homes where they would be well cared for. I hesitated, because I knew that when my husband lost his beloved spaniel he had sworn never to let another dog into his heart again. But then it occurred to me that this charming little puppy might be just the thing for Mrs Limpley, and I promised my friend to let her know next day. That evening I put my idea to the Limpleys. Mrs Limpley was silent; she seldom expressed an opinion of her own. However, Limpley himself agreed with his usual enthusiasm. Yes, yes, he said, that was all that had been missing from their lives! A house wasn't really a home without a dog. Impetuous as he was, he tried persuading me to go to Bath with him that very night, rouse my friend and collect the puppy. But when I turned down this fanciful idea he had to wait, and not until the next day did the bulldog puppy arrive at their house in a little basket, yapping and scared by the unexpected journey.

The outcome was not quite what we had expected. I had meant to provide the quiet woman who spent her days alone in an empty house with a companion to share it. However, it was Limpley himself who turned the full force of his inexhaustible need to show affection on the dog. His delight in the comical little creature was boundless, and as always excessive and slightly ridiculous. Of course Ponto, as he called the puppy, I don't know why, was the best-looking, cleverest dog on earth, and Limpley discovered new virtues and talents in him every day, indeed every hour. He spent lavishly on the best equipment for his four-footed friend, on grooming tools, leashes, baskets, a muzzle, food bowls, toys, balls and bones. Limpley studied all the articles and advertisements in the newspapers offering information on the care and nutrition of dogs, and took out a subscription to a dog magazine with a view to acquiring expert knowledge. The large dog industry that makes its money exclusively from such enthusiastic dog-lovers found a new and assiduous customer in him. The least little thing was a reason for a visit to the vet. It would take volumes to describe all the foolish excesses arising in unbroken succession from this new passion of his. We often heard loud barking from the house next door, not from the dog but from his master as he lay flat on the floor, trying to engage his pet in dialogue that no one else could understand by imitating dog language. He paid more attention to the spoilt animal's care than to his own, earnestly following all the dietary advice of dog experts. Ponto ate better than Limpley and his wife, and once, when there was something in the newspaper about typhoid—in a completely different part of the country—the animal was given only bottled mineral water to drink. If a disrespectful flea ventured to come near the sacrosanct puppy and get him scratching or biting in an undignified manner, the agitated Limpley would take the wretched business of flea-hunting upon himself. You would see him in his shirtsleeves, bent over a bucket of water and disinfectant, getting to work with brush and comb until the last unwanted guest had been disposed of. No trouble was too much for him to take, nothing was beneath his dignity, and no prince of the realm could have been more affectionately and carefully looked after than Ponto the puppy. The only good thing to come of all this foolishness was that as a result of Limpley's emotional fixation on his new object of affection, his wife and we were spared a considerable amount of his exuberance; he would spend hours walking the dog and talking to him, although that did not seem to deter the thick-skinned little creature from snuffling around as he liked, and Mrs Limpley watched, smiling and without the slightest jealousy, as her husband carried out a daily ritual at the altar of his four-footed idol. All he withdrew from her in the way of affection was the irritating excess of it, for he still lavished tenderness on her in full measure. We could not help noticing that the new pet in the house had perhaps made their marriage happier than before.

Meanwhile Ponto was growing week by week. The thick puppy folds of his skin filled out with firm, muscular flesh, he grew into a strong animal with a broad chest, strong jaws, and muscular hindquarters that were kept well brushed. He was naturally good-tempered, but he became less pleasant company when he realised that his was the dominant position in the household, and thanks to that he began behaving with lordly arrogance. It had not taken the clever, observant animal long to work out that his master, or rather his slave, would forgive him any kind of naughtiness. First it was just disobedience, but he soon began behaving tyrannically, refusing on principle to do anything that might make him seem subservient. Worst of all, he would allow no one in the house any privacy. Nothing could be done without his presence and, in effect, his express permission. Whenever visitors called he would fling himself imperiously against the door, well knowing that the dutiful Limpley would make haste to open it for him, and then Ponto would jump up proudly into an armchair, not deigning to honour the visitors with so much as a glance. He was showing them that he was the real master of the house, and all honour and veneration were owed to him. Of course no other dog was allowed even to approach the garden fence, and certain people to whom he had taken a dislike, expressed by growling at them, were obliged to put down the post

281

or the milk bottles outside the gate instead of bringing them right up to the house. The more Limpley lowered himself in his childish passion for the now autocratic animal, the worse Ponto treated him, and improbable as it may sound the dog even devised an entire system of ways to show that he might put up with petting and enthusiastic encomiums, but felt not in the least obliged to respond to these daily tributes with any kind of gratitude. As a matter of principle, he kept Limpley waiting every time his master called him, and in the end this unfortunate change in Ponto went so far that he would spend all day racing about as a normal, full-blooded dog who has not been trained in obedience will do, chasing chickens, jumping into the water, greedily devouring anything that came his way, and indulging in his favourite game of racing silently and with malice aforethought down the slope to the canal with the force of a small bomb, head-butting the baskets and tubs of washing stand-ing there until they fell into the water, and then prancing around the washerwomen and girls who had brought them with howls of triumph, while they had to retrieve their laundry from the water item by item. But as soon as it was time for Limpley to come home from the office Ponto, that clever actor, abandoned his high-spirited pranks and assumed the unapproachable air of a sultan. Lounging lazily about, he waited without the slightest welcoming expression for the return of his master, who would fall on him with a hearty, "Hello there, Ponty!" even before he greeted his wife or took off his coat. Ponto did not so much as wag his tail in response. Sometimes he magnanimously rolled over on his back to have his soft, silky stomach scratched, but even at these gracious moments he took care not to show that he was enjoying it by snuffling or grunting with pleasure. His humble servant was to notice that Ponto was doing him a favour by accepting his attentions at all. And with a brief growl that was as much as to say, "That's enough!" he would suddenly turn and put an end to the game. Similarly, he always had to be implored to eat the chopped liver that Limpley fed him piece by piece. Sometimes he merely sniffed at it and despite all persuasions lay down, scorning it, just to show that he was not always to be induced to eat his dinner when his two-legged slave served it up. Invited to go out for a walk, he would begin by stretching lazily, yawning so widely that you could see down to the black spots in his throat. He always insisted on doing something to make it clear that personally he was not much in favour of a walk, and would get off the sofa only to oblige Limpley. All his spoiling made him badly behaved, and he thought up any number of tricks to make sure that his master always assumed the attitude of a beggar and petitioner with him. In fact Limpley's servile passion could well have been described as more like doglike devotion than the conduct of the insubordinate animal, who played the part of oriental pasha to histrionic perfection.

Neither my husband nor I could bear to watch the outrageous behaviour of the tyrannical dog any longer. Clever as he was, Ponto soon noticed our lack of respect for him, and took care to show us his disapproval in the most obvious way. There was no denying that he was a dog of character. After the day when our maid turned him out of the garden in short order when he had left his unmistakable visiting card in one of our rose beds, he never again slipped through the thick hedge that formed the boundary between our two properties, and despite Limpley's pleas and persuasions could not be induced to set foot inside our house. We were glad to dispense with his visits; more awkward was the fact that when we met Limpley in his company walking down the road or outside our house, and that good-natured, talkative man fell into friendly conversation, the tyrannical animal's provocative behaviour made it impossible for us to talk at any length. After two minutes Ponto would begin to howl angrily, or growl and butt Limpley's leg, clearly meaning, "Stop it! Don't talk to these unpleasant people!" And I am sorry to say that Limpley always caved in. First he would try to soothe the disobedient animal. "Just a minute, and then we'll go on." But there was no fobbing off the tyrant, and his unfortunate servant—rather ashamed and confused—would say goodbye to us. Then the haughty animal trotted off, hindquarters proudly raised, visibly triumphant after demonstrating his unlimited power. I am not a violent woman, but my hand always itched to give the spoilt creature a smart blow with a dog whip, just once.

By these means Ponto, a perfectly ordinary dog, had managed to cool our previously friendly relations with our neighbours to a considerable extent. It obviously annoyed Limpley that he could no longer drop in on us every five minutes as he used to; his wife, for her part, was upset because she could see how ridiculous her husband's servile devotion to the dog made him in everyone else's eyes. And so another year passed in little skirmishes of this kind, while the dog became, if possible, even bolder and more demanding, and above all more ingenious in humiliating Limpley, until one day there was a change that surprised all concerned equally. Some of us, indeed, were glad of it, but it was a tragedy for the one most affected.

I had been unable to avoid telling my husband that for the last two or three weeks Mrs Limpley had been curiously shy, avoiding a conversation of any length with me. As good neighbours we lent each other this or that household item from time to time, and these encounters always led to a comfortable chat. I really liked that quiet, modest woman very much. Recently, however, I had noticed that she seemed embarrassed to approach me, and would rather send round her housemaid when she wanted to ask a favour. If I spoke to her, she seemed obviously self-conscious and wouldn't let me look her in the eye. My husband, who had a special liking for her, persuaded me just to go over to her house and ask straight out if we had done something to offend her without knowing it. "One shouldn't let a little coolness of that kind come between neighbours. And maybe it's just the opposite of what you fear. Maybe—and I do think so—she wants to ask you a favour and can't summon up the courage."

I took his advice to heart. I went round to the Limpleys' house and found her sitting in a chair in the garden, so lost in reverie that she didn't even hear me coming. I put a hand on her shoulder and said, speaking frankly, "Mrs Limpley, I'm an old woman and you needn't be shy with me. Let me speak first. If you are annoyed with us about something, do tell me what the matter is."

The poor little woman was startled. How could I think such a thing, she asked? She had kept from visiting me only because... And here she blushed instead of going on, and began to sob, but her sobs were, if I may say so, happy and glad. Finally she told me all about it. After nine years of marriage she had long ago given up all hope of being a mother, and even when her suspicion that the unexpected might have happened had grown stronger in the last few weeks, she said she hadn't felt brave enough to believe in it. The day before yesterday, however, she had secretly gone to see the doctor, and now she was certain. But she hadn't yet brought herself to tell her husband. I knew what he was like, she said, she was almost afraid of his extreme joy. Might it be best—and she hadn't been able to summon up the courage to ask us—might we be kind enough to prepare him for the news?

I said we'd be happy to do so. My husband in particular liked the idea, and he set about it with great amusement. He left a note for Limpley asking him to come round to us as soon as he got home from the office. And of course the good man came racing round, anxious to oblige, without even stopping to take his coat off. He was obviously afraid that something was wrong in our house, but on the other hand delighted to let off steam by showing how friendly and willing to oblige us he was. He stood there, breathless. My husband asked him to sit down at the table. This unusual ceremony alarmed him, and he hardly knew what to do with his large, heavy, freckled hands.

"Limpley," my husband began, "I thought of you yesterday evening when I read a maxim in an old book saying that no one should wish for too much, we should wish for only a single thing. And I thought to myself—what would our good neighbour, for instance, wish for if an angel or a good fairy or some other kindly being were to ask him—Limpley, what do you really want in life? I will grant you just one wish."

Limpley looked baffled. He was enjoying the joke, but he did not take it seriously. He still had an uneasy feeling that there was something ominous behind this solemn opening.

"Come along, Limpley, think of me as your good fairy," said my husband reassuringly, seeing him so much at a loss. "Don't you have anything to wish for at all?"

Half-in-earnest, half-laughing, Limpley scratched his short red hair.

"Well, not really," he finally confessed. "I have everything I could want, my house, my wife, my good safe job, my…" I noticed that he was going to say 'my dog', but at the last moment he felt it was out of place. "Yes, I really have all I could wish for."

"So there's nothing for the angel or the fairy to grant you?"

Limpley was getting more cheerful by the minute. He was delighted to be offered the chance to tell us, straight out, how extremely happy he was. "No… not really."

"What a pity," said my husband. "What a pity you can't think of anything." And he fell silent.

Limpley was beginning to feel a little uncomfortable under my husband's searching gaze. He clearly thought he ought to apologise.

"Well, one can always do with a little more money, of course… maybe a promotion at work… but as I said, I'm content… I really don't know what else I could wish for."

"So the poor angel," said my husband, pretending to shake his head sadly, "has to leave his mission unaccomplished because Mr Limpley has nothing to wish for. Well, fortunately the kind angel didn't go straight away again, but had a word with Mrs Limpley first, and he seems to have had better luck with her."

Limpley was taken aback. The poor man looked almost simple-minded, sitting there with his watery eyes staring and his mouth half-open. But he pulled himself together and said with slight irritation, for he didn't see how anyone who belonged to him not be perfectly happy, "My wife? What can *she* have to wish for?"

"Well—perhaps something better than a dog to look after."

Now Limpley understood. He was thunderstruck. Instinctively he opened his eyes so wide in happy surprise that you could see the whites instead of the pupils. All at once he jumped up and ran out, forgetting his coat and without a word of apology to us, storming off to his wife's room like a man demented.

We both laughed. But we were not surprised; it was just what we would have expected of our famously impetuous neighbour.

Someone else, however, *was* surprised. Someone who was loung-ing on the sofa idly, eyes half-open and blinking, waiting for the homage that his master owed him, or that he thought his master owed him—the well-groomed and autocratic Ponto. But what on earth had happened? The man went rushing past him without a word of greeting or flattery, on into the bedroom, and he heard laughter and weeping and talk and sobs, going on and on, and no one bothered about him, Ponto, who by right and custom received the first loving greeting. An hour passed by. The maid brought him his bowl of food. Ponto scornfully left it untouched. He was used to being begged and urged to eat until he was hand-fed. He growled angrily at the maid. They'd soon find out he wasn't to be fobbed off with indifference like that! But in their excitement his humans never even noticed that he had turned down his dinner that evening. He was forgotten, and forgotten he remained. Limpley was talking on and on to his wife, never stopping, bombarding her with concern and advice, lavishing caresses on her. In the first flush of his delight he had no eyes for Ponto, and the arrogant animal was too proud to remind his master of his existence by intruding. He crouched in a corner and waited. This could only be a misunderstanding, a single if inexcusable oversight. But he waited in vain. Even next morning, when the countless admonitions Limpley kept giving his wife to take it easy and spare herself almost made him miss his bus, he raced out of the house and past Ponto without a word to the dog.

There's no doubt that Ponto was an intelligent animal, but this sudden change was more than he could understand. I happened to be standing at the window when Limpley got on the bus, and I saw how, as soon as he had disappeared inside it, Ponto very slowly—I might almost say thoughtfully—slunk out of the house and watched the vehicle as it drove away. He waited there without moving for half-an-hour, obviously hoping that his master would come back and make up for the attention he had forgotten to pay him the evening before. He did not rush about playing, but only went round and round the house all day slowly, as if deep in thought. Perhaps—who knows how and to what extent sequences of thought can form in an animal mind?—he was brooding on whether he himself had done something clumsy to earn the incomprehensible withdrawal of the favours he was used to. Towards evening, about half-an-hour before Limpley usually came home, he became visibly nervous and kept patrolling the fence with his ears back, keeping an eye open to spot the bus in good time. But of course he wasn't going to show how impatiently he had been waiting; as soon as the bus came into view at its usual hour he hurried back into the living room, lay down on the sofa as usual and waited.

Once again, however, he waited in vain. Once again Limpley hurried past him. And so it went on day after day. Now and then

Limpley noticed him, gave him a fleeting, "Oh, there you are, Ponto," and patted him in passing. But it was only an indifferent, casual pat. There was no more flattering, servile attention, there were no more caresses, no games, no walks, nothing, nothing, nothing. Limpley, that fundamentally kindly man, can hardly be blamed for this painful indifference, for he now had no thought in his head but to look after his wife. When he came home from work he accompanied her wherever she went, taking her for walks of just the right length, supporting her with his arm in case she took a hasty or incautious step; he watched over her diet, and made the maid give him a precise report on every hour of her day. Late at night, when she had gone to bed, he came round to our house almost daily to ask me, as a woman of experience, for advice and reassurance; he was already buying equipment in the big department stores for the coming baby. And he did all this in a state of uninterrupted busy excitement. His own personal life came nowhere; sometimes he forgot to shave for two days on end, and sometimes he was late at the office because the constant stream of advice he gave his wife had made him miss the bus. So it was not malice or unfaithfulness if he neglected to take Ponto for walks or pay him attention; only the confusion of a passionate man with an almost monomaniac disposition concentrating all his senses, thoughts and feelings on a single object. But if human beings, in spite of their ability to think logically of the past and the future, are hardly capable of accepting a slight inflicted on them without bearing resentment, how can a dumb animal take it calmly? Ponto was more and more nervous and agitated as the weeks went by. His self-esteem could not tolerate being overlooked and downgraded in importance, when he was the real master of this house. It would have been sensible of him to adopt a pleading, flattering attitude to Limpley, who would then surely have been aware of his dereliction of duty. But Ponto was too proud to crawl to anyone. It was not he but his master who was to make the first approach. So the dog tried all kinds of ruses to draw attention to himself. In the third week he suddenly began limping, dragging his left hind leg as if he had gone lame. In normal circumstances, Limpley would have examined him at once in affectionate alarm, to see if he had a thorn in his paw. He would anxiously have phoned the vet, he would have got up three or four times in the night to see how the dog was doing. Now, however, neither he nor anyone else in the house took the slightest notice of Ponto's pathetically assumed limp, and the embittered dog had no alternative but to put up with it. A couple of weeks later he tried again, this time going on hunger strike. For two days he made the sacrifice of leaving his food untouched. But no one worried about his lack of appetite, whereas usually, if he failed to lick the last morsel out of his bowl in one of his tyrannical moods, the attentive Limpley would fetch him special dog biscuits or a slice of sausage. Finally animal hunger was too much for Ponto, and he secretly and guiltily ate all his food with little enjoyment. Another time he tried to attract attention by hiding for a day. He had prudently taken up quarters in the disused henhouse, where he would be able to listen with satisfaction to anxious cries of "Ponto! Ponto, where are you?" But no one called him, no one noticed his absence or felt worried. His masterful spirit caved in. He had been set aside, humiliated, forgotten, and he didn't even know why.

I think I was the first to notice the change that came over the dog in those weeks. He lost weight, and his bearing was different. Instead of strutting briskly with his hindquarters proudly raised in the old way, he slunk about as if he had been whipped, and his coat, once carefully brushed every day, lost its silky gloss. When you met him he bowed his head so that you couldn't see his eyes and hurried past. But although he had been miserably humiliated, his old pride was not yet entirely broken; he still felt ashamed to face the rest of us, and his only outlet for his fury was to attack those baskets of washing. Within a week he pushed no less than three of them into the canal to make it clear, through his violence, that he was still around and he demanded respect. But even that was no good, and the only effect was that the laundry maids threatened to beat him. All his cunning ruses were in vain—leaving his food, limping, pretending to go missing, assiduously looking for his master—and he racked his brain inside that square, heavy head—something mysterious that he didn't understand must have happened that day. After it, the house and everyone in it had changed, and the despairing Ponto realised that he was powerless in the face of whatever had happened or was still happening. There could be no doubt about it—someone, some strange and ill-disposed power was against him. He, Ponto, had an enemy. An enemy who was stronger than he was, and this enemy was invisible and out of his reach. So the enemy, that cunning, evil, cowardly adversary who had taken away all his authority in the household, couldn't be seized, torn to pieces, bitten until his bones cracked. No sniffing at doorways helped him, no alert watchfulness, no lying in wait with ears pricked, no brooding—his enemy, that thief, that devil, was and remained invisible. In those weeks Ponto kept pacing along the garden fence like a dog deranged, trying to find some trace of his diabolical, unseen enemy.

All that his alert senses did pick up was the fact that preparations of some kind were being made in the house; he didn't understand them, but they must be to do with his arch-enemy. Worst of all, there was suddenly an elderly lady staying there—Mrs Limpley's mother—who slept at night on the dining-room sofa where Ponto used to lounge at his ease if his comfortably upholstered basket didn't seem luxurious enough. And then again, all kinds of things kept being delivered to the house—what for?—bedclothes, packages, the doorbell was ringing all the time. Several times a black-clad man with glasses turned up smelling of something horrible, stinking of harsh, inhuman tinctures. The door to the mistress of the house's bedroom was always opening and closing, and there was constant whispering behind it, or sometimes the two ladies would sit together snipping and clicking their sewing things. What did it all mean, and why was he, Ponto, shut out and deprived of his rights? All his brooding finally brought a vacant, almost glazed look to the dog's eyes. What distinguishes an animal's mind from human understanding, after all, is that the animal lives exclusively in the past and the present, and is unable to imagine the future or speculate on what may happen. And here, the dumb animal felt in torments of despair, something was going on that meant him ill, and yet he couldn't defend himself or fight back.

It was six months in all before the proud, masterful, Ponto, exhausted by his futile struggle, humbly capitulated, and oddly enough I was the one to whom he surrendered. I had been sitting in the garden one fine summer evening while my husband played patience indoors, and suddenly I felt the light, hesitant touch of something warm on my knee. It was Ponto, his pride broken. He had not been in our garden for a year-and-a-half, but now, in his distress, he was seeking refuge with me. Perhaps, in those weeks when everyone else was neglecting him, I had spoken to him or patted him in passing, so that he thought of me in this last moment of despair, and I shall never forget the urgent, pleading expression in his eyes as he looked up at me. The glance of an animal in great need can be a more penetrating, I might even say a more speaking look than the glance of a human being, for we put most of our feelings and thoughts into the words with which we communicate, while an animal, incapable of speech, expresses feelings only with its eyes. I have never seen perplexity more touchingly and desperately expressed than I did in that indescribable look from Ponto as he pawed gently at the hem of my skirt, begging. Much moved, I realised that he was saying, "Please tell me what my master and the rest of them have against me. What horrible thing are they planning to do to me in that house? Help me, tell me what to do." I really had no idea what to do myself in view of that pleading look. Instinctively I patted him and murmured under my breath, "Poor Ponto, your time is over. You'll have to get used to it, just as we all have to get used to things we don't like." Ponto pricked up his ears when I spoke to him, and the folds of skin on his brow moved painfully, as if he were trying to guess what my words meant. Then he scraped his paw impatiently on the ground. It was an urgent, restless gesture, meaning something like, "I don't understand you! Explain! Help me!" But I knew there was nothing I could do for him. He must have sensed, deep down, that I had no comfort to offer. He stood up quietly and disappeared as soundlessly as he had come, without looking back.

Ponto was missing for a whole day and a whole night. If he had been human I would have been afraid he had committed suicide. He did not turn up until the evening of the next day, dirty, hungry, scruffy and with a couple of bites; in his helpless fury he must have attacked other dogs somewhere. But new humiliation awaited him. The maid wouldn't let him into the house, but instead put his bowl of food outside the door and then took no more notice of him. It so happened that special circumstances accounted for this cruel insult, because Mrs Limpley had gone into labour, and the house was full of people bustling about. Limpley stood around helplessly, red-faced and trembling with excitement; the midwife was hurrying back and forth, assisted by the doctor; Limpley's mother-in-law was sitting by the bed comforting her daughter; and the maid had her hands more than full. I had come round to the Limpleys' house myself and was waiting in the dining room in case I could be useful in any way. All things considered, Ponto's presence could only have been a nuisance. But how was his dull, doggy brain to understand that? The distressed animal realised only that for the first time he had been turned out of the house—*his* house—like a beggar, unwanted. He was being maliciously kept away from something important going on there behind closed doors. His fury was indescribable, and with his powerful teeth he cracked the bones that had been thrown to him as if they were his unseen enemy's neck. Then he snuffled around; his sharpened senses could tell that other strangers had gone into the house—again, *his* house—and on the drive he picked up the scent of the black-clad man he hated, the man with the glasses. But there were others in league with him as well, and what were they doing in there? The agitated animal listened with his ears pricked up. Pressing close to the wall, he heard voices both soft and loud, groaning, cries, then water splashing, hurried footsteps, things being moved about, the clink of glass and metal—something was going on in there, something he didn't understand. But instinctively he sensed that it was hostile to him. It was to blame for his humiliation, the loss of his rights—it was the invisible, infamous, cowardly, malicious enemy, and now it was really there, now it would be in visible form, now at last he could seize it by the scruff of its neck as it richly deserved. Muscles tense and quivering with excitement, the powerful animal crouched beside the front door so that he could rush in the moment it opened. He wasn't going to get away this time, the evil enemy, the usurper of his rights and privileges who had murdered his peace of mind!

Inside the house no one gave a thought to the dog. We were too busy and excited. I had to reassure and console Limpley—no mean task—when the doctor and the midwife banished him from the bedroom; for those two hours, considering his vast capacity for sympathy, he may well have suffered more than the woman in labour herself. At last came the good news, and after a while Limpley, his feelings vacillating between joy and fear, was cautiously let into the bedroom to see his child—a little girl, as the midwife had just announced—and the new mother. He stayed there for a long time, while his mother-in-law and I, who had been through childbirth ourselves, exchanged reminiscences in friendly conversation.

At last the door opened and Limpley appeared, followed by the doctor. The proud father was coming to show us the baby, and was carrying her lying on a changing pad, like a priest bearing a monstrance; his broad, kind, slightly simple face almost transfigured by radiant happiness. Tears kept running unstoppably down his cheeks, and he didn't know how to dry them, because his broad hands were holding the child like something inexpressibly precious and fragile. Meanwhile the doctor behind him, who was familiar with such scenes, was putting on his coat. "Well, my job here is done," he said, smiling, and he shook hands and went to the door, suspecting no harm.

But in the split second when the doctor opened the door, with no idea what was about to happen, something shot past his legs, something that had been crouching there with muscles at full stretch, and there was Ponto in the middle of the room, filling it with the sound of furious barking. He had seen at once that Limpley was holding some new object that he didn't know, holding it tenderly, something small and red and alive that mewed like a cat and smelled human—aha! There was the enemy, the cunning, hidden enemy he had been searching for all this time, the adversary who had robbed him of his power, the creature that had destroyed his peace! Bite it! Tear it to bits! And with bared teeth he leapt up at Limpley to snatch the baby from him. I think we all screamed at the same time, for the powerful animal's movement was so sudden and violent that Limpley, although he was a heavy, sturdily built man, swayed under the weight of the impact and staggered back against the wall. But at the last moment he instinctively held the changing pad up in the air with the baby on it, so that no harm could come to her, and I myself, moving fast, had taken her from Limpley before he fell. The dog immediately turned against me. Luckily the doctor, who had rushed back on hearing our cries, with great presence of mind picked up a heavy chair and flung it. It landed with a heavy impact on the furious animal, cracking bones, as Ponto stood there with his eyes bloodshot and foaming at the mouth. The dog howled with pain and retreated for a moment, only to attack again in his frenzied rage. However, that brief moment had been long enough for Limpley to recover from his fall and fling himself on the dog, in a fury that was horrifyingly like Ponto's own. A terrible battle began. Limpley, a broad, heavy, powerful man, had landed on Ponto with his full weight and was trying to strangle him with his strong hands. The two of them were now rolling about on the floor in a tangle of limbs as they fought. Ponto snapped, and Limpley went on trying to choke him, his knee braced on the animal's chest, while Ponto kept wriggling out of his grasp. We old women fled into the next room to protect the baby, while the doctor and the maid, joining the fray, now joined the attack on the furious dog. They struck Ponto with anything that came to hand—wood cracked, glass clinked—they went for him with hands and feet, hammering and kicking his body, until the mad barking turned to heavy, stertorous breathing. Finally the animal, now completely exhausted, his breath coming irregularly, had his front and back legs tied by the doctor, the maid and my husband, who had come running from our house when he heard the noise. They used Ponto's own leather leash and some cord, and stuffed a cloth snatched off the table into his mouth. Now entirely defenceless and half-conscious, he was dragged out of the room. Outside the door they got him into a sack, and only then did the doctor hurry back to help.

Limpley, meanwhile, swaying like a drunk, staggered into the other room to make sure his child was all right. The baby was uninjured, and stared up at him with her sleepy little eyes. Nor was his wife in any danger, although she had been woken from her deep, exhausted sleep by all the noise. With some difficulty, she managed to give her husband a wan, affectionate smile as he stroked her hands. Only now was he able to think of himself. He looked terrible, his face white, mad-eyed, his collar torn open and his clothes crumbled and dusty. We were alarmed to see that blood was dripping from his torn right sleeve to the floor. In his fury he had not even noticed that, as he tried to throttle the animal, it had bitten him deeply twice in desperate self-defence. He removed his coat and shirt, and the doctor made haste to bandage his arm. Meanwhile the maid fetched him a brandy, for exhausted by his agitation and the loss of blood he was close to fainting, and it was only with some difficulty that we got him lying down on a sofa. Since he had had little rest for the last two nights as he waited in suspense for the baby's birth, he fell into a deep sleep.

Meanwhile we considered what to do with Ponto. "Shoot him," said my husband, and he was about to go home to fetch his revolver. But the doctor said it was his own duty to take him to have his saliva tested without a moment's delay, in case he was rabid, because if so then special measures must be taken to treat Limpley's bites. He would get Ponto into his car at once, he said. We all went out to help the doctor. The animal was lying defenceless outside the door, bound and gagged—a sight I shall never forget—but he was rolling his bloodshot eyes as if they would pop out of his head. He ground his teeth and retched and swallowed, trying to spit out the gag, while his muscles stood out like cords. His entire contorted body was vibrating and twitching convulsively, and I must confess that although we knew he was well trussed up we all hesitated to touch him. I had never in my life seen anything like such concentrated malice and fury, or such hatred in the eyes of any living creature as in his bloodshot and bloodthirsty gaze. I instinctively wondered if my husband had not been right in suggesting that the dog should be shot at once. But the doctor insisted on taking him away, and so the trussed animal was dragged to his car and driven off, in spite of his helpless resistance.

With this inglorious departure, Ponto vanished from our sight for quite a long time. My husband found out that he had tested negative for rabies under observation for several days at the Pasteur Institute, and as there could be no question of a return to the scene of his crime Ponto had been given to a butcher in Bath who was looking for a strong, aggressive dog. We thought no more of him, and Limpley himself, after wearing his arm in a sling for only two or three days, entirely forgot him. Now that his wife had recovered from the strain of childbirth, his passion and care were concentrated entirely on his little daughter, and I need hardly say that he showed as much extreme and fanatical devotion as to Ponto in his time, and perhaps made even more of a fool of himself. The powerful, heavy man would kneel beside the baby's pram like one of the Magi before the crib in the Nativity scenes of the old Italian masters; every day, every hour, every minute he discovered some new beauty in the little rosy creature, who was indeed a charming child. His quiet, sensible wife smiled with far more understanding on this paternal adoration than on his old senseless idolising of his four-footed friend, and we too benefited, for the presence of perfect, unclouded happiness next door could not help but cast its friendly light on our own house.

We had all, as I said, completely forgotten Ponto when I was surprisingly reminded of him one evening. My husband and I had come back from London late, after going to a concert conducted by Bruno Walter, and I could not drop off to sleep, I don't know why. Was it the echo of the melodies of the Jupiter Symphony that I was unconsciously trying to replay in my head, or was it the mild, clear, moonlit summer night? I got up—it was about two in the morning—and looked out of the window. The moon was sailing in the sky high above, as if drifting before an invisible wind, through clouds that shone silver in its light, and every time it emerged pure and bright from those clouds it bathed the whole garden in snowy brightness. There was no sound; I felt that if a single leaf had stirred it would not have escaped me. So I started in alarm when, in the midst of this absolute silence, I suddenly noticed something moving stealthily along the hedge between our garden and the Limpleys', something black that stood out distinctly as it moved quietly but restlessly against the moonlit lawn. With instinctive interest, I looked more closely. It was not a living creature, it was nothing corporeal moving there, it was a shadow. Only a shadow, but a shadow that must be cast by some living thing cautiously stealing along under cover of the hedge, the shadow of a human being or an animal. Perhaps I am not expressing myself very well, but the furtive, sly silence of that stealthy shape had something alarming about it. My first thought—for we women worry about such things—was that this must be a burglar, even a murderous one, and my heart was in my mouth. But then the shadow reached the garden hedge on the upper terrace where the fence began, and now it was slinking along past the railing of the fence, curiously hunched. Now I could see the creature itself ahead of its shadow—it was a dog, and I recognised the dog at once. Ponto was back. Very slowly, very cautiously, obviously ready to run away at the first sound, Ponto was snuffling around the Limpleys' house. It was—and I don't know why this thought suddenly flashed through my mind—it was as if he wanted to give notice in advance of something, for his was not the free, loose-limbed movement of a dog picking up a scent; there was something about him suggesting that he had some forbidden or ill-intentioned plan in mind. He did not keep his nose close to the ground, sniffing, nor did he walk with his muscles relaxed, he made his way slowly along, keeping low and almost on his belly, to make himself more inconspicuous. He was inching forward as if stalking prey. I instinctively leant forward to get a better look at him. But I must have moved clumsily, touching the window frame and making some slight noise, for with a silent leap Ponto disappeared into the darkness. It seemed as if I had only dreamt it all. The garden lay there in the moonlight empty, white and brightly lit again, with nothing moving.

I don't know why, but I felt ashamed to tell my husband about this; it could have been just my senses playing a trick on me. But when I happened to meet the Limpleys' maid in the road next morning, I asked her casually if she had happened to see Ponto again recently. The girl was uneasy, and a little embarrassed, and only when I encouraged her did she admit that yes, she had in fact seen him around several times, and in strange circumstances. She couldn't really say why, but she was afraid of him. Four weeks ago, she told me, she had been taking the baby into town in her pram, and suddenly she had heard terrible barking. As the butcher's van rolled by with Ponto in it, he had howled at her or, as she thought, at the baby in the pram, and looked as if he were crouching to spring, but luckily the van had passed so quickly that he dared not jump out of it. However, she said, his furious barking had gone right through her. Of course she had not told Mr Limpley, she added; the news would only have upset him unnecessarily, and anyway she thought the dog was in safe keeping in Bath. But only the other day, one afternoon when she went out to the old woodshed to fetch a few logs, there had been something moving in there at the back. She had been about to scream in fright, but then she saw it was Ponto hiding there, and he had immediately shot away through the hedge and into our garden. Since then she had suspected that he hid there quite often, and he must have been walking around the house by night, because the other day, after that heavy storm in the night, she had clearly seen paw prints in the wet sand showing that he had circled the whole house several times. Did I think he might want to come back, she asked me? Mr Limpley certainly wouldn't have him in the house again, and living with a butcher Ponto could hardly be hungry. If he were, anyway, he would have come to her in the kitchen first to beg for food. Somehow she didn't like the way he was slinking about the place, she added, and did I think she ought to tell Mr Limpley after all, or at least his wife? We thought it over, and agreed that if Ponto turned up again we would tell his new master the butcher, so that he could put an end to his visits. For the time being, at least, we wouldn't remind Limpley of the existence of the hated animal.

I think we made a mistake, for perhaps—who can say—that might have prevented what happened next day, on that terrible and never-to-be-forgotten Sunday. My husband and I had gone round to the Limpleys', and we were sitting in deckchairs on the small lower terrace of the garden, talking. From the lower terrace, the turf ran down quite a steep slope to the canal. The pram was on the flat lawn of the terrace beside us, and I hardly need say that the besotted father got up in the middle of the conversation every five minutes to enjoy the sight of the baby. After all, she was a pretty child, and on that golden sunlit afternoon it was really charming to see her looking up at the sky with her bright blue eyes and smiling—the hood of the pram was put back—as she tried to pick up the patterns made by the sunlight on her blanket with her delicate if still rather awkward hands. Her father rejoiced at this, as if such miraculous reasoning as hers had never been known, and we ourselves, to give him pleasure, acted as if we had never known anything like it. That sight of her, the last happy moment, is rooted in my mind for ever. Then Mrs Limpley called from the upper terrace, which was in the shade of the veranda, to tell us that tea was ready. Limpley spoke soothingly to the baby as if she could understand him, "There, there, we'll be back in a minute!" We left the pram with the baby in it on the lawn, shaded from the hot sunlight by a cool canopy of leaves above, and strolled slowly to the usual place in the shade where the Limpleys drank afternoon tea. It was about twenty yards from the lower to the upper terrace of their garden, and you could not see one terrace from the other because of the rose-covered pergola between them. We talked as we walked, and I need hardly say what we talked about. Limpley was wonderfully cheerful, but his cheerfulness did not seem at all out of place today, when the sky was such a silky blue, it was such a peaceful Sunday, and we were sitting in the shade in front of a house full of blessings. Today, his mood was like a reflection of that fine summer's day.

Suddenly we were alarmed. Shrill, horrified screams came from the canal, voices of children and women's cries of alarm. We rushed down the green slope with Limpley in the lead. His first thought was for the child. But to our horror the lower terrace, where the pram had been standing only a few minutes ago with the baby dozing peacefully in it in perfect safety, was empty, and the shouting from the canal was shriller and more agitated than ever. We hurried down to the water. On the opposite bank several women and children stood close together, gesticulating and staring at the canal. And there was the pram we had left safe and sound on the lower terrace, now floating upside down in the water. One man had already put out in a boat to save the child, another had dived in. But it was all too late. The baby's body was not brought up from the brackish water, which was covered with green waterweed, until quarter-of-an-hour later.

I cannot describe the despair of the wretched parents. Or rather, I will not even try to describe it, because I never again in my life want to think of those dreadful moments. A police superintendent, informed by telephone, turned up to find out how this terrible thing had happened. Was it negligence on the part of the parents, or an accident, or a crime? The floating pram had been fished out of the water by now, and put back on the lower terrace on the police officer's instructions, just where it had been before. Then the Chief Constable himself joined the superintendent, and personally tested the pram to see whether a light touch would set it rolling down the slope of its own accord. But the wheels would hardly move through the thick, long grass. So it was out of the question for a sudden gust of wind, perhaps, to have made it roll so suddenly over the terrace, which itself was level. The superintendent also tried again, pushing a little harder. The pram rolled about a foot forward and then stopped. But the terrace was at least seven yards wide, and the pram, as the tracks of its wheels showed, had been standing securely some way from the place where the land began to slope. Only when the superintendent took a run up to the pram and pushed it really hard did it move along the terrace and begin to roll down the slope. So something unexpected must have set the pram suddenly in motion. But who or what had done it?

It was a mystery. The police superintendent took his cap off his sweating brow and scratched his short hair ever more thoughtfully. He couldn't make it out. Had any object, he asked, even just a ball when someone was playing with it, ever been known to roll over the terrace and down to the canal of its own accord? "No, never!" everyone assured him. Had there been a child nearby, or in the garden, a high-spirited child who might have been playing with the pram? No, no one! Had there been anyone else in the vicinity? Again, no. The garden gate had been closed, and none of the people walking by the canal had seen anyone coming or going. The one person who could really be regarded as an eyewitness was the labourer who had jumped straight into the water to save the baby, but even he, still dripping wet and greatly distressed, could say only that he and his wife had been walking beside the canal, and nothing seemed wrong. Then the pram had suddenly come rolling down the slope from the garden, going faster and faster, and tipped upside down as soon as it reached the water. As he thought he had seen a child in the water, he had run down to the bank at once, stripping off his jacket, and tried to rescue it, but he had not been able to make his way through the dense tangles of waterweeds as fast as he had hoped. That was all he knew.

The police superintendent was more and more baffled. He had never known such a puzzling case, he said. He simply could not imagine how that pram could have started rolling. The only possibility seemed to be that the baby might suddenly have sat up, or thrown herself violently to one side, thus unbalancing the lightweight pram. But it was hard to believe that, and he for one couldn't imagine it. Was there anything else that occurred to any of us?

I automatically glanced at the Limpleys' housemaid. Our eyes met. We were both thinking the same thing at the same moment. We both knew that the dog hated the child. We knew that he had been seen several times recently slinking around the garden. We knew how he had often head-butted laundry baskets full of washing and sent them into the canal. We both—I saw it from the maid's pallor and her twitching lips—we both suspected that the sly and now vicious animal, finally seeing a chance to get his revenge, had come out of hiding as soon as we left the baby alone for a few minutes, and had then butted the pram containing his hated rival fiercely and fast, sending it rolling down to the canal, before making his own escape as soundlessly as usual. But we neither of us voiced our suspicions. I knew the mere idea that if he had shot the raving animal after Ponto's attack, he might have saved his child would drive Limpley mad. And then, in spite of the logic of our thinking, we lacked any solid evidence. Neither the maid nor I, and none of the others, had actually seen the dog slinking around or running away that afternoon. The woodshed where he liked to hide—I looked there at once—was empty, the dry trodden earth of its floor showed no trace at all, we had not heard a note of the furious barking in which Ponto had always triumphantly indulged when he pushed a basket of washing into the canal. So we could not really claim that he had done it. It was more of a cruelly tormenting assumption. Only a justified, a terribly well justified suspicion. But the final, clinching certainty was missing.

And yet I have never since shaken off that dreadful suspicion—on the contrary, it was even more strongly confirmed over the next few days, almost to the point of certainty. A week later—the poor baby had been buried by then, and the Limpleys had left the house because they could not bear the sight of that fateful canal—something happened that affected me deeply. I had been shopping in Bath for a few household items when I suddenly had a shock. Beside the butcher's van I saw Ponto, of whom I had subconsciously been thinking in all those terrible hours, walking along at his leisure, and at the same moment he saw me. He stopped at once, and so did I. And now something that still weighs on my mind happened; in all the weeks that had passed since his humiliation, I had never seen Ponto looking anything but upset and distressed, and he had avoided any encounter with me, crouching low and turning his eyes away. Now he held his head high and looked at me—I can't put it any other way—with self-confident indifference. Overnight he had become the proud, arrogant animal of the old days again. He stood in that provocative position for a minute. Then, swaggering and almost dancing across the road with pretended friendliness, he came over to me and stopped a foot or so away, as if to say, "Well, here I am! Now what have you got to say? Are you going to accuse me?"

I felt paralysed. I had no power to push him away, no power to bear that self-confident and, indeed, I might almost say self-satisfied look. I walked quickly on. God forbid I should accuse even an innocent animal, let alone a human being, of a crime he did not commit. But since that day I cannot get rid of the terrible thought: "He did it. He was the one who did it."

AMOK

I N MARCH 1912 a strange accident occurred in Naples harbour during the unloading of a large ocean-going liner which was reported at length by the newspapers, although in extremely fanciful terms. Although I was a passenger on the *Oceania*, I did not myself witness this strange incident—nor did any of the others—since it happened while coal was being taken on board and cargo unloaded, and to escape the noise we had all gone ashore to pass the time in coffee-houses or theatres. It is my personal opinion however, that a number of conjectures which I did not voice publicly at the time provide the true explanation of that sensational event, and I think that, at a distance of some years, I may now be permitted to give an account of a conversation I had in confidence immediately before the curious episode.

When I went to the Calcutta shipping agency trying to book a passage on the *Oceania* for my voyage home to Europe, the clerk apologetically shrugged his shoulders. He didn't know if it would be possible for him to get me a cabin, he said; at this time of year, with the rainy season imminent, the ship was likely to be fully booked all the way from Australia, and he would have to wait for a telegram from Singapore. Next day, I was glad to hear, he told me that yes, he could still reserve me a cabin, although not a particularly comfortable one; it would be below deck and amidships. As I was impatient to get home I did not hesitate for long, but took it.

The clerk had not misinformed me. The ship was over-crowded and my cabin a poor one: a cramped little rectangle of a place near the engine room, lit only dimly through a circular porthole. The thick, curdled air smelled greasy and musty, and I could not for a moment escape the electric ventilator fan that hummed as it circled overhead like a steel bat gone mad. Down below the engines clattered and groaned like a breathless coal-heaver constantly climbing the same flight of stairs, up above I heard the tramp of footsteps pacing the promenade deck the whole time. As soon as I had stowed my luggage away amidst the dingy girders in my stuffy tomb, I then went back on deck to get away from the place, and as I came up from the depths I drank in the soft, sweet wind blowing off the land as if it were ambrosia.

But the atmosphere of the promenade deck was crowded and restless too, full of people chattering incessantly, hurrying up and down with the uneasy nervousness of those forced to be inactive in a confined space. The arch flirtatiousness of the women, the constant pacing up and down on the bottleneck of the deck as flocks of passengers surged past the deckchairs, always meeting the same faces again, were actually painful to me. I had seen a new world, I had taken in turbulent, confused images that raced wildly through my mind. Now I wanted leisure to think, to analyse and organise them, make sense of all that had impressed itself on my eyes, but there wasn't a moment of rest and peace to be had here on the crowded deck. The lines of a book I was trying to read blurred as the fleeting shadows of the chattering passengers moved by. It was impossible to be alone with myself on the unshaded, busy thoroughfare of the deck of this ship.

I tried for three days; resigned to my lot, I watched the passengers and the sea. But the sea was always the same, blue and empty, and only at sunset was it abruptly flooded with every imaginable colour. As for the passengers, after seventy-two hours I knew them all by heart. Every face was tediously familiar, the women's shrill laughter no longer irritated me, even the loud voices of two Dutch officers quarrelling nearby were not such a source of annoyance any more. There was nothing for it but to escape the deck, although my cabin was hot and stuffy, and in the saloon English girls kept playing waltzes badly on the piano, staccato-fashion. Finally I decided to turn the day's normal timetable upside down, and in the afternoon, having anaesthetized myself with a few glasses of beer, I went to my cabin to sleep through the evening with its dinner and dancing.

When I woke it was dark and oppressive in the little coffin of my cabin. I had switched off the ventilator, so the air around my temples felt greasy and humid. My senses were bemused, and it took me some minutes to remember my surroundings and wonder what the time was. It must have been after midnight, anyway, for I could not hear music or those restless footsteps pacing overhead. Only the engine, the breathing heart of the leviathan, throbbed as it thrust the body of the ship on into the unseen.

I made my way up to the deck. It was deserted. And as I looked above the steam from the funnel and the ghostly gleam of the spars, a magical brightness suddenly met my eyes. The sky was radiant, dark behind the white stars wheeling through it and yet radiant, as if a velvet curtain up there veiled a great light, and the twinkling stars were merely gaps and cracks through which that indescribable brightness shone. I had never before seen the sky as I saw it that night, glowing with such radiance, hard and steely blue, and yet light came sparkling, dripping, pouring, gushing down, falling from the moon and stars as if burning in some mysterious inner space. The white-painted outlines of the ship stood out bright against the velvety dark sea in the moonlight, while all the detailed contours of the ropes and the yards dissolved in that flowing brilliance; the lights on the masts seemed to hang in space, with the round eye of the lookout post above them, earthly yellow stars amidst the shining stars of the sky. And right above my head stood the magical constellation of the Southern Cross, hammered into the invisible void with shining

311

diamond nails and seeming to hover, although only the ship was really moving, quivering slightly as it made its way up and down with heaving breast, up and down, a gigantic swimmer passing through the dark waves. I stood there looking up; I felt as if I were bathed by warm water falling from above, except that it was light washing over my hands, mild, white light pouring around my shoulders, my head, and seeming to permeate me entirely, for all at once everything sombre about me was brightly lit. I breathed freely, purely, and full of sudden delight I felt the air on my lips like a clear drink. It was soft, effervescent air carrying on it the aroma of fruits, the scent of distant islands, and making me feel slightly drunk. Now, for the first time since I had set foot on the ship's planks, I knew the blessed joy of reverie, and the other more sensual pleasure of abandoning my body, woman-like, to the softness surrounding me. I wanted to lie down and look up at the white hieroglyphs in the sky. But the loungers and deckchairs had been cleared away, and there was nowhere for me to rest and dream on the deserted promenade deck.

So I made my way on, gradually approaching the bows of the ship, dazzled by the light that seemed to be shining more and more intensely on everything around me. It almost hurt, that bright, glaring, burning starlight, and I wanted to find a place to lie on a mat in deep shade, feeling the glow not on me but only above me, reflected in the ship's gear around me as one sees a landscape from a darkened room. At last, stumbling over cables and past iron hoists, I reached the ship's side and looked down over the keel to see the bows moving on into the blackness, while molten moonlight sprayed up, foaming, on both sides of their path. The ship kept rising and falling, rising and falling in the flowing dark, cutting through the black water as a plough cuts through soil, and in that sparkling interplay I felt all the torment of the conquered element and all the pleasures of earthly power. As I watched I lost all sense of time. Did I stand there for an hour, or was it only minutes?

The vast cradle of the ship moving up and down rocked me away from time, and I felt only a pleasant weariness coming over me, a sensuous feeling. I wanted to sleep, to dream, yet I did not wish to leave this magic and go back down into my coffin. I instinctively felt around with my foot and found a coil of ropes. I sat down on it with my eyes closed yet not fully darkened, for above them, above me, that silver glow streamed on. Below me I felt the water rushing quietly on, above me the white torrent flowed by with inaudible resonance. And gradually the rushing sound passed into my blood; I was no longer conscious of myself, I didn't know if I heard my own breathing or the distant, throbbing heart of the ship, I myself was streaming, pouring away in the never-resting midnight world as it raced past.

A dry, harsh cough quite close to me made me jump. I came out of my half-intoxicated reverie with a start. My eyes, which even through closed lids had been dazzled by the white brightness, now searched around: quite close, and opposite me in the shadow of the ship's side, something glinted like light reflected off a pair of glasses, and now I saw the concentrated and circular glow of a lighted pipe. As I sat down, looking only below at the foaming bows as they cut through the waves or up at the Southern Cross, I had obviously failed to notice my neighbour, who must have been sitting here perfectly still all the time. Instinctively, my reactions still slow, I said in German, "Oh, I do apologise!" "Don't mention it," replied the voice from the darkness, in the same language.

I can't say how strange and eerie it was to be sitting next to someone like that in the dark, very close to a man I couldn't see. I felt as if he were staring at me just as I was staring at him, but the flowing, shimmering white light above us was so intense that neither of us could see more of the other than his outline in the shadows.

And I thought I could hear his breathing and the faint hissing sound as he drew on his pipe, but that was all.

The silence was unbearable. I wanted to move away, but that seemed too brusque, too sudden. In my embarrassment I took out a cigarette. The match spluttered, and for a second its light flickered over the narrow space where we were sitting. I saw a stranger's face behind the lenses of his glasses, a face I had never seen on board at any meal or on the promenade deck, and whether the sudden flame hurt the man's eyes, or whether it was just an illusion, his face suddenly seemed dreadfully distorted, dark and goblin-like. But before I could make out any details, darkness swallowed up the fleetingly illuminated features again, and I saw only the outline of a figure darkly imprinted on the darkness, and sometimes the circular, fiery ring of the bowl of his pipe hovering in space. Neither of us spoke, and our silence was as sultry and oppressive as the tropical air itself.

Finally I could stand it no longer. I stood up and said a civil, "Goodnight."

"Goodnight," came the reply from the darkness, in a hoarse, harsh, rusty voice.

I stumbled forward with some difficulty, over hawsers and past some posts. Then I heard footsteps behind me, hasty and uncertain. It was my companion of a moment ago. I instinctively stopped. He did not come right up to me, and through the darkness I sensed something like anxiety and awkwardness in his gait.

"Forgive me," he said quickly "if I ask you a favour. I… I…" he stammered, for a moment too embarrassed to go on at once. "I… I have private… very private reasons for staying out of sight… a bereavement… I prefer to avoid company on board. Oh, I didn't mean you, no, no… I'd just like to ask… well, I would be very much obliged if you wouldn't mention seeing me here to anyone on board. There are… are private reasons, I might call them, to keep me from mingling with people just now… yes, well, it would

put me in an awkward position if you mentioned that someone…
here at night… that I…" And he stopped again. I put an end to his
confusion at once by assuring him that I would do as he wished.
We shook hands. Then I went back to my cabin and slept a heavy,
curiously disturbed sleep, troubled by strange images.

I kept my promise, and told no one on board of my strange meeting,
although the temptation to do so was great. For on a sea voyage
every little thing becomes an event: a sail on the horizon, a dolphin
leaping, a new flirtation, a joke made in passing. And I was full
of curiosity to know more about the vessel's unusual passenger. I
searched the ship's list for a name that might be his, I scrutinized
other people, wondering if they could be somehow related to him;
all day I was a prey to nervous impatience, just waiting for evening
and wondering if I would meet him again. Odd psychological states
have a positively disquieting power over me; I find tracking down
the reasons for them deeply intriguing, and the mere presence of
unusual characters can kindle a passionate desire in me to know
more about them, a desire not much less strong than a woman's wish
to acquire some possession. The day seemed long and crumbled
tediously away between my fingers. I went to bed early, knowing
that my curiosity would wake me at midnight.

Sure enough, I woke at the same time as the night before. The
two hands on the illuminated dial of my clock covered one another
in a single bright line. I quickly left my sultry cabin and climbed up
into the even sultrier night.

The stars were shining as they had shone yesterday, casting a
diffuse light over the quivering ship, and the Southern Cross blazed
high overhead. It was all just the same as yesterday, where days
and nights in the tropics resemble each other more than in our
latitudes, but I myself did not feel yesterday's soft, flowing, dreamy

315

sensation of being gently cradled. Something was drawing me on, confusing me, and I knew where it was taking me: to the black hoist by the ship's side, to see if my mysterious acquaintance was sitting immobile there again. I heard the ship's bell striking above me, and it urged me on. Step by step, reluctantly yet fascinated, I followed my instincts. I had not yet reached the prow of the ship when something like a red eye suddenly hovered in front of me: the pipe. So he was there.

I instinctively stepped back and stopped. Next moment I would have left again, but there was movement over there in the dark, something rose, took a couple of steps, and suddenly I heard his voice very close to me, civil and melancholy.

"Forgive me," he said. "You obviously want to sit there again, and I have a feeling that you hesitated when you saw me. Do please sit down, and I'll go away."

I made haste to say he was very welcome to stay so far as I was concerned. I had stepped back, I said, only for fear of disturbing him.

"Oh, you won't disturb me," he said, with some bitterness. "Far from it, I'm glad to have company for a change. I haven't spoken a word to anyone for ten days… well, not for years, really, and then it seems so difficult, perhaps because forcing it all back inside myself chokes me. I can't sit in my cabin any more, in that… that coffin, I can't bear it, and I can't bear the company of human beings either because they laugh all day… I can't endure that now, I hear it in my cabin and stop my ears against it. Of course, they don't know that I… well, they don't know that… they don't know it, and what business is it of theirs, after all, they're strangers…"

He stopped again, and then very suddenly and hastily said, "But I don't want to bother you… forgive me for speaking so freely."

He made a bow, and was about to leave, but I urged him to stay. "You're not bothering me in the least. I'm glad to have a few quiet words with someone up here myself… may I offer you a cigarette?"

He took one, and I lit it. Once again his face moved away from the ship's black side, flickering in the light of the match, but now he turned it fully to me: his eyes behind his glasses looking inquiringly into my face, avidly and with demented force. A shudder passed through me. I could feel that this man wanted to speak, had to speak. And I knew that I must help him by saying nothing.

We sat down again. He had a second deckchair there, and offered it to me. Our cigarettes glowed, and from the way that the ring of light traced by his in the darkness shook, I could tell that his hand was trembling. But I kept silent, and so did he. Then, suddenly, he asked in a quiet voice, "Are you very tired?"

"No, not at all."

The voice in the dark hesitated again. "I would like to ask you something… that's to say, I'd like to tell you something. Oh, I know, I know very well how absurd it is to turn to the first man I meet, but… I'm… I'm in a terrible mental condition, I have reached a point where I absolutely must talk to someone, or it will be the end of me… You'll understand that when I… well, if I tell you… I mean, I know you can't help me, but this silence is almost making me ill, and a sick man always looks ridiculous to others…"

Here I interrupted, begging him not to distress himself. He could tell me anything he liked, I said. Naturally I couldn't promise him anything, but to show willingness is a human duty. If you see someone in trouble, I added, of course it is your duty to help…

"Duty… to show willing… a duty to try to… so you too think it is a man's duty… yes, his duty to show himself willing to help."

He repeated it three times. I shuddered at the blunt, grim tone of his repetition. Was the man mad? Was he drunk?

As if I had uttered my suspicions aloud, he suddenly said in quite a different voice, "You may think me mad or drunk. No, I'm not—not yet. Only what you said moved me so… so strangely, because that's exactly what torments me now, wondering if it's a duty… a duty…"

He was beginning to stammer again. He broke off for a moment, pulled himself together, and began again.

"The fact is, I am a doctor of medicine, and in that profession we often come upon such cases, such fateful cases… borderline cases, let's call them, when we don't know whether or not it is our duty… or rather, when there's more than one duty involved, not just to another human being but to ourselves too, to the state, to science… yes, of course, we must help, that's what we are there for… but such maxims are never more than theory. How far should we go with our help? Here are you, a stranger to me, and I'm a stranger to you, and I ask you not to mention seeing me… well, so you don't say anything, you do that duty… and now I ask you to talk to me because my own silence is killing me, and you say you are ready to listen. Good, but that's easy… suppose I were to ask you to take hold of me and throw me overboard, though, your willingness to help would be over. The duty has to end somewhere… it ends where we begin thinking of our own lives, our own responsibilities, it has to end somewhere, it has to end… or perhaps for doctors, of all people, it ought *not* to end? Must a doctor always come to the rescue, be ready to help one and all, just because he has a diploma full of Latin words, must he really throw away his life and water down his own blood if some woman… if someone comes along wanting him to be noble, helpful, good? Yes, duty ends somewhere… it ends where no more can be done, that's where it ends…"

He stopped again, and regained control.

"Forgive me, I know I sound agitated… but I'm not drunk, not yet… although I often am, I freely confess it, in this hellish isolation… bear in mind that for seven years I've lived almost entirely with the local natives and with animals… you forget how to talk calmly. And then if you do open up, everything comes flooding out… but wait… Yes, I know… I was going to ask you, I wanted to tell you about a certain case, wondering whether you think one has a duty to help…

just help, with motives as pure as an angel's, or whether... Although I fear it will be a long story. Are you sure you're not tired?"

"No, not in the least."

"Thank you... thank you. Will you have a drink?"

He had been groping in the dark behind him somewhere. There was a clinking sound: two or three, at any rate several bottles stood ranged there. He offered me a glass of whisky, which I sipped briefly, while he drained his glass in a single draught. For a moment there was silence between us. Then the ship's bell struck half-past midnight.

"Well then... I'd like to tell you about a case. Suppose that a doctor in a small town... or right out in the country, a doctor who... a doctor who..." He stopped again, and then suddenly moved his chair closer to mine.

"This is no good. I must tell you everything directly, from the beginning, or you won't understand it... no, I can't put it as a theoretical example, I must tell you the story of my own case. There'll be no shame about it, I will hide nothing... people strip naked in front of me, after all, and show me their scabs, their urine, their excrement... if someone is to help there can be no beating about the bush, no concealment. So I won't describe the case of some fictional doctor, I will strip myself naked and say that I... I forgot all shame in that filthy isolation, that accursed country that eats the soul and sucks the marrow from a man's loins."

I must have made a movement of some kind, for he interrupted himself.

"Ah, you protest... oh, I understand, you are fascinated by India, by its temples and palm trees, all the romance of a two-month visit. Yes, the tropics are magical when you're travelling through them by rail, road or rickshaw: I felt just the same when I first arrived seven years ago. I had so many dreams, I was going to learn the language and read the sacred texts in the original, I was going to study the diseases, do scientific work, explore the native psyche—as we would put it in European jargon—I was on a mission for humanity and civilisation. Everyone who comes here dreams the same dream. But then a man's strength ebbs away in this invisible hothouse, the fever strikes deep into him—and we all get the fever, however much quinine we take—he becomes listless, indolent, flabby as a jellyfish. As a European, he is cut off from his true nature, so to speak, when he leaves the big cities for some wretched swamp-ridden station. Sooner or later we all succumb to our weaknesses, some drink, others smoke opium, others again brawl and act like brutes—some kind of folly comes over us all. We long for Europe, we dream of walking down a street again some day, sitting among white people in a well-lit room in a solidly built house, we dream of it year after year, and if a time does come when we could go on leave we're too listless to take the chance. A man knows he's been forgotten back at home, he's a stranger there, a shell in the sea, anyone can tread on him. So he stays, he degenerates and goes to the bad in these hot, humid jungles. It was a bad day when I sold my services to that filthy place…

Not that I did it entirely of my own free will. I had studied in Germany, I was a qualified doctor, indeed a good doctor with a post at the big hospital in Leipzig; in some long-forgotten issue of a medical journal a great deal was made of a new injection that I was the first to introduce. And then I had trouble over a woman, I met her in the hospital; she had driven her lover so crazy that he shot her with a revolver, and soon I was as crazy as he had been. She had a cold, proud manner that drove me to distraction—bold domineering women had always had a hold over me, but she tightened that hold until my bones were breaking. I did what she wanted, I—well, why not say it? It's eight years ago now—I dipped into the hospital funds for her, and when it came out all hell was let loose. An uncle of mine covered up for me when I was dismissed, but my career was over. It was then that I heard the Dutch government was recruiting doctors for the colonies, offering a lump sum in payment. Well, I understood at once the kind of job it would be if they were offering payment like that. For I knew that the crosses on graves in the fever-zone plantations grow three times as fast as at home, but when you're young you think fever and death affect only others. However, I had little choice; I went to Rotterdam, signed up for ten years, and was given a big bundle of banknotes. I sent half home to my uncle, and as for the other half, a woman in the harbour district got it out of me, just because she was so like the vicious cat I'd loved. I sailed away from Europe without money, without even a watch, without illusions, and I wasn't particularly sorry to leave harbour. And then I sat on deck like you, like everyone, and saw the Southern Cross and the palm trees, and my heart rose. Ah, forests, isolation, silence, I dreamed! Well—I'd soon had enough of isolation. I wasn't stationed in Batavia or Surabaya, in a city with other people and clubs, golf, books and newspapers, instead I went to—well, the name doesn't matter—to one of the district stations, two days' journey from the nearest town. A couple of tedious, desiccated officials and a few half-castes were all the society I had, apart from that, nothing for miles around but jungle, plantations, thickets and swamps.

It was tolerable at first. I pursued all kinds of studies; once, when the vice-resident was on a journey of inspection, had a motor accident and broke a leg, I operated on him without assistants, and there was a lot of talk about it. I collected native poisons and weapons, I turned my attention to a hundred little things to keep my mind alert. But that lasted only as long as the strength of Europe was still active in me, and then I dried up. The few Europeans on the station bored me, I stopped mixing with them, I drank and I dreamed. I had only two more years to go before I'd be free, with a pension, and could go back to Europe and begin life again. I wasn't really doing anything but waiting; I lay low and waited. And that's what I would be doing today if she… if it hadn't happened."

The voice in the darkness stopped. The pipe had stopped glowing too. It was so quiet that all of a sudden I could hear the water foaming as it broke against the keel, and the dull, distant throbbing of the engines. I would have liked to light a cigarette, but I was afraid of the bright flash of the lit match and its reflection in his face. He remained silent for a long time. I didn't know if he had finished what he had to say, or was dozing, or had fallen asleep, so profound was his silence.

Then the ship's bell struck a single powerful note: one o'clock. He started. I heard his glass clink again. His hand was obviously feeling around for the whisky. A shot gurgled quietly into his glass, and then the voice suddenly began again, but now it seemed tenser and more passionate.

"So… wait a moment… so yes, there I was, sitting in my damned cobweb, I'd been crouching motionless as a spider in its web for months. It was just after the rainy season. Rain had poured down on the roof for weeks on end, not a human being had come along, no European, I'd been stuck there in the house day after day with my yellow-skinned women and my good whisky. I was feeling very 'down' at the time, homesick for Europe. If I read a novel describing clean streets and white women my fingers began to tremble. I can't really describe the condition to you, but it's like a tropical disease, a raging, feverish, yet helpless nostalgia that sometimes comes over a man. So there I was, sitting over an atlas, I think, dreaming of journeys. Then there's a hammering at the door. My boy is there and one of the women, eyes wide with amazement. They make dramatic gestures: there's a woman here, they say, a lady, a white woman.

I jump up in surprise. I didn't hear a carriage or a car approaching. A white woman, here in this wilderness?

I am about to go down the steps, but then I pull myself together. A glance in the mirror, and I hastily tidy myself up a little. I am nervous, restless, I have ominous forebodings, for I know no one in the world who would be coming to visit me out of friendship. At last I go down.

The lady is waiting in the hall, and hastily comes to meet me. A thick motoring veil hides her face. I am about to greet her, but she is quick to get her word in first. 'Good day, doctor,' she says in fluent English—slightly too fluent, as if she had learnt her speech by heart in advance. 'Do forgive me for descending on you like this, but we have just been visiting the station, our car is over there'—here a thought flashes through my mind: why didn't she drive up to the house?—'And then I remembered that you live here. I've heard so much about you—you worked miracles for the vice-resident, his leg is perfectly all right now, he can play golf as well as ever. Oh yes, imagine all of us in the city are still talking about it, we'd happily dispense with our own cross-grained surgeon and the other doctors if you would only come to us instead. Now, why do you never go to the city? You live like a yogi here... '

And so she chatters on, faster and faster, without letting me get a word in. Her loquacity is nervous and agitated, and makes me uneasy. Why is she talking so much, I ask myself, why doesn't she introduce herself, why doesn't she put that veil back? Is she feverish? Is she ill? Is she mad? I feel increasingly nervous, aware that I look ridiculous, standing silently in front of her while her flood of chatter sweeps over me. At last she slows down slightly, and I am able to ask her upstairs. She signs to the boy to stay where he is, and goes up the stairs ahead of me.

'You have a nice place here,' she says, looking around my room. 'Ah, such lovely books! I'd like to read them all!' She goes up to the bookcase and looks at the titles. For the first time since I set eyes on her, she falls silent for a minute.

'May I offer you a cup of tea?' I ask.

She doesn't turn, but just looks at the spines of the books. 'No thank you, doctor… we have to be off again in a moment, and I don't have much time… this was just a little detour. Ah, I see you have Flaubert as well, I love him so much… *L'Education sentimentale*, wonderful, really wonderful… So you read French too! A man of many talents! Ah, you Germans, you learn everything at school. How splendid to know so many languages! The vice-resident swears by you, he always says he wouldn't go under the knife with anyone else… our residency surgeon is good for playing bridge but… the fact is,' she said, still with her face turned away, 'it crossed my mind today that I might consult you myself some time… and since we happened to be passing anyway, I thought… oh, but I'm sure you are very busy… I can come back another time.'

Showing your hand at last, I thought. But I didn't show any reaction, I merely assured her that it would be an honour to be of service to her now or whenever she liked.

'It's nothing serious,' she said, half-turning and at the same time leafing through a book she had taken off the shelf. 'Nothing serious… just small things, women's troubles… dizziness, fainting. This morning I suddenly fainted as we were driving round a bend, fainted right away, the boy had to prop me up in the car and fetch water… but perhaps the chauffeur was just driving too fast, do you think, doctor?'

'I can't say, just like that. Do you often have fainting fits?'

'No… that is, yes… recently, in fact very recently. Yes, I have had such fainting fits, and attacks of nausea.' She is standing in front of the bookcase again, puts the book back, takes another out and riffles the pages. Strange, I think, why does she keep leafing through the pages so nervously, why doesn't she look up behind that veil?

324

Deliberately, I say nothing. I enjoy making her wait. At last she starts talking again in her nonchalant, loquacious way.

'There's nothing to worry about, doctor, is there? No tropical disease… nothing dangerous… ?'

'I'd have to see if you are feverish first. May I take your pulse?'

I approach her, but she moves slightly aside.

'No, no, I'm not feverish… certainly not, certainly not, I've been taking my own temperature every day since… since this fainting began. Never any higher, always exactly 36.4°. And my digestion is healthy too.'

I hesitate briefly. All this time a suspicion has been lurking at the back of my mind: I sense that this woman wants something from me. You certainly don't go into the wilderness to talk about Flaubert. I keep her waiting for a minute or two, then I say, straight out, 'Forgive me, but may I ask you a few frank questions?'

'Of course, doctor! You are a medical man, after all,' she replies, but she has her back turned to me again and is playing with the books.

'Do you have children?'

'Yes, a son.'

'And have you… did you previously… I mean with your son, did you experience anything similar?'

'Yes.'

Her voice is quite different now. Very clear, very firm, no longer loquacious or nervous.

'And is it possible… forgive my asking… that you are now in the same situation?'

'Yes.'

She utters the word in a tone as sharp and cutting as a knife. Her averted head does not move at all.

'Perhaps it would be best, ma'am, if I gave you a general examination. May I perhaps ask you to… to go to the trouble of coming into the next room?'

Then she does turn, suddenly. I feel a cold, determined gaze bent straight on me through her veil.

'No, that won't be necessary… I am fully aware of my condition.'"

The voice hesitated for a moment. The glass that he had refilled shone briefly in the darkness again.

"So listen… but first try to think a little about it for a moment. A woman forces herself on someone who is desperate with loneliness, the first white woman in years to set foot in his room… and suddenly I feel that there is something wrong here, a danger. A shiver runs down my spine: I am afraid of the steely determination of this woman, who arrived with her careless chatter and then suddenly came out with her demand like a knife. For I knew what she wanted me to do, I knew at once—it was not the first time women had made me such requests, but they approached me differently, ashamed or pleading, they came to me with tears and entreaties. But here was a steely… yes, a virile determination. I felt from the first second that this woman was stronger than me, that she could force me to do as she wanted. And yet, and yet… there was some evil purpose in me, a man on his guard, some kind of bitterness, for as I said before… from the first second, indeed even before I had seen her, I sensed that this woman was an enemy.

At first I said nothing. I remained doggedly, grimly silent. I felt that she was looking at me under her veil—looking at me straight and challengingly, I felt that she wanted to force me to speak, but evasively, or indeed unconsciously, I emulated her casual, chattering manner. I acted as if I didn't understand her, for—I don't know if you can understand this—I wanted to force her to speak clearly, I didn't want to offer anything, I wanted to be asked, particularly by her, because her manner was so imperious… and because I knew that I am particularly vulnerable to women with that cold, proud manner.

So I remained non-committal, saying there was no cause for concern, such fainting fits occurred in the natural course of events, indeed they almost guaranteed a happy outcome. I quoted cases from the medical press… I talked and talked, smoothly and effortlessly, always suggesting that this was something very banal, and… well, I kept waiting for her to interrupt me. Because I knew she wouldn't stand for that.

Then she did interrupt me sharply, waving aside all my reassuring talk.

'That's not what worries me, doctor. When my son was born I was in a better state of health, but now I'm not all right any more… I have a heart condition… '

'Ah, a heart condition,' I repeated, apparently concerned. 'We must look into that at once.' And I made as if to stand up and fetch my stethoscope.

But she stopped me again. Her voice was very sharp and firm now—like an officer's on a parade ground.

'I *do* have a heart condition, doctor, and I must ask you to believe what I tell you. I don't want to waste a lot of time with examinations— I think you might show a little more confidence in me. For my part, I've shown sufficient confidence in you.'

Now it was battle, an open challenge, and I accepted it.

'Confidence calls for frank disclosure, with nothing held back. Please speak frankly. I am a doctor. And for heaven's sake take that veil off, sit down, never mind the books and the roundaboutation. You don't go to visit a doctor in a veil.'

Proud and erect, she looked at me. For one moment she hesitated. Then she sat down and lifted her veil. I saw the kind of face I had feared to see, an impenetrable face, hard, controlled, a face of ageless beauty, a face with grey English eyes in which all seemed at peace, and yet behind which one could dream that all was passion. That narrow, compressed mouth gave nothing away if it didn't want to.

For a moment we looked at each other—she commandingly and at the same time inquiringly, with such cold, steely cruelty that I couldn't hold her gaze, but instinctively looked away.

She tapped the table lightly with her knuckles. So she was nervous too. Then she said, quickly and suddenly, 'Do you know what I want you to do for me, doctor, or don't you?'

'I believe I do. But let's be quite plain about it. You want an end put to your condition... you want me to cure you of your fainting fits and nausea by... by removing their cause. Is that it?'

'Yes.'

The word fell like a guillotine.

'And do you know that such attempts are dangerous... for both parties concerned?'

'Yes.'

'That I am legally forbidden to do such a thing?'

'There are cases when it isn't forbidden but actually recommended.'

'They call for medical indications, however.'

'Then you'll find such indications. You're a doctor.'

Clear, fixed, unflinching, her eyes looked at me as she spoke. It was an order, and weakling that I am, I trembled with admiration for her demonically imperious will. But I was still evasive, I didn't want to show that I was already crushed. Some spark of desire in me said: don't go too fast! Make difficulties. Force her to beg!

'That is not always within a doctor's competence. But I am ready to ask a colleague at the hospital... '

'I don't want your colleague... I came to you.'

'May I ask why?'

She looked coldly at me. 'I have no reservations about telling you. Because you live in seclusion, because you don't know me—because you are a good doctor, and because,' she added, hesitating for the first time, 'you probably won't stay here very much longer, particularly if you... if you can go home with a large sum of money.'

I felt cold. The adamant, commercial clarity of her calculation bemused me. So far her lips had uttered no request—she had already worked it all out, she had been lying in wait for me and then tracked me down. I felt the demonic force of her will enter into me, but embittered as I was—I resisted. Once again I made myself sound objective, indeed almost ironic.

'Oh, and you would... would place this large sum of money at my disposal?'

'For your help, and then your immediate departure.'

'Do you realise that would lose me my pension?'

'I will compensate you.'

'You're very clear in your mind about it... but I would like even more clarity. What sum did you envisage as a fee?'

'Twelve thousand guilders, payable by cheque when you reach Amsterdam.'

I trembled... I trembled with anger and... yes, with admiration again too. She had worked it all out, the sum and the manner of its payment, which would oblige me to leave this part of the world, she had assessed me and bought me before she even met me, had made arrangements for me in anticipation of getting her own way. I would have liked to strike her in the face, but as I stood there shaking—she too had risen to her feet—and I looked her straight in the eye, the sight of her closed mouth that refused to plead, her haughty brow that would not bend, a... a kind of violent desire overcame me. She must have felt something of it, for she raised her eyebrows as one would to dismiss a trouble-maker; the hostility between us was suddenly in the open. I knew she hated me because she needed me, and I hated her because... well, because she would not plead. In that one single second of silence we spoke to each other honestly for the first time. Then an idea suddenly came to me, like the bite of a reptile, and I told her... I told her...

But wait a moment, or you'll misunderstand what I did... what I said. First I must explain how... well, how that deranged idea came into my mind."

Once again the glass clinked softly in the dark, and the voice became more agitated.

"Not that I want to make excuses, justify myself, clear myself of blame... but otherwise you won't understand. I don't know if I have ever been what might be called a good man, but... well, I think I was always helpful. In the wretched life I lived over there, the only pleasure I had was using what knowledge was contained in my brain to keep some living creature breathing... an almost divine pleasure. It's a fact, those were my happiest moments, for instance when one of the natives came along, pale with fright, his swollen foot bitten by a snake, howling not to have his leg cut off, and I managed to save him. I've travelled for hours to see a woman in a fever—and as for the kind of help my visitor wanted, I'd already given that in the hospital in Europe. But then I could at least feel that these people *needed* me, that I was saving someone from death or despair—and the feeling of being needed was my way of helping myself.

But this woman—I don't know if I can describe it to you—she had irritated and intrigued me from the moment when she had arrived, apparently just strolling casually in. Her provocative arrogance made me resist, she caused everything in me that was—how shall I put it?—everything in me that was suppressed, hidden, wicked, to oppose her. Playing the part of a great lady, meddling in matters of life and death with unapproachable aplomb... it drove me mad. And then... well, after all, no woman gets pregnant just from playing golf. I knew, that is to say I reminded myself with terrible clarity—and this is when my idea came to me—that this cool, haughty, cold woman, raising her eyebrows above her steely eyes

330

if I so much as looked at her askance and parried her demands, had been rolling in bed with a man in the heat of passion two or three months ago, naked as an animal and perhaps groaning with desire, their bodies pressing as close as a pair of lips. That was the idea burning in my mind as she looked at me with such unapproachable coolness, proud as an English army officer... and then everything in me braced itself, I was possessed by the idea of humiliating her. From that moment on, I felt I could see her naked body through her dress... from that moment on I lived for nothing but the idea of taking her, forcing a groan from her hard lips, feeling this cold, arrogant woman a prey to desire like anyone else, as that other man had done, the man I didn't know. That... that's what I wanted to explain to you. Low as I had sunk, I had never before thought of exploiting such a situation as a doctor... and this time it wasn't desire, the rutting instinct, nothing sexual, I swear it wasn't, I can vouch for it... just a wish to break her pride, dominate her as a man. I think I told you that I have always been susceptible to proud and apparently cold women... and add to that the fact that I had lived here for seven years without sleeping with a white woman, and had met with no resistance... for the girls here, twittering, fragile little creatures who tremble with awe if a white man, a 'master' takes them... they efface themselves in humility, they're always available, always at your service with their soft, gurgling laughter, but that submissive, slavish attitude in itself spoils the pleasure. So can you understand the shattering effect on me when a woman full of pride and hostility suddenly came along, reserved in every fibre of her being, glittering with mystery and at the same time carrying the burden of an earlier passion? When such a woman boldly enters the cage of a man like me, a lonely, starved, isolated brute of a man... well, that's what I wanted to tell you, just so that you'll understand the rest, what happened next. So, full of some kind of wicked greed, poisoned by the thought of her stripped naked, sensuous, submitting, I pulled myself together with pretended indifference. I said coolly, 'Twelve thousand guilders? No, I won't do it for that.'

She looked at me, turning a little pale. She probably sensed already that my refusal was not a matter of avarice, but she said, 'Then what do you want?'

I was not putting up with her cool tone any more. 'Let's show our hands, shall we? I am not a tradesman... I'm not the poor apothecary in *Romeo and Juliet* who sells his poison for 'corrupted gold'. Perhaps I'm the opposite of a tradesman... you won't get what you want by those means.'

'So you won't do it?'

'Not for money.'

All was very still between us for a second. So still that for the first time I heard her breathing.

'What else can you want, then?'

Now I could control myself no longer. 'First, I want you to stop... stop speaking to me as if I were a tradesman and address me like a human being. And when you need help, I don't want you to... to come straight out with your shameful offer of money, but to ask me... ask me to help you as one human being to another. I am not just a doctor, I don't spend all my time in consultations... I spend some of it in other ways too, and perhaps you have come at such a time.'

She says nothing for a moment, and then her lip curls very slightly, trembles, and she says quickly, 'Then if I were to ask you... would you do it?'

'You're trying to drive a bargain again—you won't ask me unless I promise first. You must ask me first—then I will give you an answer.'

She tosses her head like a defiant horse, and looks angrily at me.

'No, I will not ask you. I'd rather go to my ruin!'

At that anger seized upon me, red, senseless anger.

'Then if you won't ask, I will make my own demand. I don't think I have to put it crudely—you know what I want from you. And then—then I will help you.'

She stared at me for a moment. Then—oh, I can't, I can't tell you how terrible it was—then her features froze and she... she suddenly *laughed*, she laughed at me with unspeakable contempt in her face, contempt that was scattered all over me... and at the same time intoxicated me. That derisive laughter was like a sudden explosion, breaking out so abruptly and with such monstrous force behind it that I... yes, I could have sunk to the ground and kissed her feet. It lasted only a second... it was like lightning, and it had set my whole body on fire. Then she turned and went quickly to the door. I instinctively moved to follow her... to apologise, to beg her... well, my strength was entirely broken. She turned once more and said... no, *ordered*, 'Don't dare to follow me or try to track me down. You would regret it.'

And the door slammed shut behind her."

Another hesitation. Another silence... again, there was only the faint rushing sound, as if of moonlight pouring down. Then, at last, the voice spoke again.

"The door slammed, but I stood there motionless on the spot, as if hypnotized by her order. I heard her go downstairs, open the front door... I heard it all, and my whole will urged me to follow her... to... oh, I don't know what, to call her back, strike her, strangle her, but to follow her... to follow. Yet I couldn't. My limbs were crippled as if by an electric shock... I had been cut to the quick by the imperious gleam of those eyes. I know there's no explaining it, it can't be described... it may sound ridiculous, but I just stood there, and it was several minutes, perhaps five, perhaps ten, before I could raise a foot from the floor...

But no sooner had I moved that foot than I instantly, swiftly, feverishly hurried down the stairs. She could only have gone along the road back to civilisation… I hurry to the shed for my bicycle, I find I have forgotten the door key, I wrench the lock off, splitting and breaking the bamboo of the shed door… and next moment I am on my bicycle and hurrying after her… I have to reach her, I must, before she gets back to her car. I must speak to her. The road rushes past me… only now do I realise how long I must have stood there motionless. Then, where the road through the forest bends just before reaching the buildings of the district station, I see her hurrying along, stepping firmly, walking straight ahead accompanied by her boy… but she must have seen me too, for now she speaks to the boy, who stays behind while she goes on alone. What is she doing? Why does she want to be on her own? Does she want to speak to me out of his hearing? I pedal fast and furiously… then something suddenly springs into my path. It's the boy… I am only just in time to swerve and fall. I rise, cursing… involuntarily I raise my fist to hit the fool, but he leaps aside. I pick up my bicycle to remount it, but then the scoundrel lunges forward, takes hold of the bicycle, and says in his pitiful English, 'You not go on.'

You haven't lived in the tropics… you don't know how unheard-of it is for a yellow bastard like that to seize the bicycle of a white 'master' and tell him, the master, to stay where he is. Instead of answering I strike him in the face with my fist. He staggers, but keeps hold of the bicycle… his eyes, his narrow, frightened eyes are wide open in slavish fear, but he holds the handlebars infernally tight. 'You not go on,' he stammers again. It's lucky I don't have my revolver with me, or I'd shoot him down. 'Out of the way, scum!' is all I say. He cringes and stares at me, but he does not let go of the handlebars. At this rage comes over me… I see that she is well away, she may have escaped me entirely… and I hit him under the chin with a boxer's punch and send him flying. Now I have my bicycle back, but as I jump on it the mechanism jams. A spoke has bent in our tussle. I try to straighten it with trembling hands. I can't, so I fling the bicycle across the road at the scoundrel, who gets up, bleeding, and flinches aside. And then—no, you won't understand how ridiculous it looks to everyone there for a European... well, anyway, I didn't know what I was doing any more. I had only one thought in my mind: to go after her, to reach her. And so I *ran*, ran like a madman along the road and past the huts, where the yellow riff-raff were gathered in amazement to see a white man, the doctor, *running*.

I reach the station, dripping with sweat. My first question is: where is the car? Just driven away... People stare at me in surprise. I must look to them like a lunatic, arriving wet and muddy, screaming my question ahead of me before coming to a halt... Down in the road, I see the white fumes of the car exhaust. She has succeeded... succeeded, just as all her harsh, cruelly harsh calculations must succeed.

But flight won't help her. There are no secrets among Europeans in the tropics. Everyone knows everyone else, everything is a notable event. And not for nothing did her driver spend an hour in the government bungalow... in a few minutes, I know all about it. I know who she is, I know that she lives in... well, in the capital of the colony, eight hours from here by rail. I know that she is... let's say the wife of a big businessman, enormously rich, distinguished, an Englishwoman. I know that her husband has been in America for five months, and is to arrive here next day to take her back to Europe with him...

And meanwhile—the thought burns in my veins like poison— meanwhile she can't be more than two or three months pregnant...

So far I hope I have made it easy for you to understand... but perhaps only because up to that point I still understood myself, and as a doctor I could diagnose my own condition. From now on, however, something began to work in me like a fever… I lost control. That's to say, I knew exactly how pointless everything I did was, but I had no power over myself any more… I no longer understood myself. I was merely racing forward, obsessed by my purpose… No, wait. Perhaps I can make you understand it after all. Do you know what the expression 'running amok' means?"

"'Running amok?' Yes, I think I do… a kind of intoxication affecting the Malays…"

"It's more than intoxication… it's madness, a sort of human rabies, an attack of murderous, pointless monomania that bears no comparison with ordinary alcohol poisoning. I've studied several cases myself during my time in the East —it's easy to be very wise and objective about other people—but I was never able to uncover the terrible secret of its origin. It may have something to do with the climate, the sultry, oppressive atmosphere that weighs on the nervous system like a storm until it suddenly breaks… well then, this is how it goes: a Malay, an ordinary, good-natured man, sits drinking his brew, impassive, indifferent, apathetic… just as I was sitting in my room… when suddenly he leaps to his feet, snatches his dagger and runs out into the street, going straight ahead of him, always straight ahead, with no idea of any destination. With his *kris* he strikes down anything that crosses his path, man or beast, and this murderous frenzy makes him even more deranged. He froths at the mouth as he runs, he howls like a lunatic… but he still runs and runs and runs, he doesn't look right, he doesn't look left, he just runs on screaming shrilly, brandishing his bloodstained *kris* as he forges straight ahead in that dreadful way. The people of the villages know that no power can halt a man running amok, so they shout warnings ahead when they see him coming —'Amok! Amok!'—and everyone flees… but he runs on without hearing, without seeing, striking down anything he meets… until he is either shot dead like a mad dog or collapses of his own accord, still frothing at the mouth…

I once saw a case from the window of my bungalow. It was a terrible sight, but it's only because I saw it that I can understand myself in those days... because I stormed off like that, just like that, obsessed in the same way, going straight ahead with that dreadful expression, seeing nothing to right or to left, following the woman. I don't remember exactly what I did, it all went at such breakneck speed, with such mindless haste... Ten minutes, no, five—no, two— after I had found out all about the woman, her name, where she lived and her story, I was racing back to my house on a borrowed bicycle, I threw a suit into my case, took some money and drove to the railway station in my carriage. I went without informing the district officer, without finding a locum for myself, I left the house just as it was, unlocked. The servants were standing around, the astonished women were asking questions. I didn't answer, didn't turn, drove to the station and took the next train to the city... only an hour after that woman had entered my room, I had thrown my life away and was running amok, careering into empty space.

I ran straight on, headlong... I arrived in the city at six in the evening, and at ten past six I was at her house asking to see her. It was... well, as you will understand, it was the most pointless, stupid thing I could have done, but a man runs amok with empty eyes, he doesn't see where he is going. The servant came back after a few minutes, cool and polite: his mistress was not well and couldn't see anyone.

I staggered away. I prowled around the house for an hour, possessed by the insane hope that she might perhaps come looking for me. Only then did I book into the hotel on the beach and went to my room with two bottles of whisky which, with a double dose of veronal, helped to calm me. At last I fell asleep... and that dull, troubled sleep was the only momentary respite in my race between life and death."

*

The ship's bell sounded. Two hard, full strokes that vibrated on, trembling, in the soft pool of near-motionless air and then ebbed away in the quiet, endless rushing of the water washing around the keel, its sound mingling with his passionate tale. The man opposite me in the dark must have started in alarm, for his voice hesitated. Once again I heard his hand move down to find a bottle, and the soft gurgling. Then, as if reassured, he began again in a firmer voice.

"I can scarcely tell you about the hours I passed from that moment on. I think, today, that I was in a fever at the time; at the least I was in a state of over-stimulation bordering on madness—as I told you, I was running amok. But don't forget, it was Tuesday night when I arrived, and on Saturday—as I had now discovered—her husband was to arrive on the P&O steamer from Yokohama. So there were just three days left, three brief days for the decision to be made and for me to help her. You'll understand that I knew I must help her at once, yet I couldn't speak a word to her. And my need to apologise for my ridiculous, deranged behaviour drove me on. I knew how valuable every moment was, I knew it was a matter of life and death to her, yet I had no opportunity of approaching her with so much as a whisper or a sign, because my tempestuous foolishness in chasing after her had frightened her off. It was… wait, yes… it was like running after someone warning that a murderer is on the way, and that person thinks you are the murderer yourself and so runs on to ruin… She saw me only as a man running amok, pursuing her in order to humiliate her, but I… and this was the terrible absurdity of it… I wasn't thinking of that any more at all. I was destroyed already, I just wanted to help her, do her a service. I would have committed murder, any crime, to help her… but she didn't understand that. When I woke in the morning and went straight back to her house, the boy was standing in the doorway, the servant whose face I had punched, and when he saw me coming—he must have been looking out for me—he hurried in through the door. Perhaps he went in only to announce my arrival discreetly... perhaps... oh, that uncertainty, how it torments me now... perhaps everything was ready to receive me, but then, when I saw him, I remembered my disgrace, and this time I didn't even dare to try calling on her again. I was weak at the knees. Just before reaching the doorway I turned and went away again... went away, while she, perhaps, was waiting for me in a similar state of torment.

I didn't know what to do in this strange city that seemed to burn like fire beneath my feet. Suddenly I thought of something, called for a carriage, went to see the vice-resident on whose leg I had operated back at my own district station, and had myself announced. Something in my appearance must have seemed strange, for he looked at me with slight alarm, and there was an uneasiness about his civility... perhaps he recognised me as a man running amok. I told him, briefly, that I wanted a transfer to the city, I couldn't exist in my present post any longer, I said, I had to move at once. He looked at me... I can't tell you how he looked at me... perhaps as a doctor looks at a sick man. 'A nervous breakdown, my dear doctor?' he said. 'I understand that only too well. I'm sure it can be arranged, but wait... let's say for four weeks, while I find a replacement.'

'I can't wait, I can't wait even a day,' I replied. Again he gave me that strange look. 'You must, doctor,' he said gravely. 'We can't leave the station without a medical man. But I promise you I'll set everything in motion this very day.' I stood there with my teeth gritted; for the first time I felt clearly that I was a man whose services had been bought, I was a slave. I was preparing to defy him when, diplomat that he was, he got his word in first. 'You're unused to mixing with other people, doctor, and in the end that becomes an illness. We've all been surprised that you never came here to the city or went on leave. You need more company, more stimulation. Do at least come to the government reception this evening. You'll find the entire colony, and many of them have long wanted to meet you, they've often asked about you and hoped to see you here.'

That last remark pulled me up short. People had asked about me? Could he mean *her*? I was suddenly a different man: I immediately thanked him courteously for his invitation and assured him that I would be there punctually. And punctual I was, over-punctual. I hardly have to tell you that, driven by my impatience, I was the first in the great hall of the government building, surrounded by the silent, yellow-skinned servants whose bare feet hurried back and forth, and who—so it seemed to me in my confused state of mind—were laughing at me behind my back. For a quarter of an hour I was the only European among all the soundless preparations, so alone with myself that I could hear the ticking of my watch in my waistcoat pocket. Then a few government officials at last appeared with their families, and finally the Governor too entered, and drew me into a long conversation in which I assiduously and I think skilfully played my part, until… until suddenly, attacked by a mysterious attack of nerves, I lost all my diplomatic manner and began stammering. Although my back was to the entrance of the hall, I suddenly felt that she must have entered and was present there. I can't tell you how that sudden certainty confused me, but even as I was talking to the Governor and heard his words echo in my ears, I sensed her presence somewhere behind me. Luckily the Governor soon ended the conversation—or I think I would suddenly and abruptly have turned, so strong was that mysterious tugging of my nerves, so burning and agitated my desire. And sure enough, I had hardly turned before I saw her exactly where my senses had unconsciously guessed she would be. She wore a yellow ball-dress that made her slender, immaculate shoulders glow like dull ivory, and was talking to a group of guests. She was smiling, but I thought there was a tense expression on her face. I came closer—she either could not or would not see me—and looked at the attractive smile civilly hovering on her narrow lips. And that smile intoxicated me again, because… well, because I knew it was a lie born of art or artifice, a masterpiece of deception. Today is Wednesday, I thought, on Saturday the ship with her husband on board will arrive… how can she smile like that, so… so confidently, with such a carefree look, casually playing with the fan she holds instead of crushing it in her fear? I… I, a stranger, had been trembling for two days at the thought of this moment… Strange to her as I was, I experienced her fear and horror intensely… and she herself went to this ball and smiled, smiled, smiled…

Music started to play at the back of the hall. The dancing began. An elderly officer had asked her to dance; she left the chattering circle with a word of excuse and walked on his arm towards the other hall and past me. When she saw me her face suddenly froze—but only for a second, and then, before I could make up my mind whether or not to greet her, she gave me a civil nod of recognition, as she would to a chance acquaintance, said, 'Good evening, doctor,' and was gone. No one could have guessed what that grey-green glance concealed; I didn't know myself. Why did she speak to me… why did she suddenly acknowledge me? Was it rejection, was it a *rapprochement*, was it just the embarrassment of surprise? I can't describe the agitation into which I was cast; everything was in turmoil, explosively concentrated within me, and as I saw her like that—casually waltzing in the officer's arms, with such a cool, carefree look on her brow, while I knew that she… that she, like me, was thinking of only one thing… that we two alone, out of everyone here, had a terrible secret in common… and she was waltzing… well, in those few seconds my fear, my longing and my admiration became more passionate than ever. I don't know if anyone was watching me, but certainly my conduct gave away no more than hers—I just could not look in any other direction, I had to… I absolutely had to look at her from a distance, my eyes fastening on her closed face to see if the mask

341

would not drop for a second. She must have found the force of my gaze uncomfortable. As she moved away on her dancing partner's arm, she glanced my way for a split second with imperious sharpness, as if repelling me; once again that little frown of haughty anger, the one I knew already, disfigured her brow.

But… but, as I told you, I was running amok; I looked neither to right nor to left. I understood her at once—her glance said: don't attract attention! Control yourself! I knew that she… how can I put it?… that she expected me to behave discreetly here in the hall, in public. I realised that if I went home at this point, I could be certain she would see me in the morning… that all she wanted to avoid just now was being exposed to my obvious familiarity with her, I knew she feared—and rightly—that my clumsiness would cause a scene. You see, I knew everything, I understood that imperious grey gaze, but… but my feelings were too strong, I had to speak to her. So I moved unsteadily over to the group where she stood talking, joined its loose-knit circle although I knew only a few of the people in it, merely in the hope of hearing her speak, yet always flinching from her eyes timidly, like a whipped dog, when they coldly rested on me as if I were one of the linen curtains hanging behind me, or the air that lightly moved it. But I stood there thirsty for a word spoken to me, for a sign of our understanding, I stood like a block, gazing at her amidst all the chatter. It cannot have passed unnoticed, for no one addressed a word to me, and she had to suffer my ridiculous presence.

I don't know how long I would have stood there… for ever, per-haps… I *could* not leave that enchantment of my own volition. The very force of my frenzy crippled me. But she could not bear it any more… she suddenly turned to the gentlemen, with the magnificent ease that came naturally to her, and said, 'I am a little tired… I think I'll go to bed early for once. Good night!' And she was walking past me with a distant social nod of her head… I could still see the frown on her face, and then nothing but her back, her white, cool, bare back. It was a second before I realised that she was leaving... that I wouldn't be able to see her or speak to her again this evening, this last evening before I could help her. For a moment I stood there rooted to the spot until I realised it, and then... then...

But wait... wait, or you will not understand how stupid and pointless what I did was. I must describe the whole room to you first. It was the great hall of the government building, entirely illuminated by lights and almost empty... the couples had gone into the other room to dance, gentlemen had gone to play cards... only a few groups were still talking in the corners, so the hall was empty, every movement conspicuous and visible in the bright light. And she walked slowly and lightly through that great hall with her shoulders straight, exchanging greetings now and then with indescribable composure, with the magnificent, frozen, proud calm that so enchanted me. I... I had stayed behind, as I told you, as if paralysed, before I realised that she was leaving... and then, when I did realise, she was already at the far side of the hall and just approaching the doors. Then... and I am still ashamed to think of it now... something suddenly came over me and I *ran*... I ran, do you hear?... I did not walk but *ran* through the hall after her, my shoes clattering on the floor. I heard my own footsteps, I saw all eyes turning to me in surprise... I could have died of shame... even as I ran I understood my own derangement, but I could not... could not go back now. I caught up with her in the doorway. She turned to me... her eyes stabbed like grey steel, her nostrils were quivering with anger... I was just going to stammer something out when... when she suddenly *laughed* aloud... a clear, carefree, whole-hearted laugh, and said, in a voice loud enough for everyone to hear, 'Oh, doctor, have you only just remembered my little boy's prescription? Ah, you learned scientists!' A couple of people standing nearby laughed kindly... I understood, and was shattered by the masterly

343

way she had saved the situation. I put my hand in my wallet and tore a blank leaf off my prescription block, and she took it casually before… again with a cold smile of thanks… before she went. For one second I felt easy in my mind… I saw that her skill in dealing with my blunder had made up for it and put things right—but next moment I also knew that all was over for me now, she hated me for my intemperate folly… hated me worse than death itself. I could come to her door hundreds upon hundreds of times, and she would always have me turned away like a dog.

I staggered through the room… I realised that people were looking at me, and I must have appeared strange. I went to the buffet and drank two, three, four glasses of cognac one after another, which saved me from collapsing. My nerves could bear no more, they were in shreds. Then I slunk out through a side entrance, as secretly as a criminal. Not for any principality in the world could I have walked back through that hall, with her carefree laughter still echoing from its walls. I went… I really can't say now exactly where I went, but into a couple of bars where I got drunk, like a man trying to drink his consciousness away… but I could not numb my senses, the laughter was there in me, high and dreadful… I could not silence that damned laughter. I wandered around the harbour… I had left my revolver in my room, or I would have shot myself. I could think of nothing else, and with that thought I went back to the hotel with one idea in my mind… the left-hand drawer of the chest where my revolver lay… with that single idea in mind.

The fact that I didn't shoot myself after all… I swear it wasn't cowardice, it would have been a release to take off the safety catch and press the cold trigger… how can I explain it? I still felt I had a duty… yes, that damned duty to help. The thought that she might still need me, that she did need me, made me mad… it was Thursday morning before I was back in my room, and on Saturday, as I have told you, on Saturday the ship would come in, and I knew that *this* woman, this proud and haughty woman would not survive being shamed before her husband and the world... Oh, how my thoughts tortured me, thoughts of the precious time I had unthinkingly wasted, the crazy haste that had thwarted any prospect of bringing her help in time... for hours, I swear, for hours on end I paced up and down my room, racking my brains to think of a way to approach her, put matters right, help her... for I was certain that she wouldn't let me into her house now. Her laughter was still there in all my nerves, I still saw her nostrils quivering with anger. For hours I paced up and down the three metres of my cramped room... and day had dawned, morning was here already.

Suddenly an idea sent me to the desk... I snatched up a sheaf of notepaper and began to write to her, write it all down... a whining, servile letter in which I begged her forgiveness, called myself a madman, a criminal, and begged her to entrust herself to me. I swore that the hour after it was done I would disappear from the city, from the colony, from the world if she wanted... only she must forgive me and trust me to help her at the last, the very last minute. I feverishly wrote twenty pages like this... it must have been a mad, indescribable letter, like a missive written in delirium, for when I rose from the desk I was bathed in sweat... the room swayed, and I had to drink a glass of water. Only then did I try reading the letter through again, but the very first words horrified me, so I folded it up, trembling, found an envelope... and suddenly a new thought came to me. All at once I knew the right, the crucial thing to say. I picked up the pen again, and wrote on the last sheet, 'I will wait here in the beach hotel for a word of forgiveness. If no answer comes by seven this evening, I shall shoot myself.'

Then I took the letter, rang for a boy, and told him to deliver the envelope at once. At last I had said everything—everything!"

*

Something clinked and fell down beside us. As he moved abruptly he had knocked over the whisky bottle; I heard his hand feeling over the deck for it, and then he picked it up with sudden vigour. He threw the empty bottle high in the air and over the ship's side. The voice fell silent for a few minutes, and then feverishly continued, even faster and more agitated than before.

"I am not a believing Christian any more… I don't believe in heaven or hell, and if hell does exist I am not afraid of it, for it can't be worse than those hours I passed between morning and evening… think of a small room, hot in the sunlight, red-hot at blazing noon… a small room, just a desk and a chair and the bed… and nothing on the desk but a watch and a revolver, and sitting at the desk a man… a man who does nothing but stare at that desk and the second hand of his watch, a man who eats and drinks nothing, doesn't smoke, doesn't move, who only… listen to me… who only stares for three long hours at the white circle of the dial and the hand of the watch ticking as it goes around. That… that was how I spent the day, just waiting, waiting, waiting… but waiting like a man running amok, senselessly, like an animal, with that headlong, direct persistence.

Well, I won't try to describe those hours to you… they are beyond description. I myself don't understand now how one can go through such an experience without going mad. Then, at twenty-two minutes past three… I remember the time exactly, I was staring at my watch… there was a sudden knock at the door. I leap up… leap like a tiger leaping on its prey, in one bound I am across the room and at the door, I fling it open, and there stands a timid little Chinese boy with a folded note in his hand. As I avidly reach for it, he scurries away and is gone.

I tear the note open to read it… and find that I can't. A red mist blurs my vision… imagine my agony, I have word from her at last, and now everything is quivering and dancing before my eyes. I dip my head in water, and my sight clears… once again I take the note and read it. 'Too late! But wait where you are. I may yet send for you.'

No signature on the crumpled paper torn from some old brochure… the writing of someone whose handwriting is usually steady, now scribbling hastily, untidily, in pencil. I don't know why that note shook me so much. Some kind of horror, some mystery clung to it, it might have been written in flight, by someone standing in a window bay or a moving vehicle. An unspeakably cold aura of fear, haste and terror about that furtive note chilled me to the heart… and yet, and yet I was happy. She had written to me, I need not die yet, I could help her… perhaps I could… oh, I lost myself in the craziest hopes and conjectures. I read the little note a hundred, a thousand times over, I kissed it… I examined it for some word I might have forgotten or overlooked. My reverie grew ever deeper and more confused, I was in a strange condition, sleeping with open eyes, a kind of paralysis, a torpid yet turbulent state between sleep and waking. It lasted perhaps for quarter of an hour or so, perhaps for hours.

Suddenly I gave a start. Wasn't that a knock at the door? I held my breath for a minute, two minutes of perfect silence… and then it came again, like a mouse nibbling, a soft but urgent knock. I leaped to my feet, still dizzy, flung the door open, and there outside it stood her boy, the same boy whom I had once struck in the face with my fist. His brown face was pale as ashes, his confused glance spoke of some misfortune. I immediately felt horror. 'What… what's happened?' I managed to stammer. He said, 'Come quickly!' That was all, no more, but I was immediately racing down the stairs with the boy after me. A *sado*, a kind of small carriage, stood waiting. We got in. 'What's happened?' I asked him. He looked at me, trembling, and remained silent, lips compressed. I asked again… still he was silent. I could have struck him with my fist once more, but his doglike devotion to her touched me, and I asked no more questions. The little carriage trotted through the crowded street so fast that people scattered, cursing. It left the European quarter near the beach in the lower town and went on into the noisy turmoil of the city's Chinatown district. At last we reached a narrow, very remote alley… and the carriage stopped outside a low-built house. The place was dirty, with a kind of hunched look about it and a little shop window where a tallow candle stood… one of those places where you would expect to find opium dens or brothels, a thieves' lair or a receivers' cellar full of stolen goods. The boy quickly knocked… a voice whispered through a crack in the door, which stood ajar, there were questions and more questions. I could stand it no longer. I leaped up, pushed the door right open, and an old Chinese woman shrank back with a little scream. The boy followed me, led me along the passage… opened another door… another door, leading to a dark room with a foul smell of brandy and clotted blood. Something in the room groaned. I groped my way in…"

Once again his voice failed. And what he next uttered was more of a sob than words.

"I… I groped my way in… And there… there on a dirty mat, doubled up with pain… a groaning piece of human flesh… there she lay…

I couldn't see her face in the darkness. My eyes weren't yet used to it… so I only groped about and found… found her hand, hot, burning hot… she had a temperature, a very high one, and I shuddered, for I instantly knew it all… how she had fled here from me, had let some dirty Chinese woman mutilate her, only because she hoped for more silence in that quarter… she had allowed some diabolical witch to murder her rather than trust me… because, deranged as I was, I hadn't spared her pride, I hadn't helped her at once… because she feared me more than she feared death.

I shouted for light. The boy ran off; the appalling Chinese woman, her hands trembling, brought a smoking oil lamp. I had to stop myself taking her by her filthy yellow throat as she put the lamp on the table. Its light fell bright and yellow on the tortured body. And suddenly... suddenly all my emotions were gone, all my apathy, my anger, all the impure filth of my accumulated passion... I was nothing but a doctor now, a human being who could understand and feel and help. I had forgotten myself, I was fighting the horror of it with my senses alert and clear... I felt the naked body I had desired in my dreams only as... how can I put it?... as matter, an organism. I did not see *her* any more, only life defending itself against death, a human being bent double in dreadful agony. Her blood, her hot, holy blood streamed over my hands, but I felt no desire and no horror, I was only a doctor. I saw only her suffering... and I saw...

And I saw at once that barring a miracle, all was lost... the woman's criminally clumsy hand had injured her, and she had bled half to death... and I had nothing to stop the bleeding in that stinking den, not even clean water. Everything I touched was stiff with dirt...

'We must go straight to the hospital,' I said. But no sooner had I spoken than her tortured body reared convulsively.

'No... no... would rather die... no one must know... no one... home... home...'

I understood. She was fighting now only to keep her secret, to preserve her honour... not to save her life. And—and I obeyed. The boy brought a litter, we placed her in it... and so we carried her home, already like a corpse, limp and feverish, through the night, fending off the frightened servants' inquiries. Like thieves, we carried her into her own room and closed the doors. And then... then the battle began, the long battle with death..."

*

Suddenly a hand clutched my arm, and I almost cried out with the shock and pain of it. His face in the dark was suddenly hideously close to mine, I saw his white teeth gleam in his sudden outburst, saw his glasses shine like two huge cat's eyes in the pale reflection of the moonlight. And now he was not talking any more but screaming, shaken by howling rage.

"Do you know, stranger, sitting here so casually in your deckchair, travelling at leisure around the world, do you know what it's like to watch someone dying? Have you even been at a deathbed, have you seen the body contort, blue nails scrabbling at the empty air while breath rattles in the dying throat, every limb fights back, every finger is braced against the terror of it, and the eye stares into horror for which there are no words? Have you ever experienced that, idle tourist that you are, you who call it a duty to help? As a doctor I've often seen it, seen it as… as a clinical case, a fact… I have studied it, so to speak—but I *experienced* it only once, there with her, I died with her that night… that dreadful night when I sat there racking my brains to think of something, some way to staunch the blood that kept on flowing, soothe the fever consuming her before my eyes, ward off death as it came closer and closer, and I couldn't keep it from her bed. Can you guess what it means to be a doctor, to know how to combat every illness—to feel the duty of helping, as you so sagely put it, and yet to sit helpless by a dying woman, knowing what is happening but powerless… just knowing the one terrible truth, that there is nothing you can do, although you would open every vein in your own body for her? Watching a beloved body bleed miserably to death in agonising pain, feeling a pulse that flutters and grows faint… ebbing away under your fingers. To be a doctor yet know of nothing, nothing, nothing you can do… just sitting there stammering out some kind of prayer like a little old lady in church, shaking your fist in the face of a merciful god who you know doesn't exist… can you understand that? Can you understand it? There's just one thing I don't understand myself: how... how a man can manage not to die too at such moments, but wake from sleep the next morning, clean his teeth, put on a tie... go on living, when he has experienced what I felt as her breath failed, as the first human being for whom I was really wrestling, fighting, whom I wanted to keep alive with all the force of my being... as she slipped away from me to somewhere else, faster and faster, minute after minute, and my feverish brain could do nothing to keep that one woman alive...

And then, to add to my torment, there was something else too... as I sat at her bedside—I had given her morphine to relieve the pain—and I saw her lying there with burning cheeks, hot and ashen, as I sat there, I felt two eyes constantly fixed on me from behind, gazing at me with terrible expectation. The boy sat there on the floor, quietly murmuring some kind of prayer, and when my eyes met his I saw... oh, I cannot describe it... I saw something so pleading, so... so grateful in his doglike gaze! And at the same time he raised his hands to me as if urging me to save her... to me, you understand, he raised his hands to *me* as if to a god... to me, the helpless weakling who knew the battle was lost, that I was as useless here as an ant scuttling over the floor. How that gaze tormented me, that fanatical, animal hope of what my art could do... I could have shouted at him, kicked him, it hurt so much... and yet I felt that we were both linked by our love for her... by the secret. A waiting animal, an apathetic tangle of limbs, he sat hunched up just behind me. The moment I asked for anything he leaped to his bare, silent feet and handed it to me, trembling... expectantly, as if that might help, might save her. I know he would have cut his veins to help her... she was that kind of woman, she had such power over people... and I... I didn't even have the power to save her from bleeding... oh, that night, that appalling night, an endless night spent between life and death!

Towards morning she woke again and opened her eyes... they were not cold and proud now... there was a moist gleam of fever in them as they looked around the room, as if it were strange… Then she looked at me. She seemed to be thinking, trying to remember my face… and suddenly, I saw, she did remember, because some kind of shock, rejection… a hostile, horrified expression came over her features. She flailed her arms as if to flee… far, far away from me… I saw she was thinking of *that*… of the time back at my house. But then she thought again and looked at me more calmly, breathing heavily… I felt that she wanted to speak, to say something. Again her hands began to flex… she tried to sit up, but she was too weak. I calmed her, leaned down to her… and she gave me a long and tormented look… her lips moved slightly in a last, failing sound as she said, 'Will no one ever know? No one?'

'No one,' I said, with all the strength of my conviction. 'I promise you.'

But her eyes were still restless. Her fevered lips managed, indistinctly, to get it out.

'Swear to me… that no one will know… swear.'

I raised my hand as if taking an oath. She looked at me with… with an indescribable expression… it was soft, warm, grateful… yes, truly, truly grateful. She tried to say something else, but it was too difficult for her. She lay there for a long time, exhausted by the effort, with her eyes closed. Then the terrible part began… the terrible part… she fought for another entire and difficult hour. Not until morning was it all over…"

He was silent for some time. I did not notice until the bell struck from amidships, once, twice, three times—three o'clock. The moon was not shining so brightly now, but a different, faint yellow glow was already trembling in the air, and the wind blew light as a breeze from time to time. Half-an-hour more, an hour more, and it would be day, the grey around us would be extinguished by clear light. I saw his features more distinctly now that the shadows were not so dense and dark in the corner where we sat—he had taken off his cap, and now that his head was bared his tormented face looked even more terrible. But already the gleaming lenses of his glasses were turned to me again, he pulled himself together, and his voice took on a sharp and derisive tone.

"It was all over for her now—but not for me. I was alone with the body—but I was also alone in a strange house and in a city that would permit no secrets, and I… I had to keep hers. Think about it, think about the circumstances: a woman from the colony's high society, a perfectly healthy woman who had been dancing at the government ball only the evening before, suddenly dead in her bed… and a strange doctor with her, apparently called by her servant… no one in the house saw when he arrived or where he came from… she was carried in by night in a litter, and then the doors were closed… and in the morning she was dead. Only then were the servants called, and suddenly the house echoes with screams… the neighbours will know at once, the whole city will know, and there's only one man who can explain it all… I, the stranger, the doctor from a remote country station. A delightful situation, don't you agree?

I knew what lay ahead of me now. Fortunately the boy was with me, the good fellow who read every thought of mine in my eyes— that yellow-skinned, dull-minded creature knew that there was still a battle to be fought. I had said to him only, 'Your mistress did not want anyone to know what happened.' He returned my glance with his moist, doglike, yet determined gaze. All he said was, 'Yes, sir.' But he washed the blood off the floor, tidied everything—and his very determination restored mine to me.

Never in my life before, I know, was I master of such concentrated energy, and I never shall be again. When you have lost everything, you fight desperately for the last that is left—and the last was her legacy to me, my obligation to keep her secret. I calmly received the servants, told them all the same invented story: how the boy she had sent for the doctor happened to meet me by chance on his way. But while I talked, apparently calmly, I was waiting… waiting all the time for the crucial appearance of the medical officer who would have to make out the death certificate before we could put her in her coffin, and her secret with her. Don't forget, this was Thursday, and her husband would arrive on Saturday…

At last, at nine o'clock, I heard the medical officer announced. I had told the servants to send for him—he was my superior in rank and at the same time my rival, the same doctor of whom she had once spoken with such contempt, and who had obviously already heard about my application for a transfer. I sensed his hostility at once, but that in itself stiffened my backbone.

In the front hall he immediately asked, 'When did Frau… naming her by her surname—when did she die?'

'At six in the morning.'

'When did she send for you?'

'Eleven last night.'

'Did you know that I was her doctor?'

'Yes, but this was an emergency… and then… well, she asked especially for me. She wouldn't let them call any other doctor.'

He stared at me, and a flush of red came into his pale, rather plump face. I could tell that he felt bitter. But that was exactly what I needed—all my energies were concentrating on getting a quick decision, for I could feel that my nerves wouldn't hold out much longer. He was going to return a hostile reply, but then said more mildly, 'You may think that you can dispense with my services, but it is still my official duty to confirm death—and establish the cause of death.'

I did not reply, but let him go into the room ahead of me. Then I stepped back, locked the door and put the key on the table. He raised his eyebrows in surprise.

'What's the meaning of this?'

I faced him calmly. 'We don't have to establish the cause of death, we have to think of a different one. This lady called me to treat her after... after suffering the consequences of an operation that went wrong. It was too late for me to save her, but I promised I would save her reputation, and that is what I'm going to do. And I am asking you to help me.'

His eyes were wide with astonishment. 'You surely aren't saying,' he stammered, 'that you're asking me, as medical officer, to conceal a crime?'

'Yes, I am. I must.'

'So I'm to pay for your crime?'

'I've told you, I didn't touch this lady, or... or I wouldn't be here talking to you, I would have put an end to myself by now. She has paid for her transgression, if that's what you want to call it. There's no need for the world to know about it. And I will not allow this lady's reputation to be tarnished now for no good reason.'

My firm tone made him even angrier. 'You will not allow... oh, so I suppose you're my superior, or at least you think you are! Just try giving me orders... when you were summoned here from your country outpost I thought at once there was something fishy going on... nice practices you get up to, I must say, here's a pretty sample of your skill! But now *I* will examine her, *I* will do it, and you may depend upon it that any account to which my name is signed will be correct. I won't put my name to a lie.'

I kept quite calm. 'This time you must. You won't leave the room until you do.'

I put my hand in my pocket. In fact I did not have my revolver with me, but he jumped in alarm. I came a step closer and looked at him.

'Listen, let me tell you something... and then we need not resort to desperate measures. I have reached a point where I set no store by my life or anyone else's... I am anxious only to keep my promise that the manner of this death will remain secret. And listen to this too: I give you my word of honour that if you will sign the certificate saying that this lady died of… well, died accidentally, I will leave this city and the East Indies too in the course of this week… and if you want, I will take my revolver and shoot myself as soon as the coffin is in the ground and I can be sure that no one… *no one*, you understand—can make any more inquiries. That ought to satisfy you—it *must* satisfy you.'

There must have been something menacing in my voice, something quite dangerous, because as I instinctively came closer he retreated with the obvious horror of… of someone fleeing from a man in frenzy running amok, wielding a *kris*. And suddenly he had changed… he cringed, so to speak, he was bemused, his hard attitude crumbled. He murmured something with a last faint protest. 'It will be the first time in my life that I've signed a false certificate… still, I expect some form of words can be found… Who knows what would happen if… but I can't simply… '

'Of course not,' I said helpfully, to strengthen his will—only move fast, move fast, said the tingling sensation in my temples—'but now that you know you would only be hurting a living man and doing a terrible injury to a dead woman, I am sure you will not hesitate.'

He nodded. We approached the table. A few minutes later the certificate was made out; it was published later in the newspaper, and told a credible story of a heart attack. Then he rose and looked at me.

'And you'll leave this week, then?'

'My word of honour.'

He looked at me again. I realised that he wanted to appear stern and objective. 'I'll see about a coffin at once,' he said, to hide his embarrassment. But whatever it was about me that made me so… so dreadful, so tormented—he suddenly offered me his hand and shook mine with hearty good feeling. 'I hope you will be better soon,' he said—I didn't know what he meant. Was I sick? Was I... was I mad? I accompanied him to the door and unlocked it—and it was with the last of my strength that I closed it again behind him. Then the tingling in my temples returned, everything swayed and went round before my eyes, and I collapsed beside her bed... just as a man running amok falls senseless at the end of his frenzied career, his nerves broken."

Once again he paused. I shivered slightly: was it the first shower carried on the morning wind that blew softly over the deck? But the tormented face, now partly visible in the reflected light of dawn, was getting control of itself again.

"I don't know how long I lay on the mat like that. Then someone touched me. I came to myself with a start. It was the boy, timidly standing before me with his look of devotion and gazing uneasily at me.

'Someone wants come in... wants see her... '

'No one may come in.'

'Yes... but... '

There was alarm in his eyes. He wanted to say something, but dared not. The faithful creature was in some kind of torment.

'Who is it?'

He looked at me, trembling as if he feared a blow. And then he said—he named a name—how does such a lowly creature suddenly come by so much knowledge, how is it that at some moments these dull human souls show unspeakable tenderness?—then he said, very, very timidly, 'It is *him*.'

I started again, understood at once, and I was immediately avid, impatient to set eyes on the unknown man. For strangely enough, you see, in the midst of all my agony, my fevered longing, fear and haste, I had entirely forgotten 'him', I had forgotten there was a man involved too… the man whom this woman had loved, to whom she had passionately given what she denied to me. Twelve, twenty-four hours ago I would still have hated him, I would have been ready to tear him to pieces. Now… well, I can't tell you how much I wanted to see him, to… to love him because she had loved him.

I was suddenly at the door. There stood a young, very young fair-haired officer, very awkward, very slender, very pale. He looked like a child, so… so touchingly young, and I was unutterably shaken to see how hard he was trying to be a man and maintain his composure, hide his emotion. I saw at once that his hands were trembling as he raised them to his cap. I could have embraced him… because he was so exactly what I would have wished the man who had possessed her to be, not a seducer, not proud… no, still half a child, a pure, affectionate creature to whom she had given herself.

The young man stood before me awkwardly. My avid glance, my passionate haste as I rushed to let him in confused him yet more. The small moustache on his upper lip trembled treacherously… this young officer, this child, had to force himself not to sob out loud.

'Forgive me,' he said at last. 'I would have liked to see Frau… I would so much have liked to see her again.'

Unconsciously, without any deliberate intention, I put my arm around the young stranger's shoulders and led him in as if he were an invalid. He looked at me in surprise, with an infinitely warm and grateful expression… at that moment, some kind of understanding existed between the two of us of what we had in common. We went over to the dead woman. There she lay, white-faced, in white linen—I felt that my presence troubled him, so I stepped back to leave him alone with her. He went slowly closer with… with such reluctant, hesitant steps. I saw from the set of his shoulders the kind of turmoil that was ranging in him. He walked like… like a man walking into a mighty gale. And suddenly he fell to his knees beside the bed, just as I had done.

I came forward at once, raised him and led him to an armchair. He was not ashamed any more, but sobbed out his grief. I could say nothing—I just instinctively stroked his fair, childishly soft hair. He reached for my hand... very gently, yet anxiously... and suddenly I felt his eyes on me. 'Tell me the truth, doctor,' he stammered. 'Did she lay hands on herself?'

'No,' I said.

'And... I mean... is anyone... is someone to blame for her death?'

'No,' I said again, although a desire was rising in me to cry out, 'I am! I am! I am! And so are you! The pair of us! And her obstinacy, her ill-starred obstinacy.' But I controlled myself. I repeated, 'No... no one is to blame. It was fate!'

'I can't believe it,' he groaned, 'I can't believe it. She was at the ball only the day before yesterday, she waved to me. How is it possible, how could it happen?'

I told a lengthy lie. I did not betray her secret even to him. We talked together like two brothers over the next few days, as if irradiated by the emotion that bound us... we did not confess it to each other, but we both felt that our whole lives had depended on that woman. Sometimes the truth rose to my lips, choking me, but I gritted my teeth, and he never learned that she had been carrying his child, or that I had been asked to kill the child, his offspring, and she had taken it down into the abyss with her. Yet we talked of nothing but her in those days, when I was hiding away with him—for I forgot to tell you that they were looking for me. Her husband had arrived after the coffin was closed, and wouldn't accept the medical findings. There were all kinds of rumours, and he was looking for me... but I couldn't bear to see him when I knew that she had suffered in her marriage to him... I hid away, for four days I didn't go out of the house, we neither of us left her lover's apartment. He had booked me a passage under a false name so that I could get away easily. I went on board by night, like a thief, in case anyone recognised me. I have left everything I own behind… my house, all my work of the last seven years, my possessions, they're all there for anyone who wants them… and the government gentlemen will have struck me off their records for deserting my post without leave. But I couldn't live any longer in that house or in that city… in that world where everything reminded me of her. I fled like a thief in the night, just to escape her, just to forget. But… as I came on board at night, it was midnight, my friend was with me… they… they were just hauling something up by crane, something rectangular and black… her coffin… do you hear that, her coffin? She has followed me here, just as I followed her… and I had to stand by and pretend to be a stranger, because he, her husband, was with it, it's going back to England with him. Perhaps he plans to have an autopsy carried out there… he has snatched her back, she's his again now, not ours, she no longer belongs to the two of us. But I am still here… I will go with her to the end… he will not, must not ever know about it. I will defend her secret against any attempt to… against this ruffian from whom she fled to her death. He will learn nothing, nothing… her secret is mine alone…

So now do you understand… do you realise why I can't endure the company of human beings? I can't bear their laughter, to hear them flirting and mating… for her coffin is stowed away down there in the hold, between bales of tea and Brazil nuts. I can't get at it, the hold is locked, but I'm aware of it with all my senses, I know it is there every second of the day… even if they play waltzes and tangos up here. It's stupid, the sea there washes over millions of dead, a corpse is rotting beneath every plot of ground on which we step… yet I can't bear it, I cannot bear it when they give fancy dress balls and laugh so lasciviously. I feel her dead presence, and I know what she wants. I know it, I still have a duty to do… I'm not finished yet, her secret is not quite safe, she won't let me go yet…"

*

Slow footsteps and slapping sounds came from amidships; the sailors were beginning to scour the deck. He started as if caught in a guilty act, and his strained face looked anxious. Rising, he murmured, "I'll be off... I'll be off." It was painful to see him: his devastated glance, his swollen eyes, red with drink or tears. He didn't want my pity; I sensed shame in his hunched form, endless shame for giving his story away to me during the night. On impulse, I asked him, "May I visit you in your cabin this afternoon?"

He looked at me—there was a derisive, harsh, sardonic set to his mouth. A touch of malevolence came out with every word, distorting it.

"Ah, your famous duty—the duty to help! I see. You were fortunate enough to make me talk by quoting that maxim. But no thank you, sir. Don't think I feel better now that I have torn my guts out before you, shown you the filth inside me. There's no mending my spoiled life any more... I have served the honourable Dutch government for nothing, I can wave goodbye to my pension—I come back to Europe a poor, penniless cur... a cur whining behind a coffin. You don't run amok for long with impunity, you're bound to be struck down in the end, and I hope it will soon all be over for me. No thank you, sir, I'll turn down your kind offer... I have my own friends in my cabin, a few good bottles of old whisky that sometimes comfort me, and then I have my old friend of the past, although I didn't turn it against myself when I should have done, my faithful Browning. In the end it will help me better than any talk. Please don't try to... the one human right one has left is to die as one wishes, and keep well away from any stranger's help."

Once more he gave me a derisive, indeed challenging look, but I felt that it was really only in shame, endless shame. Then he hunched his shoulders, turned without a word of farewell and crossed the foredeck, which was already in bright sunlight, making for the cabins and holding himself in that curious way, leaning sideways, footsteps dragging. I never saw him again. I looked for him in our usual place that night, and the next night too. He kept out of sight, and I might have thought he was a dream of mine or a fantastic apparition had I not then noticed, among the passengers, a man with a black mourning band around his arm, a Dutch merchant, I was told, whose wife had just died of some tropical disease. I saw him walking up and down, grave and grieving, keeping away from the others, and the idea that I knew about his secret sorrow made me oddly timid. I always turned aside when he passed by, so as not to give away with so much as a glance that I knew more about his sad story than he did himself.

Then, in Naples harbour, there was that remarkable accident, and I believe I can find its cause in the stranger's story. For most of the passengers had gone ashore that evening—I myself went to the opera, and then to one of the brightly lit cafés on the Via Roma. As we were on our way back to the ship in a dinghy, I noticed several boats circling the vessel with torches and acetylene lamps as if in search of something, and up on the dark deck there was much mysterious coming-and-going of *carabinieri* and of other policemen. I asked a sailor what had happened. He avoided giving a direct answer in a way that immediately told me the crew had orders to keep quiet, and next day too, when all was calm on board again and we sailed on to Genoa without a hint of any further incident, there was nothing to be learned on board. Not until I saw the Italian newspapers did I read accounts, written up in flowery terms, of the alleged accident in Naples harbour. On the night in question, they wrote, at a quiet time in order to avoid upsetting the passengers, the coffin of a distinguished lady from the Dutch colonies was to be moved from the ship to a boat, and it had just been let down the ship's side on a rope ladder in her husband's presence when something heavy fell from the deck above, carrying the coffin away into the sea, along with the men handling it and the woman's husband, who was helping them to hoist it down. One newspaper said that a madman had flung himself down the steps and onto the rope ladder; another stated that the ladder had broken of itself under too much weight. In any case, the shipping company had done all it could to cover up what exactly had happened. The handlers of the coffin and the dead woman's husband had been pulled out of the water and into boats, not without some difficulty, but the lead coffin itself sank straight to the bottom, and could not be retrieved. The brief mention in another report of the fact that, at the same time, the body of a man of about forty had been washed ashore in the harbour did not seem to be connected in the public mind with the romantic account of the accident. But as soon as I had read those few lines, I felt as if that white, moonlit face with its gleaming glasses were staring back at me again, in ghostly fashion, from behind the sheet of newsprint.

THE STAR ABOVE
THE FOREST

A STRANGE THING HAPPENED one day when the slender, elegantly groomed waiter François was leaning over the beautiful Polish Baroness Ostrovska's shoulder to serve her. It lasted for only a second, it was not marked by any start or sudden movement of surprise, any restlessness or momentary agitation. Yet it was one of those seconds in which thousands of hours and days of rejoicing and torment are held spellbound, just as all the wild force of a forest of tall, dark, rustling oak trees, with their rocking branches and swaying crowns, is contained in a single tiny acorn dropping through the air. To outward appearance, nothing happened during that second. With a supple movement François, the waiter in the grand hotel on the Riviera, leaned further down to place the serving platter at a more convenient angle for the Baroness's questing knife. For that one moment, however, his face was just above her softly curling, fragrant waves of hair, and when he instinctively opened the eyes that he had respectfully closed, his reeling gaze saw the gentle white radiance of the line of her neck as it disappeared from that dark cascade of hair, to be lost in her dark red, full-skirted dress. He felt as if crimson flames were flaring up in him. And her knife clinked quietly on the platter, which was imperceptibly shaking. But although in that second he foresaw all the fateful consequences of his sudden enchantment, he expertly mastered his emotion and went on serving at the table with the cool, slightly debonair stylishness of a well-trained waiter with impeccable good taste. He handed the platter calmly to the Baroness's usual companion at table, an elderly aristocrat with gracefully assured manners, who was talking of unimportant matters in crystal-clear French with a very faint accent. Then he walked away from the table without a gesture or a backward glance.

Those minutes were the beginning of his abandoning himself to a very strange kind of devotion, such a reeling, intoxicated sensation that the proud and portentous word 'love' is not quite right for it. It was that faithful, dog-like devotion without desire that those in mid-life seldom feel, and is known only to the very young and the very old. A love devoid of any deliberation, not thinking but only dreaming. He entirely forgot the unjust yet ineradicable disdain that even the clever and considerate show to those who wear a waiter's tailcoat, he did not look for opportunities and chance meetings, but nurtured this strange affection in his blood until its secret fervour was beyond all mockery and criticism. His love was not a matter of secret winks and lurking glances, the sudden boldness of audacious gestures, the senseless ardour of salivating lips and trembling hands; it was quiet toil, the performance of those small services that are all the more sacred and sublime in their humility because they are intended to go unnoticed. After the evening meal he smoothed out the crumpled folds of the tablecloth where she had been sitting with tender, caressing fingers, as one would stroke a beloved woman's soft hands at rest; he adjusted everything close to her with devout symmetry, as if he were preparing it for a special occasion. He carefully carried the glasses that her lips had touched up to his own small, musty attic bedroom, and watched them sparkle like precious jewellery by night when the moonlight streamed in. He was always to be found in some corner, secretly attentive to her as she strolled and walked about. He drank in what she said as you might relish a sweet, fragrantly intoxicating wine on the tongue, and responded to every one of her words and orders as eagerly as children run to catch a ball flying through the air. So his intoxicated soul brought an ever-changing, rich glow into his dull, ordinary life. The wise folly of clothing the whole experience in the cold, destructive words of reality was an idea that never entered his mind: the poor waiter François was in love with an exotic Baroness who would be for ever unattainable. For he did not think of her as reality, but as something very distant, very high above him, sufficient in its mere reflection of life. He loved the imperious pride of her orders, the commanding arch of her black eyebrows that almost touched one another, the wilful lines around her small mouth, the confident grace of her bearing. Subservience seemed to him quite natural, and he felt the humiliating intimacy of menial labour as good fortune, because it enabled him to step so often into the magic circle that surrounded her.

So a dream suddenly awakened in the life of a simple man, like a beautiful, carefully raised garden flower blooming by a roadside where the dust of travel obliterates all other seedlings. It was the frenzy of someone plain and ordinary, an enchanting narcotic dream in the midst of a cold and monotonous life. And such people's dreams are like a rudderless boat drifting aimlessly on quiet, shining waters, rocking with delight, until suddenly its keel grounds abruptly on an unknown bank.

However, reality is stronger and more robust than any dreams. One evening the stout hotel porter from Waadland told him in passing, "Baroness Ostrovska is leaving tomorrow night on the eight o'clock train." And he added a couple of other names which meant nothing to François, and which he did not note. For those words had turned to a confused, tumultuous roaring in his head. A couple of times he mechanically ran his fingers over his aching brow, as if to push away an oppressive weight lying there and dimming his understanding. He took a few steps; he was unsteady on his feet. Alarmed and uncertain, he passed a tall, gilt-framed mirror from which a pale strange face looked back at him, white as a sheet. No ideas would come to him; they seemed to be held captive behind a dark and misty wall. Almost unconsciously, he felt his way down by the hand-rail of the broad flight of steps into the twilit garden, where tall pines stood alone like dark thoughts. His restless figure took a few more shaky steps, like the low reeling flight of a large dark nocturnal bird, and then he sank down on a bench with his head pressed to its cool back. It was perfectly quiet. The sea sparkled here and there beyond the round shapes of shrubs. Faint, trembling lights shone out on the water, and the monotonous, murmuring sing-song of distant breakers was lost in the silence.

Suddenly everything was clear to him, perfectly clear. So painfully clear that he could almost summon up a smile. It was all over. Baroness Ostrovska was going home, and François the waiter would stay at his post. Was that so strange? Didn't all the foreign guests who came to the hotel leave again after two, three or four weeks? How foolish not to have thought of it before. It was so clear, it was enough to make you laugh or cry. And ideas kept whirring through his head. Tomorrow evening on the eight o'clock train to Warsaw. To Warsaw—hours and hours of travel through forests and valleys, passing hills and mountains, steppes and rivers and noisy towns. Warsaw! It was so far away! He couldn't even imagine it, but he felt it in the depths of his heart, that proud and threatening, harsh and distant word Warsaw. While he…

For a second a small, dream-like hope fluttered up in his heart. He could follow. He could hire himself out there as a servant, a secretary, could stand in the street as a freezing beggar, anything not to be so dreadfully far away, just to breathe the air of the same city, perhaps see her sometimes driving past, catch a glimpse of her shadow, her dress, her dark hair. Daydreams flashed hastily through his mind. But this was a hard and pitiless hour. Clear and plain, he saw how unattainable his dreams were. He worked it out: at the most he had savings of a hundred or two hundred francs. That would scarcely take him half the way. And then what? As if through a torn veil he suddenly saw his own life, knew how wretched, pitiful, hateful it must be now. Empty, desolate years working as a waiter, tormented by foolish longing—was something so ridiculous to be his future? The idea made him shudder. And suddenly all these trains of thoughts came stormily and inevitably together. There was only one way out...

The treetops swayed quietly in an imperceptible breeze. A dark, black night menacingly faced him. He rose from his bench, confident and composed, and walked over the crunching gravel up to the great building of the hotel where it slumbered in white silence. He stopped outside her windows. They were dark, with no spark of light at which his dreamy longing could have been kindled. Now his blood was flowing calmly, and he walked like a man whom nothing will ever confuse or deceive again. In his room, he flung himself on the bed without any sign of agitation, and slept a dull, dreamless sleep until the alarm summoned him to get up in the morning.

Next day his demeanour was entirely within the bounds of carefully calculated reflection and self-imposed calm. He carried out his duties with cool indifference, and his gestures were so sure and easy that no one could have guessed at the bitter decision behind his deceptive mask. Just before dinner he hurried out with his small savings to the best florist in the resort and bought choice flowers whose colourful glory spoke to him like words: tulips glowing with fiery, passionate gold—shaggy white chrysanthemums resembling light, exotic dreams—slender orchids, the graceful images of longing—and a few proud, intoxicating roses. And then he bought a magnificent vase of sparkling, opalescent glass. He gave the few francs he still had left to a beggar child in passing, with a quick and carefree movement. Then he hurried back. With sad solemnity, he put the vase of flowers down in front of the Baroness's place at table, which he now prepared for the last time with slow, voluptuously meticulous attention.

Then came the dinner. He served it as usual: cool, silent, skilful, without looking up. Only at the end did he embrace her supple, proud figure with an endlessly long look of which she never knew. And she had never seemed to him so beautiful as in that last, perfect look. Then he stepped calmly back from the table, without any gesture of farewell, and left the dining room. Bearing himself like a guest to whom the staff would bow and nod their heads, he walked down the corridors and the handsome flight of steps outside the reception area and out into the street: any observer must surely have been able to tell that, at that moment, he was leaving his past behind. He stood outside the hotel for a moment, undecided, and then turned to the bright villas and wide gardens, following the road past them, walking on, ever on with his thoughtful, dignified stride, with no idea where he was going.

He wandered restlessly like this until evening, in a lost, dreamy state of mind. He was not thinking of anything any more. Not about the past, or the inevitable moment to come. He was no longer playing with ideas of death, not in the way one might well pick up a shining revolver with its deep, menacing mouth in those last moments, weighing it in the hand, and then lower it again. He had passed sentence on himself long ago. Only images came to him now in rapid flight, like swallows soaring. First images of his youthful days, up to a fateful moment at school when a foolish adventure had suddenly closed an alluring future to him and thrust him out into the turmoil of the world. Then his restless wanderings, his efforts to earn a living, all the attempts that kept failing, until the great black wave that we call destiny broke his pride and he ended up in a position unworthy of him. Many colourful memories whirled past. And finally the gentle reflection of these last few days glowed in his waking dreams, suddenly pushing the dark door of reality open again. He had to go through it. He remembered that he intended to die today.

For a while he thought of the many ways leading to death, assessing their comparative bitterness and speed, until suddenly an idea shot through his mind. His clouded senses abruptly showed him a dark symbol: just as she had unknowingly, destructively driven over his fate, so she should also crush his body. She herself would do it. She would finish her own work. And now his ideas came thick and fast with strange certainty. In just under an hour, at eight, the express carrying her away from him left. He would throw himself under its wheels, let himself be trampled down by the same violent force that was tearing the woman of his dreams from him. He would bleed to death beneath her feet. The ideas stormed on after one another as if in jubilation. He knew the right place too: further off, near the wooded slope, where the swaying treetops hid the sight of the last bend in the railway line nearby. He looked at his watch; the seconds and his hammering blood were beating out the same rhythm. It was time to set off. Now a spring returned to his sluggish footsteps, along with the certainty of his destination. He walked at that brisk, hasty pace that does away with dreaming as one goes forward, restlessly striding on in the twilight glory of the Mediterranean evening towards the place where the sky was a streak of purple lying embedded between distant, wooded hills. And he hurried on until he came to the two silver lines of the railway track shining ahead of him, guiding him on his way. The track led him by winding paths on through the deep, fragrant valleys, their veils of mist now silvered by the soft moonlight, it took him into the hilly landscape where the sight of sparkling lights along the beach showed how far away the nocturnal, black expanse of the sea was now. And at last it presented him with the deep, restlessly whispering forest that hid the railway line in its lowering shadows.

It was late when, breathing heavily, he reached the dark wooded slope. The trees stood around him, black and ominous, but high above, in their shimmering crowns, faint, quivering moonlight was caught in the branches that moaned as they embraced the slight nocturnal breeze. Sometimes this hollow silence was broken by the strange cries of night birds. In this alarming isolation, his thoughts froze entirely. He was merely waiting, waiting and straining his eyes to see the red light of the train appearing down by the curve of the first bend. Sometimes he looked nervously at his watch again, counting seconds. Then he listened once more, thinking that he heard the distant whistle of the locomotive. But it was a false alarm. All was perfectly silent again. Time seemed to stand still.

At last, far away, he saw the light. At that moment he felt a pang in his heart, and could not have said if it was fear or jubilation. He flung himself down on the rails with a brusque movement. At first he felt the pleasantly cool sensation of the strips of iron against his temples for a moment. Then he listened. The train was still far off. It might be several minutes yet. There was nothing to be heard but the whispering of the trees in the wind. His thoughts went this way and that in confusion, until suddenly one stopped and pierced his heart painfully, like an arrow: he was dying for her sake, and she would never know. Not a single gentle ripple of his life as it came to its turbulent end had ever touched hers. She would never know that a stranger's life had depended on her own, and had been crushed by it.

Very quietly, the rhythmic chugging of the approaching engine came through the breathless air from afar. But that idea burned on, tormenting the dying man in his last minutes. The train rattled closer and closer. Then he opened his eyes once more. Above him was a silent, blue-black sky, with the tops of a few trees swaying in front of it. And above the forest stood a shining, white star. A single star above the forest… the rails beneath his head were already beginning to vibrate and sing faintly. But the idea burned on like fire in his heart, and in his eyes as they saw all the fire and despair of his love. His whole longing and that last painful question flowed

into the white and shining star that looked mildly down on him.
Closer and closer thundered the train. And once more, with a last
inexpressible look, the dying man took the sparkling star above the
forest to his heart. Then he closed his eyes. The rails were trembling
and swaying, closer and closer came the rattling of the express train,
making the forest echo as if great bells were hammering out a rhythm.
The earth seemed to sway. One more deafening, rushing, whirring
sound, a whirlwind of noise, then a shrill scream, the terrifyingly
animal scream of the steam whistle, and the screech and groan of
brakes applied in vain…

The beautiful Baroness Ostrovska had a reserved compartment to
herself in the express. She had been reading a French magazine
since the train left, gently cradled by the rocking movement of the
carriage. The air in the enclosed space was sultry, and drenched with
the heavy fragrance of many fading flowers. Clusters of white lilac
were already hanging heavily, like over-ripe fruit, from the magnificent
farewell baskets that she had been given, flowers hung limp on their
stems, and the broad, heavy cups of the roses seemed to be withering
in the hot cloud of intoxicating perfumes. Even in the haste of the
express as it rushed along, a suffocatingly close atmosphere heated
the heavy drifts of perfume weighing oppressively down.

Suddenly she lowered her book with limp fingers. She herself
did not know why. Some secret feeling was tearing at her. She felt
a dull but painful pressure. A sudden sense of constriction that she
couldn't explain clutched her heart. She thought she would choke
on the heavy, intoxicating aroma of the flowers. And that terrifying
pain did not pass, she felt every revolution of the rushing wheels,
their blind, pounding, forward movement was an unspeakable torment. Suddenly she longed to be able to halt the swift momentum
of the train, to haul it back from the dark pain towards which it

was racing. She had never in her life felt such fear of something terrible, invisible and cruel seizing on her heart as she did now, in those seconds of incomprehensible, incredible pain and fear. And that unspeakable feeling grew stronger and stronger, tightening its grasp around her throat. The idea of being able to stop the train was like a prayer moaned out loud in her mind...

Then she hears a sudden shrill whistle, the wild, warning scream of the locomotive, the wailing groan and crunch of the brakes. And the rhythm of the flying wheels slackens, goes slower and slower, until there is a stuttering rattle and a faltering jerk.

With difficulty, she makes her way to the window to fill her lungs with fresh air. The pane rattles down. Dark figures are hurrying around... words fly back and forth, different voices: a suicide... under the wheels... dead... yes, out here in the open...

She starts. Instinctively, her eyes go to the high and silent sky and the dark trees whispering above it. And beyond them, a single star is shining over the forest. She is aware of its gaze on her like a sparkling tear. Looking at it, she abruptly feels such grief as she has never known before. A fiery grief, full of a longing that has not been part of her own life...

Slowly, the train rattles on. She leans back in the corner and feels soft tears running down over her cheeks. That dull fear has gone away, she feels only a deep, strange pain, and seeks in vain to discover its source. A pain such as terrified children feel when they suddenly wake on a dark, impenetrable night, and feel that they are all alone...

DATE OF FIRST
PUBLICATION IN GERMAN

THE MIRACLES OF LIFE
Die Wunder des Lebens   1903

THE STAR ABOVE THE FOREST
Der Stern über dem Walde   1904

TWILIGHT
Geschichte eines Unterganges   1910

A STORY TOLD IN TWILIGHT
Geschichte in der Dämmerung   1911

WONDRAK [UNFINISHED]
Wondrak   1990
[published posthumously but written during the First Word War]

AMOK
Der Amokläufer   1922

THE INVISIBLE COLLECTION
Die unsichtbare Samlung   1925

DOWNFALL OF A HEART
Untergang eines Herzens   1927

LEPORELLA
Leporella   1929

DID HE DO IT?
War er es?   1987
[written between 1934–40]

PUSHKIN PRESS

Pushkin Press was founded in 1997, and publishes novels, essays, memoirs, children's books—everything from timeless classics to the urgent and contemporary.

Our books represent exciting, high-quality writing from around the world: we publish some of the twentieth century's most widely acclaimed, brilliant authors such as Stefan Zweig, Marcel Aymé, Antal Szerb, Paul Morand and Yasushi Inoue, as well as compelling and award-winning contemporary writers, including Andrés Neuman, Edith Pearlman and Ryu Murakami.

Pushkin Press publishes the world's best stories, to be read and read again. Here are just some of the titles from our long and varied list. For more amazing stories, visit www.pushkinpress.com.

====

THE SPECTRE OF ALEXANDER WOLF
GAITO GAZDANOV
'A mesmerising work of literature' Antony Beevor

BINOCULAR VISION
EDITH PEARLMAN
'A genius of the short story' Mark Lawson, *Guardian*

TRAVELLER OF THE CENTURY
ANDRÉS NEUMAN
'A beautiful, accomplished novel: as ambitious as it is generous, as moving as it is smart' Juan Gabriel Vásquez, *Guardian*

BEWARE OF PITY
STEFAN ZWEIG
'Zweig's fictional masterpiece' *Guardian*

THE BREAK

PIETRO GROSSI

'Small and perfectly formed… reaching its end leaves the reader desirous to start all over again' *Independent*

FROM THE FATHERLAND, WITH LOVE

RYU MURAKAMI

'If Haruki is The Beatles of Japanese literature, Ryu is its Rolling Stones' David Pilling

BUTTERFLIES IN NOVEMBER

AUÐUR AVA ÓLAFSDÓTTIR

'A funny, moving and occasionally bizarre exploration of life's upheavals and reversals' *Financial Times*

BARCELONA SHADOWS

MARC PASTOR

'As gruesome as it is gripping… the writing is extraordinarily vivid… Highly recommended' *Independent*

THE LAST DAYS

LAURENT SEKSIK

'Mesmerising… Seksik's portrait of Zweig's final months is dignified and tender' *Financial Times*

BY BLOOD

ELLEN ULLMAN

'Delicious and intriguing' *Daily Telegraph*

WHILE THE GODS WERE SLEEPING

ERWIN MORTIER

'A monumental, phenomenal book' *De Morgen*

THE BRETHREN

ROBERT MERLE

'A master of the historical novel' *Guardian*

COIN LOCKER BABIES

RYU MURAKAMI

'A fascinating peek into the weirdness of contemporary Japan' Oliver Stone

TALKING TO OURSELVES

ANDRÉS NEUMAN

'This is writing of a quality rarely encountered… when you read Neuman's beautiful novel, you realise a very high bar has been set' *Guardian*

CLOSE TO THE MACHINE

ELLEN ULLMAN

'Astonishing… impossible to put down' *San Francisco Chronicle*

MARCEL

ERWIN MORTIER

'Aspiring novelists will be hard pressed to achieve this quality' *Time Out*

JOURNEY INTO THE PAST

STEFAN ZWEIG

'Lucid, tender, powerful and compelling' *Independent*

POPULAR HITS OF THE SHOWA ERA

RYU MURAKAMI

'One of the funniest and strangest gang wars in recent literature' *Booklist*

LETTER FROM AN UNKNOWN WOMAN AND OTHER STORIES

STEFAN ZWEIG

'Zweig's time of oblivion is over for good… it's good to have him back' Salman Rushdie

ONE NIGHT, MARKOVITCH

AYELET GUNDAR-GOSHEN

'A remarkable first novel, trenchant and full of love, highly impressive in its maturity and wisdom' Eshkol Nevo

MY FELLOW SKIN

ERWIN MORTIER

'A Bildungsroman which is related to much European literature from Proust and Mann onwards… peculiarly unforgettable' AS Byatt, *Guardian*